CONTENTS

To see the complete list of titles available
from Susan Mallery, please visit SusanMallery.com.

THE LADIES' MAN

Susan Mallery

Chapter 1

Rachel Harper had always longed to be more sophisticated. It was right there on her to-do list between "be more aware of current events" and "don't let your handwashing pile up so much."

While she *had* started watching the national news nearly every night, she wasn't doing so well keeping up with her delicates. And the sophistication thing? A total loss.

Which was why she found herself, at the ripe old age of twenty-five, sitting in a bar and feeling as if she didn't have a clue as to how to act. Not that she was here to do normal barlike things. Instead, she'd agreed to accompany Diane, a new teacher at her school, who was breaking up with her boyfriend and had asked Rachel to come along for moral support. As the next item of Rachel's to-do list—right under the issue with the handwashing—was "get out more," she'd agreed to tag along to the Blue Dog Bar.

Rachel wasn't sure what dog, blue or not, had inspired the name. There seemed to be a lot more men than women in the bar. She swirled the margarita she'd ordered, then took a big sip.

"The jerk isn't even going to show up," Diane said from her seat across the small table they'd chosen by the wall. "That is so like him. I swear, I'm going to kick him in the head when I see him." Diane paused, then smiled. "See, I'm talking in 'I' sentences, just like that book said."

"Yes, you are," Rachel murmured, deciding not to point out that the "I" sentences the self-help manual referred to probably didn't fall into the "I'm going to kick you in the head" category.

"There he is," Diane said as she stood. "Wish me luck."

Rachel glanced at the tall, dark-haired man who strolled into the bar, looking as if he could take just about every other guy there. "Good luck," she said and meant it.

Carter Brockett eyed the curvy brunette in the prim dress and knew he was seconds away from all kinds of trouble. The cool, logical side of his brain reminded him that all the pain and suffering in his life could be traced back to one source: women. Life was always better when he walked away.

The part of his brain—and the rest of him—that enjoyed a warm body, a sharp mind and a purely feminine take on the world said she looked interesting. And that last bit of consciousness, shaped by a very strong-willed mother who had drilled into him that he was always to protect those weaker than him, told him that the attractive brunette was in way over her head.

#1 *New York Times* bestselling author **Susan Mallery** has won the hearts of millions of readers around the world with books described as "immensely entertaining, intensely emotional" (*RT Book Reviews*), "hilarious" (*Fort Worth Star-Telegram*) and "heartwarming" (*Publishers Weekly*). One major retailer recently described her as "the queen of romantic fiction." While she deeply appreciates the accolades of critics and booksellers, Mallery is even more honored by the enthusiasm of her readers and the word of mouth that catapults her toward the top of the bestsellers lists time and again.

Mallery lives in not-so-sunny Seattle with her husband and a toy poodle who makes her laugh every day and who's not even a little bit impressed by her growing fame. Visit Susan online at SusanMallery.com.

USA TODAY bestselling author **Sarah Morgan** writes hot, happy contemporary romance. Her trademark humor and sensuality have gained her fans across the globe and two RITA® Awards from the Romance Writers of America. Sarah lives near London with her family. Visit her at sarahmorgan.com.

#1 *New York Times* **Bestselling Author**

SUSAN MALLERY

THE LADIES' MAN

&

USA TODAY **Bestselling Author**

SARAH MORGAN

SOME KIND OF WONDERFUL

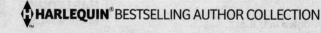

HARLEQUIN® BESTSELLING AUTHOR COLLECTION

ISBN-13: 978-0-373-01036-3

The Ladies' Man & Some Kind of Wonderful
Copyright © 2016 by Harlequin Books S.A.

The publisher acknowledges the copyright holders
of the individual works as follows:

The Ladies' Man
Copyright © 2006 by Susan Macias Redmond

Some Kind of Wonderful
Copyright © 2015 by Sarah Morgan

Recycling programs
for this product may
not exist in your area.

www.Harlequin.com

Printed in U.S.A.

He could be wrong of course. For all he knew, she was a leather-wearing dominatrix who came to the Blue Dog because of the place's reputation. But he had his doubts.

The Blue Dog was a cop bar. But not just any hangout for those in uniform. It was a place where guys showed up to get lucky and the women who walked in counted on that fact. Carter usually avoided the place—he worked under-cover and couldn't afford to be seen here. But one of his contacts had insisted on the location, so Carter had agreed and prayed no one from the force would speak to him.

No one had. He'd concluded his business and had been about to leave when the brunette had walked in with her friend, who was currently involved in a heated conver-sation with Eddy. Eddy wasn't exactly a prince when it came to his dating habits, so Carter had a feeling the chat wasn't going to go well. He nodded at Jenny, the bartender on duty, then pointed to the brunette. Jenny raised her eyebrows.

Carter didn't have to guess what she was thinking. Jenny, an ex-girlfriend, knew him pretty well. Yeah, well, maybe after a few months of self-induced celibacy, he was ready to give the man-woman thing another try. Even though he knew better. Even though it was always a di-saster.

He glanced around and saw he wasn't the only one who'd noticed the contrast between the brunette's made-for-sin body and her Sunday-school-teacher clothes. So if he was going to protect her from the other big bad cops, he'd better get a move on.

He walked to the bar, where Jenny handed him a beer and a margarita. He ignored her knowing grin and crossed to the brunette's table.

"Hi. I'm Carter. Mind if I join you?"

As he asked the question, he set down the margarita and gave her his best smile.

Yeah, yeah, a cheap trick, he thought, remembering all the hours he'd spent perfecting it back in high school. He'd taught himself to smile with just the right amount of interest, charm and bashfulness. It never failed.

Not even tonight, when the woman looked up, flushed, half rose, then sat back down, and in the process knocked over her nearly empty drink and scattered the slushy contents across the table and down the front of her dress.

"Oh, no," she said, her voice soft and almost musical. "Darn. I can't believe I…" She pressed her lips together, then looked at him.

He'd already sopped up the mess on the table with a couple of napkins. He completely ignored the dampness on her dress. Sure, he was interested, but he wasn't stupid.

"You okay?" he asked, curious about a woman who actually said *darn*.

"Yes. Thank you."

He passed over the drink he'd brought.

She glanced first at it, then at him. "I'm, ah, with someone."

He kept his gaze on her. "Your girlfriend. I saw you come in together."

She nodded. "She's breaking up with her boyfriend and wanted moral support. I don't usually… This isn't…" She sighed. "She'll be back soon."

"No problem," he said easily. "I'll keep you company until she's finished."

Even in the dim light of the bar, he could see her eyes were green. Her long, dark hair hung in sensuous waves to just past her shoulders.

Carter held in a snort. Sensuous waves? He'd sure been without for a little too long if he were thinking things like that.

She shifted uncomfortably and didn't touch the drink.

"Is it me or the bar?" he asked.

"What? Oh, both, I suppose." Instantly, she covered her mouth, then dropped her hand to her damp lap. "Sorry. I shouldn't have said that."

"It's fine. I'm a great believer in the truth. So which is more scary?"

She glanced around the Blue Dog, then returned her attention to him. "Mostly you."

He grinned. "I'm flattered."

"Why? You *want* me to think you're scary?"

He leaned forward and lowered his voice just enough to get her to sway toward him. "Not scary. Dangerous. All guys want to be dangerous. Women love that."

She surprised him by laughing. "Okay, Carter, I can see you're a pro and I'm way out of my league with you. I cheerfully confess I'm not the bar type and being in this setting makes me horribly uncomfortable." She glanced at her friend. "I can't tell if the fight's going well or badly. What do you think?"

He looked at Eddy, who'd backed the blonde into a corner. "It depends on how you're defining 'well.' I don't think they're actually breaking up. Do you?"

"I'm not sure. Diane was determined to tell him what she thought, once and for all. In 'I' sentences."

He frowned. "In what?"

She smiled. "*I* think you're not treating me with respect. *I* think you're always late on purpose. That kind of thing. Although she did say something about wanting to kick him in the head, which is unlikely to help. Of course, I don't know Eddy. He may like that sort of thing."

Carter was totally and completely charmed. "Who *are* you?" he asked.

"My name is Rachel."

"You don't swear, you don't hang out in bars, so what do you do?"

"How do you know I don't swear?" she asked.

"You said 'darn' when you spilled your drink."

"Oh. Right. It's a habit. I teach kindergarten. There's no way I can swear in front of the children, not that I ever used a lot of bad words, so I trained myself to never say them. It's just easier. So I use words like 'darn' and 'golly.'" She grinned. "Sometimes people look at me like I'm at the dull-normal end of the IQ scale, but I can live with that. It's for the greater good. So who are you?"

A complicated question, Carter thought, knowing he couldn't tell her the truth. "Just a guy."

"Uh-huh." She eyed his too-long hair. "More than just a guy. What do you do?"

That changed with the assignment, he thought. "I'm working for a chopper shop. Motorcycles," he added.

She straightened her spine and squared her shoulders. "I know what a chopper is. I'm not some innocent fresh out of the backwoods."

Her indignation made him want to chuckle. She reminded him of a kitten facing down a very large and powerful dog. All the arched back and hissing fury didn't make the kitten any bigger.

"Not a lot of backwoods around here," he said easily. "Desert, though. You could be an innocent fresh out of the desert."

Her lips twitched, as if she were trying not to smile. He pushed her margarita toward her.

"You're letting all the ice melt," he told her.

She hesitated, then took a sip. "Are you from around here?" she asked.

"Born and raised. All my family's here."

"Such as?"

Now it was his turn to pause. He didn't usually give out personal information. In his line of work, it could get him into trouble. But he had a feeling Rachel wasn't going to be a threat to much more than his oath of celibacy.

"Three sisters, a mom. Their main purpose in life is to make me crazy." He made the statement with equal parts love and exasperation.

Rachel looked wistful. "That's nice. Not the crazy part, but that you're close."

"You're not close to your family?"

"I don't have any."

He didn't know what to say to that and reminded himself too late that he was supposed to be charming her, not reminding her that she was alone in the world.

"Are you from around here?" he asked.

"Riverside?" She shook her head. Her hair swayed and caught the light and, for the moment, totally mesmerized him. "I moved here after I graduated from college. I wanted a nice, quiet, suburban sort of place." She sighed. "Not very exciting."

"Hey, I've lived here all my life. I can show you the best spots for viewing the submarine races."

She grinned. "Where I grew up, we went parking over by the river. Well, not really a river. More of a gully. Part of the year, it even had water in it."

"Parking, huh?"

She shrugged. "I had my moments."

"And now?"

Her gaze drifted to where her friend still talked to Eddy. "Not so much." She looked back at him. "Why'd you come over?"

He smiled. "Have you looked in the mirror lately?"

She ducked her head and blushed. Carter couldn't remember the last time he'd seen a woman blush. He wanted to make her do it again.

"Thank you," she said. "I spend my days with five-year-olds whose idea of being charming is to put glue in my hair. You're a nice change."

"You're comparing me to a five-year-old?" he asked, pretending outrage.

"Well, a lot of guys have maturity issues."

"I'm totally mature. Responsible, even."

She didn't look convinced. "Of course you are."

Carter was…interesting, Rachel thought, then nearly laughed out loud at the wild understatement. Okay, he was gorgeous, in a California blond, male-model sort of way. Classically handsome with shaggy hair. She couldn't stop looking at him, which told her she needed to get out more. No wait—that was already on her to-do list.

He was big, with broad shoulders and a smile that made her toes curl inside her sensible, low-heeled pumps even as she wondered if there were any interesting tattoos underneath the chambray shirt and jeans. What would it be like to be a leather-and-lace kind of woman—someone who knew what to do with a guy like Carter? As it was she was blushing, practically stammering and wishing Diane would hurry up so they could go.

Except she wasn't ready to leave. Not just yet. Carter

wasn't the kind of guy who usually came on to her, but it was fun to play "what-if" even if only in her head.

So she took a drink of her margarita and imagined herself to be wearing a wicked red-lace bra and a matching thong under black leather and some low-cut bustier. What would *that* Rachel say to a man like him?

"So tell me a secret," she said, surprising herself and, from the way his eyebrows lifted, him.

Her instinct was to take it back and say he didn't have to, but she refused to crumble now.

He thought for a second, then shrugged. "I keep trying to give up on women. They invade every part of my life and I know I'd be better off if I could just stay away from them. I was raised to do the right thing, so once I'm involved it's hard to get out."

Not the answer she'd expected. "You know I'm a woman, right?" she asked, only half kidding.

He grinned. "Oh, yeah. I noticed."

"You're going to give up women by not avoiding them?"

He sipped his beer. "It's a work in progress," he admitted. "I avoid them for a few months and then I walk into somewhere safe and I'm sucker punched by someone I didn't expect."

Did that mean her?

"So tell me your secret," he said.

"I dance," she admitted without thinking, then immediately wished she could call back the words. "I mean, I used to. When I was growing up and in college. I wanted to be a dancer, but I don't have the right body type."

He was polite enough to keep his gaze firmly fixed on her face.

"What kind of dance?" he asked.

"Everything. Ballet, jazz, modern. I still take classes,

which is silly because it's not like I'm going to do something with it."

"Why is it silly? Does everything have to have a purpose?"

She didn't know how to answer. She'd never told anyone about her dancing and she wasn't sure why she'd admitted it now. Maybe because it was easier than talking about her leather-and-lace fantasy.

Before she could answer his question, Diane's sharp voice cut across the floor.

"You're a jerk, Eddy. I don't know why I ever bothered with you."

"Hey, babe, don't be that way."

Eddy reached for Diane, who pushed his arm away. "I hate you. How's that for an *I* sentence. Go to hell."

Eddy threw up both hands. "I don't need this from you. Just forget it."

Diane glared at him. "Fine, I will. This is the end. Don't bother coming around again. Understand?"

"Clearly. Don't you come crawling back. I'm not interested."

"Me, either."

With that, Diane whirled around and marched out of the bar.

Rachel stared after her. "She said she wanted to break up with him, but I didn't think she meant it." She looked at the exit, wondering if her friend would be all right. "I need to go check on her."

"Sure thing."

Rachel stood, as did Carter. She glanced from him to the door and back.

"Thanks for the drink and the conversation," she said, suddenly feeling awkward. "You were really nice."

His easy smile gave her toes another miniworkout. "Words every guy longs to hear."

"What? Oh." She laughed. "Right. Sorry. You were especially dangerous tonight. I was terrified."

"Better."

He stepped around the table and lightly kissed her. She had no warning. One second he was moving and the next she felt a soft, tempting pressure on her mouth that was gone before she could fully grasp it.

"Take care, Rachel," he said and headed back to the bar.

She watched him go, then turned and walked out into the still warm evening. Who could have known she could meet such a great guy in a bar? She glanced at the sign showing a sitting, tail-wagging, blue dog in bright neon. And here, of all places.

At least she could check "get out more" off her to-do list, she thought as she moved toward Diane's car. That was—

The car was gone.

Rachel distinctly remembered where her friend had parked because the ghostly blue from the sign had turned her dress purple as she'd climbed out of the car. As Diane wasn't standing around in hysterics, it was unlikely the car had been stolen.

"But she was my ride home," Rachel said aloud to no one.

Diane had left her? Was that possible? Sure, her friend had been upset, but…

Rachel walked to the edge of the parking lot and glanced up and down the street. Nothing. No familiar blue sedan cruised in her direction.

Her mouth opened and closed. This could not be happening. Sure she didn't know Diane all that well, but how flaky would the other woman have to be to go off and forget her?

"Is there a problem?"

The familiar voice made her want to groan, and not in a good way. She'd been so happy with how things had gone in the bar. She'd managed to act sophisticated and bar-worldly...sort of. But to have all that blown now was really unfair.

She turned until she faced Carter, then shrugged.

"So your girlfriend was more upset than either of us realized," he said, obviously grasping what had happened.

"Apparently."

"Come on," he said with a smile. "I'll take you home."

She wanted to tell him that wasn't necessary. That she would call another friend or a cab. But it was late and she hated to disturb anyone because of what had happened, and this was Riverside, not New York. There weren't exactly cabs cruising around looking for fares.

He held up both hands, as if surrendering. "I'm perfectly safe."

"Ha. You said you were dangerous."

"Only in my dreams."

He tilted his head in invitation. She sighed, then nodded.

"Thank you," she said as she followed him to a large black truck.

"No problem. This can be my good deed for the week. It'll make my mom happy."

Him mentioning his mother eased a little of her tension. She felt awkward as she climbed onto the passenger seat, which felt about thirty feet above the ground.

"Nice truck," she said when he slid in on the driver's side. "Great visibility."

"Macho," he corrected with a grin. "Macho truck."

She couldn't help laughing. "Of course. My mistake. Imagine how high it would be if you got those really big tires."

"Not my style."

Oh, but a truck was? And people said women were confusing.

He started the engine, then glanced at her. "Where to?"

She fastened her seat belt and gave him directions.

After Carter pulled out of the parking lot, he said, "You need to have a talk with your friend. Driving off and leaving you alone at a bar is not okay."

"I agree. I couldn't believe it when I stepped out and her car was gone. I don't know her all that well, but still…" She shrugged.

"You work together?" he asked.

"Yes. She just started this term. Diane teaches fourth grade."

"Big kids," he teased.

"Bigger than mine. Plus I suspect by the time they're nine there's a whole lot less paste eating. But I wouldn't trade. I love the little kids. Everything is exciting and new to them. They see all the possibilities. If I do my job right, I can help them love school for the rest of their lives."

Just then his cell phone rang. He pulled it out of his shirt pocket and flipped it open.

"Brockett. Uh-huh. Yeah. How'd you know?" He laughed. "No. I've got it. Night." He hung up. "Your friend came back, looking for you."

"Really? Good. I didn't want to have to yell at her tomorrow. Who called?"

"Jenny, the bartender. She'll tell Diane that you're good."

Rachel opened her mouth, then closed it. She wasn't sure "good" covered it. There was every possibility that Diane would think she was going home with a guy she just met. Perhaps not the most awful thing in the world, but not a reality Rachel was comfortable with.

As she couldn't discuss that with Carter, she asked the next logical question.

"How does the bartender know your cell number?"

"Don't panic," he told her. "I'm not that much of a regular. Jenny and I go way back. We've been friends for years."

Friends, huh? And before that?

He pulled up in front of her small apartment building. It was in an older part of town. Rachel had chosen the place specifically because she loved the higher ceilings and custom touches of the Craftsman-style architecture.

Carter turned off the engine, then looked at the carport. "Let me guess," he said, eyeing the cars parked there. "The gray sedan."

She unfastened her seat belt and had the satisfaction of knowing she was about to shock him. "The little red, two-seater convertible."

His eyes widened. "No way."

"Way."

His gaze settled on her face. "Why wasn't my kindergarten teacher more like you?"

"Maybe she was. Five-year-olds tend not to notice stuff like that."

"I guess."

Before she could thank him for the ride, he climbed out of the truck. She did the same and they met on the sidewalk.

"You don't have to walk me up," she said.

"I want to. This is a full-service rescue."

She felt nervous and out of her element, but not afraid. She liked Carter and while she knew she would probably never see him again, she couldn't help being glad he didn't want to run right off.

She led the way up the stairs to the far apartment. As they passed between her overflowing plant stands, he asked, "Yours?"

She pulled her keys out of her purse. "Another hobby. I like to grow things."

"A kindergarten teacher who dances and has a green thumb. Interesting." He stepped a little closer and lightly touched her cheek with his fingertips. "I'm going to kiss you, Rachel. I'm telling you this in advance, so you can race inside, slap me or go with it and kiss me back. We all know what my choice would be, but you get a say in this, too."

The porch light brought out the gold in his blond hair. He was both handsome and sexy, a fairly irresistible combination. She hadn't been on a date in months or been kissed in nearly two years and until this exact moment, hadn't realized how much she'd missed having a man in her life.

"I'm not the slapping type," she murmured, her gaze locked with his.

He gave her a slow, knowing smile that made her shiver.

"Good to know," he said, right before he kissed her.

Chapter 2

Carter's mouth was warm and firm on hers, but tender. Rachel had thought he might be one of those pushy kissers, claiming what he wanted. Instead he moved back and forth against her mouth, giving just enough to make her want more.

One of them moved toward the other. She wasn't sure who was responsible for the sudden closeness, but she wasn't going to complain about the feel of his hard, muscled body pressing against hers. He smelled good—like the outdoors, with a hint of masculine temptation. Heat radiated from him, making her want to cuddle even closer, like a cat looking for a sunny spot.

One of his hands continued to stroke her cheek, lightly brushing against her skin, while the other rested on her waist. She wondered if he were holding her in place. Had her mouth not been so busy pressing up against his, she would have told him that she had no intention of going anywhere.

He brushed the very tip of his tongue against her lower lip. The tiny movement was both exciting and erotic. She parted for him, then held her breath in anticipation of him deepening the kiss.

He moved forward slowly, cautiously, as if giving her time to retreat. Instead all she could think was how long it had been since she'd really kissed a man. Not since she'd broken off her engagement nearly two years ago.

At the exact moment his tongue gently stroked hers, need exploded inside of her. The intensity was as shocking as it was unexpected. She wanted more, needed more. Her body suddenly ached to have him touching her. Skin tightened, her breasts swelled. She let her purse slip to the ground, then wrapped both arms around his neck and leaned into him.

He accepted her with a low groan that made her nipples tighten. He pulled her against him, even as he ran his hands up and down her back. She tilted her head and he deepened the kiss, exploring all of her mouth with an urgency that made her tremble.

The depth of passion stunned her. She'd never felt like this from just a kiss and certainly never with a man she'd just met. It was insane. It was also thrilling and arousing and so not anything she was used to.

Carter pulled back slightly. He kissed her cheeks, then along her jaw and down her neck.

"You're so beautiful," he murmured. "Are you trying to make guys crazy on purpose?"

She could barely breathe, let alone speak, but she forced herself to gather her thoughts. "What are you talking about?"

"Those damn curves in that prim little dress," he muttered as he licked the sensitive skin just below her ear. "It shouldn't be legal."

Her eyes popped open and she stared into the darkness of the night. "Me?" she asked in a voice that squeaked. "But I need to lose about fifteen pounds." Twenty, really, but she couldn't bring herself to say that aloud. "I'm not…"

"Incredible?" he asked, brushing her mouth with his. "Sexy? Stunning?" He straightened and smiled. "If this wasn't the first time I'd kissed you and if I hadn't been raised to know better, I'd show you exactly what you've done to me."

Curiosity exploded. Was he talking about what she thought he was talking about? Had she really aroused him?

For her own part, she felt more than a little tingly, but he was so much more cool than she could ever hope to be.

She looked into his dark eyes and saw fire burning there. His desire matched her own growing need.

"I've never…" she said, then cleared her throat. "I don't…"

"I know," he said with more than a little regret. "I swore off sex on the first date about the time I turned twenty. You're not the type." He smiled ruefully. "I'll tell you what, Rachel. You're enough to make me rethink my plan of swearing off women."

He kissed her again, then bent down and picked up her purse. She took it from him and held it in both hands. It was that or reach for him again.

He drew in a deep breath. "Here's what I think. You're gonna go inside your place, smile, thank me for a great evening and close the door." He frowned. "You need to lock it, too."

That made her smile. "You're not the type to break in."

"I don't know. I haven't been this tempted before."

His words made her tremble. She knew his advice was sound, but it was amazingly difficult to force herself to open her door, then step inside alone. Still, she did it. She set her keys and her purse on the small table by the door, then drew in a breath and prepared to tell him goodbye.

She was in his arms. She wasn't sure who made the move, but it didn't matter because holding him and being held felt so good. Even as his mouth claimed hers in a kiss that stirred her to her soul, she savored the feel of his hands as he ran them up and down her back. She could feel the pressure of his fingers, the heat of him. When he lingered on her hips, she instinctively arched toward him. Her belly brushed against his erection.

Need rushed through her. He hadn't been kidding—he *did* want her. Just as she wanted him. Nothing about this made any sense at all, but where men were concerned, she'd always been cautious. She'd had exactly two lovers in her life and she'd waited until she'd been sure they were in love and talking about getting married before giving in. She'd never been with a stranger. Until tonight she'd never even kissed a stranger. She was sure that in the bright light of day she would have given herself a stern talking-to, but right now she didn't care.

She placed her hands on his chest and allowed herself to explore him. As their tongues circled and danced and mated, she learned how she liked to breathe in the scent of his skin.

He set his hands on her waist and moved them up. Slowly, slowly, as if giving her time to protest. Without thinking, she covered his hands with hers and brought them to her breasts.

She was jolted both by her own actions, something she'd never done before, and the exquisite pleasure of having him touch her there. She decided to deal with her guilt later and simply enjoy the feel of him caressing her curves, brushing against her nipples and making her body melt.

The ever-present need grew. She was already wet and swollen and she wanted to be touched everywhere. She squirmed to get closer even as he started unbuttoning the front of her dress.

Yes, she thought hazily. Without clothes they could touch each other. She tugged at his T-shirt. He stepped back, unfastened the buttons and ripped it off. Passion darkened his eyes to the color of the night sky. There was light from a single small lamp in the corner but it was enough to let her see how hard he was breathing and how his desire pushed at the zipper of his jeans.

They came together again. Now she could touch his back and chest, feeling the warmth and smoothness of his skin. He managed to unfasten the front buttons on her dress and push the fabric aside. Her arms were caught for a moment, then she freed herself and shoved it out of the way. Her dress fell to the floor and pooled at her feet.

Under any other circumstances, she would have been embarrassed, but there was no time. Carter bent down and, through her bra, took her nipple in his mouth. She lost herself in the wet heat and gentle sucking. She touched his head, his back, his arms and wished there was a way to touch all of him.

He nudged her backward. She went willingly, then let herself fall onto the sofa. He eased on top of her until they were a tangle of arms and legs. His arousal pressed between her thighs and, even with multiple layers of clothing, he managed to excite that one sensitive spot.

More, she thought frantically, knowing it had been so long and that she would be close in a matter of seconds. She needed more.

He unfastened her bra and pulled it away. Now she felt his mouth on her bare skin and it was nearly enough to send her over the edge. He slipped one hand between them and even as his tongue teased her aching nipple and brought her close to the edge, he eased between her legs and under her panties to get lost in paradise.

He found her center immediately. She didn't know if it was good luck or a lot of practice, and at that moment, she didn't care. He rubbed around the swollen spot before brushing over it. She gasped as her body tightened and every cell waited breathlessly for that one moment of release.

Again and again he touched her, moving steadily, then slower, then faster, pushing her into madness until she could only wait, unable to breathe until her body gave in to the pure pleasure and convulsed into release.

She clung to him as the waves rippled through her. He continued to touch her and she continued to climax until he swore, pulled back, unfastened his jeans, jerked down her panties and plunged inside of her.

He was thick and he filled her until she had no choice but to climax again. They held on to each other, kissing, straining, reaching. He called out her name, then stiffened as his body found its own release, and then they were still.

Rachel savored the weight of him, unable to believe that she, of all people, had really made love with a stranger, on her slip-covered sofa, with the scent of night-blooming jasmine in the air.

Rachel woke a few minutes before her alarm clock went off, to find the sun streaming into the room. That didn't make sense, she thought in sleepy confusion. She always closed the blinds and then pulled the pale curtains. But this morning the curtains were all that were between her and an east-facing window. Huh. Shouldn't she have...

Reality crashed in on her. She suddenly remembered why, exactly, she hadn't bothered to lower the blinds. In truth, she hadn't pulled the curtains, but someone else had. Probably the same person who had urged her into her bed so their second round of lovemaking could take place in more leisurely comfort.

She sat up, then immediately squealed and sank back under the covers. She was naked. Totally, completely naked. She never slept naked, but then she never brought a man she'd barely met back to her apartment and had sex with him.

Embarrassment heated her cheeks. What had she been thinking? Easy answer—she hadn't. She'd been too busy *feeling*.

But that was no excuse, she told herself as she clutched the sheets to her chest and slowly sat up again. There were no excuses, no way to justify what she'd done. Momentary insanity, she thought glumly. What other explanation could there be?

She glanced around the room, looking for evidence that Carter was still around. There was no noise from the bathroom and she didn't see any of his clothes. Had he left? Would that make things better or worse?

Before she could decide, she spotted a piece of paper resting at the foot of the bed. Cautiously, careful to stay covered by the sheet, she reached for it.

Morning, Rachel. Sorry to duck out without saying goodbye, but I have to be at work really early and I didn't let you get a whole lot of sleep last night, so I didn't want to wake you before dawn. You're amazing and I hope I can see you again. Here's my cell number.

He'd left a phone number and signed his name.

Rachel read the note over a couple of times before setting it on the nightstand. He was gone. That was a relief. She didn't have to deal with any awkward "morning after" conversation. In truth, she didn't have to deal with anything. Last night had been a weird, unexplainable phenomenon. Like a bubble in the space-time continuum. She would accept it as such and move on.

Right, she thought as she got out of bed and ran to the closet so she could pull on her robe. Moving on was an excellent plan. Last night had never even happened. She wouldn't think about it ever again.

Except, as she walked to the kitchen to start her morning coffee, she noticed that specific parts of her felt a little sore. Her hips and thighs had that stretched-too-far ache and there was a faint sort of throb in more intimate places.

No wonder, she thought with a smile. The first time had been all heat and speed, but the second had been incredibly slow and seductive and—

"Stop!" she said aloud in a firm voice. "No thinking, remember? This is thinking. Stop it."

Right. She had to remember it had all been a big mistake. Not one she would ever repeat, under any circumstances. Carter could have been a serial killer. Right now her body could be in chunks all over the place. She'd been stupid and for reasons not clear to anyone, she'd gotten out unscathed.

As for calling Carter, that wasn't going to happen. What was she supposed to say to him? How could she explain she wasn't that type of woman, when as far as he was concerned, she obviously was. She hated that he would think she was slutty, but she couldn't think of a way to change his mind. He was good-looking enough that this sort of thing probably happened to him all the time. He wouldn't even give her another thought, just as she'd get him out of her mind immediately. Starting right now.

But when she reached for her coffeepot, she realized it was full and that the aroma of the fresh brew filled the room.

He'd made coffee before he'd left, she realized with a little sigh. Talk about thoughtful.

The phone rang. Rachel's heart fluttered briefly before she consciously squashed the sensation. No fluttering, no anticipation, no hoping, no Carter. Besides, the man might know where she lived and be on very intimate terms with her body, but he didn't know her phone number.

"Hello?"

"Rachel? It's Diane. Are you okay?"

"I'm fine."

Diane sighed. "I'm so sorry about last night. I can't believe I took off like that and left you. I nearly had a heart attack when I got home and realized what I'd done. I came right back but the bartender said you'd already gotten a ride home. I would have called then, but it seemed so late. Are you sure you're fine?"

"I am," she said, determined to make it true by sheer force of will.

"Okay. Good. Obviously Eddy makes me crazy. I'm so not going out with him anymore." Diane sighed. "I should be more like you. You're so sensible when it comes to men."

Rachel held in a wince. "I have my moments, like everyone else."

Diane laughed. "Oh, please. When was the last time you did anything impetuous with a guy?"

Rachel wasn't about to answer *that* question. "Thanks for checking on me. I'll see you later at school."

"Right. Bye."

Rachel hung up the phone and poured herself a mug of coffee. It was a new day and she had a new plan. No more wild nights with men she didn't know. She would go back to being the kind of woman Diane assumed she was. Better for everyone, especially herself.

The rhythmic click of the knitting needles was a good memory for Rachel. One of her years in foster care had been with an older woman who had taught her to knit. She associated the feel of the soft yarn and the sound of the needles with calm evenings spent by a fire with plenty of hot cocoa on hand.

"She's going to throw me out of class," Crissy said in a low voice.

Noelle grinned at Rachel, then turned to their friend. "She's not. She likes you."

"Ha. She has to." Crissy tugged at her tangled knitting.

"I gave her a free month at one of my gyms. I know it's wrong to bribe people but I didn't know what else to do."

Rachel held in a smile. "Gee, Crissy, have you thought of actually paying attention to your knitting? It *is* why we're here."

Crissy laughed. "Oh, please. You know I only come here so we can go to dinner afterward. The first set of classes wasn't too bad, but now things are so complicated. Who writes these patterns?"

"We could meet you for dinner after knitting class," Noelle offered.

"This is fine," Crissy told her as she held out her needles to Rachel. "I'll muddle through."

"*Muddle* being the key word," Rachel said as she took the disaster and began unraveling it. "How can you mess up casting on? It's just not that complicated."

"I'm a businesswoman. I can run my company, but I'm not very good with my hands," Crissy said. "Big deal."

Noelle, ever the peacemaker, patted her arm. "You could try a little harder."

"I could also wish to be taller," Crissy said. "It's not happening."

Rachel looked at Noelle. "She's hopeless."

"Pretty much," Noelle said cheerfully. "But we love her anyway."

Noelle set down her needles and stretched her arms above her head. "I'm getting creaky," she said. "I'm only twenty and I'm already stiff and old."

Crissy leaned over and hugged Noelle. "You're pregnant. There's a difference." She patted her friend's round belly. "I can't believe how long it took you to show. You're into your sixth month and you're not big at all."

"I feel big," Noelle said with a contented smile. "I feel huge. But it's good."

"Of course it is," Rachel told her. "How's Dev?"

Noelle's expression turned dreamy. "Perfect in every way. He wants us to go away before the baby's born. Sort of a belated honeymoon. But he doesn't want me to worry about flying. So he's been looking into a cruise on the Mexican Riviera. Maybe in late January."

Rachel couldn't help smiling at her friend. Noelle radiated happiness. Her marriage to Devlin Hunter had started out as a purely practical arrangement that had turned into something wonderful when they'd fallen in love. Even their brief scare that something might be wrong with the baby had ended well when the tests had come back with the good news that everything was fine.

Noelle tucked her blond hair behind her ears. "So, what's new with you two?" she asked.

Crissy laughed. "Since last week? Gee, nothing. What about you, Rach? Any deep, dark secrets you want to share?"

"Not really," Rachel murmured. She was still a little sore from her wild adventure three nights before, but she sure wasn't going to mention that to her friends. While she didn't think they would actually disapprove, she wasn't ready to confess all. Maybe she never would be.

In truth, she couldn't figure out why she'd allowed things to get so out-of-hand with Carter. Okay, he'd been funny and charming and sexy. In her line of work, she didn't meet a lot of guys like that. Most of the men in her circle were married and fathers of five-year-olds.

And yes, it had been long time since her last relationship, so maybe she'd been in a weakened condition. But still—that was hardly an excuse for what she'd done.

Just as bad, she was starting to regret throwing away Carter's note, which was crazy. It wasn't as if she would have ever called the man. And say what? Invite him out on a date? He would think she was only interested in him for sex. How humiliating. Not that she wasn't interested in him that way, but there would have to be more than just that. Just thinking about it all was confusing, which meant that a relationship would be difficult and if there were this many questions now, what was the point?

She knew better than to get involved. Caring meant losing and she'd already had enough pain in her life.

"Earth to Rachel," Noelle said. "Are you all right?"

"What? Oh." Rachel handed Crissy her knitting project. "I'm fine. Just a little distracted."

"I would normally assume work," Crissy said, "but you had the oddest look on your face."

Rachel willed herself not to blush. "It's nothing."

Crissy didn't look convinced. "I make it a rule never to pry, but I'm tempted this one time. Just promise me you won't do what Noelle did and turn up pregnant."

"Of course not," Rachel said. "I'm not dating anyone."

"Dating isn't actually required," Crissy informed her with a grin. "Sometimes proximity is enough."

Noelle laughed. Rachel forced herself to smile, despite the dark, ugly pit that had opened up in her stomach.

Pregnant? No! It wasn't possible. No, no, no. She couldn't be. They'd only done it those two times. Just twice.

Without protection.

Rachel wanted to run screaming into the early evening. She wanted to pound her head against the table, or at the very least, turn back time and not invite Carter into her apartment that night.

She couldn't be pregnant. She was single and a kindergarten teacher. This wasn't part of her plan. Not yet. Of course she wanted a husband and a family, just like most women. But in that order. Someday. When she was feeling brave enough to risk her heart.

It wasn't possible, she told herself firmly, fighting the need to throw up. She would be fine.

Seventeen days after her night with Carter and fourteen days after considering the possibility of pregnancy, Rachel sat on the edge of her tub and told herself not to break into hysterics.

She'd waited an extra two days just to be sure. She'd been patient, she'd done her best not to think about it. She'd willed her period to start exactly on time and when it hadn't, she'd gone the extra mile just to be sure.

Now, she stared at the seven plastic sticks she'd neatly lined up on two paper towels. They were from three different kits and they all said exactly the same thing.

Positively pregnant.

Chapter 3

Rachel hadn't planned on ever returning to the Blue Dog Bar. Unfortunately, since she'd tossed the note with Carter's cell number on it, she had no way to get in touch with the man. But she had remembered that one of the bartenders—Rachel couldn't remember her name—had known Carter well enough to have his number and so here she was, showing up at three-thirty in the afternoon, with a nervous stomach and several spots of drying paste on the hem of her skirt.

Kindergarteners were hard on their teacher's clothes, she thought as she glanced down at the dark patches. At least the paste would wash out. If only her problem with Carter could be solved as easily.

She drew in a deep breath, wished she hadn't been so hasty with that note he'd left and walked into the dim building.

It was early enough that there weren't many customers. Rachel ignored the few patrons and made her way to the bar, where she sighed in relief when she recognized the same woman who had been here that night three weeks ago.

The woman behind the bar smiled. "Hi. Can I help you?" She was pretty—late twenties, with a cute, short haircut and big green eyes.

"I hope so," Rachel said, wishing she weren't so nervous. She could feel herself shaking. "I'm, ah, looking for Carter."

The bartender continued to smile. "Okay. Carter who?"

Rachel held in a moan of humiliation. "I don't know," she admitted in a rush. "I met him here three weeks ago. I didn't mean to. I was here with a friend and she was breaking up with this guy and…" She sucked in a breath and clutched the large envelope of papers to her chest. "That's not important, right? Because no one cares. Okay. We, ah, met and I need to talk to him. It's really important. Carter. He's about six-two with dark blond hair."

Honestly, how many Carters could there be? Rachel swallowed hard, then blurted out, "He has a scar shaped like a lightning bolt on his thigh right by his…"

"Oh," the woman said, knowing. "*That* Carter. Have a seat. I'll see if I can get in touch with him."

Carter couldn't decide if he was annoyed or relieved. He couldn't believe it had been three weeks and Rachel was only now getting in touch with him. Sure, hard-to-get was a time-honored game between the sexes, but hey— it was him. He'd never had to wait to get a call before.

Logically, this was probably better. He knew better

than to get involved and if she were the kind of female totally into games, he wouldn't be into her. Problem solved.

Except he had a feeling it wouldn't be that simple. He hadn't been able to get Rachel out of his mind. He knew where she lived and could have gone to see her, but that wasn't his style. Besides, he'd left her his number and she hadn't called. What did that say about what she thought about him?

He walked into the Blue Dog Bar determined to make her want him, even though he didn't know if he wanted her. His male pride was at stake. He nodded at Jenny, who pointed to a booth in the back. He squared his shoulders and strolled casually in that direction.

Only to get broadsided by a two-by-four.

It didn't matter that the hunk of wood was metaphorical. His gut twisted, the air rushed out of his lungs and he would swear he could hear angels singing. Damn, she looked good.

Rachel sat facing the bar, her back all straight, her clothes prissy enough for a preacher's wife and her hair tied back in some kind of fancy braid. But he knew the truth. He knew that behind that don't-touch-me-I'm-a-good-girl exterior beat the heart of a wanton. She kissed like a dream and made love as if it were her last time.

Heat poured through him and he had a brief but intense fantasy about dragging her onto the table and taking her right there. Only he'd never been one to show off in front of strangers. Besides, she hadn't called and that might have hurt his feelings.

"Rachel," he said as he approached.

She half stood, then sank back into the seat. "Hello, Carter."

He slid into the seat across from her, then noticed

the large legal-sized envelope she'd placed on the table. What was that about?

"It's been awhile," he said.

She nodded. "Three weeks."

She licked her lips, which made his whole body clench. Damn, why did she have to get to him?

She put her hands on the table, laced her fingers together, then pulled back and dropped them to her lap. Nervousness radiated from her like a fine mist. He half expected her to clutch her stomach and run for the bathroom.

He'd decided to play it cool, to let her do all the talking. Not only was it a power play, but he would learn more that way. So he got really annoyed with himself when he blurted out, "You didn't call."

She blinked at him. "Excuse me?"

"You didn't call. I was polite. I had to be up early and I didn't want to wake you, so I left a note. And my phone number." He leaned toward her. "I don't go home with just anyone. Is that what you thought? You could use me and forget about me?"

He swore silently. Had those words come out of his mouth? If anyone ever found out he'd said them, he would be drummed out of the male gender and forced to live as a eunuch.

Her eyes widened. "I didn't use you."

"What would you call it? You had your way with me and then walked away without a second thought." Until today, but he doubted she would think of that.

"I'm the woman. I can't use you," she said.

"Right. Because only guys can be jerks. Women always act perfectly."

"Well, no. Of course not." She stared at him. "I wasn't trying to use you."

"You could have called."

"I didn't know what to say."

"How about 'Thanks for the great night. We should go out sometime.'" Unless she hadn't wanted to go out with him again, which wasn't possible.

She drew in a deep breath. "Carter, I'm sorry I didn't call, but we have something else more important to discuss."

Important, huh? With women, that generally meant one thing. The relationship. But he and Rachel didn't have a relationship.

"I'm listening," he said.

She nodded, then exhaled. "There are ramifications from our night together."

It took a second for her words to sink in. He swore under his breath and felt all desire bleed from his body.

"If you have something, you should have told me," he growled.

Dammit all to hell, he had no one but himself to blame. He hadn't used anything and he knew better. Not that he usually traveled with a condom. But he should have stopped to think, to ask, to be a responsible adult.

How bad was it? Would his…would it fall off?

"What?" she asked, sounding slightly outraged. "*Have something?* I'm not sick. There's nothing wrong with me."

"There's nothing wrong with me, either," he told her. "I'm fine. So if we're both fine, what's the problem?"

She glared at him. "Seeing you know everything about women, you should have already figured it out. I'm pregnant."

Had he mentioned that all of his trouble came from

the women in his life? Timing being what it was, Jenny chose that moment to come up and ask if they wanted something to drink.

He looked up at her and sighed. "Give us a minute," he said.

"Sure thing."

Jenny glanced at Rachel and then headed back to the bar.

Carter knew what would happen next. He figured they had maybe fifteen minutes more of privacy and, given the topic, they were going to need a lot more.

He turned his attention back to Rachel and let her words wash over him. Pregnant. *Pregnant?*

"You're not on the Pill?" he asked, more to himself than her. Because he hadn't asked before…when it had mattered.

"No," she said, her voice low and annoyed.

"You let yourself have sex with me without protection or birth control?"

She opened her mouth and then closed it. "Not on purpose," she told him. "It wasn't as if I'd planned the night. It just sort of happened. I lost my head."

And that was going to be his fault.

"I don't do this sort of thing very much," she said, obviously still annoyed, although he couldn't figure out what *her* problem was. He was the injured party here.

"Meaning?" he asked.

She glanced around, then lowered her voice. "I've only been with two other guys and I was engaged to both of them."

"You've been married before?" he asked, feeling slightly outraged. "Twice?"

"No." She leaned back against the seat and groaned.

"I was engaged, not married. That isn't the point. I'm pregnant."

"I got that."

"There's going to be a baby."

That stopped him. Because until she'd said the "b" word, he hadn't put the two together. Pregnant was a scary, dangerous condition used to trap men, but a baby was something pretty miraculous.

He felt himself smile. "Yeah?"

"Don't you dare be happy," she told him. "Neither of us planned this. We don't even know each other." She thrust the envelope toward him. "I've been to a lawyer. This is a very straightforward agreement. I'm not asking you for anything now or ever. In return, you sign away all rights to the child."

"Why would I do that?"

She rolled her eyes. "Because it makes the most sense. Like I said, we barely know each other. We can't have a baby together."

"I'd say we already are."

From the corner of his eye, he saw Jenny on the phone. She was quick, he would give her that.

A baby. He didn't know what he felt, exactly, except a certainty that the kid would be a girl. As for signing away his rights, that wasn't going to happen in this lifetime.

"We need to talk," he said, then winced. Was Jenny spiking the beer? Was he turning into a woman?

"There's nothing to talk about. You should look at the papers."

He leaned toward her. "I'm not discussing this in a bar."

She flinched. "I'm not taking you home with me. Look what happened last time."

He wanted to tell her that he wasn't interested in her that way—except he was. Now that he knew all his parts were going to stay in place, he could appreciate her pale skin and the way her mouth curved when she smiled. Not that she'd done so in recent memory.

"I'm not trying to sleep with you," he said. "We can go to my place. Follow me in your car. Keep the damn engine running if you want. My point is, I'm not talking about this here."

He didn't mention that his ex-girlfriend was still friends with his mother and likely on the phone with her this exact second. Hence the need for speed.

Rachel considered his words, then nodded slowly. "Fine. Your place. But I want you to consider my offer. I'm not trying to trap you."

"Good to know."

Rachel enjoyed her little convertible and she'd always liked driving the manual transmission. Only this afternoon she couldn't stop shaking, which made it difficult to shift.

The conversation with Carter hadn't gone at all the way she'd imagined. For one thing, he'd kept talking about the fact that she hadn't called him. As if he'd wanted her to.

Honestly, the thought had never crossed her mind. She'd figured he slept with different women all the time and one more wasn't going to make an impact on his life. Had she been wrong? Did he really care that she hadn't called?

The thought was so foreign, she didn't know how to process it in her brain. Adding to the confusion was his refusal to instantly sign off on the baby. She'd never

thought he would *want* to take on that kind of responsibility. Weren't women always complaining that men
hated the idea of being tied down?

She had to make him understand they weren't in this
together. Dealing with being pregnant was hard enough,
and not something she'd even begun to accept, but having to deal with Carter, too, was unimaginable.

She followed his large, black truck into a pleasant
neighborhood, the kind populated by young families.
When he pulled into the driveway of a pretty, one-story
house, she parked in front and climbed out.

For a second, she looked around and felt herself get
lost in the past. This was the sort of street where she'd
grown up. Modest homes filled with parents and kids
and lots of laughter. Even after all these years, she could
remember everything about her old bedroom. The color
of the wallpaper, the bookshelves on the wall, the way
her mother would tease her about the mess on the floor.

Happy memories, she thought wistfully. Happy and
so very, very sad.

"Rachel?"

She looked up and saw Carter waiting by the front
door. She walked up the path and into his house.

The living room was open, with cream-colored drapes
and pretty sage paint on the walls. The furniture looked
relatively new and not the least bit like bachelor leather.

"Have a seat," he said, closing the front door behind
her. "You want something to drink?"

"I'm fine."

She set the paperwork on the coffee table, then sank
on the sofa. Now what?

Apparently Carter didn't know, either. He paced the
length of the room, paused in front of her, started to

speak, shook his head and started pacing again. She reminded herself that she'd had several days to attempt to get used to the news and she still wasn't dealing with it. The poor man would need some time.

"I didn't plan this," she said by way of a peace offering. "I want you to know that. What happened between us was totally unexpected."

He looked at her and smiled. "I know. I was there."

Somehow, she found herself getting lost in his brown eyes. She felt a pull between them. Something strong and powerful that made her want to stand up and step into his arms. Once there he would draw her close and...

Whoa! That's what had gotten her in trouble in the first place, she thought.

She cleared her throat. "My point is, I don't want you to be concerned. I can take care of myself." She wasn't sure how yet and thinking about being a single mother made her hyperventilate, but that wasn't his problem. "I have no intention of trapping you. You can take as long as you'd like to look over the papers."

His expression hardened. "Let's get this clear right now. I'm not signing away my kid."

He couldn't mean that. "Do you want to be a father?"

"I didn't plan on it this week, no. But we're talking about my child." He gave a strangled laugh. "Who am I kidding? My daughter. And you can't have her."

He stopped and put his hands on his hips. From her seated position, he looked very powerful and masculine and just a little intimidating.

"You can't mean that," she murmured, as caught off guard by his presence as by his words. "I never thought you'd be interested. You don't know me."

"Knowledge isn't required. We did it, it happened, now we'll deal with it."

What he said sounded perfectly logical, but this was not the conversation she thought they'd be having.

But before she could say that, the front door burst open and three women entered. One was in her fifties, the others were about Carter's age. Rachel stood and stared at them.

Carter groaned. "Mama, this is not a good time."

"You're one to talk about timing," the older woman said, pushing past him to stand in front of Rachel. "A man who gets a woman pregnant without meaning to should talk about timing. Apparently he's very good at it."

Mama? As in…his mother?

She was about five foot two, with short blond hair and Carter's eyes. Tiny, but Rachel could feel the energy pouring off her. The other two women were taller and pretty, but they were a little intimidating, too.

"H-how did you know?" she asked, not sure she wanted the answer.

Carter slumped into one of the club chairs opposite the sofa. "Jenny called her. Rachel, this is my mother, Nina Brockett, and two of my sisters, Liz and Merry. You don't need to know who is who because they won't be staying. Mama, this is Rachel."

"Of course we're staying," his mother told him, then turned to Rachel. "You should sit."

"Why would the bartender call you?" Rachel asked, wondering if this would ever make sense.

"Jenny's a friend of the family," Nina told her.

"We stay in touch with most of Carter's old girl-friends," one of his sisters offered. "There have been lots, but you're the first one to get pregnant."

Jenny from the bar was his *ex-girlfriend?*

"She's married," Carter said, as if he could read her mind. "I doubt you can make your escape now. You might as well sit."

"Of course she should sit," Nina said, moving next to Rachel, taking her hand and urging her back on the sofa. "She needs to rest. She's going to have a baby."

"The baby is maybe four cells big," Carter told her. "I doubt it's going to tire her out."

Rachel looked at him. "You went out with Jenny?" she asked, feeling herself blush. "She pretended not to know who you were. She made me describe…"

She suddenly became aware of the other three women in the room and sank onto the sofa.

"It doesn't matter," she whispered.

"That Jenny has a real sense of humor," Carter muttered.

One of the sisters smiled. "She's great. Carter was an usher in her wedding and she was a bridesmaid in mine."

This was way too much information, Rachel thought frantically, glancing at the door and wondering if she could make a run for it. This wasn't happening. She hadn't just met Carter's mother, two sisters *and* his ex-girlfriend.

Nina patted her hand. "You'll be fine. This is shocking now, but that's because Carter didn't tell you about us. Why my only son wouldn't mention his family to the mother of his child, I don't know. But I'm *only* the mother. No one tells me anything."

"Save me," Carter muttered as he rubbed his temples. "Mama, you're not helping."

"Of course I'm helping," his mother insisted. "I want

to help. It's what I do best. So, what were the two of you talking about when we got here?"

Rachel glanced at the envelope on the table. Suddenly Carter's unwillingness to walk away from his unborn child made a little more sense.

"That's private," Carter told her.

"You might as well tell us," one of his sisters said. "We'll find out anyway."

"No, you won't," Carter told her. He looked at Rachel. "If you want to make a run for it, I'll cover your back."

"She's not running," Nina said and it was only then Rachel realized the older woman still had a firm grip on her hand.

Rachel tugged it free. "Carter and I have some things we need to work out," she said weakly.

"Of course you do." Nina smiled at her. "You're a nice girl, I can tell. You didn't mean to get pregnant. But it happens. So we'll deal with it."

We? No, no. There was no *we*. "Technically, I'm the one who's pregnant," she began.

Carter's gaze narrowed. "And I'm the father."

"I'm not denying that," Rachel said, bristling. "I'm the one who came to you."

"I would have been happy to do things the other way," he reminded her. "You didn't call."

The sisters looked at each other. "Really? You went out with Carter and didn't call the next day?" one of them asked.

"Ah…"

"The women always call," the other sister said. "Some of them won't stop calling."

"Ah…"

"It gets embarrassing," the first one continued. "I want to take them aside and tell them to have a little pride."

"It's not their fault," Nina said with a proud smile. "It's my son."

Rachel raised her eyebrows. "Really?"

Carter groaned. "Ignore them. I mean that."

"Maybe I want to hear about 'the women.'"

"You don't," he told her. "Trust me."

"About the baby," Nina said, breaking the mood. "We need to talk." Nina patted the back of her hand. "I understand. If you young people insist on putting the cart before the horse, then they need to turn the horse around."

"What?" Rachel and Carter asked together.

Nina glanced between them. "Isn't it obvious? You have a baby coming. You need to get married."

Chapter 4

Carter stood. He'd been willing to let the moment run its course. Thirty years of being his mother's son had taught him that was the easiest way to deal with her. He would listen and then do exactly what he wanted. But mother or not, she'd just crossed the line.

"Okay, that's enough," he said flatly and walked to the door. "Great to see you all. Thanks for stopping by."

His mother was about a foot shorter, but that never seemed to bother her. She rose and walked over until she was in front of him, staring up, glaring.

"Carter Brockett, I'm serious."

"So am I, Mama. This isn't about you. This is between me and Rachel. We're going to deal with it and we don't need your help."

Her brown eyes narrowed. "You're going to have a baby, Carter. This is serious."

He knew she meant well. He knew she loved him and would gladly throw herself in front of a train for him. But sometimes she was the biggest pain in the butt.

He bent down and kissed her. "I know, Mama. Trust me, okay?"

She sighed heavily, then nodded. As she stepped out of the house, his sisters trailed after her. Merry grinned.

"You're in big trouble, now," she murmured as she passed.

"Thanks for the support."

"Any time."

He closed the door behind them.

Rachel still sat on the sofa, although she looked a little shell-shocked. His family had that effect on people. He'd seen it many times.

He walked into the kitchen and got her a glass of ice water, then returned to the living room. She stared at him, her green eyes wide, her mouth slightly parted.

"You doing okay?" he asked.

"No." She took the glass he offered. "Who *were* those people?"

He sank back into his chair. "My family. Most of them, anyway. I have another sister around somewhere. She must not have been home or she would have been part of the parade, too."

"You have three sisters, right?"

"I'm the youngest and the only boy. My dad died before I was born so it was just me and them. A world of women."

She sipped the water. "When you said women were the cause of all the trouble in your life, I thought you meant romantically."

"That would have made things too easy. I'm surrounded by them. Even my dog, a stray Lab who showed up one day all skinny and pathetic, is female. Welcome to my world."

She managed a small smile. "It's not so bad. Your family obviously cares about you." She took another drink. "Did Jenny really call your mother to tell her what she'd heard?"

"Oh, yeah. Jenny stayed pretty tight with her and my sisters. As have a lot of my ex-girlfriends. They show up at holidays or parties. I never know when I'm going to run into one." Or twenty, he thought grimly. Why couldn't his ex-girlfriends be like other women? Bitter and vindictive. Right now the idea of someone slashing his tires was a whole lot easier to deal with than someone like Jenny, who simply stayed in his world.

Not that he didn't like Jenny—he did. She'd married a great guy, but damn, whose side was she on? Calling his mother and telling her Rachel was pregnant.

Rachel set down her glass and glanced at him. "I didn't get pregnant on purpose."

"I know. Neither of us planned on that. We just weren't thinking."

She ducked her head, but he saw her smile. "I was kind of swept away. Nothing like that has ever happened to me before."

"Me, either."

She looked up and rolled her eyes. "Oh, please. I might not know you very well, but I'm getting a clear idea about your past. You seem to have women lined up around the block."

"Sure, a lot of relationships, but that kind of heat?" He shrugged, trying to remember the last time he'd felt it. "It doesn't happen very often."

"Are you just saying that?"

The uncertainty in her voice added to her charm. They were already in so much trouble, Carter almost felt still being attracted to her couldn't make things worse. Except he knew it could. A relationship would only complicate the situation. Better to keep his head and think clearly. If only she didn't smell so good.

"I don't do lines," he told her. "You're beautiful and sexy and funny. You dress like a nun and you have a body made for...ah, making love," he said, self-editing to something less graphic. "What's not to like?"

"Wow. When you say it like that, you were lucky to have me."

He smiled. "Yes, I was. Only now there are consequences for us to deal with."

"The baby."

"Right. Rachel, I'm not giving up my daughter."

"You don't actually know the baby is a girl."

"Yes, I do, but that doesn't matter. We're going to have to work something out, because I won't sign those papers."

He'd understood why she'd thought he might. Many guys would jump at the chance to walk away from this kind of responsibility, but he couldn't. He'd been raised to believe family mattered more than anything.

She leaned forward and fingered the thick envelope. "I know. I mean I didn't know before, but I do now." She straightened and touched her stomach. "So what do we do? No offense, but I'm not going to accept your mother's suggestion."

"You don't want to marry me?" he asked, his voice teasing.

"I don't know you."

"I'm a great catch."

"You certainly don't seem to have an ego problem."

He grinned. "I have references."

"Apparently in the hundreds."

"Not that many." He stood and moved to the sofa, where he angled toward her. "How about this. We have what, eight months until the baby is born?"

"Just about."

"Okay, let's take that time and figure out what we want to do. Not what my mother says is best. We'll talk about the situation and come up with a plan." He hesitated. "You're going to keep the baby, aren't you?"

She stiffened. "Of course. I want this child."

"Me, too. So what do you say? We'll take our time and consider our options. You live in the area, I live in the area, we could easily share custody. Or figure out something else that works. Let's get to know each other and find out what works best for us."

She bit her lower lip, which made him think about doing that for her, which made him think about other things. They *were* alone in the house.

Only that wasn't a very good idea right now.

"You're right," she said, obviously oblivious to the temptation she represented. "We have time. We should use it."

"Great." He grabbed a pen and paper from the end table and wrote down his home and cell number. Then he held the sheet out to her. "You're not going to throw it out again, are you?"

"No, I promise I won't."

She reached for the paper, but he held it out of reach. "Why didn't you call me?"

She sighed. "Are you ever going to let that go?"

"Probably not until you answer the question."

She sank back against the sofa. "I couldn't call you, Carter. I honestly didn't know what to say. I'd never done anything like that in my life. I was afraid of what you'd think of me. And I was afraid of what I'd think of myself."

He dropped the paper in her lap and gave an exaggerated sigh. "I knew it. You were just using me for sex."

She groaned. "You're impossible."

"Sometimes I'm even better than that."

"Give me those."

She reached across the sofa and grabbed the pen and paper from him. Suddenly they were very close, with her breasts pressing against his arm and one of her hands lightly touching his stomach.

His reaction was instant and predictable. Blood rushed south, and his brain went blank, except for the burning need to pull her into his arms.

Her gaze locked with his and he was gratified to see an answering fire there. Unfortunately, she had more self-control.

"I'll, ah, give you my number," she murmured as she drew back and quickly wrote down the information. "We should plan to get together and talk some more."

"How about Saturday?" he asked.

She handed him back the pad. "Okay. Do you want to go out or…" She shook her head. "No matter what I say, it's going to sound like a date."

"It's not a date," he told her, suddenly wishing it was. "Let's go casual. I'll bring dinner to your place. That way we won't be interrupted."

She blinked several times.

"While we talk," he added, emphasizing the last word. "Just talk."

"Okay. That's fine. We'll talk."

Carter went out back and whistled for Goldie. The golden Lab, named by one of his nieces, strolled out of her plush doghouse, stretched and ambled toward him. She gave him a quick lick on the hand by way of greeting, then bumped her head against his thigh so he would rub her ears.

"Have you noticed everything in this relationship is about you?" he asked conversationally as he obliged her for a couple of minutes. "Come on. We're going to see Mama."

The magic name perked up Goldie and she trotted eagerly to the side gate. Carter let her out, then followed her down the street. Goldie paused at the curb until he'd checked for traffic, then dashed across to a tidy front yard. She sniffed the big tree in front, raced up the two steps, rose on her back legs and pressed her paw against the bell.

The front door opened and his mother appeared.

"Goldie. Such a pretty dog. Come in, come in. I have some nice pot roast from last night. I saved you some." His mother held open the screen door for the dog, then glanced at him. "If you're going to tell me to mind my own business, you can go home now."

"That's exactly what I'm going to tell you and you know you'd never send me away without feeding me first."

"You think you know everything," his mother grumbled, but held the screen door open for him, too, then shooed him into the kitchen.

Carter had grown up in this house. He'd painted walls, laid tile and, when he was nine, broke the front window with a high fly ball hit from Billy Hinton's front yard. There were a lot of memories under this roof. Mostly good ones.

The kitchen was large and open, with painted cabinets and a six-burner stove that was always in use. Right now marinara sauce bubbled away.

He glanced around at the table. "Where are the girls?" He'd expected an inquisition.

"I sent them home. I wanted to talk to you alone."

That was never good news, he thought glumly as he pulled up a stool at the island and took a cookie from the ever-present plate of them. Neither the alone part nor her confidence that he would stop by.

"I appreciate your interest," he told his mother. "I love you, but stay out of this. Rachel and I have to figure out what to do ourselves."

"What to do?"

His mother might be short, but she was formidable when she got her back up. Right now, with him on the stool, they were perilously close to eye level. She glared at him.

"*What to do?*" she repeated, sounding both outraged and furious. "If you get a girl pregnant, Carter, you marry her. I raised you to know that."

There was something mythic about his mother. Carter had never figured out the source of her power, but he respected it. With the right look and tone of voice, she could make him feel as if he were ten years old again.

"Things have changed," he said. "Lots of women have babies on their own. That's what Rachel wants to do." The woman had tried to get him to sign away his own child. Nothing about those actions indicated a burning desire to marry him.

"Did you propose? Did you offer to take responsibility?"

"I said I wanted to be a part of my child's life. I want to share custody with her."

His mother walked to the sink, where she began rinsing pots. "Share custody. What does that mean? Half a life with a child? You're having a baby, Carter. This isn't a game. You have to marry this girl."

"She doesn't want to marry me."

"How do you know? Have you asked?"

He didn't mention the legal paperwork. She wouldn't understand a woman expecting a man to walk away from a child and it might make her dislike Rachel. Nina Brockett was a wonderful woman, but she could hold a grudge for decades. Better to take the fall himself. After all, Rachel was going to be his baby's mother, so there would be plenty of contact between Rachel and *his* mother.

"I already know the answer," he said.

"You think you do, but you could be wrong. Stranger things have happened."

"Mama, give it a rest."

She flung down a dishcloth and spun to face him. "I won't give it a rest. You're my son. We're talking about your firstborn child. You have to be a father to that baby."

He put down the cookie. "I'm going to be," he said quietly. "I'll be there."

Her expression softened. "I know, Carter. I'm sorry. You know more than anyone what it's like to grow up without a father."

"Then trust me to do the right thing," he said.

"I can't even trust you to wear a condom."

Every now and then she surprised the hell out of him. Desperate to escape he looked around for Goldie, who was nosing the now licked-clean dish on the floor by the pantry.

"I gotta go," he said as he stood, then whistled for his dog.

"Marry the girl."

"I love you, Mama."

"I love you, too. I'd love you more if you'd marry Rachel."

"Good to know."

He let himself out and made his way back to his house, knowing he could run but he couldn't hide. Once his mother had something lodged in her brain, she never let it go. She would be all over him until he and Rachel had tied the knot.

The thing was he didn't object to marriage in theory… for other people. But honestly, he didn't see the point. Why be with one person forever?

His sisters kept telling him he didn't understand because he'd never been in love. That one day he would fall and fall hard, and they all couldn't wait to be there.

He told them hell would freeze over first, but he hadn't meant it. He wouldn't mind falling in love. He wanted to feel that he couldn't live without the one person who made him want to get up every morning. Only he'd never found anyone who came close to that. Eventually he'd decided that romantic love was a myth—a product of greeting card advertisers.

If Rachel had wanted to get married to give the baby his name, he probably would have said yes, as long as she understood he wasn't about to fall in love with her. But from what he'd seen, that was the last thing on her mind.

So they would work something out—a sensible plan that took care of all their needs and the baby's as well. Because he knew one thing for sure—he might not believe in romantic love, but he knew about a parent's love for a child and no one was going to keep him from that.

"I'm having wine," Crissy said as they took their seats in the restaurant after knitting class. "I need it. I swear, I have an anti-knitting gene. If it wasn't that I wanted to hang out with you two so much, I would have given up that first week."

"You're not that bad," Noelle said kindly.

"Jan flinched when I showed her what I'd done. Did you see that?" Crissy asked, then shook her head. "I know you're going to want to take the advanced class and she's never going to let me. She'll probably hire a security guard just to keep me out."

Rachel laughed. "I don't think she cares that much. You're doing fine."

Crissy picked up her menu. "You mean you're able to rework what I've messed up and it looks okay." She shook her head. "I need to let it go. I'm a good person with a successful career."

"And a really nice car," Noelle added.

"Very upscale," Rachel said, remembering the too-cute coupe her friend had leased that week.

"I have good friends," Crissy said. "That should be enough, right? I don't date, but that's by choice. Another first date is the last thing I need. So I'm good. I can let the knitting thing go."

"Let it fly free," Rachel told her. "The yarn will thank you."

Noelle chuckled. Crissy rolled her eyes. "It's not my

fault," she muttered as she opened her menu. "I hate the yarn."

"It knows," Rachel said, hiding her smile. "It knows and it flinches when it sees you coming."

Crissy set down her menu and leaned across the table. "It's not fair. I have absolutely no crafty or homemaking type talents."

Rachel thought of her friend's minichain of women-only gyms. She'd opened her fourth the previous year and was looking at locations for a fifth.

"Want to trade paychecks?" Rachel asked brightly.

Crissy grinned. "Thanks, but no. You do a good thing, teaching those little kids, and you'll get your reward in heaven. Mine is more immediate."

"That's okay," Rachel assured her. "I've always wanted to be a kindergarten teacher." She'd planned to dance for ten or fifteen years, then go teach. As it was, the teaching had started a little early.

Crissy picked up her menu. "What are we all having? Rachel, have some wine, please. I hate to drink alone and Noelle is obviously out of the running on that."

Rachel opened her mouth, then closed it. She wasn't sure what to say, or how. Of course she'd planned on telling her friends about the baby, but now? Like this?

Noelle glanced at her. "Are you all right? You've been a little quiet all evening."

"I'm good," Rachel said.

Crissy smiled. "So what's going on? It had to be something, because I know you're not pregnant like this one here."

Rachel drew in a breath. "Actually, I am."

Noelle's eyes widened. "Rachel, are you serious? Really? That's so great."

Crissy blinked twice, then raised her arm. "Waiter, I need a margarita here. Right away." She lowered her arm. "Pregnant? As in 'with child'? Are you sure?"

Rachel nodded. "I peed on seven sticks. It was quite the event."

"So there's a guy," Crissy said. "There has to be a guy. But I didn't know you were seeing anyone." She looked at Noelle. "Did you know?"

"No." Noelle glanced between them. "She's right. There's a guy. So who is he?"

"A complicated question," Rachel admitted.

The waiter appeared with Crissy's drink. They placed their food order and when he was gone, Noelle leaned forward and rested her forearms on the table.

"Spill," she said.

Rachel sipped her water. "Okay, I'll tell you, but please don't judge me. I never do this sort of thing. I don't date much and I never ever sleep with a guy right away."

Crissy picked up her drink. "You slept with a guy on the first date? Wow—my respect was linked to your ability to knit and hang out with little kids, but this is even better. Tell everything. Start at the beginning and talk slowly."

Rachel explained about going to the bar with Diane and how Carter bought her a drink and that they got to talking. She detailed Diane driving off without her and that Carter had offered her a lift.

"It was supposed to just be a good-night kiss," Rachel admitted. "I never expected to lose control like that."

"It must have been some kiss," Crissy said.

Rachel willed herself not to blush. "We, ah, got swept away. Like in the movies. He left the next morning for an early meeting. He wrote me a note and gave me his phone number."

Noelle folded her arms over her chest. "You've been going out all this time and never told us?"

"We haven't been dating," Rachel said.

Crissy sipped her drink. "You met a guy who kisses so great you were compelled to have sex with him and you're not dating?"

"I didn't call him."

"Why not?" Noelle and Crissy asked together.

Rachel moved her fork around on her napkin. "I don't know. I didn't know what to say. I mean, what would he think of me after that night we'd spent together? I'm not really that kind of person."

Crissy rolled her eyes. "You didn't call him because you thought he'd think you were slutty." She paused. "Do we still say 'slutty'? Am I dating myself?"

"You're doing fine," Noelle told her, then turned to Rachel. "I know you'd feel awkward, but why wouldn't you want to see him again?"

Rachel honestly didn't have an answer. Now that she'd talked to Carter again, even under really difficult circumstances, she'd seen that she liked him, even without the sex thing.

"It's complicated," she said. "I thought avoiding him was for the best."

"But then you turned up pregnant," Crissy said. "That had to have been an interesting conversation. Or have you told him yet?"

"I told him," she said. "Actually, first I went to a lawyer."

She explained about the paperwork she'd had drawn up.

Noelle gasped. "Did he sign it? Did he really sign away his baby?"

"No," Rachel admitted. "He refused. I think he was kind of insulted I'd even asked. Then his mother and two of his sisters walked in and they know I'm pregnant."

Crissy and Noelle exchanged a confused look. "Where did his mother come from?" Crissy asked.

Rachel explained about meeting at the bar and Jenny and then following Carter home.

"His mother thinks we should get married."

"She's right," Noelle said primly. "You're having a baby together. It's the right thing to do."

"It's the twenty-first century," Crissy said. "No one has to get married anymore. At least not here. Rachel, honey, you do whatever you want. If that means being a single mom, then yay you."

"Work isn't a problem," she said slowly. "One of the other teachers got pregnant and had a baby last year and she's not married."

Noelle leaned forward. "Of course you can be a single parent if you want to be, but isn't that the question? Do you *want* to do this on your own? Dev and I had a marriage of convenience and look how that turned out."

"You're the one in a million," Crissy said. "Rachel, you don't have to marry a complete stranger."

"Actually he's not a complete stranger," Noelle said smugly. "She's seen him naked."

"There is that," Crissy said. "What do you want?"

Rachel sighed. "I don't know. Carter and I have agreed to get to know each other and then figure things out. And don't forget, the marriage was his mother's idea, not his. He never mentioned it at all."

"What would you have said if he had?" Noelle asked.

"I don't know that, either," she admitted. She thought

about her conversation with Carter. "Do I dress like a nun?"

Noelle had been drinking her water and now she choked as she tried not to spit. "What?"

"My clothes. I try to dress low-key for the kids. Plus I need things that are washable. But do I dress… I don't know…too conservative?"

Crissy eyed her short-sleeved blouse and long skirt. "You're not on the fashion cutting edge, but you always look nice. Who said you dressed like a nun?"

Rachel shrugged.

"Carter," Crissy said knowingly.

"He didn't mean it in a bad way," Rachel told her. "He was talking about finding me attractive, even though I dress like a nun."

"She's defending him," Noelle said conversationally. "That's step one."

"It's not step anything," Rachel said. "I'm explaining."

"Oooh, step two," Crissy teased. Then her smile faded. "Look, you have to do what feels right for you, Rachel. Whether it's your clothes or your job or your baby. It *is* your baby, so don't let anyone else make the decisions for you."

"It's also Carter's baby," Noelle said gently. "He sounds like a man who wants to be a father."

"He is," Rachel said, more confused than ever. "Plus there's his whole family. They seem really nice."

The kind of family she remembered hers being. Could she be a part of that now? Under these circumstances?

"Carter said we should take our time," Rachel told him. "We're going to meet and talk and figure it all out."

"Sounds like a sensible plan to me," Crissy said. "Just don't be rash."

"I don't do rash," Rachel said.

"All evidence to the contrary," Crissy said, with a pointed glance at Rachel's midsection.

"Okay. Just that one time. My point is, in one way or another I've been on my own since I was twelve. I know how to take care of myself."

"Maybe that's not the issue," Noelle said. "Now there's going to be someone else."

"A baby," Rachel murmured. "I'm still having trouble dealing with that. I don't feel pregnant."

"I didn't for a long time, either," Noelle said, "but I wasn't talking about the baby. I meant there was going to be Carter."

"But he's not in my life."

"If you're going to have a baby together," Crissy told her, "then I would say he is. Permanently."

Chapter 5

Rachel paced nervously the last twenty minutes before Carter was due to arrive. Despite his promise for them to just "talk," she couldn't help remembering what had happened the last time he'd been here. Even worse, she couldn't seem to twist that remembering in such a way that she felt bad about it.

Okay, yes, the pregnancy had her totally freaked, and given the chance to magically undo the moment of conception, she was fairly sure she would. But she couldn't help breathing just a little faster every time she recalled what she'd felt like when he'd touched her. Which meant she would have to be extra careful tonight and make sure there wasn't a repeat of those events. Things between them were complicated enough without adding that to the mix.

She glanced around at the dining alcove in her apartment. She'd set the table three different ways and had finally settled on the more casual place mats and paper napkins. This wasn't a date, after all. Just friends getting together to discuss some issues. Only she and Carter weren't friends and a baby counted for more than just an "issue."

She'd worked herself into such a frenzy that she was actually grateful when she heard footsteps on the balcony.

"Hi," she said, pulling open the front before he could knock.

"Hi, yourself." Carter smiled, then stepped inside. "I'd forgotten your thing for plants."

"It's a hobby," she admitted, motioning to the hanging baskets and overflowing tiered plant stands in the living room.

He handed her a picnic basket. "Dinner," he said. "I hope you like pasta."

"Sure. Who doesn't?"

He looked good. Normally she liked guys who were the more button-down-collar type, with short hair and loafers. Carter's shaggy dark blond hair hung nearly to his shoulders. He wore his faded red shirt outside his battered jeans and while he'd put on loafers, they were old and he wasn't wearing socks.

She should have been disapproving or at least unimpressed. Instead she found herself wanting to run her hands up and down his chest to see if the shirt was really as soft as it looked and he was as...

She hurried into the kitchen. Danger, she thought as she set the basket on the narrow counter. She had to keep her mind from wandering. She had to be smart and careful and...something else she couldn't remember right now.

She opened the basket and stared at the stacked glass containers inside. "What is all this?"

Carter moved close and peered over her shoulder. "Ravioli, extra sauce, salad, dressing, garlic bread and something for dessert. I can't tell what it is."

"You don't know what you made?"

He looked at her and grinned. "I didn't cook any of this. My sisters make regular contributions to my refrigerator. Word got out that we were having dinner together tonight and this appeared. I only dragged it along."

"Interesting system," she said, thinking it would be pretty nice to find dinner waiting for her when she got home after a long day.

"I like it. I never know what's for dinner, but then I enjoy surprises."

Even mine? Except she didn't ask the question—mostly because she wasn't sure she wanted to hear the answer.

"There are instructions," he said, reaching around her and pulling a piece of paper out of the basket.

She was aware of how close they were standing and the way his forearm almost brushed against her waist.

He handed her a typed sheet and for a second she couldn't unclog her brain enough to read. Then she blinked and the words came into focus.

"Ravioli on the stove with the extra sauce," she said, telling herself it was a good thing that he moved back and refusing to feel disappointed that he hadn't spun her in his arms and kissed her. "Garlic bread in the oven. Salad and dressing in the refrigerator along with the dessert. Oh, it's tiramisu. Did one of your sisters really make it?"

"I guess."

"I've never had it homemade before. I can't wait."

"Merry will be delighted to know she's made a good impression."

He gave her a smile that made her insides quiver. Okay, she had to get a grip. She was reacting to his superficial good looks and some chemistry. But there were things that were much more important than that. Such as who Carter was as a man. She should focus on the insides and ignore the pretty package.

She put the food away, started the oven to preheat it, then asked if he'd like something to drink.

"I got a six-pack of that beer you were drinking at the bar," she said. "Would you like a bottle?"

"Sure. Thanks."

She collected it and a bottle of water for herself, then led the way back into her small living room. As they sat on the sofa, Rachel did her best to ignore the fact that these cushions had been the scene of the crime less than a month ago.

"Your sisters must live close to you," she said. "If they're bringing over food."

He leaned back and took a drink of his beer. "Too close. In a weak moment I bought a house on the same street as my mom and sisters. I like the free food delivery, but they're always dropping in, as you saw. I would like to be a little farther away, but right now moving would take too much time."

"Still, so much family nearby is nice."

He studied her with his dark eyes. "What happened to your family?"

She smoothed the front of her khakis. "My parents and my brother were killed in a car accident when I was twelve. There were no other relatives."

"I'm sorry," he said, leaning toward her. "What happened to you? Where did you go?"

"Into foster care." She shrugged. "Don't worry. It wasn't awful. The people who took me in were actually pretty nice. I grew up, finished high school and then went to college."

"You make it sound easy," he told her. "It can't have been. In one second, everything changed for you."

She still had nightmares about those days after the accident. About being all alone and knowing nothing would ever feel right again. She remembered vowing she would never, ever feel that much pain again and so far she'd managed to keep her word. She had friends, of course, but no one she couldn't imagine living without.

"It was hard," she admitted. "If I'd had grandparents or aunts or uncles, I think it would have been better. Some family to care about me."

"Now you take care of other people's children."

She smiled. "I know—it's not hard to figure out why I went into teaching. I wanted to be there for my kids."

"How long have you been teaching?"

People usually asked more questions about her loss. She sensed that Carter wanted more information and she appreciated his sensitivity in changing the subject. "This is my fourth year. I love everything about it. Even the messes. I asked the principal about starting a small garden in the spring and she okayed a nice open area near the play yard. That will be fun."

He glanced at the tangle of plants on the coffee table. "Just don't bring anything home. You're already at risk of becoming a pod person."

She laughed. "My plants know I love them. They'd never hurt me."

"You say that now, but wait until you wake up with a thorn growing out of your neck and stalks instead of arms."

"I'm not worried. What about you? Tell me about your work."

"I can't believe you're interested in carburetors and timing belts. You're too much a girl."

"Excuse me?" She raised her eyebrows. "Are you saying because of my gender, I'm not into cars?"

"Are you?"

"Well, no, but I could be if I wanted."

"Sure you could. So are you seeing anyone?"

The shift in subject startled her. "You mean like a guy?"

"I'm comfortable with your relationship with the plants."

She fought against the need to spring to her feet and glare down at him. "I wouldn't have slept with you if I'd been seeing someone else. How can you even ask? Are you seeing someone else?"

"I told you, I was off women until you came along and tempted me. It's not an unreasonable question."

"It is to me. I'm not that kind of person."

She regretted the words as soon as she spoke them. Gee, wow—talk about a moral code. She wasn't the kind of woman to sleep with one man while dating another, but she would bring a guy home from a bar and have sex with him.

"I've never done anything like that before," she murmured. "I shouldn't have…."

Carter slid across the sofa and touched her arm. "Hey, no beating yourself up. It's not allowed. Sometimes things happen and we deal with them. That's what we're doing right now. Dealing."

"But you think I'm awful."

"I don't. I think you got swept away, just like I did. Of course, I blame you for that."

She made a sound that was both a laugh and something way too close to a sob. No tears, she thought. Not over this. She preferred to save her crying for something more tragic. While she didn't know how she felt about being pregnant by a man she barely knew, no one had died. They would get through this.

"You okay?" he asked.

She nodded.

He moved back to his side of the sofa, which was both good and bad. She liked having him close and touching her. Of course that would only lead to trouble.

"So we get to know each other," he said. "Then we make some decisions about how we're going to handle the baby."

"I agree." She picked up her bottle of water and looked at him. "You never proposed."

His reaction was almost comical. His whole body stiffened. His eyes darted from side to side and he looked ready to bolt.

"Did you want me to?"

She was impressed by how calm he sounded as he asked the question, and she did her best to hide her smile.

"It is traditional," she pointed out.

His gaze narrowed. "You're screwing with me."

She felt the corners of her mouth turn up. "Maybe a little."

He grinned. "I like that in a woman."

By the time they finished dinner, there was a whole lot more that he liked about Rachel. She was smart, and she was funny. She held her own when he pushed back and yet he could make her blush without trying.

"I would have expected lots of dance trophies all around the place," he said when they'd cleared the table and returned to the living room. "Didn't you say it was your secret passion?"

"It was. I had big plans to be a professional ballerina. If that didn't work out, I was willing to go be on Broadway."

"I'm sure New York theater was delighted to be your backup plan."

She laughed. "Yeah, I know. The arrogance of youth. Eventually I figured out I wasn't going to be a professional dancer, so I switched dreams."

There was something in the way she said the words that told him the decision hadn't been an easy one. "You kept on dancing, though."

"Sure. I take a couple of classes every week. More in the summer. I'm not sure how long I'll be able to keep them up." She touched her stomach as she spoke.

He eyed her belly and wondered when she would start showing. All his sisters had kids, but he'd never paid much attention to their pregnancies except to hope they had boys—which they never did.

"Any symptoms?" he asked.

"Aside from panic? Not yet. I'll be making a doctor's appointment to find out what I should and shouldn't be doing. I know to avoid alcohol and medications. Neither is really a problem for me. Aside from that, I'm in the dark."

"Me, too."

"You're a guy. That's expected. Shouldn't I have some maternal instincts that are activated just by me being pregnant?"

"Maybe they wait for the baby to be born."

She tucked her hair behind her ears. "I hope so, because otherwise, I'm pretty clueless."

"There's time."

"That's what I tell myself."

He looked around at the bright colors on the wall and the little touches like candles and bowls of stuff that smelled. "Your place is nice."

"Thanks. I like to decorate. Your house was nice, too. I only saw the living room, but it wasn't bachelor pad central."

"My sisters," he said by way of explanation. "They meddled."

She smiled. "In some cultures, that would be called helping."

"Yeah, well, in some cultures they'd ask first. But I didn't mind too much. They had some good ideas. I did most of the work myself. I remodeled the kitchen and did all the painting."

"Really? You know how to do that kind of thing?"

He nodded. "My mom worried about me growing up without a father and with only sisters in the house so she was always sending me off to spend the weekend with my friends and their dads. I learned to do basic carpentry, change oil in a car, ride a motorcycle. I don't think she was too excited about that last one."

"Not many mothers would be. But that was good of her, to take care of you that way."

"She's all right." He wasn't going to have a discussion about how much he loved his mother. That was too twisted for the already complicated situation. Time to get back to the one thing that had been on his mind since before dinner.

He leaned toward Rachel. He knew she'd been kidding before, but he wasn't sure if she'd been hinting. "Did you want to get married, Rachel?"

Her eyes widened as she shook her head. "No. It's okay. No proposals are required. Really."

That was a relief. "So what do you want to do?"

She bit her lower lip, which probably meant she was confused. Most of him got that. But the real male part of him interpreted that little movement as an invitation. Sort of a "come kiss me" kind of invitation.

He wanted her. Even knowing she was pregnant didn't change that. He wanted to touch her and taste her and claim her. That single night together had been a good start, but there were so many things they hadn't done.

"What we're doing. Talking. Figuring it out without making any rash decisions."

"I can avoid rash," he said.

She smiled. "Have you ever been married?"

"No. Not my thing."

"Is it the fidelity issue? Being with just one woman?"

"I've only ever been with one woman at a time," he said. "Never cheated."

He'd never wanted to. It wasn't as if he needed *more* women in his life.

"You're not that into marriage, either," he said, remembering that she'd been engaged twice but never married.

"I will be," she told him. "It wasn't right before."

He almost asked what would make it right, because that's what he had trouble with. How did anyone know when it was right?

"Will you stay here?" he asked, nodding at the apartment.

"I haven't thought that far ahead. There are two bedrooms, but… Gee, now I have to think about moving. I guess the baby will want a yard."

"Not the first week."

She laughed. "Good point. I have time."

"If money's an issue, I could help."

She shifted on the sofa. "Okay, we've officially crossed into uncomfortable territory. Let's avoid talk of moving and money for a while."

"Fair enough."

She shook her head. "Carter, I'm really sorry this happened. I didn't mean to mess up your life. Or mine."

"We'll make it through. Kids aren't that bad."

"You don't actually know that."

"My sisters are doing fine and between them they have a bunch."

"So you're an uncle."

"Many times over. And now that they're married, there are finally guys around."

"There aren't *that* many women in your family."

He looked at her. "I only have nieces."

"You're kidding."

"No. Chances are you're having a girl."

She smiled. "I'd like that."

Under other circumstances, the relaxed body language and gentle smile would have been his cue to move in for a kiss and whatever else was being offered. Under these circumstances, that wouldn't be the wisest move.

Instead he stood and stretched. "I should get going. Thanks for dinner."

"I only heated it. I should thank you. And your sisters."

"I'll tell them you had seconds. That's thanks enough for them."

"Everything was great. Thanks for bringing it." She

followed him to the front door. "We didn't really get any-thing resolved."

He smiled at her and fought against the need to feel her mouth on his. "Sure we did. I know you're a sucker for tiramisu and that dancing on Broadway was your second choice."

She swayed toward him. "You know what I mean. About the baby. But you're right. We have time. I…" She ducked her head, then looked at him. "I know neither of us wanted this to happen, but since it did, I'm glad it was you."

She blushed bright red. "I mean, you're really nice and I know you want me to think you're dangerous, but you're really not and I think you'll be a good dad. That's all I meant. Nothing, you know…"

"Mushy?"

She smiled. "Yeah. Mushy."

He gave in because after that little speech, how could he not? He put one hand on her shoulder, leaned toward her and lightly brushed her mouth with his.

Her lips were as warm and soft as he remembered. His body went on instant alert, but he ignored the want-ing and drew back.

"I'll give you a call the first part of next week," he said. "We'll do this again."

"I'd like that. Night, Carter."

"Night."

He walked to his truck and climbed inside. It was barely ten on a Saturday night and he didn't feel like going home.

He made a U-turn and headed the couple of miles to the Blue Dog Bar. Once he arrived, he parked a street away and walked in through the kitchen entrance, so he wouldn't be seen by anyone up front.

George stood by the deep fryer where most of the snacks were made. "Hey, Carter. What's up?"

"Not much. Is Jenny around?"

"Sure. Watch this. They need to come out when the buzzer sounds. I'll go get her."

Carter monitored a basket of what looked like chicken wings until George returned with Jenny in tow.

"Hey, you," she said. "How are things?"

"Okay. Can you take a break?"

"Already told Dan I'd be gone for a few minutes."

Jenny followed him into a small breakroom in the back. At this hour it was empty. They settled on some plastic chairs placed around a round table.

"Dan was a little hurt," Jenny said. "You know he hates it when you talk to me instead of him."

"He's a typical guy, same as me. How is he going to help?"

"He's not," Jenny said with a grin. "But he has delusions of grandeur."

"Is that why you married him?"

"I couldn't wait for you forever, darlin'."

"I don't remember you waiting at all." He leaned back in the chair. "You called my mother."

"I know. I was there."

"You're supposed to be *my* friend. That means being on my side."

"There's a baby now, Carter. You don't get a side."

"Still, you could have waited."

"Actually I called more for Rachel than for you."

He didn't question how Jenny knew Rachel's name.

Her sisters were close to Jenny and would have filled her in on everything they knew.

"Rachel's fine."

"I wanted to be sure," Jenny said. "I have to tell you, I'm surprised. You were always compulsively careful."

There was something about the way she said it. "Was that a problem for you?"

"Not a problem, more of a symptom. You made it clear you wouldn't be trapped and while I wasn't interested in that, a woman likes to think a man can be swept away from time to time."

"Look what happens when he is."

Jenny nodded. "You don't seem too angry."

"I'm not. I'm…" He wasn't sure what he felt. He'd always liked kids and had thought he'd want them in his life. It was the whole marriage thing he couldn't relate to.

"Think I have what it takes to be a good father?" he asked lightly, although he was deadly serious about the question.

"Absolutely," she said. "You'll be great. You know your mom thinks you should marry Rachel."

"I think she mentioned that. What do you think?"

"That a baby changes everything. For what it's worth, marriage is pretty cool."

"I can't believe you're happy with Dan when you had me."

She laughed. "He loves me and you never did. Besides, you're not all that."

"Sure I am."

"Okay, yes you are, but you were never the one for me and I wasn't the one for you."

He didn't think he had a "one" but there was no point in saying that to Jenny.

She stood, walked around the table, then bent over and kissed him on the cheek. "You're going to be a daddy, Carter. It's time to stop playing and grow up."

"I'm plenty grown-up."

"You're still fooling around. Look at what you're doing with your life. Get a real job."

He frowned. "I have a real job."

"You know what I mean." She touched his hair. "You've always gotten by on charm and looks, that body and a great personality. Now it's time for some substance."

"Ouch."

"I only say this because I love you. I have to get back to work."

She left the breakroom. Carter stayed where he was.

Jenny had always been able to say the words. For her, professing love was as easy as folding socks. But not for him. Oh, he knew he loved his family and cared about his friends. But love, romantic love?

Not even once.

He told himself it didn't matter. That he was still a great guy. He almost believed it, too. Only he couldn't figure out why his heart had never been touched and what about him would change if it was.

Rachel picked up the containers of paint and carried them to the sink. The mess was indescribable, but it had been worth it. Her class had met all its goals for the week and because of that, they'd been able to pick their reward. Unfortunately for her, the reward had been finger painting. Both she and the room were now brightly colored and smudgy, but the water-based product would wash off and she and her class had had a great time together. She'd even created a finger-painting masterpiece of her own, although she had no idea what she was going to do with it.

She'd just finished washing off the tables when she noticed three men walking toward her classroom. They'd come through the play area, so they were visible through the large set of windows in her room. All three were in uniform, two from the local police and one in what looked like a firefighter uniform.

Her first thought was that they were coming to arrest her, only she hadn't done anything wrong. Her second was that her apartment had burned down. She met them at the door.

"Is it bad?" she asked fearfully. "Is everything gone?"

The firefighter smiled. "Everything's fine. You're Rachel Harper, right?"

Everything was all right? "Yes, that's me."

"Good," one of the cops said. "We'd hate to welcome the wrong person into the family."

Rachel blinked. "Excuse me?"

One of the guys nudged the other two. "This works better if we introduce ourselves. I'm Frank and I'm married to Liz. This is Adam. He's with Merry." He pointed to the other police officer. "Gordon's married to Shelly. This is complicated enough without worrying about last names. You can learn them later."

It took her a second to figure out what they were talking about. "You're married to Carter's sisters," she said more to herself than to them.

Gordon, the firefighter, said, "The family is kind of crazy close, but that's what makes them so special. Our wives have been talking about you, so we thought we'd come down and introduce ourselves when things were quiet. It will make it easier to get to know the family."

"It was really nice of you to stop by," she said, "and I don't mean to sound rude; but why did you?"

"Because of Carter. Now that the two of you are getting married," Frank said.

"Married?" Rachel took a step back. "I don't think so. Not married. Carter and I barely..." She hesitated, thinking that due to her pregnancy, saying she and Carter barely knew each would be really tacky. She cleared her throat. "We're not getting married."

All three men glanced at her midsection. "You have to," Gordon said. "You're going to have Carter's baby."

That was the theory, she thought, still not sure any of this was real, although thinking about it too much sent her into a panic.

"Once you start to show," Adam said, "won't you want to be married? I know this is sudden, but Carter's a good guy to have at your back. I'd trust him with my life. I have."

She frowned. "Excuse me? How? He works in a motorcycle shop."

"Right." Adam shrugged. "Still, I'd let him date my sister."

There was a recommendation, Rachel thought, not sure if she should laugh or run for the hills.

"You're all being terrific," she said carefully. "I really appreciate the support and the welcome, but Carter and I..."

Three pairs of disapproving eyes focused on her.

"That is, I don't think we..." She pressed her lips together. This was her life. She didn't have to answer to anyone. If Carter was happy to not marry her, why did these guys get a vote?

But she didn't know how to say that and for reasons

not clear to her, she couldn't seem to tell the three of them to mind their own business. Maybe it was because they were part of a family and she'd wanted that ever since she'd lost hers.

"We're dating," she said at last, doing her best not to wince at the lie. "We're dating and we're really hopeful."

She smiled brightly and prayed that was enough. The three guys nodded.

"Good," Frank said. "Okay, then. We'll let you get back to work now. But if you need anything—I mean anything—just call. One of us can always get to you. Okay? You're not alone anymore, Rachel. You're one of us."

With that, they left. She stared after them knowing that the smart, independent side of her should resent the implication that she couldn't handle things on her own. When in truth, she was really touched by their visit and envious of their closeness. What would it be like to be a part of a family like that?

She drew in a deep breath and reminded herself that she had a more pressing problem. Namely informing Carter that they were now a dating couple. Honestly, she had no idea how he was going to take the news.

Chapter 6

Carter arrived at Rachel's house after work. She'd left a message for him on his cell, saying that his brothers-in-law had stopped by and that she needed to talk to him. She hadn't said much else, but then she hadn't had to. He could imagine how the conversation had gone.

As he climbed up the stairs to her apartment, he wondered if any of the three had told her about his real job. Some women were fine with it but others freaked.

She opened the door before he could knock. "Thanks for coming. I just didn't…" She drew in a breath. "Okay. Come in and we'll talk, right? Because that's what rational grown-ups do. We talk. We don't panic, we don't allow ourselves to be influenced by the thoughts of others. Especially people we don't know. I mean, I'm sure your family is perfectly lovely, but they don't have the right to dictate how I live my life. Plus, I have to say, I hated the disapproval. I understand it, sort of. They care about you and they want you to get what you want. I don't mind that, either, but you've made it really clear you're not interested in marrying me and who am I to complain? I don't want to get married, either."

He'd been content to let her wind down, but when it became obvious that wasn't going to happen anytime soon, he stepped in to fix the problem.

He moved into the apartment, grabbed Rachel by her upper arms, drew her to him and kissed her firmly on the mouth.

He had a brief impression of heat and softness, then he pulled back. The reaction was exactly what he'd hoped. She stopped talking and stared at him.

"You kissed me."

"I know," he said with a grin. "I was there."

"I didn't think there would be kissing."

"There doesn't have to be if you don't like it. I didn't know how else to get you to take a breath. Whatever happened, we can fix it."

She closed the front door behind him and shook her head. "You'd think so, wouldn't you? But I have my doubts."

He had a feeling she was going to get wound up again, and while he wouldn't mind the excuse to kiss her a second time, they needed to make a little progress on the information front.

"Tell me what happened," he said as he led her to the brightly colored sofa and urged her to sit. "Start at the beginning."

She sank down. He settled next to her and waited.

"Your brothers-in-law came to visit me at school today."

He groaned. "During class?"

"No, after." She flopped against the back of the sofa. "How on earth would I have explained them if they'd showed up in the middle of the day? Five-year-olds can ask a lot of questions. I can only imagine the phone calls from worried parents after a visit like that."

"There won't be another visit like that," he told her, knowing when he got home, he was going to have a little talk with his sisters. He appreciated their concern, but this wasn't their business.

"I hope you're right," Rachel told him. "I mean it was really nice to meet them, even if I wasn't sure who was who, let alone which guy had which sister. But, Carter, they think we're getting married. They sort of implied it was required. I don't know what I want. I haven't even accepted the fact that I'm pregnant. I saw the truth on the test sticks, so I have the information in my head, but I really don't believe it. Not yet. And when I do try to convince myself that it's real, I start to hyperventilate, and that can't be good."

She was adorable, he thought as he watched her sit up and give a good imitation of someone unable to catch her breath.

"Relax," he told her. "Take a deep breath and hold it."

She did as he suggested.

"Now let it out."

She exhaled.

"You're fine," he said, wishing he had another excuse to kiss her or even touch her soft wavy curls. Her hair was a tempting combination of reds and browns and gold. He remembered how it had felt in his fingers the one night they'd made love. Of course touching her hair was only one of several experiences he would like to repeat.

"I don't feel fine," she admitted. "I feel weird. I don't

want to disappoint your family. I know they're important to you. But I won't be dictated to."

"No one's dictating."

"It felt like that."

"That doesn't make it real. This is between the two of us. We'll work it out in the best way for us."

She ducked her head. "It's not that simple," she whispered. "There were three of them and I felt trapped."

He could imagine. "What did you say?"

She looked at him. "That we were dating and hoping for the best."

He could live with that. Besides, she looked so dejected and guilty that he couldn't be annoyed with her. "So you didn't promise to marry me."

"Of course not." She narrowed her gaze. "Are you smiling? This is *not* funny."

He kept his expression as neutral as he could make it. "I'm not smiling."

"It looks like you are. Nothing about this is funny. We're talking about lives on the line here. We've made a baby. When I think about that, I can't breathe anymore. Besides, this is all your fault."

"Hey, how do you figure? There were two of us doing the wild thing that night."

"Exactly. But if you hadn't kissed me like that, I wouldn't have given in."

He'd been about to get defensive, but now there was no need. "My kissing won you over, huh?"

She shifted away from him. "Don't take that as a compliment. I didn't mean it that way."

"Right. Being a good kisser is a bad thing."

"It is when it gets two strangers in trouble," she muttered. "Don't you dare get smug on me. I couldn't stand it."

He was feeling a lot of things, but smug wasn't one of them. Right now what he wanted most was a chance to kiss her again and cause her to lose control. Not his most sensible plan, he admitted, but a guy could dream.

"Besides," she continued, "our more pressing problem is your family. You know those guys are going to talk to your sisters and then what? They'll tell your mom and everyone will think we're dating."

And that statement was the answer, he thought suddenly. "Dating isn't a bad idea."

She stared at him. "Excuse me? How is that going to help?"

"We can use this. Dating would be the next logical step, under the circumstances. If we were serious about working on a relationship, I mean. So we date. Or tell my family we're dating. We can even act like we're dating. Then, in a couple of months, we'll tell everyone things didn't work out. Relationships fail all the time. The family will think we really tried and get off our backs and we'll be free to work out things as we want to."

She tilted her head. "I like it," she said slowly. "You'll be okay with your family and they won't think I'm awful."

"They don't think that now."

"You didn't see the looks on those guys' faces," she told him.

Carter felt his fingers curl into his palms. He had been delighted when his sisters had gotten married. The more guys in the family, the better, as far as he was concerned. But knowing they'd made Rachel uncomfortable had him thinking about pounding each one of them into a bloody pulp.

"Okay, we're pretend dating," she said. "We'll need

some sort of plan and schedule. You won't be able to see anyone else while this is going on. It wouldn't look right."

"Not a problem," he told her, consciously letting go of his anger. "I'm swearing off women again."

"Are you sure you want to do that?" she asked, her voice teasing. "Look at what happened the last time."

"Not my fault. You were too tempting to resist."

She leaned back and laughed. "Oh, please. Me?"

"Yes, you. Don't you consider yourself a temptation?"

The smile lingered, bringing light to her green eyes. "Not even on my best day, but it's sweet of you to say so. Now about your job."

The quick change in topic didn't give him much time to brace himself. Had they told her the truth or not?

"Want to see a pay stub?" he asked.

"Not especially. But why did Frank and the others act so strange when I reminded them you worked in a motor-cycle shop? You're not on probation, are you?"

He chuckled and held up his right hand. Good news— they hadn't told her. "I swear I have never been arrested, convicted or incarcerated. Ever."

"That's encouraging. They're all cops and firefighters. Don't they approve of what you do?"

"I…"

He found himself not wanting to lie to her. She was going to have to know eventually and if she reacted badly, better now than later.

There were rules about who could know and mothers of unborn children fell in the "yes" category. But it was more than just that. There was the woman herself and how carefully she would protect the information.

"What are you thinking?" she asked. "Should I be scared?"

"No. But I will need you to give your word that you won't tell anyone what I'm going to tell you."

"Or you'll have to shoot me?" she asked. "What are we talking about? I can't figure out if I should laugh or make a run for my car."

"I'm a cop working undercover. This job at the motorcycle shop is part of my cover. I'm working on a case involving counterfeit parts brought into this country from overseas."

She blinked. "You're a…"

"Police officer."

"But your hair is so long."

He laughed then and, without thinking, pulled her close. "Damn, Rachel, you're never boring."

She held herself stiffly for a second before relaxing into his embrace. "You haven't known me long enough to be bored," she murmured. "That could come later."

"I don't think so."

His body reacted to her nearness with a predictable rush of blood and need. But he kept the embrace light. They weren't going to do that again, remember?

He released her and straightened. She studied him.

"They know about the hair, then?" she asked.

He grinned. "It's all part of the assignment. I have a gun and a badge if you want to see them."

"No, thanks. I believe you. So that's why your brothers-in-law acted so strange. They were surprised I didn't know the truth."

He shrugged. "Probably."

"Your mom can't like what you do. She must worry all the time."

"She's used to it. I come from a long line of cops. My

grandfather, my great-grandfather. My dad was one. He died before I was born."

She winced. "I'm sorry. Was it work-related?"

He nodded. "A drunk driver got him while he was on patrol."

"Oh, Carter. That must have been so awful for your mom and your sisters. And for you, growing up without a dad."

"I appreciate the sympathy," he said, "but it's not necessary. I don't know any different."

"Everything is so complicated," she said. "How did that happen?"

"We made a baby."

Her eyes widened slightly. "I'm still not comfortable thinking about that. Could we avoid the topic?"

"Not for much longer."

"I know, but we have a plan, right? Pretend dating." She grinned. "Does that mean you bring me plastic flowers instead of real ones?"

"Would you like that?"

She glanced around the apartment. "I have plenty of real ones, so I'm good."

He started to ask what she would like instead, but stopped himself. Pretend dating meant putting on a show, not getting involved in any way. They could be friends, but nothing more.

Friends who sleep together, he thought hopefully, and then reminded himself he'd sworn off women again. He had to. Look at what had happened with Rachel.

Women were the root of all the trouble in his life and he would be better off if he could simply walk away from them.

Then Rachel smiled and he found himself wanting

her again. Okay, so he would swear off women *after* they worked this pretend dating thing out. Maybe they could figure out a way to have pretend sex. That could be fun.

Rachel smoothed the foil on top of the casserole she carried. "I hope this is okay. I didn't know what to make. I don't cook a lot but my seven-layer bean dip is really popular at all the teacher potlucks at school. Of course, free food is rarely criticized, so maybe that's not a good standard. Should I have made something else? An entrée? Or dessert? Is bean dip enough?"

Carter pulled his front door shut and stared at her. "You do that a lot, don't you?"

Rachel found herself momentarily caught up in his brown eyes and the little crinkly lines that formed when he smiled, like now. She had to shake her head to clear her brain.

"I'm sorry, what was the question?"

He chuckled and took the casserole dish from her. "You get wound up when you're nervous. I like it. Of course the best way to get you back on earth seems to be to kiss you and we both know that's not a good idea, so we're going to need another plan."

She wasn't so sure. Carter's kisses tended to totally clear her mind and as nervous as she felt right now, she wouldn't mind forgetting the reason.

"We're walking?" she asked as they moved past his truck and her car.

"No point in driving." He paused and pointed across the street and down one house. "That's where Mama lives. Merry is next to her. Liz and Shelly live in the other direction. Three houses down and that one on the corner."

"That's really close," she said, surprised he would plant himself in the middle of all that family.

He sighed as they crossed the street. "Yeah, I know," he muttered. "I wasn't thinking when I bought this place. It's too close. One of these days I'm going to move."

"Still, you enjoy your family and that's nice." She could appreciate the need to stay connected. If her parents and brother were still alive...

She pushed the thought away. Not going there right now. She was nervous enough without adding a little heartache to the mix.

She distracted herself by remembering how great Carter had been about the dating issue. He could have gotten upset, but he hadn't, which made him a good guy in her eyes. Of course he'd already proved himself a good guy by how he'd reacted to her pregnancy. Now that she thought about it, she'd pretty much been one disaster after the other where he was concerned.

They reached the front door of his mother's house. Carter walked in without knocking and yelled, "We're here."

Rachel could hear voices coming from the back of the house, then Nina Brockett hurried out to greet them.

"Late as always. Some mothers would take that as a message. Some mothers would think their only son was trying to say he was no longer interested in visiting his old mother."

"Some mothers are just a little too dramatic for their own good," he said, bending down and kissing her on the cheek. "You remember Rachel."

His mother, an attractive, petite woman, smiled broadly at Rachel, then held out both her arms. "Of course. Welcome, welcome."

Rachel found herself hugged, then kissed on the cheek. "Thanks for having me, Mrs. Brockett."

"Nina. I insist." She nudged Carter with her elbow. "We'll have her calling me Mama like everyone else before too long, eh? So what's this? You made something. See? A girl who can cook. That's new for you. A step up. Come, come. We're all in the kitchen. No matter how nice I make the rest of the house, everyone wants to be in the kitchen."

"It's Carter and Rachel," Nina called as she led the way into the overly crowded kitchen. "Carter, remind her who everyone is. Oh, what's this, dear?" She took the casserole dish from Carter.

"A seven-layer dip," Rachel said. "Carter mentioned you always had chips on hand."

"You didn't have to bring anything, but I appreciate that you did. Very thoughtful. Carter, she's thoughtful. Did you notice?"

Rachel felt herself blush but before she could say anything, she was caught up in another confusing round of introductions.

There were too many people in the small space. Adults, kids, a large dog.

Carter pointed to his sisters. "Merry, Liz and Shelly," he said. "Their husbands are Adam, Frank and Gordon."

She recognized the three men who had visited her the previous week, although now that they were in casual clothes instead of their uniforms, she wasn't sure who was who. As for Carter's sisters, she was pretty sure that Merry had short dark hair and Shelly had long brown hair, but if anyone got a haircut, she was in trouble for sure.

"And you remember Jenny, from the Blue Dog Bar, right?" Carter asked.

Jenny?

Rachel turned and found herself staring into the smiling face of the pretty female bartender.

"Hi," Jenny said. "Good to see you again."

"Hello."

Rachel opened her mouth and closed it. She didn't know how to politely ask what the woman was doing here. Staying in touch was one thing, but like this?

"I'm an ex-girlfriend," Jenny said, obviously reading Rachel's confusion. "Carter and I dated for a while about…what, five years ago, I guess."

Carter put his arm around Rachel's shoulder. "We broke up, but would she go away? Not even for money."

Jenny lightly punched him in the arm. "You *never* offered to pay me to leave. I might have left then." She smiled at Rachel. "Carter's a great guy, but he does seem to hang on to his women. Even when he dumps us."

Rachel didn't know what to think. She'd never been in a situation like this, and she wasn't sure what she should say or do.

"You dumped me," Carter said. "I'm sure of it."

"Sorry, no," Jenny said with a smile. "But don't sweat it. I'm grateful." She turned back to Rachel. "Carter broke my heart, so I decided to date someone totally inappropriate. It turns out, Dan was the love of my life." She held up her left hand and wiggled her ring finger. The diamond band there sparkled impressively. "We've been married three years now."

Just then a little girl burst into the kitchen. "Tanya stole the ball and she won't let me play." After her announcement, she burst into tears.

"I'll handle this," Merry said. She picked up the child and carried her back outside. Jenny excused herself and went with her.

Rachel found herself being offered a drink—she chose flavored water—and a chair, which she declined. A few minutes later, in a relatively private moment, she turned to Carter.

"You and Jenny really went out?" she asked.

He shrugged. "Yeah. But it was a long time ago. It doesn't mean anything."

"I don't mean to be rude or too curious, but why is she here?"

"Sometimes my mom and sisters like one of my girlfriends enough to keep her around even after we stop going out. It's made for some entertaining holidays, I can tell you."

"You mean several of them will join in with the family?"

"Sure. It's okay if they bring a date, but when they're single, it's a little uncomfortable. Or they become close friends. I dated this other woman, Shawna. She and Jenny got so close they were in each other's weddings."

She was torn between wanting to get the facts and wondering if she'd crossed the line into the land of too much information.

"I'm not sure this is a completely normal family," she murmured.

He leaned close enough for her to feel his breath on her ear. "I can tell you that it's not, but that's what makes it so much fun."

She was aware of every part of his body. The need to lean in—to touch and be touched—was powerful and just a little scary.

"So, how are you two getting along?"

Rachel jumped as Nina appeared from nowhere with a plate of tiny quiches.

"We're good," Carter said as he took three quiches, placed them on a napkin and handed them to Rachel. "How about you? Having fun?"

His mother ignored the question. "A baby changes everything. Have you thought of that? It's not just you anymore. There's another life."

Rachel was glad she hadn't taken a bite. She had a bad feeling that she would have choked.

"You're kidding," Carter said as he collected a couple of quiches for himself. "Another life. Huh. I didn't know that. I just thought, 'Hey, a baby. We'll keep it on the bookcase.'"

His mother glared at him. "I'm being serious."

"You're meddling," he said. "We talked about that."

His mother turned to Rachel. "You're a sensible girl. What do your parents say about all this?"

Rachel opened her mouth, then closed it. She cleared her throat. "My parents are gone. They died in a car accident when I was twelve. My baby brother was with them and he was killed as well."

She felt Carter's gaze on her. Nina touched her arm. "So it's just you? You have no other relatives?"

Rachel managed a smile. "I'm okay."

"Of course you are," the older woman said. "You have us, now. We're your family. We'll be there for you. No matter what. You have a problem, you call. Promise?"

Rachel felt a tightness in her throat. "Thank you."

Nina smiled and moved away.

"She's trying to be supportive," Carter said when they were alone.

."I know. She wants me to feel welcome. Better that than stoning me or something."

"We gave up stoning awhile ago."

"Good to know."

"Mama's a little over-the-top," he said. "But she's right. You do have all of us now."

"Wherever will I put you?" she asked, her voice deliberately teasing. There was already so much going on today, she didn't need an emotional moment to push her over the edge.

Just then one of Carter's sisters walked over. Rachel was pretty sure it was Liz.

"I'm glad you two agreed to get married," she said. "Mama is so excited. She was starting to think no one would ever trap Carter."

Rachel winced. "I didn't exactly trap him."

"Sure you did, but don't worry about it. He's had it coming for years."

Carter sighed. "Thanks for the support, sis."

"No problem. I've always taken care of my baby brother. Oh, Tanya, honey, no. That's breakable. You put that down right now."

Liz fled across the room.

"You didn't trap me," Carter said in a low voice. "We're in this together, making our own decisions."

Rachel nodded, but inside she felt funny. She'd never thought of herself as the kind of woman who would have to trap a man into being involved with her. And she hadn't. As he'd said, she and Carter were figuring out what they wanted for themselves. They weren't a couple. This wasn't even a real date. So why did she feel guilty?

"Do you want this baby?" she asked.

"Absolutely," he said without hesitating. "I might have

issues with women, but all my life I've wanted to be a father. I don't know anything about it, but I'm willing to learn. I want to be there for my kid. I want to make a difference in her life."

She smiled. "Still convinced we're having a girl?"

"It's just my luck."

"What about my luck?" she asked.

He grinned. "You have me. How much luckier could you get?"

It was dark when Rachel and Carter walked back to his house. She felt tired, but in a good way. There were still complications to be dealt with, and she doubted she would ever figure out who was who in his family, but she'd felt welcomed with open arms.

"I like them," she said as he opened his front door and let Goldie push into the house first. "Everyone was great."

He sighed heavily. "I knew it. This always happens. A guy thinks he's getting lucky because he's charming or smart and then he finds out that the only thing his girl is interested in is his family."

He was teasing, of course, but even more intriguing was his use of the words *his girl*. She wasn't. That wasn't the deal. But for a moment, she felt a shiver of something very close to longing.

"I find it hard to believe you've ever had trouble getting women on your own," she said. "So don't look for sympathy here."

"Ouch. After my family *and* heartless. I'm crushed."

He looked good crushed, she thought, studying the strong, handsome lines of his face before finding her interest settling on his mouth. Carter had a lot of good qualities but right at the top was his amazing ability to kiss her until her entire body turned to mush.

"You'll survive," she murmured, knowing she should look away but finding it difficult to do so. Just one little kiss. What could it hurt?

"Rachel."

He spoke her name in a low growl that caused goose bumps to break out on her arms and the little hairs on the back of her neck to prickle.

She forced herself to take a step back. Right. Be sensible. "Complications," she said as she reached for her car keys in her purse's outside pocket. "We don't need any more complications. There are other things we need to deal with." Although at the moment, she couldn't remember what they were.

"Don't look at me like that," he told her.

"Like what?"

"Like you mean it."

Before she could decide if she did or not, he leaned in and kissed her. As it was exactly what she'd been hoping for, she did little more than melt against him and wish she could purr.

His arms came around her, supporting her, comforting and arousing. She felt his strong hands on her back. Her purse slipped to the ground, but she managed to keep hold of her car keys. That was something, right? That meant she wasn't totally losing control.

But it was hard to stay sane when he moved his lips against hers in a way designed to make her go crazy. She couldn't figure out if it was the pressure, the intensity or some chemical connection that defied description. Whatever the cause, she wanted him right then. The fact that they were still on his front porch didn't matter.

She parted for him. He nipped her lower lip before slipping his tongue inside.

The first erotic stroke made her thighs tremble. The second had her insides clenching and the third had her wet and swollen and nearly whimpering with need.

He moved his hands up and down her back. She wanted to grab his wrists and guide him so that his clever fingers could touch her breasts. She wanted to be swept away by the most intense passion she'd ever experienced. She wanted…

He drew back.

Every cell in her body screamed in protest as he stepped away and gave her a regretful smile.

"Not a good idea," he said.

Of course it wasn't a good idea. But wasn't that the point? How could he be rational at a time like this?

Still, she wouldn't let him know that she hadn't wanted him to stop.

"I'll be going," she said, proud of herself to being able to speak in a steady, nearly normal tone of voice. "Have a nice evening."

"You, too."

A few deep breaths helped clear her mind enough for her to remember their plan. Pretend dating only. Nothing more. A smart woman would quit while she was ahead and Rachel had always been one of the brightest girls in her class.

Chapter 7

"You don't have to do this," Carter said, sounding more apprehensive than he should have.

Rachel held in a grin as she slipped her hand into the crook of his arm and sighed. "I *want* to do this. You did a beautiful job remodeling your kitchen. Now it's time to finish it off."

"It *is* finished," he grumbled as they walked through the aisles of the large home-improvement store.

"White walls? Come on. Have a little imagination. Color is our friend. Besides, you get to pick any color you want. You don't have to run it by your landlord and then plead for your choice."

"My choice is white."

She chuckled. "No, it's not. Besides, it's too stark against the maple cabinets. Quite the bold selection here in Southern California, where most people favor oak."

He shrugged. "I thought they looked nice."

"They do. They're beautiful and they deserve something better than white walls."

He mumbled something under his breath, but Rachel didn't mind. If Carter really had wanted to keep those stark white walls, he wouldn't have asked her to come with him after work to look at paint chips.

The invitation might fall under the category of "pretend dating" but she intended to enjoy every minute of it.

"You're lucky to have your own house," she said. "I'm saving, but with real estate prices what they are, it's going to take me awhile. But I have a whole shoe box full of articles and pictures I've cut out of magazines, or downloaded off Web sites. I have this dream about the perfect closet, all organized with shoe shelves and hooks for belts and purses."

He eyed her suspiciously. "We're just here for paint."

"I know that. Don't worry. I don't expect you to completely redo your closets just to satisfy my urges. At least not this week."

He groaned and she laughed.

They walked into the paint department. Carter held out the small drawer she'd insisted they bring along to help with the color choices.

"So maybe cream?" he said. "Cream would look nice with the maple."

"I don't think so." She ignored the chips of cream and white and headed to the yellows. "Nothing superbright," she murmured more to herself than him. "It has to blend. But nothing too boring."

Carter had gone with black appliances, which made it easy, and a fairly neutral black, gray and cream flecked granite. The cabinets were light, and that meant a bland paint color would cause the whole room to fade away.

"A warm color," she said. "You get that great morning sun in there."

She plucked out three different yellows, then moved to peach. "Hmm, more on the orange side or more salmon?"

Carter took a step back. "That's a lot of color."

"I know. We'll grab all the ones that interest us, then narrow the choice down to three or four. Then we buy samples. Better to paint big squares of color on the wall and live with it for a week, than get the wrong color."

She fanned out her selections. Rather than pick, he made a strangled sound in his throat.

"Are you always like this?" she asked. "It's paint, not a room full of snakes."

"I could deal with snakes."

"What a typical guy."

"That's me. Mr. Beige."

She discarded a couple of samples until they had four she liked and he didn't flinch at. After collecting the samples, she dragged him over to the fabric department.

He stared at the bolts of cloth. "Why are we here?"

"I was thinking I could make some valances for your windows. Nothing fancy, but they'd dress them up."

He looked as if he was about to run for cover. "Those go on the top of the window, right?"

"Uh-huh. The miniblinds are practical, but not especially attractive. Roman shades would be nice, but I can't see you agreeing to that, what with how you've reacted to a little color."

He stiffened. "I'm reacting fine. I have samples here. I'm going to put them on the wall."

"I know, but you're pretty whiny about it."

He looked outraged. "I do not whine."

"Of course not."

"I am rational and completely in control of the situation."

She held in a smile. "Okay, so I was thinking of something like this."

She pulled out a bolt of fabric and spread out the cloth, then put the paint chips on top. "See how they all go."

He frowned. "How did you do that? You just picked that one out and it's perfect? That's not right."

"I'm gifted. Now, do you like this?"

He studied the striped fabric. "Yeah. There aren't any flowers on it."

"You're not the flower type. So we'll get the fabric, then when you choose the paint color, we'll use the valance material to pick out coordinating chair mats and a tablecloth for that little table. The simple stripe in the valance means you can get a different pattern for those or none at all."

He nodded slowly. "My sisters talk like that, too. Is it a chick thing?"

"Yes. Most of us are born with the ability to coordinate fabric."

He rubbed the cloth. "It's nice. I like it better than white."

"It's a miracle."

"Carter?"

The woman's voice came from behind them. Rachel turned and saw a pretty, petite redhead holding a bolt of fabric.

"Hi, Nora," Carter said. "How are you?"

"Okay."

"Good. Rachel, this is Nora."

The other woman nodded. "Hi. Nice to meet you. So you're with Carter now, huh? We used to go out." The hunger in her expression said she would like to again. "You look…great."

"You, too," he said as he gently put his hand on Rachel's shoulder.

Rachel felt both awkward and uncomfortable. Should she excuse herself so Carter and Nora could speak in private? Good manners dictated that she at least offer, but she couldn't seem to form the words or make her feet move.

Nora cleared her throat. "I thought maybe, you know, sometime we could go out for coffee."

"Thanks, but this isn't a good time for me. You take care, Nora."

"Yeah. Okay. Well, bye."

She shuffled off.

Carter watched her go, then shook his head. "Sorry about that."

"It's fine. I take it you two had a bad breakup?"

"Yeah. Usually I can stay friends, but Nora wanted marriage or nothing."

"You weren't interested in her that way?"

Carter looked at her. "I'm not interested in anyone that way. All my life I've been told I'll meet someone, fall in love and get married. So far, it hasn't happened. I love women—all women. I don't cheat, I'm more interested in quality than volume, but forever? Not my style. I don't need to grow old with anyone."

As he spoke his expression tightened.

"What?" she asked. "Do you expect me to get mad?"

He shrugged. "I'm braced for the criticism. Most women don't appreciate my position."

"I do," she told him and meant it. "Why marry someone you don't love?" She drew in a breath. "That's what happened to me with my two engagements. I thought I loved the guys, but as time passed, I realized I didn't. I started to feel trapped. Neither of them understood."

He relaxed a little. "So what do you think of marriage?"

She thought of what she remembered of her parents' relationship. "I think with the right person, it can be the best part of anyone's life. I want that, but only when it's right. And it needs to be for the right reasons."

"I won't ever want to get married."

She smiled. "I'm okay with that, Carter. I don't plan to be one of your groupies."

"I don't have groupies."

"Oh, you're wrong, but that's okay. I can totally respect not wanting to make a commitment to someone you don't love. What I don't understand is not making a commitment to one of these beautiful paints. Now *that* would break my heart."

He grinned. "Fine. I'll put the damn paint on the damn wall and pick one."

"You promise?"

"Yes."

"Good. I'll make valances."

"You can't."

"Actually, I'm pretty good with my old, trusty sewing machine. I learned while I was still dancing. Costumes cost too much to buy. None of my foster families could afford it, so I learned to sew."

"I don't mean that. I'll owe you."

"And that's bad why?"

"I don't know how to pay you back."

Images of them naked and touching and joining instantly filled her brain. Okay, she could give him a list of ways to pay her back, starting with a few long, slow, deep kisses, followed by some serious naked time.

Without meaning to, she remembered how his hands had felt on her body. How he touched her with an irresistible combination of aggressive tenderness that had left her weak and hungry for more. He could...

"Earth to Rachel."

"What? Oh." She blinked at him. "Sorry. What was the question?"

"If you're going to do this for me, I want to do something for you. What do you need? Heavy furniture moved? A tree planted in your honor?"

She laughed. "Nothing like that. But I do have the fall festival coming up at school. Each class has to build a booth. Now that I've seen your handiwork, I think maybe you're the right one to take on the job of being in charge."

"Done."

"Are you sure? We're talking about ten five-year-olds and some fairly inept parents."

"I like kids, and parents find me very charming."

"Especially the moms."

He flashed her a smile. "Especially."

Carter tucked his too-long hair under a baseball cap and then turned up the collar of his jacket. The truck stop diner was several miles north of Riverside on I-15. As this was the main drag to Las Vegas, there were plenty of people coming and going. A good place for a private meeting.

He'd already seen his captain's car in the parking lot, so he walked in and looked for the table.

Captain Don Killian was known for protecting his men, so Carter wasn't surprised to see the older man at a booth in the back. Carter slid in across from him and realized a large pole would conceal him from view.

"Nicely done," he said with a grin.

Killian shrugged. "I had to wait for an old couple to clear out, but I figured this was the best seat in the house. How's it going, Carter?"

"Good."

The waitress appeared. Both men ordered burgers and sodas. When she left, Carter leaned forward.

"There's going to be a big shipment out next week. I've got a copy of the parts inventory heading out. The drop is in Chicago, and from there it goes all across the country."

Carter was part of a team investigating counterfeit auto parts brought in from other countries.

While Carter went over the details, Killian wrote down the information.

"We can intercept this," his captain said. "I'll talk to the Feds on the case, but the current plan is we'll make it look like a highway accident so no one gets suspicious. We're thinking maybe four or five more weeks on the job. You okay with that?"

The waitress arrived with their drinks. Carter waited until she'd left before saying, "Sure. I'm good. No one suspects anything."

"They will if you keep hanging out at the Blue Dog Bar."

Carter grimaced. "That wasn't my idea. My contact insisted. He thought it would make me nervous to be around so many cops. It did, but not in the way he thought."

"You calling ahead helped," Killian told him. "Jenny

put out the word. She's a great girl. Too bad you let that one get away."

"She wasn't for me." Jenny had been great, but he'd let her go as easily as everyone else. Most of the time he was fine with his life and appreciated the women he'd dated and then walked away from, but sometimes he wondered if there was something wrong with him...a reason he couldn't settle down like everyone else.

"Just as well," his boss said. "With this assignment, you don't need the added pressure of being involved. But when it's over, what next?"

Carter looked at him. "What do you mean? I take the next job."

"Another undercover assignment? Come on, Carter. You passed the tests, you're ready to move up to detective. So what's stopping you? Why do you always turn down the job?"

"I turned down one."

"Most guys would jump at the chance to make detective."

Carter shrugged. "I'll get there."

"Why take the test if you're not interested?"

"I am interested." If the man talking had been anyone but his boss, Carter would have told him to back off.

"Then act like it. Take the next opening. You can't play forever. Maybe it's time to grow up."

Carter glared at Killian. "What I do is damned important. I make a difference."

"You could make a bigger difference as detective. You know it and I know it. So what's holding you back?"

Saturday morning started with complete chaos. Ten five-year-olds running through the open classroom, their parents talking in groups and Rachel sorting through supplies left in the small yard off her classroom.

She knew nothing about lumber or tools, so she wasn't sure if she had everything she was supposed to have. While she could figure out which wood was which from the size, she wasn't sure if she had the right braces or not.

"Need some help?" Carter asked as he stepped out into the yard.

"Desperately," she said and held out her list. "Do I have all this? I've never made a booth before and to be honest, I have no big plans to make one now. That's why you and the parents are here. Well, some of you will help me with the card kits, but that's the easy part. It's mostly sorting and counting."

She was aware she was talking too much, which frequently happened the first time she saw Carter after any kind of absence. She wanted to explain that, technically, it wasn't her fault. There was something about looking at him that unhinged her brain. Something that made her remember what it was like to touch him and kiss him and…

He moved close and smiled at her. "You about wound down?"

If she said no, would he stop her talking in the most interesting way possible?

"Pretty much. The kindergarteners have never had to have a booth before. I was very comfortable in that position. Suddenly, someone decided we were capable, or at least the parents were. I know nothing about building. Can you take charge of this and coordinate the work? In theory, the build should take no more than two hours."

"I've built cabinets. I can handle a festival booth." He glanced over the instructions. "It'll be fun. Are the kids supposed to help?"

"If they want. I'm going to have some of them with me, putting together our card kits."

"Which are?"

"Greeting cards. Some are preprinted and some can be made by hand with decorations and trims."

He took a step back. "Don't make me do that."

She grinned. "I promise. You can stay out here and be macho with the wood and paint."

"Perfect."

He smiled at her and she felt her insides shimmy a little. Despite her urge to throw herself at him, she drew in a deep breath and walked toward the classroom. "Let's go gather the troops and divide into teams."

Back in the classroom, Rachel explained their two projects and let the parents and kids divide up themselves. She felt someone tugging on the hem of her T-shirt and turned.

"Morning, Christian," she said to the small boy. "Are you excited to help build the booth?"

Christian nodded. "Is he your boyfriend?" he asked, pointing at Carter.

Rachel's mind went blank. Under the circumstances it was a reasonable question and one she should have expected. "Ah, well, to be honest…"

"Yes," Carter said easily.

Christian giggled. "Are you gonna kiss her?"

"Maybe later. If she's very good."

A couple of the mothers exchanged glances as if they wouldn't mind being rewarded by Carter for excellent behavior.

"Okay, then," Rachel said, ignoring the heat on her cheeks. "Let's get started."

Carter led the construction crew outside while she put

the card kit folks to work in the classroom. She had set up several stations for the kids, showing how many of each items went in to the various bags. White cardboard signs showed five buttons inside a bag at one station and three bows in another bag at a different station.

Soon kids and parents alike were counting greeting cards and filling bags. When she was sure everything was going smoothly, she walked to her desk and pulled out her parent list. There were a few she wanted to talk to today. It was more casual than an official parent-teacher conference.

"Helen, do you have a second?" Rachel asked a pretty, dark-haired woman who was helping with the bow counting.

"Sure, Rachel."

Rachel let the way into the classroom next door. It was empty and quiet.

When they were seated on the two adult-sized chairs Rachel had brought in earlier that morning, she leaned forward.

"I'm a little worried about Anastasia. She's a wonderful girl. So bright and friendly and she loves learning. But she's obviously exhausted. She falls asleep during storytime nearly every day."

Helen stiffened. "I don't know what you mean. We put her to bed at nine. That should be enough sleep."

"She's only five. I think an earlier bedtime might help. Does she try to stay up later? Some kids are natural night owls." Rachel didn't think that was the problem, but she'd found it was usually more productive to start by getting the parent on her side than to make an outright accusation.

Helen shook her head. "Anastasia is always ready to

go to bed when it's time. In fact, if we've been out after seven, she falls asleep in the car on the way home."

"Then I would suggest moving her bedtime back fifteen minutes every four or five days until you find a time that gives her enough sleep. It's probably going to be about seven-thirty."

Helen's eyes widened. "But that's not possible. She has her classes."

"Hmm, yes. She's mentioned that she has a lot of activities outside of school. Dance, Spanish, some kind of martial arts."

Helen nodded. "Gymnastics, piano, soccer. We have a schedule. Some are in the afternoon, but a few are in the evening. She couldn't attend them and get to bed earlier."

Rachel tried to figure out the most tactful way to make her point. "I think it's wonderful when caring parents take such an interest in their children. I wish all parents were like you. But sometimes kids get overscheduled. Anastasia needs time to just be a little girl. She needs time to play and dream and imagine as well as learn Spanish."

Helen opened her mouth, then closed it. "We have her doing too much, don't we? I've wondered. It's just both Martin and I have siblings who are gross underachievers. We didn't want that for Anastasia. We want her to have every advantage, but also to understand that she needs to push herself."

"Pushing her now won't teach her that lesson," Rachel said gently. "Anastasia is exceptional because of who she is on the inside, not because of what she does. She's not going to be your little girl for a very long time and that goes so quickly. I would hate for you two to miss these special years because your daughter is never home."

"I'll talk to Martin," Helen said. "Maybe we can back off on the classes."

"Don't give them up all together," Rachel said. "It's good to expose her to a few things. Maybe try a couple this semester and next semester try some different ones. Then you can sit down as a family and figure out what you think is important and she likes to do."

"Okay. Thanks."

"You're more than welcome. Anastasia is wonderful. I'm glad she's in my class."

Helen smiled. "I am, too."

The other woman left. Rachel made some notes on her file, then glanced up when Carter walked into the room.

"Impressive," he said. "I came to tell you the booth is coming together, but I didn't want to interrupt. You handled that really well."

His praise made her feel a little bit floaty inside. "Thanks. I'm with the kids for several hours a day. Because I'm not the parent, I can usually see both the good and bad that's happening. Unfortunately, parents tend to get stuck on one or the other."

"Helen got the message."

Rachel closed her file and stood. "I hope so. I hate seeing these kids dragging because their parents plan for them to be the next Secretary General of the United Nations. But balance is tricky to find."

Carter tucked a strand of hair behind her ear. "My mom did a great job at it. We were all convinced we were her favorite. She made us believe we could do anything."

"My parents were like that, too," Rachel said, remembering the loving support they'd offered her. "I wanted to be an astronaut/ballerina and no one ever said it was a dumb idea. Of course I was only twelve and no one takes career plans seriously at that age. There was this one time that they—"

Unexpected tears filled her eyes. Rachel was so surprised, she stopped in midsentence.

"What's wrong?" Carter asked.

"I don't know." She blinked several times, but the tears wouldn't go away. "I was going to say something about my parents, but I know if I do, I'll burst into tears."

"I can handle it."

She sniffed and smiled at the same time. "I appreciate you saying that. It's just I don't understand. I don't cry very much, especially not about the loss of my family. It's been fourteen years. I'm sad they're gone, but I've recovered, emotionally."

"Hey, it happens."

He drew her close and wrapped his arms around her. She let him because, for reasons she couldn't explain, she needed the comfort.

"This is crazy," she murmured against his shoulder as tears trickled down her cheeks. "I have no reason to cry. This is not like me."

"You're having a baby," he said.

She drew back and stared at him. "I hardly think that's a reason to break down when I talk about my parents. I know the situation is stressful, but speaking as someone who is firmly in denial about the whole thing, I can't believe that's why I'm losing it."

She wiped her face and tried to think happy thoughts. Maybe she should get a kitten. A fluffy white one that would play with a ball of yarn. Only the image of it caused her eyes to fill again.

"I'm not saying it's because you're stressed," he said. "It's hormones. Trust me. I have three sisters who have all been pregnant at least twice. You might not want to think about being pregnant, but your body is seriously busy producing all kinds of chemicals. You're reacting to them."

Was that possible?

"Are you saying I'm going to be an emotional basket case for the next seven months?"

"Possibly."

"I'll never survive."

"Sure you will. Besides, I'll be right here. You can cry on my shoulder anytime."

She laughed, which helped ease the need to sob. He cupped her face in his hands and used his thumbs to wipe her cheeks.

"Better?" he asked.

She nodded, then found her gaze lingering on his mouth.

"Yeah," he murmured. "Me, too. Think anyone would mind?"

"Hurry up," a small voice called out. "He's gonna kiss her."

Rachel turned and saw Christian and his friend lurking in the doorway. "Great. An audience."

Carter laughed. "I don't do requests. Rain check?"

"Absolutely."

Chapter 8

Crissy set the pitcher of iced tea on the table, then put her hands on her hips. "Let me just say for the record, I'm bitter about the lack of wine, okay?"

Noelle smiled. "I'm only twenty. I couldn't drink the wine anyway."

"You could be with us in spirit," Crissy grumbled. "But you're right. So, Rachel, what's your excuse?"

"I'm pregnant."

"I meant for getting pregnant."

Rachel didn't have an actual answer for that. Fortunately the phone rang…again.

Noelle's smile broadened. "That's probably Dev," she murmured. "I'll take it in the other room."

Crissy stared after her. "We've been here less than two hours and this is his third call. It's amazing he can get any work done."

"I'm thinking he's not," Rachel said, wondering what it would be like to be that in love. She'd wanted that for herself, had tried twice. So what had gone wrong? Did she just have bad taste in men or did she not know how to have a good relationship?

"I'm sure he misses her," Crissy said as she poured Rachel a glass of iced tea. "I still can't believe they're so much in love, but they are. Talk about lucky."

Crissy sounded both happy for her friend and a little wistful, which Rachel could relate to.

"She's glowing," Rachel said. "Now that they know the baby's all right, they can be happy."

"Are you happy?" Crissy asked. "You haven't said much about your own pregnancy."

For good reason, Rachel thought. "I'm doing okay. Physically I don't feel any different. At least not yet. I had an emotional meltdown the other day, which isn't like me, but I guess now I have hormones to deal with." She leaned toward Crissy. "Honestly? I can't seem to get my mind around the fact that I'm having a baby. I've tried to think about it as far as what all I have to plan for and deal with, and when I do I start to panic. It seems easier to ignore the whole thing. But that can't be good, either."

"You have time," Crissy told her. "What? Seven more months? Trust me, as you begin to completely lose control of your body, you'll get that it's real."

Rachel grinned. "Lose control? You make me feel like aliens have invaded and will soon be bursting out."

"Pretty much."

"You have personal experience in the matter?" Rachel asked teasingly.

Crissy shrugged. "I've been doing some reading so I can relate to what Noelle's going through. And now you."

She reached in her purse and held up a bottle of water. "But to be on the safe side, I'm avoiding any liquids that come from a tap. What is it with you two?"

"We're just lucky," Noelle said as she walked back into the kitchen and took her seat at the table. "Dev says hi and promises he won't call again until after you guys are gone."

"I'm not a big believer in happy endings," Crissy said, "but looking at you is kinda making me a believer. You look good in love."

"Thanks. I feel good. Now I just have to get you two married off."

Crissy scooted back her chair. "I'm fine being single. Did I mention my charming cat? He's more than enough company, thank you very much. I hate first dates enough to never want to go on one again!"

"You're going to be a tough one," Noelle said. "I thought we'd start with someone easier." She turned to Rachel. "So how's Carter?"

Rachel laughed. "He's fine, but you're wasting your time setting us up. It's not going to happen."

"Why not?" Noelle passed around the large bowl of Chinese chicken salad. "You said he's a great guy."

"He is. He's funny and charming and I think he's dated nearly every age-appropriate woman in a tristate area."

Noelle nodded. "You don't think he's good husband material."

Rachel considered the statement. "Actually, I think he is. He cares a lot about his family. They're all wonderful. He's responsible and caring. He helped me out with my fall festival booth last weekend, which was great."

"He sounds perfect," Crissy said as she took a roll. "Which makes me instantly not want to trust him. But

I'm the cynical member of the team. What's your excuse?"

"For one thing, he's made it really clear that he's not interested in anything long-term. Carter doesn't believe in romantic love. Not for himself anyway."

Noelle dismissed the problem with a flick of her fingers. "That just means he hasn't met the right someone yet. Which could be you. But I don't understand. Doesn't it bother you that he doesn't want to get married for the sake of the baby?"

"Not really," Rachel admitted. "I know that decision was right for you, but it's not right for me. I don't need to be married to have a child. Carter will be part of the baby's life and that's enough."

Crissy and Noelle exchanged a glance that told Rachel they'd been discussing this without her.

"You've always talked about wanting a family," Crissy said slowly. "I thought you meant in the traditional sense. Husband and kids."

"I do want that. Just not with Carter."

Noelle took some salad for herself. "At the risk of sounding stupid, why not? If he's all that you said, how can you keep from falling in love with him?"

"I just can."

Rachel had been in love twice, or so she'd thought. She'd agreed to marry two terrific guys, only to have second thoughts a few weeks later. She'd hated hurting them by ending the relationships, but she hadn't been willing to go forward with their plans when her feelings had changed.

This was when she missed her mother the most. She wanted to ask questions about her parents' courtship and hear how they'd known that each other was the one. She wanted to be told that there was nothing wrong with her, that when she met the right guy, she would just know.

Apparently Carter wasn't that guy. He was wonderful and she liked being with him and she still went weak remembering their one night together, but was that enough to hold a marriage together? Shouldn't there be some defining moment when she just *knew?*

"I'll find Mr. Right," Rachel said. "He's out there."

"Waiting," Crissy said with a grin. "Longing for you. Desperate and needy."

Rachel rolled her eyes. "Stop it or I'll spike your bottled water with something from the tap and then you'll get pregnant, too."

"Never," Crissy said firmly.

The morning of the fall festival promised perfect Southern California weather. Blue skies and a cool start to the day with afternoon temperatures in the low eighties.

Rachel had arrived before eight to supervise the setup. The booth had turned out great, with bright colors and plenty of room for the sale of greeting cards. Now she checked the inventory against the numbers on her master list and made a note that she had to count the change.

"Coffee," Brady's mom said as she walked over with a tray filled with steaming paper cups. "I stopped on the way."

"Thanks," Rachel said as she took one of the small cups and set it on the booth. She'd never been much of a coffee drinker and these days she was avoiding caffeine, but it seemed easier to take the drink and get rid of it discreetly at a later time than to explain why she was refusing.

"I'm excited," Brady's mom continued. "He's our oldest, so this is the first time we're able to get involved in school activities. I can't wait to get started."

Rachel knew there were two other younger children at home. "Okay, but hold on to that enthusiasm," she teased. "We don't want you burning out before the baby hits kindergarten."

"I won't," she promised.

"Morning, ladies."

Rachel didn't have to turn around and see the speaker to recognize the voice. "Carter," she said. "You're early."

"It's the fall festival. How could I resist?"

How could *she?* He looked good in his worn jeans and dark T-shirt. Why was it a man could step out of the shower, pull on any old thing and look fabulous while women had to sweat makeup and stylish clothes to achieve any kind of gorgeous?

"You have a burning need for greeting cards?" she asked.

"I might. You never know."

"Carter? Is that you?"

Rachel stepped back to avoid being pushed aside as a woman flung herself at Carter, wrapping her arms around him as she pressed her body against his.

"It is you. Ohmygosh! I can't believe it. What are you doing here?"

Rachel blinked. "Eden?"

The woman glanced at Rachel and grinned. "Oh, hi, Rachel."

Eden Baker was one of the teachers at Rachel's school and obviously another of Carter's exes.

Carter reached up and carefully loosened Eden's grip

from around his neck. "Good to see you, Eden. How's John?"

"He's great." Eden released Carter and stepped back. She smiled at Rachel. "Sorry. I didn't mean to be rude. I was just so shocked to see Carter here. I could never get him to come to any school events. It's been what? Five years?"

"About that," he said.

Eden's smile widened. "I'm a happily married woman now and I wouldn't change a thing, but we had some good times." She patted Rachel's arm. "Enjoy him, honey. Enjoy him for all of us."

Rachel watched Eden head back to her booth, then she turned to Carter. "I'm thinking maybe you could just give me a list. You know, names, occupations, addresses, so I can be prepared for the next round of women I'm going to meet."

Carter shuffled his feet and shoved his hands into his front pockets. "There aren't that many."

"Really? I seem unable to leave the house with you without us running into someone you used to date. And I use the term 'date' very loosely."

All his exes weren't excited to see him because he'd known how to pick a great movie.

"Are you mad?" he asked.

"No, not mad. Just out of my element. I've never known a guy like you."

"Is that a bad thing?" he asked.

He was so obviously uncomfortable, she wanted to laugh. He could have strutted around and bragged about his conquests. The fact that he didn't made her willing to deal with all the Edens and Jennys she was bound to meet.

"I'm thinking you should give lessons to less fortunate males," she teased. "It would be a great side job. Think of the money you'd make."

"You're exaggerating," he told her. "I—"

"Carter? Carter Brockett? As I live and breathe, is that you, honey?"

Rachel patted him on the arm. "I'll go take care of my booth. You handle the fans."

By that afternoon, the festival was officially a success. Rachel went over her inventory and was pleased to see they'd already sold about eighty percent of the greeting-card kits. Parents were showing up on time to man the booth, the kids were having a blast—running through the playground and getting in the way—and money was being made for the school.

Carter had ducked out before lunch, although he'd promised to return later. Now Rachel found herself watching for him, which she didn't like. Their deal of pretend dating didn't have any room for the real thing.

Still, she scanned the crowd, then smiled when she saw a familiar older woman heading in her direction.

Rachel walked into the main path to greet Nina Brockett.

"What are you doing here?" she asked as Carter's mom gave her a hug.

"I always come to the fall festival. I have grandchildren, you know."

"I do know. I've met nearly all of them. Your entire family has stopped by to say hi."

Rachel hadn't expected their appearance but had enjoyed it. The Brocketts were obviously willing to take her in and accept her as one of them. Unfortunately, their warmth left her feeling guilty about her secret plan with Carter.

"So what are you selling?" Nina asked as she moved to the booth. "Oh, cards. Very nice."

"Um, you might want to buy something else," Rachel told her. "All three of your daughters bought cards, so you're all at risk of sending each other exactly the same one."

"Still, I want to support your class." She leaned close. "Children are a blessing and I love every one of mine, but grandchildren are the reward. You wait. You'll see what I mean. Have you seen Carter?"

"He was here this morning to help me set up."

"Good. He talked about how important the festival was to you. How it's the major fundraiser for the school. He asked us all to come and stop by."

Had he? That was unexpected, but nice to hear.

"Carter's a good man," his mother said. "He's always thinking about the people he cares about. He's responsible, too."

Rachel silently groaned at the obvious matchmaking. "Nina, you don't have to sell him to me."

Nina smiled. "Of course I do. I want to make sure you both fall in love and get married. Not just for the baby, although he or she is going to need a name, but for yourself. There's nothing better than a happy marriage. I know. I had ten wonderful years with Carter's father."

Rachel held in the need to point out that her baby would have a name even if it wasn't Carter's and decided it was much safer to shift the topic of conversation.

"You've been a widow for a long time. Didn't you ever want to remarry?"

"I thought about it," Nina told her. "I wanted a man around for my children. I decided that when I fell in love again, I'd marry, but not for any other reason. Like you."

Rachel blinked. "Excuse me?"

"Carter mentioned you'd been engaged before but had broken things off. I'm glad. That means you're sensible *and* romantic. A good combination."

While she appreciated the praise, she wasn't sure she deserved it. "I made a mistake with each of them," Rachel admitted. "I thought I was in love, which is why I said yes. But I wasn't."

"Exactly. Romantic enough to see the possibilities and sensible enough to know what was required to make things work. Now you have Carter. He's my son so I'm biased, but where are you going to do better?"

Nina patted her hand and walked toward the booth. Rachel stayed where she was as the other woman's question echoed in her brain.

Where *was* she going to do better? Carter was everything she'd ever wanted in a man and she practically became a puddle every time they were close. So why wasn't she pushing for a real relationship? Why was she content to keep her distance?

She didn't have any answers, and it was a little unsettling. When she tried to dig deeper, emotionally, she found only that dark scary place that made her want to ignore the whole issue.

Love meant loss. She'd learned the lesson early and well when her family had been killed and she'd been left totally alone. Since then she'd found the courage to let some people in to her life. Her friends, her kids. She could care about them and survive the fear. But anything more was out of the question. The potential for loss was too great—she wouldn't risk it. Which was why Carter was perfect for her. He didn't want any more than she could give.

"I confess, I never thought of the 'after' part," Rachel said as Carter took the end of a hammer to the booth and started pulling out nails.

"What did you think happened?" he asked. "That the festival would end and the booths would disappear?"

"Sure. I thought they went back to their festival booth village and lived happily with others of their own kind."

He looked at her. "Sometimes you're a little weird, you know that?"

"I've been told."

She ached from the long day spent at the booth. She'd had a full contingent of parents to handle the sales, but she'd been in charge. Except for a quick lunch break, she'd been on her feet since seven that morning.

"I need a long bath," she said as she moved her feet to shoulder-width apart, then bent over. Her fingers curled against the asphalt of the playground. She put her palms on the rough surface and pressed down until she felt a stretch in the back of her legs.

After grabbing her left ankle, she pulled herself to the side, then repeated the movement on her right side. When she straightened, she found Carter staring at her.

"What?" she asked.

"You're really limber."

She grinned. "Yes, I am. I haven't had much time for dance class lately, but I do my stretching."

He muttered something and went back to work on disassembling the booth.

Had that been a flicker of hunger in his eyes? she wondered happily. Did he, too, feel the pull between them? She started to tease him about it, then stopped herself.

She and Carter had a good working plan. Getting intimate again would only complicate the situation and neither of them wanted that. She was still feeling a little unsettled by his mother's visits and her claims that Carter was the perfect man. Or if not perfect, then at least perfect for her.

"Your family all stopped by," she said to change the subject. "Your mom told me you'd mentioned the festival to them and they came by to be supportive."

He twisted the booth into three separate parts. "It's a fundraiser. I wanted to help."

"The booth building and destruction was more than enough. You didn't have to do that, but thank you for saying something. It was nice."

"They like you." He tossed the smaller pieces into the back of his truck.

"I like them. You're lucky, Carter."

"I know."

He straightened and suddenly they were standing way too close together. His dark eyes seem to draw her in, so that she took a step toward him without even meaning to.

His broad shoulders offered the perfect resting place for her hands, so it wasn't really her fault that she put them there. He was warm and strong and she couldn't seem to stop looking at his mouth.

Nearly everyone had already left and there was only the call of a few birds in the playground. To Rachel, it felt as if they were alone in the world.

He rested his hands on her waist. "We have to stop doing this," he told her.

"Why?" she asked.

"Hell if I can remember."

And then he kissed her. He bent down and claimed her mouth with a possessive heat that branded her. Even as she wrapped her arms around his neck, she surged toward him, her body moving without permission. As if it had no choice but to be next to him. His thighs pressed against hers, his chest flattened her breasts and she knew she could stay in his embrace forever.

She parted and he swept inside her mouth. His tongue touched hers with a slow, erotic stroke. The thrill stole her breath. She clung to him, letting him claim her, then following him back and claiming him.

Need grew until she had to have him or die. She was already aroused and hungry. There were—

The sound of a child's laughter echoed in the late afternoon. She told herself it didn't matter, that she was allowed to kiss Carter, but she didn't quite believe it and even if she did, he'd already pulled back.

"Great idea, bad timing," he said.

His eyes were dark with passion. Wanting tightened his expression until she knew for certain he was a man in need.

She wanted to know that his desire was specifically for her. That she was different from all those who had come before. Except she wasn't, and she couldn't be. None of this was real, remember?

"You all right?" he asked.

She nodded. "I get a little confused. It's the kissing. You do it better than anyone I've ever, well, kissed."

"You're pretty good, yourself."

"So speaks the voice of experience."

He winced. "Ouch."

She smiled. "Come on, Carter, you can't avoid the

truth. You've dated more women than the average professional football team."

"I doubt that."

"Close enough. I've had two serious boyfriends in my life and I was engaged to each of them."

"Not at the same time, right?"

Even hungry for his kiss and not sure how to reconcile what was happening, she liked that he could still make her laugh.

"Not at the same time. There were a couple of years between them. My point is I've never done the casual thing before."

"Probably for the best, considering what happened that first night."

She touched her stomach. "Right. So we should stay with our plan. Pretend dating." And that meant there should be a whole lot less kissing.

"I can do that," he said.

"Me, too. So we don't have a problem."

"Not even a little one."

"Good."

"Great."

They stared at each other and she fought against the need to throw herself at him. Just one more night, she thought. One long, slow, sexy night in his bed, his arms. She wanted his hands on her body, his tongue in her mouth and his...

"Rachel?" His voice sounded strangled.

"Yes?" Was that breathy whisper really her?

"You gotta stop thinking like that. I can't stand it. In fact, why don't you head home? I'll finish up here."

She almost said no. She almost issued the invitation she sensed he would accept. But then what? Could she make love with Carter a second time and not get emotionally involved?

What if the worst happened? What if she fell for him? He was the guy most likely to walk away, which would leave her emotionally broken and bleeding on the side of the road.

"I can't do this," she told him.

"I'm not asking you to."

"Right. You're not."

She made the rational choice then and collected her car keys. Then she walked across the parking lot and into the relative safety of her small car.

Once she'd started the engine, she drove directly home without once looking back. She knew if she looked back, she would turn around. And if she turned around, she might be lost forever.

Chapter 9

Rachel handed over her car keys and walked into the waiting room of the local auto repair shop. She was diligent about regular oil changes for her little car, although this might be one of the last ones she'd have to have done. The two-seater convertible wasn't practical for a single mom with a newborn. She would have to start looking around for something bigger. Maybe a four-door of some kind. Something with a good safety record and side airbags.

Maybe Carter could help her find one that was…

She flopped down onto one of the plastic chairs and held in a groan. Not Carter. She hadn't seen or talked to him since the fall festival the previous weekend and she preferred things that way. Better to take some time and get him off her mind and out of her system.

She'd been doing a pretty good job, too, not thinking

about him more than three or four hundred times a day. Now if she could get that down to an even hundred, she could consider herself on the road to recovery.

The problem was she missed him. He was so good to have around. Not just because he was gorgeous—which he was—but because he was fun and charming and caring and thoughtful. And those qualities made her once again wonder why she was so dead set on avoiding anything personal with him.

But every time she thought about talking to him about something more than their pretend relationship, she felt shaky and afraid. Nope, this was better.

She opened a home decorating magazine, but couldn't concentrate on any of the articles. Then she flipped through a travel magazine, but that didn't hold her interest, either. She was the only customer and knew she wouldn't be waiting long, but still she felt restless. Giving in to the need to move, she walked out of the waiting room and paced the sidewalk of the main road.

This was the part of town that catered to those with cars. There were several body shops, a place that sold custom wheels and a motorcycle sales-and-repair place. She stared at the latter because it made her think of Carter. That's where he was working. Or at least pretend work while undercover.

Pretend work, pretend relationship. Was anything in his life real?

A beautiful blonde stepped out of the sales office and onto the sidewalk. Three men followed her. They were all talking intently. Then a fourth man joined them and Rachel nearly shrieked in surprise. It was Carter!

She glanced around, not sure what she should do. Not

call out to him, of course. That was his police world and she wasn't supposed to know him.

She turned and hurried to the waiting room. When she was safely back in the small, glass space, she hid behind a magazine, while watching the ongoing conversation. The men seemed to come to some kind of agreement, because they all shook hands. Then Carter put his arm around the blonde and gave her a long, lingering kiss on the lips.

The magazine fell to the floor. Rachel half rose, then sank back onto the seat. She blinked several times, but the image didn't go away. There was Carter sharing a very intimate moment with another woman.

Her chest ached, it was difficult to breathe and she had the strongest urge to cry. Only this time the tears wouldn't be brought on by pregnancy hormones. Instead they would be the result of anger and betrayal.

How could he do that? How could he kiss someone else? They were…

What? she thought. What were they doing? Not dating. Not for real. It was all fake, done for the benefit of his family. Hadn't she made it clear that she didn't want anything from him? Hadn't she made it clear she wasn't any more interested in getting involved than he was? So none of this should matter.

Except it did and she hurt.

"Hey, Rach, the car's done. Oil's changed and everything else checks out fine."

She turned toward her mechanic. "Thanks, Evan. What do I owe you?"

Twenty minutes later she found herself driving around town. Her work day was finished, she was tired and confused and the best place for her was home. Only she couldn't seem to make herself go in that direction, so she made turns until she pulled in to the parking lot of the Blue Dog Bar.

She stared at the neon sign, then at the door. The need to go inside got stronger and stronger until she finally climbed out of her car and walked across the parking lot.

It took her eyes a second to adjust from the bright afternoon to the dimness of the bar. She glanced around and saw Jenny drying glasses. Rachel wasn't sure why she thought Carter's ex-girlfriend could help. Maybe it was because Jenny knew the man but seemed to have let him go and moved on. Maybe it was because Carter's sisters and mother liked and trusted her. Maybe it was the first symptom of a pregnancy-induced insanity. Regardless, Rachel made her way to the bar and slid onto a stool.

Jenny put down her dishtowel. "Hi, Rachel. This is a surprise. Looking for Carter again?"

"No. I have his cell number now."

Jenny grinned. "Good for you. So what's up? You want something to drink?" Her gaze dipped to Rachel's midsection. "A seltzer or soda?"

"Just water, please." She glanced around at the quiet room and remembered how busy it had been that first night, when she'd come here with Diane. "How long have you worked here?"

"Mostly all my life," Jenny said. "My dad owns the place. Or he used to. I'm buying him out, a little every month. Dan jokes that when we finally own the place outright, we'll license the name and become a chain. I'm thinking one bar is plenty." She handed Rachel a tall glass of water with ice and a slice of lemon. "Here you go."

"Thanks." Rachel sipped the water. "I, ah, I'm not sure why I'm here. I didn't know where else to go. You know Carter and you seem nice."

Jenny shook her head. "That doesn't sound good. Is there a problem?"

"I don't know. Maybe. I was getting my oil changed and I went for a walk while I was waiting. I saw Carter across the street with a bunch of guys. There was a blonde there, too. Tall and really beautiful. He kissed her. Seriously kissed her. For a long time. I know what he does and I know this is probably some part of that, but still…"

Jenny pulled up a stool and sat down. "Carter doesn't cheat. He has a lot of flaws, but that's not one of them. He doesn't lie or even bend the truth. If you two are together and he was kissing someone else, then it was about work. Trust me. I've known him for a lot of years. Despite plenty of opportunity, he's never once strayed."

If he were in a relationship, Rachel thought glumly. But they weren't. Not really. So who was the woman?

Jenny leaned toward her. "Look, I'm sorry about before. That I told his mom you were pregnant. I didn't know you and I wanted to protect Carter. He's important to me. Now, I kinda wish I'd kept my mouth shut."

Rachel smiled. "It worked out okay, but thanks for apologizing. I adore his family, but they're a lot to deal with."

"I know. That's what's so great about him. Listen, Carter is terrific, but there will always be women in his life. His family, his old girlfriends, even me. He adores women and they adore him."

"I've met a few of the old girlfriends. Some of them are scary."

"I know." Jenny smiled. "There were a couple who made it clear that they wanted him back and they didn't care that we were together."

"I ran across one of those, too. They're everywhere.

He says he's sworn off women before, but with so many exes strolling around, I don't see how that's possible."

"They were short breaks," Jenny told her. "Sometimes measured in hours."

Rachel ran her finger down the length of the glass. "What happened with you two? Why did you break up?"

"Honestly? I wanted him to fall madly in love with me and he never did. I don't think Carter's ever been in love. Not romantically. He thinks he's immune, but I believe he's going to fall hard one day and I can't wait to see it. Maybe you'll be the one."

Rachel had her doubts about that. "He's had plenty of opportunity."

"If you're going to be with him, you have to be able to handle what happened before. Those other women exist."

"So I've seen. Some of them can't seem to let go. You did, though."

"I was pretty broken up when Carter and I split, but it worked out for the best. Dan is amazing. If I'd stayed with Carter, I never would have met him."

"But you're still a part of Carter's life. Isn't that strange?"

"It was at first," Jenny admitted with a smile. "But after a while I realized I missed his family more than I missed him. Liz and I had become close. So I just butted in. No one minded, least of all Carter. Which is good. I'm the only child of a single dad. I never had brothers or sisters. Now I have both. The Brockett clan is good at taking in strays, and I'm happy to be one of them."

Strays? Rachel had never thought of herself that way but she supposed she fit the description, which didn't make her comfortable.

"You should talk to Carter," Jenny said. "Ask him about the kiss."

"But that would be so logical and mature. I don't think I'm ready for that."

"It's your call. Better to get the question answered than wonder."

"It's not a big deal," Rachel assured her. "We're not... we're not that serious."

"Really? For someone who isn't serious, you seem plenty upset."

"I'm fine."

"Are you trying to convince me or yourself?"

Carter thought about calling first, but he didn't want to get into it on the phone with Rachel. So he swung by his mother's house, picked up lasagna, garlic bread and salad, then showed up at Rachel's place a little after five.

"I hope you haven't eaten yet," he said when she opened the door.

She wore her hair back in a ponytail and her face was scrubbed clean of makeup. He liked seeing the pale freckles on her nose and the tiny scar by her right eyebrow. She wore a T-shirt and old jeans, an intriguing contrast to her usually prissy teacher clothes. Not that he hadn't learned to appreciate the subtle sexiness of prissy.

"What?" she asked as she stepped back to let him in. "I haven't eaten. I was going to have a salad or something. Why are you here with dinner? We didn't have plans."

He carried dinner into her kitchen and set it on the counter. "I've had five phone calls in the past hour," he told her. "Word travels fast."

She groaned. "Jenny called one of your sisters?"

"Two of them, actually. They called the third and my

mom." He took her hands in his and rubbed her fingers. "I was working. Ellie is my partner. That's all. We're posing as a couple for this assignment. I would never cheat on you."

She made a halfhearted attempt to pull her hands free. When he didn't let her, she sighed.

"It's fine. I understand. Plus, it's not like we're really dating."

For once he couldn't tell what she was thinking. "Whatever we are, that can't have been fun to see."

She shrugged. "I was shocked and then I wasn't sure I had the right to be upset. Not that I was."

He tugged her a little closer and stared into her eyes. "I'm sorry you were upset. I really am doing this for work."

Her mouth twisted slightly. "Oh, sure. Talk about a yucky assignment. She's beautiful."

"She's okay. But I don't think of her that way. She's my partner. It's about as exciting as kissing one of my sisters. Besides, even if I wanted to like it, I couldn't. Her husband is a big guy and he'd beat the crap out of me."

That earned him a smile.

"I'm okay," she told him. "Thanks for worrying, but you don't have to."

"Are you sure? Because I grew up with three sisters. I know how to dig up a good worry on command."

The smile widened. "Maybe next time." She tilted her head. "Are you mad because I talked to Jenny?"

"You're allowed to talk to anyone you want."

"In theory. I wasn't spying on you or trying to dig up secrets. Honestly, I just didn't know what to think."

"Did she help you feel better?"

"Sort of. We talked about your past."

Not good, he thought glumly. "You can't hold that against me."

"I'm not. However, I think there should be some kind of club, or support group. We could come up with a name and hold meetings. You could be a guest speaker."

He released her hands. "You *are* upset."

"I'm really not. It's just you're not like any other guy I've ever known."

That didn't sound pleasant. "It's the volume thing," he muttered, knowing he wasn't going to apologize for dating a lot. Despite the gnawing in his gut, he hadn't done anything wrong. "Look, when I'm with a woman, she's the one I'm interested in. Not anyone else."

"I know that. You're loyal and honest and from what I can tell, you don't have any flaws."

"That's what I've been saying for years," he told her. "No one listens."

She smiled again. "Okay, you do have flaws, but they're not typical ones."

"Which would be?"

"I don't know. An obsession about sports. An inability to show up on time."

"I'm prompt."

"Yes, you are." She shook her head. "I don't even know what we're talking about anymore."

"We're talking about the fact that I'm sorry you were upset before. I should have told you about Ellie."

"It wasn't your fault. It was just…weird."

"Recoverable weird?" he asked.

Her green eyes sparkled with amusement and pleasure. "Yes. Recoverable weird."

He gave an exaggerated exhale. "Good, because the other kind of weird is just not for me."

"You're a little crazy," she said.

"Also a good thing. See—I have so many good qualities. I'm prompt and charming and totally into the person I'm with."

"So if this was real, you'd be totally into me?"

Awareness filled the room. Carter had a three-second battle with himself and need won over noble sacrifice. "I'm already totally into you."

Her eyes widened but she didn't look away. "You don't have to be. We're just trying to fake out your family."

He moved closer. "Is that all? So nothing else is required?"

"Not a thing." This time she eased toward him.

"So anything not related to faking out my family would be a waste of time and energy?" he asked as he put one hand on her shoulder and touched her cheek with the other.

"Totally."

"Something I can relate to."

He kissed her. Rachel had known he was going to. In fact, she'd counted on it. Maybe it *was* a complete waste of time and energy, but she couldn't think of a better way to do it.

Her body clenched in anticipation of the pleasure she always experienced when he put his mouth on hers. She wrapped her arms around him and leaned against his hard, muscled body. Her breath caught, her lips parted and she prepared herself for the ride.

He claimed her with a kiss that touched her down to her itty-bitty red blood cells. Heat poured through her making her tremble and want to rip off clothes. Desire exploded until she wondered if a kiss was going to be enough. If this time she would need more.

He plunged his tongue into her mouth. She met him stroke for stroke, savoring the tingles that accompanied every brush, every inch of contact.

Apparently he felt the pressing need, too, because he dropped his hands to her hips and urged her closer. She pulsed against him. The second she did so, she felt the hardness of his arousal. Her body remembered what it had been like to be claimed by him and she trembled.

He kept his hands on her hips, holding her in place, then rubbed against her. She desperately wanted to wrap her legs around him so he could do exactly that to her hot, swollen center.

He kissed his way along her jaw to her neck, and then down her neck. "We have dinner," he whispered against her skin. Quick flicks of his tongue followed by little bites punctuated his sentence. "Lasagna."

"I love lasagna," she moaned.

"So we could stop and eat."

Stop? Was he kidding? She slid her hands under his loose T-shirt and rested her palms on his bare belly. "Do you really want to stop?"

He raised his head and grinned. "I think the pasta will keep."

"Me, too."

That decided, she expected him to pull her into his arms again. Instead, he grabbed her hand and led her down the hallway. When they were in her bedroom, he sat on the bed and pulled off his boots. After he'd let them fall on the floor, he tugged her between his legs and unfastened the button at the waistband of her jeans.

"I've only seen you in dresses and skirts," he said. "Long dresses and skirts."

"They're more practical for my job."

She'd been planning on saying more. She had a whole speech that defended her wardrobe, but just then he pressed an openmouthed kiss to her belly and she forgot everything, even how to breathe.

"I'm not complaining," he said against her skin. "I like it. Very old-fashioned, but sexy. Still, the jeans are nice. I like seeing the curve of your hips and butt. I like thinking about touching those curves."

Her throat went dry, while other parts of her got really, really wet. "You've only been here about twenty minutes. How could you have thought all that so fast?"

He tugged her jeans and panties down to nearly her knees. "I thought it all in the first thirty seconds."

Was that true? On the heels of the question came the realization she was kind of trapped. And naked. She couldn't step out of her jeans and she was still dressed on the top half. This was not how she'd imagined things going between them.

"Carter, I…"

"Trust me."

He bent toward her and used his fingers to gently part her. She nearly lost her balance and had to put her hands on his shoulders to steady herself. Then, while she tried to figure out how to explain that she wasn't very comfortable, he licked her.

The combination of being slightly off balance, semi-naked and the erotic kiss nearly did her in. She gasped as she felt him lick her again. Just a quick, wet caress that made everything else seem unimportant.

"Okay, yeah," he murmured. "More of that."

He moved his hands to her waist, then eased her around until she was on her back on the bed. Her jeans and panties went flying, then he was between her legs and she knew that she would soon be lost.

He kissed her there as perfectly as he kissed her everywhere else. Openmouthed, slow-moving and thorough. He explored her, teasing, circling, touching until he found all the places that made her gasp and squirm and beg. Just when she started to think this was a game for him, he settled over her center and picked a rhythm that made the bottoms of her feet burn.

Over and over, he touched her. As her body tensed, he moved a little faster, making her push them to the next level. She began to pulse her hips as every part of her focused on the perfect pleasure.

Her breathing quickened. She tossed her head from side to side. Nothing had ever felt so good.

Then, just as she knew the end was as inevitable as the tide, he slipped two fingers inside of her. The unexpected fullness pushed her over the edge and she lost herself in her climax.

Her release poured through her. It went on and on, making her writhe and cry out and beg him to never stop. Finally the shudders slowed enough for her to catch her breath and open her eyes.

He'd braced himself on one arm and was lightly kissing her stomach. When he looked up, she saw the fire in his eyes and knew he was a man on the edge.

"Don't feel you have to wait," she told him.

He hesitated about an eighth of a second, then unfastened his belt and his jeans and pushed them, and his boxers, down.

"One day we're going to do it like regular people," he said as he positioned himself between her still trembling thighs. "You know, get naked first. Have a conversation."

She reached down and guided him inside of her.

He was thick and hard and he filled her until she knew she was going to have to come again.

"Conversation," she gasped as he plunged in again, "is highly overrated."

Chapter 10

Rachel woke up to find bright sunlight flooding her bedroom and a heavy arm draped across her stomach. She felt a delicious combination of contentment and exhaustion. Despite the fact that she'd slept in, she'd barely gotten four hours of sleep in the night. She would be dragging all day. But as the reason for the dragging was fairly spectacular, she wasn't about to complain.

She rolled on her side and saw Carter already awake and watching her.

"Morning," he murmured.

"Morning."

She ran her fingers across the stubble on his jaw.

"Such a bad boy," she told him.

"Smile when you say that."

She laughed. "I'm pretty sure I'm smiling about everything. What you do with a woman could be considered illegal in several states. I don't think one man is allowed to have that much sexual power."

"I can handle it."

He could sure handle her.

He kissed the palm of her hand, then rolled onto his back. "What's the plan for today? Do you have a lot to do? I'm open. Maybe we could do something together."

Her insides gave a little shimmy. "That would be nice," she said carefully, not wanting to appear too enthused. Hanging out was just that. Two friends spending time together. It didn't mean anything, except maybe the possibility of a repeat encounter in bed.

"Shopping," he said, glancing at her. "Women like shopping."

She laughed. "Or we could go to a movie."

"That sounds good. I like movie popcorn." He pulled on her hand, drawing her closer. "Or we could stay in bed. I'm kinda tired. What about you?"

Before she could answer, there was a knock on her front door. Rachel glanced at the clock. It was only a little after nine. She didn't usually get visitors. All her friends phoned rather than dropped by.

She sat up and grabbed her robe, then slipped into it and tied the belt.

"I have no idea who that is," she said as she walked into the living room.

"I do," Carter muttered from the bedroom.

He couldn't possibly know who—

Rachel opened her front door to find Nina Brockett on her plant-filled front balcony.

"I know, I know," Nina said with a bright smile as she passed over a covered basket and stepped inside. "I'm interrupting. Carter's always saying I should call instead of coming by. But it's so much nicer to talk in person. Besides, when I went to Carter's house and he wasn't home, I knew just where he was going to be and I was right."

Rachel opened her mouth, then closed it. Heat flooded her cheeks and she knew she was blushing.

"I, ah…" She pressed her lips together and struggled for control. "Good morning."

"Morning, dear." Nina tapped the basket. "Cinnamon rolls. Carter's favorite. Don't let them get cold."

Carter walked out of the bedroom. He'd pulled on jeans and his shirt. "Mama, you gotta stop doing this."

"Doing what? A mother isn't allowed to talk to her only son? I knocked. Where's the crime?"

He leaned against the door frame and sighed heavily. "Okay, fine. What are you doing here?"

"My water heater is broken. Just like that, it stopped working. Gordon is already off buying me a new one, but he's going to need your help putting it in."

"You could have called," he told her.

"You weren't home and I didn't know if you would be going home to get the message. Besides, I don't have Rachel's number."

"Cell phone, Mama," Carter said. "You could have called my cell phone."

"Oh. I didn't think of that." Nina smiled again. "Besides, it was a lovely drive over here and I'm happy to see you two getting along. It makes an old woman very happy."

"You're not an old woman," Carter said. "You're going to outlive us all."

"Don't say that. No mother wants to outlive her children. Now you two enjoy the cinnamon rolls. Carter, you should call Gordon and see when he'll need you."

With that, she waved and left.

Rachel carefully closed the front door and then crossed to the sofa. As she sank onto the cushions, she covered her face with her hands.

"I'm so embarrassed," she whispered. "That was your mother. She knows what we were doing."

"Oh, yeah. She's real clear on that." He took the basket from her and set it on the coffee table. "Rachel, it's okay."

"It's not. She's your *mother.*"

He sat next to her. His mouth twitched slightly and she guessed he was trying not to smile.

"You think this is funny?" she asked in outrage.

"It's not that big a deal. She knows about the baby, so she's probably not shocked about the sex thing."

Oh, yeah. Good point, but still. "It's just wrong. I felt so awful."

"Don't. She's the one who barged in here. This is your home." He grimaced. "Now it's going to have to be one hell of a fight to convince her we've broken up."

Broken up? Then she remembered. This wasn't real. She and Carter weren't a couple. They were just two people having a baby and trying to convince his family that they were involved, so they could end things later and get back to their original plan of just being two people having a baby.

"We'll need witnesses," she said.

"And a script."

He was being funny, but suddenly she didn't feel like laughing. Nothing about this situation was turning out how she'd thought. Carter's family wasn't supposed to matter, but she found herself hating the thought of Nina thinking less of her. Carter wasn't supposed to be important, yet she wasn't sure she was ready for the breakup they'd planned. Which meant what? That she wanted this to be real? That she wanted to get involved?

No way. Not with him. How could she be with a man who had dated nearly every single woman on the planet? He'd made it clear he didn't want a relationship with her, so she'd better get the idea out of her head.

But wouldn't getting involved with the father of her child be the most logical choice?

The following Thursday, Rachel left work a half hour early and headed for her car. She felt as if an entire team of butterflies had taken up residence in her stomach and were currently arguing on the best way to fly in formation. She was shaky and scared and telling herself that everything was fine, but it didn't seem to be helping.

Ever since she'd made the appointment with her doctor, she'd had a barely controllable urge to burst into tears. Not because she was especially nervous about the baby—having a child was still something she thought in her head rather than felt in her heart. Instead, she wrestled with the terror of being alone.

Although she'd lost her parents fourteen years ago, she still missed them. At the oddest times she longed for one or the other to be with her. Today it was her mother. She wanted familiar arms to hold her close and say everything was going to be all right. She wanted to hear stories of her mother's pregnancies and births. She wanted a connection to family.

Maybe she should have called Noelle or Crissy, she thought as she drove toward the medical building. Both of them would have been happy to be with her. Noelle was experiencing pregnancy firsthand. But she, Rachel, hadn't wanted to be a bother.

"Talk about dumb," she murmured as she parked and got out of her car. "This was not the time to be noble."

Next time, she promised herself. Next time she would call her friends. Besides, this was only a first appointment. She would be fine.

She walked into the four-story building and started for the elevator, only to come to a complete stop. There, in the center of the lobby, stood Nina, Merry and Liz.

Rachel stared at Carter's mother and sisters. "What are you doing here?" she asked, a little surprised at the coincidence.

Nina shrugged her shoulders. "When I was over on Saturday, I happened to notice the note you'd written about your doctor's appointment. I know, I know, I'm meddling. So sue me. I tried to forget you were coming here, but I couldn't. I know you don't have any family and this is your first baby. I couldn't stand for you to be here alone."

"We wanted to come, too," Merry said, giving Rachel a hug. "Shelly's sorry she couldn't make it, but the sitter we hired got the flu and she offered to stay with all the kids. But she's here in spirit."

Rachel opened her mouth to speak, then couldn't when her throat got tight and her eyes began to burn.

"You didn't have to do this," she managed to say, "but I'm really glad you did."

Nina exhaled in obvious relief. "Here I was all braced to be told to mind my own business. I'm glad you're not mad." She slipped an arm around Rachel. "All right. Let's go talk to this doctor. Between us, we've had a lot of kids and we know the right questions to ask. You'll be fine. Pregnancy is sometimes easy, sometimes hard, but then you have a baby and it's all worth it."

"She's right," Liz said, claiming her other arm. "When you're ready, we'll tell you stories about childbirth. It's not so bad."

"Take the drugs," Merry added.

"Exactly," Liz said with a grin. "Why suffer?"

They continued to offer advice all through the elevator ride and into the doctor's office. The four of them claimed a corner of the cheerful waiting room. Rachel held on to Nina's hand and found she didn't miss her own mother quite so much.

"This means a lot to me," she said. "You can't know how much."

"We're happy to be here." Nina patted her hand. "This isn't about Carter, you know. This is about you. Whatever happens with him, you're one of the family."

Rachel touched her stomach. The pregnancy had been an accident and for a while she'd thought it might be a disaster, but now she was starting to wonder if having this child was the best thing that had ever happened to her.

"Dr. Richards will see you now," the nurse said. "She'd like you to start in her office, so you can talk. She'll do the exam after."

They rose together and headed for the large office. There were plenty of chairs. Nina stayed next to Rachel while Merry and Liz were on either side of them.

When Dr. Richards entered, she grinned. "I love it when a baby brings a family together. Good afternoon, ladies."

Rachel bit her lower lip. "I know this is kind of a lot but…"

Her doctor, an attractive woman in her mid-forties, shook her head. "Don't apologize. The more support, the better. There's no better source of information for a pregnant woman than other women who have been through it already. They understand what's happening to your body and they know what questions to ask. All right, first things first. Your due date."

Rachel fought against embarrassment as she said, "I, um, know the day I got pregnant."

Liz nudged her. "I heard it was night."

Merry laughed. "I heard it was a very good night."

"Girls," Nina scolded. "Stop. You'll upset Rachel."

But Rachel didn't mind the teasing. It made her feel a little less self-conscious.

"Technically it was night," she admitted and gave the date.

"That makes the calculations easier," Dr. Richards told her. "So we have a due date."

"Not that the baby will come that day," Nina said.

"Exactly," Dr. Richards said. "But it gives us something to shoot for. I'll be giving you an examination and doing some preliminary blood work. I expect everything to go normally. You're in great health. There are some dietary changes I'd like you to make, which we'll also discuss."

"Prenatal vitamins," Liz said with a groan. "They made me constipated, so drink lots of water."

"Yeah, drink now, before the baby decides to spend all day sitting on your bladder."

They continued talking, exchanging stories and advice. Rachel listened more to their voices than their words. The information wasn't as important to her as the connection. They had meant what they said—that she was one of them now. A member of the family. It had been so very long since she'd been able to be a part of something so very precious.

* * *

Carter stopped by his mother's house after work.

"You called?" he said as he walked into the kitchen and found her stirring something on the stove.

She raised her head for his kiss, then studied him with her dark eyes. "I wanted to talk to you."

"Water heater working all right?" he asked as he grabbed a cookie from the cooling rack and then pulled out a chair at the round table by the bay window.

"It's fine. You're always good to me, Carter. You come by whenever I need you. You're the same with your sisters."

He wasn't sure he liked the sound of that. On the surface, it seemed to be a compliment, but he knew his mother and she hadn't asked him to stop by so she could give him a pat on the back. Life was never that easy.

"And?" he prompted.

"You're a good man. I appreciate that. I take some of the credit."

He grinned. "Of course you do."

Her smile faded. "Rachel went to the doctor today."

He dropped the cookie onto the table and stood. "What? Is she all right? Did anything happen?"

His mother waved him back into his chair. "She's fine. It was a routine prenatal visit."

Right—pregnant women had to go to the doctor. That made sense. "She didn't tell me," he said, more to himself than his mother. He'd seen Rachel most of the weekend. Why hadn't she said anything to him? Was she trying to keep him from getting too involved or had she thought he wouldn't be interested?

Whatever she thought of him, he had a right to be involved. He was the baby's father.

"She didn't tell anyone," his mother said. "I saw the note when I was over on Saturday and Merry, Liz and I just showed up. I thought she might be angry, but she wasn't. Do you know why?"

"Because you bullied her and she didn't want to be rude?"

His mother narrowed her gaze. "Such a smart mouth. You didn't get that from me. No, she wasn't angry because she's alone, Carter. She's pregnant and alone in the world."

He actually knew that, but still, his mother's impressive ability to make him feel guilty kicked into play.

"I would have gone," he said. "I wanted to go. She never mentioned she was going to the doctor."

"Maybe you should ask. Your sisters have been pregnant enough for you to have an idea of what goes on. You have to get involved. There's going to be a baby soon, and then what?"

And then, he didn't know. The direction of this conversation was clear. He braced himself for the familiar attack, but instead of readying his arguments, he wondered if maybe his mother was right.

Whoa—where had that thought come from? Right?

"You should marry her," Nina said. "The baby will need a father, and don't tell me you're going to be a father regardless of whether or not you get married. You can't show up every other weekend, Carter. You need to be there all the time. You need to give this baby a name. Do the right thing. And not just because it's the right thing. Do it because you want to."

Marriage. He had very particular ideas about the institution—most of them involving him running as far and fast as he could. Sure, it looked good from the outside, but then what? How could he think about forever when he wasn't sure he believed he could ever be in love?

Except, for once, the idea wasn't so uncomfortable. He could see himself with Rachel in a few years. In a lot of years. He wouldn't mind fighting with her and making up with her. He kind of liked thinking about sharing diaper duty and decorating for Christmas. He suddenly wanted to know if she liked dogs.

Was he serious about this? Could he honestly imagine spending the rest of his life with Rachel? Fidelity had never been an issue, mostly because he always knew he could move on. But this time there would be no moving on. In his mind, marriage was forever.

Could he be with just her?

The answer came more easily than he ever could have imagined. Yes, he could be with her forever. He could grow old with her. He could love her.

Love? Him?

And if he could or did love her, what did she think about him? She'd been completely comfortable with the idea of not getting married. She was one of the few women he knew who *didn't* talk about getting married. Did that mean he'd finally found "the one" only to have her not want him? His ex-girlfriends would have a party in the streets if that turned out to be true.

But he was getting ahead of himself.

"Carter, are you listening to me?" his mother asked.

"Not really."

"Then listen to this. It's time for you to grow up."

A common theme in his life, he thought. First the captain and now her.

He stood and crossed to the stove. "Mama, I love you, but you don't get a say in this. I'll do anything for you except live my life the way you want me to. It's time for you to back off."

She eyed him. "You're standing up to me."

"It's not the first time."

"I know, but I think maybe now you mean it."

"I do."

She smiled. "You're a good man, Carter. I'm very proud of you."

He kissed her again and left. As he crossed the street to his own house, he was again reminded that there were way too many women in his world. Was he really thinking of inviting in one more?

Chapter 11

Rachel pushed her cart through the grocery store. Carter had called and suggested barbecuing that night. He'd offered to bring everything, including a portable grill, but she'd insisted on providing dinner. After all, their last couple of meals had been compliments of him…or at least his family.

Carter being a typical guy, she bypassed chicken in favor of steaks, then picked up some ingredients for salad. In the dairy aisle, she grabbed a few cartons of yogurt to help with her calcium intake.

It felt strange to be shopping for two—in a guy way, not a baby way—and yet it was fun. She'd been alone for a long time and having Carter around was nice. More than nice. He was a lot of things she'd been looking for in a man. So was she being too hasty in thinking they couldn't maybe work things out?

The biggest problem was how Carter saw her. Was she someone he would get serious about? Was he—

"Hi. I know this is really weird, but are you Rachel?"

Rachel turned to see a stunning blonde in a T-shirt tight enough to cut off circulation smiling at her. Describing the woman as "pretty" was practically an insult. She defined beautiful, from her gleaming, waist-length hair to her large blue eyes.

"What?" Rachel blinked and tried to get her brain to work.

The woman smiled. That was perfect, too. "I'm sorry. I'm Pam. Liz and I go way back. She mentioned you were seeing Carter. My two kids go to your school, so I've seen you around. How is he?"

Carter had dated this…this…goddess?

"I, ah, he's fine," Rachel said, knowing she sounded about as stupid and clueless as she felt. Suddenly her sensible dress seemed drab and unflattering. Her makeup had long since worn off, although there weren't enough skin products in the world to get her face to look like Pam's.

Pam's smile widened. "I fell for Carter when I was seventeen. And eighteen and nineteen. We were young and things were a little volatile. Liz is thrilled he's finally found the one. I'm totally content in my life, but I'll admit to a twinge of envy when I heard he was settling down. Carter's one of the good guys. I hope you two are really happy."

The other woman's sincere good wishes made Rachel feel like slime, especially since she and Carter were still in the pretend dating stage of their relationship.

"Thanks," she murmured as Pam moved away.

Later, when Rachel had carried the groceries into her

apartment and set them on the counter, she stared out the window. The women were everywhere. How many had he dated? A hundred? Five hundred? She supposed that logically all that one-on-one interaction would mean that he would be completely clear on who and what he wanted. While he'd never indicated she was that one, if she was, could she handle it? Could she give her heart knowing that for the next ten or fifteen years women would be coming up to him and offering various degrees of good wishes, some sincerely, some wishing they were in her place?

She didn't have an answer, she just knew the question made her uncomfortable and she wasn't sure why.

An hour later she'd changed into a flirty skirt and a sleeveless T-shirt in what she refused to believe was any kind of attempt to compete with Pam. That relationship had been over for years, right? Carter probably didn't even remember her.

But when he arrived, barbecue and all, she invited him inside, then mentioned running into Pam in the grocery store.

He kissed her lightly, then smiled. "I haven't seen Pam in a while. How is she?"

Not exactly the "Pam who?" she'd been hoping for.

"Fine. Gorgeous. She mentioned she was friends with Liz."

He nodded. "They were always tight. Pam is my age, a couple of years younger than Liz, but she'd skipped a few grades in school, so they were in the same high school class."

Rachel held in a groan. Beautiful *and* brilliant? Was that fair?

"She seemed very nice."

"She is," he told her. "So are you. How was your day?"

"Fine." Other than the Pam encounter.

"I haven't seen you in a couple of days. How was your doctor's appointment?"

The change in subject caught her off guard. She'd planned on more Pam talk, but the doctor was a good subject, too.

"Great. I was really nervous about going. I don't know why. I've been seeing Dr. Richards since I moved here. She's great. Very approachable and patient. I'm glad she'll be delivering my baby. But this is the first time I'm pregnant, so I didn't know what to expect. Your mom and sisters showed up." She frowned. "But if you're asking about the appointment, I guess you already know that."

"Were you angry they were there?"

"Not at all. I appreciated the support. It was weird— as I was driving there, I was missing my mom. I know it's been a long time since she died, but sometimes I feel like I won't make it if I can't talk to her one more time. Seeing your family there really helped."

She paused and waited for him to say something or at least nod. Instead she couldn't figure out his expression and he seemed almost…angry.

"Carter, if I don't mind that they came, then you shouldn't," she told him.

His eyes darkened. "That's not the point. This is my baby, too. You didn't mention the doctor's appointment to me. I told you I wanted to be a part of things. This is important to me, Rachel. I don't want you shutting me out."

She opened her mouth, then closed it. Guilt and shame settled in the pit of her stomach.

"I'm sorry," she told him, meaning it. "I really never thought…"

He stiffened. "Thought what?"

She swallowed. "That you'd be interested," she whispered.

Nothing about him changed, but she had the feeling that she'd just cut him deeply. Funny how until this moment, she'd never considered that Carter had feelings like everyone else. He was always so charming and in charge of every situation.

She reached for his hand, then pulled back. Touching didn't seem like a good idea.

"I was wrong," she said, gazing directly at him. "Totally wrong. I should have told you about the appointment. I wasn't deliberately trying to shut you out. It won't happen again. I'll let you know every time I see the doctor. I promise."

Carter nodded. He was still pissed, but didn't feel he had the right anymore. Rachel had admitted the mistake and said she wouldn't repeat it. He should let it go.

The thing was, he didn't want to. He wasn't sure why this got to him, but it did.

"I mean it," she told him. "I am sorry."

"I know you are. You don't have to keep saying that."

"You're still upset."

He consciously relaxed. "I'm a guy. We don't get upset."

One corner of her mouth twitched. "Crabby, then. You're a little crabby and moody."

He growled low in his throat and she laughed. Her hand settled on his arm.

"Seriously," she said. "I'm sorry. It won't happen again."

"I know. I'm fine. Let's change the subject."

She hesitated, then tugged him over the sofa. "How was your day?"

"Good. We're getting close to making the bust."

"Will that be dangerous?"

"Not especially."

"Why don't I believe you?" she asked.

"Not a clue."

In truth, there was always a risk, but it was minor and he didn't want to worry her.

"Then what?" she asked. "Do you take another undercover assignment?"

"Maybe." He hadn't decided. "You hungry? I can set up the grill."

"Sure. I cleared a spot on the back balcony. I didn't think it would be a good idea for my plants to go up in flames."

Nearly an hour later, dinner was prepared. He brought in the steaks, while she served salad and baked potatoes.

She moved with an easy grace that made him think of other things she did well. But instead of getting lost in his ever-present passion, he pushed his need away. There were different things they had to deal with and this seemed to be as good a time as any.

"Tell me about the guys you were engaged to before," he said.

She froze in the act of passing him salad dressing. "Excuse me?"

Okay, maybe not his smoothest transition, but he'd been thinking about her previous engagements. "I've been wondering what went wrong," he admitted. "You wouldn't have agreed to marry them in the first place if they'd been jerks."

She passed over the bottle of ranch dressing and gave

him a smile that didn't reach her eyes. "Thanks for the support on that assumption," she said, her voice light but wary. "They weren't jerks. I realized I wasn't in love with either of them."

"Why?" he asked bluntly. "What changed? Was it them? Was it you?"

She picked up her fork, then set it down. "I'm not sure who changed. With Brett, we were both young. We'd met our freshman year, sort of clinging to each other for support. Neither of us had dated much before that. We started out as friends and things progressed from there. After a while the relationship turned serious."

"So he proposed?"

She nodded slowly. "I was kind of surprised, actually. But in a good way. He was nice and sweet and I thought..." She shrugged. "I thought I was in love with him."

Carter wasn't excited to hear about the other men in her life, but he knew the information was important.

"What changed your mind?" he asked.

"I just wasn't. I still cared about him, but not in a romantic way. I realized that for me the relationship hadn't really gone past friendship. I'd been excited by the thought of a serious boyfriend, but I hadn't considered that Brett wasn't the right guy for me."

Logical, he thought. He almost believed her. "And the other one?"

"This isn't exactly dinner conversation," she told him.

"I don't mind, if you don't."

He suspected she wanted to say she did mind, but couldn't figure out how.

"Okay. Well, I met Ray in my senior year of college. I was a student teaching a couple of days a week and he was a teacher at the same school. We were a lot alike. He was great with kids and funny and really smart. He was getting his Ph.D. in education at night and planned on becoming a principal."

Carter hated the guy immediately. "So what happened?"

Rachel sighed. "The usual. He asked me out, I accepted and things progressed fairly quickly. I fell in love with him. He proposed, I said yes, we set a date."

His muscles clenched. "And?"

"And I couldn't imagine myself married to him. There was nothing wrong with him. I was the problem. I broke things off and returned the ring." She looked at him. "I'm sorry this isn't more dramatic. If I'd known I was supposed to provide entertainment during dinner, I would have planned better stories."

He'd annoyed her, but that was the least of his problems. "You don't let people in," he said.

She stared at him. "Excuse me? I tell you about two relationships and you're ready to make a judgment on my character?"

"It's not a judgment. I'm stating a fact. You don't let people get close."

She put her napkin on the table and glared at him. "At least I can count the number of relationships I've had without having to get out a calculator. If you want to talk about people who aren't willing to take that next step, maybe you should look in the mirror."

"I didn't believe in the next step," he said. "You did. You wanted to get married and have kids. You wanted normal. So why did you agree to marry two different guys only to back out when it all got too real?"

She stood. "Let me guess. You're going to tell me everything that's wrong with me. How helpful. I should probably listen. After all, you have plenty of experience with women."

He'd hurt her, which he hadn't meant to do. He rose. "Rachel, stop. I'm not saying this to upset you. I'm trying to understand. You're an incredible woman. I've seen you with the kids in your class. You're warm and caring and they adore you. So why aren't you married? Why weren't either of those other guys the one?"

"You tell me," she said tightly.

Damn. He hadn't wanted the conversation to go this way. But now that it had… "You don't let people in. Your friends, my family, even me, we only get so far."

"You don't know what you're talking about," she told him. "Maybe I don't let you in because I don't want to. Based on your track record, you're not exactly a good bet in the romance department. Besides, this isn't real. Those were your rules. Pretend dating so we could break up later. I find it interesting that you weren't willing to get to know the woman having your child."

"I was interested," he told her, doing his best to stay focused and logical. "You came to me with papers for me to sign giving up the rights to my kid. You made it clear from the start that you weren't in this for anything but the baby."

"Right. So you're saying that otherwise, you would have tried to make things work with me?"

"Yes."

She rolled her eyes. "I don't believe you. You've made a career out of not committing. At least I've tried."

"What makes you think I haven't? Because I haven't gotten engaged and then changed my mind? Is that the measure of a real commitment? Because if that's what you want, let's do it. We'll get engaged. Then you can break up with me later because you've changed your mind."

He knew he'd gone too far even before she paled and then pointed to the door.

"Get out," she said, her voice low and trembling.

He stalked across the room, then turned. "You never gave me a chance," he said. "Why was that? We have great chemistry, we get along. Is it my job? Is it my past? Or is it you? We're having a baby together, Rachel. Shouldn't you be trying?"

"I am trying," she yelled. "What do you want from me? We've played all of this by your rules and now I'm in trouble because of that? Here's a news flash—I don't have to be married to have a baby. I'm fine on my own. I'm comfortable being a single parent. I'm sorry if that doesn't satisfy your fantasy, but I can't be responsible for that."

He frowned. "I thought you said you wanted a family. Husband, kids, the whole thing. Did I imagine that?"

She paused. "No. I'd always thought... Dammit, Carter, stop doing this."

He'd never heard her swear before. "You say you want it all, but you don't act like it. The way things have happened in your past tell me that you're the one in the way of the dream, not me. I stand by what I said before. You don't let anyone get inside. You might want to think about why that is."

Rachel hadn't slept much that night. She'd had big plans for a wonderful evening and Carter had ruined them with his stupid accusations.

What was up with him? Who did he think he was?

He didn't know her well enough to be critical of her or her choices. It wasn't as if he'd lived *his* life perfectly.

She was a good person and a good friend. She'd always worked hard to do the right thing. So why had he jumped all over her? Was it his ego talking because she refused to be one of a crowd? Couldn't he stand the thought that there was one woman who didn't desperately want to be with him?

But as she drove across town after work, she found that making him the bad guy didn't make her feel any better. She'd hated fighting with him and she'd been unable to forget some of what he'd said. Like the part about not letting people in. That wasn't true. She had lots of close, intimate relationships. Why did he have to think the worst of her and why did she care?

She pulled into the parking lot and walked toward the large entrance to the all-women workout center. Crissy owned four gyms in the area. This was the biggest, with her company offices on the second floor.

"Is she in?" Rachel asked Crissy's assistant, then gave her name.

After being buzzed, her friend walked out to greet her. "Hey, you. This is unexpected. What's up?"

Rachel clutched her purse in both hands. "I need to talk. Is this a good time?"

"Absolutely."

After asking her assistant to hold all calls, Crissy led Rachel into her bright and spacious office. When they were settled on the sofa, Crissy turned to her.

"I'm feeling especially nonjudgmental today," Crissy said with a warm smile. "Tell me everything."

Now that she was here, Rachel wasn't sure how to start. Maybe with last night. "Carter and I had a fight and I hate that. He was unfair and difficult and I'm not sure what he wanted, but he really bugged me."

"He's a guy. Sometimes they can't help it."

"I know, but this was different. He wanted to know about the other guys in my life. The two men I was engaged to. I thought it was a weird topic, but I gave him the five-minute version of what happened. Then he said the reason things hadn't worked out is that I'm not emotionally accessible. Can you believe it? Me? He was talking to me like I was some kind of scary loner. There's nothing wrong with me."

Crissy patted her arm. "Of course there isn't. Look, I don't know what Carter's problem is. Maybe he was threatened by your past."

"Oh, please. The man has dated thousands of women. I'm just one in a long line."

"Then he has other issues. Everyone has different emotional boundaries. Didn't you say that his family is running in and out of his place all the time? That sounds a little flaky. He's kind of a mama's boy, isn't he? And just a little too close to his sisters. If you ask me, he's the one with the issues."

Rachel drew in a breath. She'd come to her friend for a shoulder to cry on, not to get into a fight. "Carter isn't a mama's boy. That's not really fair. He's a great guy. Very responsible. Sure, he cares about his family, but he's also willing to put his life on the line in his job. He's a good guy. Trustworthy and honest and…"

She saw the corners of Crissy's mouth twitch, as if her friend were holding in a smile.

"At least we know you like him," Crissy said. "I wanted to be sure."

Rachel sighed. "You set me up."

"Just a little. If you hated the guy, that would change my advice."

"I don't hate him, but he's impossible. I think he expects me to fall at his feet and that's not going to happen."

"I agree. That whole feet-falling never really helps anyone. But I do have a question. If he is, as you said, a good guy, then why didn't you ever consider marrying him? You're having a child together and marrying the baby's father remains the traditional response."

"For one thing, he made it clear he didn't want to marry me. Why would I pursue him?"

"Okay. But if he doesn't want to marry you and you don't want to marry him, why do you care what he thinks about you? If he's wrong about you, so what?"

Rachel opened her mouth then closed it. "Good point," she said slowly. "I don't know why I care, but I do. I hated what he said."

"So his comment about not letting people in pushed a button for you."

"Maybe." Rachel drew in a deep breath. "Yes. It bugged me big-time."

"Why?"

"I'm not like that."

"So he was wrong."

"Yes. Maybe." Rachel leaned back against the sofa and closed her eyes. "I guess, maybe, he's not totally wrong. I sometimes think it hurts too much to care. You know, because I lost my family when I was so young."

She opened her eyes and saw Crissy looking at her.

"Are you upset because he saw the truth or because he articulated something you're not proud of?" her friend asked.

"Both, I think. I know I never want to feel that pain

again. It was so horrible. I kept thinking that if I could die, too, everything would be all right."

Long dormant emotions tried to surge to life, but Rachel suppressed them with a skill born of years of practice. No way she wanted to go there. Not now. Not ever.

"So you're holding back to protect yourself," Crissy said. "That makes sense. For you, the price of belonging isn't worth the risk. We all make trade-offs."

Rachel wasn't sure she liked the sound of that. "I belong."

"Where?" Crissy asked gently. "I'm not judging you, honey. I'm the last person to do that. I'm just saying, are you sure you're where you want to be? Are you acting or reacting? The past can be powerful and an influence we can't shake."

Rachel had never thought about not having a choice. "I didn't want to marry Brett or Ray. I wasn't willing to go through with it just to prove a point."

"Good for you," Crissy told her. "Are you avoiding a relationship with Carter because he's not the one or because you're afraid?"

"I don't love him," Rachel said stubbornly. "Just because I can list all his good qualities doesn't make him Mr. Right."

"What does it make him?"

Rachel didn't have an answer for that. Just as difficult, deep in her heart, she wasn't sure what she felt for Carter. "Everything is so confusing."

"Life always is."

Rachel shook her head. "Not for you. You're the most together person I know."

Crissy didn't smile. "I'm faking it as much as anyone else." She shrugged. "Okay, here's my confession. I'm nearly thirty. I've never been married. Despite what I say about hating first dates, there have been plenty of great guys. So why didn't I pick one of them?"

Rachel had never much thought about her friend's personal life. "Why didn't you?" she asked.

"Because I can't. I'm not allowed. My punishment is to never fall in love, never be romantically happy, never have a child."

"That's crazy," Rachel breathed. "Why would you think that? You don't have to be punished."

"Actually, I do." Crissy drew in a deep breath. "I got pregnant in high school. It was my senior year. I didn't mean for it to happen, but then who does? I didn't want to marry the guy and he didn't want a kid. I found out I didn't, either. So I took the easy way out. I gave up my baby."

She stood and crossed to the window. There she folded her arms over her chest. "I could have kept him. My parents were supportive and offered to help. But I wasn't interested. I knew a child would tie me down. A child would change everything, and I didn't want that. I had dreams. The irony is I gave him up without a second thought and ever since, I've been unable to let him go."

Rachel rose and joined her friend. "You've been thinking about your son?"

Crissy nodded. "It's been getting worse. Maybe because I'm nearly thirty and I can hear rumblings from my biological clock. Maybe the guilt is growing. I don't know. He's twelve. The family is local, even. They send me pictures and letters. He's a good kid. Happy. I couldn't have done as decent a job."

Rachel didn't know what to say. She couldn't believe

Crissy had carried this secret for so long. "Do you want to meet him?"

"I don't know," her friend admitted. "I have a standing invitation to come on by whenever I'd like. But what do I say? 'I'm the woman who couldn't be bothered? There's a statement."

"You were only eighteen," Rachel reminded her. "You were in high school."

"I was lazy. I did what was easy, but I don't know if it was right. Now there's no going back. Even if I go meet him, I will never be what I could have been. I will never be more than the woman who gave birth to him. Someone else is his mother."

Crissy turned and looked at Rachel. "You can't imagine what this is like. I can't know what you went through when you lost your family. It was horrible and you will always feel that pain. But you do need to figure out how it impacts you today. If you don't care about Carter, if he's just some fun guy you messed up with, then great. But if he could be more, then you need to think about that. You've always talked about wanting a family. You've always said that was important to you and I think it is. There are a lot of good men out there, but it would be so much easier if you could fall for your baby's father."

Rachel nodded slowly. "I have to figure out why I'm avoiding him."

"I would. This is a big deal. This is the rest of your life."

She hugged Crissy. "I'm sorry about what happened to you. I wish I could make it better."

"It's okay. All of this is my responsibility. I can handle it."

"You shouldn't have to handle it alone. If you want

to talk, or decide to go meet him, I'm happy to be there. Really."

"I appreciate that. Right now I'm not doing anything."

Rachel managed a smile. "That's kind of how I feel."

Crissy touched Rachel's stomach. "I have time on my side. You don't. There's going to be a baby before you know it. Trust me, they change everything. Even when you don't keep them."

Rachel nodded. She knew her friend was right. A baby *would* change everything. The question was what would she do about it?

Carter or not Carter. What did he want from her? Just as important, what did she want from him?

Chapter 12

Rachel paced her apartment restlessly. Normally she loved a day off midweek. It was unexpected and she always felt so decadent sleeping in when she would normally be rushing around to get ready. But despite the time off work, today she felt out of sorts and jumpy. She couldn't settle in to any one task. It was time to do some serious pruning on her plants and even that didn't excite her.

It was all because she hadn't talked to Carter in nearly a week, she thought grimly. She'd picked up the phone about fifty times, but hadn't made the call. Partly because she wanted him to come to her and partly because she didn't know what to say.

He'd been wrong about her. Totally and completely wrong. Absolutely wrong and maybe just a little right.

She stalked out onto her back balcony and started

plucking off dead flowers. "So I don't embrace the world with open arms," she muttered. "He does that enough for any five people. I care. I have friends. I know how to love. I…"

Love. Somehow the word got stuck in her brain. She believed in love. She desperately wanted to be *in* love. She wanted to feel safe and cared for and as if she finally belonged. She wanted to be home.

But the thought of loving and being loved and depending on that love terrified her. Loving meant losing and that was so not for her.

Rachel straightened. What did that mean? That she was letting fear rule her life?

"Of course not," she muttered. "I'm being careful and sensible, which does not define Carter."

He was all things wild, which made him exciting in bed, but what about in the real world? Did she want that kind of uncertainty every day? She still believed he'd set her up—establishing ground rules and then punishing her for following them. But if they were both wrong then neither of them could be right. She really hated that.

With her plants plucked, she returned to her apartment and glanced at the to-do list she'd prepared for herself. Nothing sounded very exciting, but folding laundry was a must. She cleared the coffee table, dumped everything on the sofa, then flipped on the TV to keep her company.

But instead of a morning talk show, she found herself staring at a helicopter shot of a street. A familiar street.

"This is live coverage of a standoff in Riverside. The police spokesman tells us that their raid on a motorcycle repair shop went bad when suspects opened fire. Two people have been shot, although they are still trapped inside. Until suspects release them, they will be unable to receive medical attention."

The reporter kept talking, but Rachel wasn't listening. She recognized the building in the center of the television as the one where Carter was working. Which meant he was inside. Had they found out he was an undercover cop?

Panic gripped her. Panic and fear. She lunged for the phone and started to dial his cell only to hang up mid-number. She couldn't phone him. She had no idea what was happening. If the phone rang at the wrong time, it could get him killed.

Now what? Her thoughts whirled frantically. Her chest hurt and she had trouble breathing. Now what?

Not knowing what else to do, she grabbed her purse and her car keys, then hurried downstairs. Fifteen minutes later, she pulled up in front of Carter's mother's house. After the fight she'd had with Carter, she wasn't sure how she would be welcomed.

Shelly answered her knock.

"I was worried," Rachel said by way of explanation.

"Of course you were. We all are."

"Is it okay that I'm here?"

Shelly smiled. "You're family, Rachel. Where else would you go?"

Some of the fear was replaced by relief. Until that moment, she hadn't realized how much she'd been worried about everyone hating her for arguing with Carter. But based on Shelly's reaction, she wondered if they even knew there'd been a falling out.

But if their plan had been to pretend date and then have a pretend fight for the sake of his relatives, why hadn't he told them about the real disagreement?

Shelly ushered her into the family room at the back of the house. Nina was sitting on the sofa with Liz and Merry on either side of her. The TV was on the same channel as Rachel's had been. When the older woman saw her, she stood and embraced her.

"We talked about calling you," Nina said as she clutched Rachel's arms. "I thought you'd be at work. You're not teaching today?"

Rachel shook her head. "No. It's one of those weird holidays where only schools close. When I saw what had happened, I didn't know what to do, so I came here. I hope you don't mind."

"Of course not," Merry said, scooting over to make room on the couch. "We're all worried. Of course Carter is going to be all right, but until we know for sure…"

Her voice trailed off. Rachel understood. She felt exactly the same way. Of course Carter was fine. How could he be anything but? Still, until she knew for sure, it was difficult to think about anything else.

Liz jumped to her feet. "I'm going to get something to drink. Is there coffee, Mama? Should I make a pot?"

"You can make some more," Nina told her. "Rachel, I have herbal tea. Would you like that? To soothe you?"

Rachel didn't think tea would help, but she sensed Liz wanted to be doing something. "That would be nice. Thank you."

"I'll help," Shelly said and joined her sister in the kitchen.

Merry clutched her mother's hand. "I can't stand this," she whispered. "The only thing worse than Carter being there would be Adam inside, too."

"Until we know better, we assume the best," Nina said firmly, even as she stroked her daughter's short, dark hair.

"Carter knows what he's doing. He's smart and capable. He's good at his job. How many people are in the building? Ten? Twenty? He's not one of the ones who was shot. You'll see. And if he is, he's strong. He'll pull through. He has Rachel and the baby to live for."

Nina held out her free hand and Rachel took it. As their fingers clutched tightly, she felt both the older woman's emotional strength and her own guilt.

Carter didn't have her to live for. Even though she hadn't intentionally kept him out of the loop with the baby, that was how he felt. So he didn't have that, either.

She told herself that Carter was a tough guy and that she wouldn't make or break his survival. But still, she worried.

The women sat together for several hours. The standoff continued. Rachel forced herself to nibble on a sandwich for the sake of the baby, even though every bite made her want to throw up. Nina stayed strong. Only the trembling in her fingers betrayed her worry. Merry, Liz and Shelly clung to each other and promised that Carter would be fine.

Shortly after one in the afternoon, someone shot tear gas into the building. Several police officers stormed inside and there was the sound of gunshots. Rachel's breath caught in her throat. She couldn't stand watching this, but not knowing was worse. Carter, she prayed desperately. Please let Carter be all right.

Twenty minutes later, the worst was over. Paramedics rushed in and three men were brought out on stretchers. The women crowded around the television, trying to see if one of them was Carter. Suddenly the phone rang.

Nina rushed to grab it.

Merry clutched Rachel's arm. "They'll let us know either way," she whispered. "If he's been hurt, his captain will call. If he's all right, he'll call."

Merry's fingers dug into Rachel's skin, but she didn't pull back. She waited and prayed until Nina said, "Carter, is that you?"

There was silence, then Nina sank into a chair and began to cry. She held up her hand and nodded through the tears.

"He's fine," she mouthed. "He's fine."

Rachel and Merry embraced, while Shelly and Liz did the same. Then they huddled in a heartfelt group hug as Rachel felt her tension begin to ease.

"It's hard," Liz told her, wiping away her own tears. "Knowing Frank risks his life every day is so hard, but I get through it. We all do. We have each other and you have us."

Rachel touched her face and was surprised to find her cheeks damp. Apparently she'd given in to tears, too.

"We stay strong for each other," Shelly said.

"I can see that." Rachel's throat was still tight, so it hurt to speak.

These women kept each other going. She envied the connection they had and how they were there for each other. She'd always wanted that.

Nina hung up the phone. "He's fine. He had to go help with the arrests and give a statement. There will be paperwork."

Her daughters groaned. "There's always paperwork," Merry said. "You get used to it."

Nina smiled at Rachel. "You get used to all of it. Would I have liked Carter's father to be in a less dangerous line of work? Of course. But he was who he was.

I didn't want to change him. So you pray, you keep busy, you love while you can."

Rachel nodded. It made sense and in a perfect world, that was what would happen. But her problems with Carter weren't about his job. They were about so much more.

"I should get going," she said. "I'm so glad he's fine."

Nina hugged her. "He's a good man, my Carter."

"Yes, he is. One of the best."

That much was true. Carter's goodness wasn't in question. Instead, she had to wonder about her feelings and his feelings and what each of them wanted and when their rules of pretend dating had suddenly changed.

Carter finished up his paperwork at about eight that night. He was exhausted, but it had been a day he'd worked hard for and it had come out right. The bad guys were in jail or the hospital, the good guys were safe and he was damn proud to be a cop.

He drove home and parked in his driveway, but instead of going inside, he crossed the street and knocked on his mother's door. He wasn't going to stay, but she'd insisted on seeing him that night, swearing she wouldn't sleep until she knew for herself that he was fine.

She opened the door and instead of speaking, she just pulled him close.

He held her awkwardly, feeling how small she was and knowing he'd put her through hell that day.

"I'm fine," he murmured.

"Of course you are. Why wouldn't you be? You were just doing your job. Still, when the bullets go flying, a mother has a right to worry."

"You're good at that."

She stepped back and smiled at him. "I've had practice. We all have."

"The girls were here?"

Dumb question, he thought. Once word spread, all three of his sisters would end up here.

"And Rachel," his mother said. "She saw the standoff live on TV and came over. I'm glad she did. A time like this, a woman needs her family around her."

"Rachel was here?"

"Where else would she go?"

Interesting question, he thought. He'd wondered about her. But they hadn't talked in a while and he'd figured she was still mad at him.

"She was worried," his mother said, poking him in the chest. "And in her condition, she shouldn't have to worry so much."

"I know. So, um, she left?"

"After you'd called to say you were safe. You haven't talked?"

He shook his head.

His mother pushed him out the door. "So go. Call. Be with her. She was frantic, Carter. This kind of thing is hard for all of us, but for Rachel it's also new. Go show her you're fine."

"Thanks, Mama," he said. "I love you."

She smiled. "I love you, too. You make me very proud."

He stepped off the porch and headed back to his place.

So Rachel had been at his mother's. What did that mean? Had her fear been bigger than her anger? Should he call? Go by? He swore under his breath and opened his front door.

He hated not knowing what to do next, mostly because it never happened to him. He always knew. Getting involved was easy. Only this time it wasn't. This time it was complicated in ways he couldn't understand.

He flipped on the light by the door then came to a stop when he saw Rachel curled up on his sofa. Goldie lay at the other end, her head on Rachel's thigh.

Rachel opened her eyes and smiled at him. "Hey. Liz showed me where you kept the spare key, so I let myself in. I fed Goldie and decided to just wait. I wanted to see if you were okay."

"I'm fine."

"I can see that." She pushed herself into a sitting position and lowered her bare feet to the floor. "I thought you might call."

"I didn't know if you wanted to hear from me."

Her green eyes were bright with emotion. "I did. Despite everything, I wanted to talk to you."

Which told him what? That she'd been worried? Okay, worry was nice, but it wasn't exactly what he was looking for.

"So talk."

He lowered himself into the club chair opposite the sofa. Goldie wagged her tail but didn't stir from her comfy place on the couch.

"Were you scared?" she asked.

Not exactly the subject he'd thought she'd bring up but if she needed to stall for a few minutes, he could respect that.

"Not really," he told her. "No one in the shop thought I was a cop, so I was safe from them. An overeager shooter could have taken me out, but I figured the odds of that were slim. It was a waiting game."

"I was terrified. So was your mom and your sisters.

We knew people had been injured, but we didn't know if it was you."

He raised both hands, then glanced down at his chest. "I'm good."

She shifted so she could stroke Goldie's head. "You didn't tell them about our fight. I thought you might, so I wasn't sure if I would be welcome." She glanced at him. "I thought you were looking for a chance for our pretend dating to end. Why didn't you take it?"

"I didn't think of it," he told her honestly. He'd been angry about what had happened, and confused, but he'd never thought to tell anyone else about it.

Her eyes widened slightly. "Okay. I'll go with that. But you set me up, Carter. You established the rules, then got mad because I followed them."

He'd known they would get around to this eventually. "Maybe," he admitted, hating that he had to. "But I made up the rules because of how you started things."

"I didn't know you," she protested. "I never thought you'd be interested in having a baby with me."

"Maybe you should have gotten to know me before you assumed I was some jerk who would walk away from his kid."

She pressed her lips together, then nodded. "You're right. I found out I was pregnant and I freaked. Totally and completely. I guess I thought if there was no father, things would be easier."

"You want to do everything on your own?"

"Not really, but I wasn't very clear at the time."

"And now?" he asked.

"Now I know you're the kind of man who wants to be involved. And you will be."

He studied her. "Is that good or bad?"

She smiled. "Both."

He drew in a breath. "I didn't set you up. Not on purpose. It just kind of happened. We had rules in place and you didn't mind them."

"Did you?" she asked, her voice sounding a little breathless.

"Some. I don't know what I feel, Rachel, but we're having a baby. I think our daughter deserves more than a halfhearted attempt to get to know each other. I think she deserves some serious effort."

"You don't know we're having a girl."

"Yeah, I do. It's the one thing I'm very clear on."

"I hope I have a boy just to shock you."

He smiled. "I'd like that."

She leaned toward him. "What do you want?"

Right that minute, he wanted her. In his arms, in his bed, under him, naked. He wanted to touch her and feel her. He wanted to close his eyes and go to sleep knowing she was there.

But that wasn't what she was talking about. She meant what did he want in the big-picture sense. As in for more than today.

He stiffened as he realized his answer was the same. He wanted Rachel in his life. He wanted to wake up and have her next to him.

The truth was a bitch, he thought, not sure what to do with the information. He'd never been the guy who did long term, so why was he thinking about it now? Why her? Was it because they were having a baby together?

He shook his head. No, this was bigger than that.

"Carter? The question wasn't supposed to be that hard."

"I want us to try," he said. "I want us to think about making it real."

He wanted to say a whole lot more, but a warning voice told him if he pushed too hard too fast he would scare Rachel away. He still believed she held back, that strong emotion scared her and the last thing he wanted was for her to run.

She bit her lower lip. "Real as in really dating? Really getting involved?"

He nodded. "Can you handle that?"

She drew in a deep breath. "Yes, I can." She smiled. "Okay, I'm a little nervous, but I'll go with it."

He didn't want to give her too much time to think so he stood. After taking her hand, he pulled her to her feet and drew her close. "Nervous? Around me?"

"You're a big, tough guy," she said. "Dangerous."

"Very dangerous," he murmured, his mouth inches from hers. "Good in bed."

She sighed. "You're okay."

That made him grin. "Just okay."

She sniffed. "Some of your techniques need a little refining."

He saw the teasing light in her eyes and heard it in her voice.

"What kind of refining? Want to tell me?" He bent down and swept her up in his arms. "Or better yet, want to show me?"

Saturday morning Carter stepped out of the shower to find Rachel waiting for him in the bathroom. Since his bust had gone down the previous week, she'd been staying with him more than she'd been at home. He'd never lived with anyone before and he found he liked having her around.

One advantage of close, constant proximity was that they got to make love like regular people. Just last night they'd managed to get naked *and* talk before he'd had to claim her. Of course this morning they'd made love on the counter, while their waffles burned.

"Want to wash my back?" he asked as he reached for a towel. "I can get back in the shower."

"I'd love to but your mom called. She asked if we could bring ice to the barbecue because her ice maker is acting up."

"I'm not surprised," he said. "It's about a hundred years old. My sisters and I tried to buy her a new refrigerator for Christmas last year, but she found out and got mad. She said it was too much money. I explained split four ways, it's not that much, but she wouldn't listen. What?"

Rachel was smiling at him.

"I love listening to you talk about your family," she told him. "There's something warm in your voice. It makes me happy."

"Yeah?" Despite the fact that he was still wet and she'd showered and dressed earlier, he pulled her close. "You make me happy."

"I'm glad."

They kissed. The second her mouth pressed against his, wanting poured through him. The instant and natural reaction jabbed her in the leg.

"You are consistent," she said as she reached down and caressed him. "Normally I would totally agree, but we have to get ice and be there in half an hour."

"Tonight," he promised.

"Oh, yeah," she said as she stepped back. "Even if I have to force you."

She glanced down at his thigh, then frowned slightly. "I noticed that scar the first night we were together. It's so unusual. What happened?"

He finished drying off, then wrapped the towel around his waist. "I was being an idiot, climbing up on the back of the sofa to hang shoelaces over the curtain rod. I was maybe six. Mama kept telling me to stop, that I'd hurt myself, and I did. I fell through the window and sliced my leg open. I remember her telling me that if it had been a couple of inches north, I would have been hating life."

She winced. "I have to agree with her. I, for one, would have been deeply disappointed. Okay, big, bad guy. Go get dressed."

She strolled out of the bathroom. He watched her go. Rachel didn't seem to notice the changes in her body, but he could see them. Her breasts were fuller and, based on her recent ecstatic reactions to his touch, more sensitive. There was a slight curve to her stomach and thickening of her waist. She looked lush, like a woman coming in to her most beautiful time.

Carter was so used to feeling trapped and pressured in a relationship that he hadn't known what it was like to feel that everything was right. He belonged with Rachel. She completed him and he wanted to be there for her. He wanted to hold her and support her and convince her that it was safe to care about him.

He wanted to love her.

Love. The one thing he never thought he would find. But he had. So what was he going to do about it?

After icing brownies, Rachel survived the water fight, then cuddled Liz's two girls as she dried them with a big towel in a sunny spot in the yard.

What a perfect day, she thought as the three of them sprawled on the grass and looked up at the clouds passing overhead.

"That one looks like Goldie," Erin, the youngest, said.

"I can see that," Rachel told her.

Around them the family laughed and talked. The guys had settled into a meaningful discussion about college bowl games, while the women kept an eye on the kids. Carter had ducked out about an hour ago and Rachel found herself listening for his arrival.

"Auntie Rachel, when I go to kindergarten next year, can I be in your class?" Erin asked.

Rachel ran her fingers through the little girl's silky hair. "I think you'll probably get Mrs. Reed for your teacher."

Erin pouted. "But I want to be in your class."

Rachel wasn't sure how to explain the complications of her having a child by Erin's uncle and how that would mean Erin would get a different teacher.

"Because I already know you and think you're so great, Mrs. Reed is going to want a chance to get to know you, too," she said. "I think you'll like her. She's a lot of fun. I'd want to be in her class."

Erin giggled. "You're too big and you're a teacher. You can't be in class."

A shadow fell across them.

"Uncle Carter!" Erin sat up and grinned. "You're back!"

"I am, Peanut." He held out a hand. "I'm going to steal Rachel away for a few minutes. Okay?"

"Don't be long."

He chuckled. "I won't." He pulled Rachel to her feet.

"Where'd you run off to?" she asked. "I turned around and you were gone. Sneaking out on me?"

"Only now and then."

He led the way to the front of the house, then across to his place. Once they were inside, he faced her.

Rachel gazed into his handsome face and felt an instant quivering low in her stomach. Just being alone with the man was enough to make her want to have her way with him. But before she could move close and kiss him, he took her hands in his.

"I want to talk to you," he said, sounding serious.

"About?"

"A couple of things. I know how we met wasn't what either of us would have planned, and then you got pregnant, which complicated things. It was a giant twist of fate and for a long time I was kind of pissed off that my life wasn't in my control anymore."

She wasn't sure where he was going with this, but so far she agreed with him.

"I've never been a forever kind of guy," he continued. "I didn't get it. Other people fell in love and got married. Not me."

There was something wrong with her ears, she thought suddenly. A faint buzzing, as if she had a cold. And her skin was all tight. Go. She had to go.

"Carter," she began, but he shook his head.

"Let me finish."

She didn't need him to finish. He'd already said too much.

"I'm making this right," he told her. "Not because I have to but because it's what we both want. I love you, Rachel. I don't know how it happened, but I do. You're the one I want to be with forever. I want to learn everything about you. I want to share your hopes and dreams. I want us to make plans and have more kids and make a life. Just you. Only you."

He let go of her hands. Before she could run, he pulled a jewelry box out of his jeans pocket, then opened it. A beautiful solitaire diamond glimmered in the afternoon.

"It's taken me a long time to get here," he said, "but there's nowhere else I'd rather be. I love you, Rachel. Will you marry me?"

Chapter 13

Rachel stared at the ring, then at Carter. Panic swept through her and with it, the need to run as far and as fast as she could. This was wrong. She didn't want to get married. Not to Carter. No. No! This wasn't happening. He couldn't be ruining everything like this.

"You're moving too fast," she said, barely able to catch her breath. The door beckoned, but she knew that she couldn't just bolt. Not without talking to him first.

"We're having a baby."

"I know, but marriage is not required."

Some of the light faded from his eyes. He closed the jewelry box. "You don't want to marry me," he said flatly.

"Carter, look. You're a great guy. You're practically perfect. You're terrific. If I had to have a baby like this, you're the one I'd pick to do it with. But why change things? We have a good relationship. Let's not change that. We don't need the pressure."

She felt herself inching backward as she spoke. The door was so close, she thought frantically. If she could just get outside, then maybe she could breathe.

Carter couldn't believe this was happening. After all this time, after all the women he'd dated, the ones who had begged him to marry them, he'd finally fallen for the only one not interested in him that way. Here he was, ring in hand, heart exposed and from the looks of things, Rachel couldn't wait to get away from him.

Was it payback? A big cosmic joke on his behalf? Except he'd never led anyone on. He'd done his best to be honest.

Everything hurt. He'd been so sure that once Rachel knew how he felt about her, she'd be able to let go and love him back. He'd believed her feelings were right there, ready to burst free. Talk about being wrong.

She touched his arm. "I'm honored. Truly. I know this is a big deal. To be honest, some of what you said before is true. I do kind of hold back emotionally. So why push that? Why risk tying yourself down with someone who isn't exactly what you want?"

"Don't try to make this about me," he told her, feeling his temper rise. Anger might just be a mask for the pain of rejection, but right now a mask seemed like a good idea. "You're the one not willing to take a chance."

She took a step back. "It's my choice to make. Just because you're willing to make a commitment doesn't mean I am, too. It's a question, not an obligation."

He knew that. She was right about all of it, but he couldn't help wanting to lash out and hurt her.

"You're not making a choice," he said angrily. "You're running. Reacting to something that happened fourteen years ago. You'll never be free of your loss if you don't let yourself love again. Let yourself trust and be vulnerable."

Her gaze narrowed. "Sure. Because this couldn't possibly be about anything else. After all, the amazing Carter proposed. If I'm not falling at your feet in gratitude, there must be something wrong with me."

"I didn't say that."

"You implied it. I don't want to marry you, Carter. I just don't. Think what you want, but that's my bottom line."

With that, she turned and left. The front door closed behind her.

Fifteen minutes later, he walked into the Blue Dog Bar. Someone yelled his name but before he could answer, the half-full bar erupted in applause.

"Good job," one of the cops yelled. "Not getting dead is always a good job."

Carter nodded and waved. He appreciated the support and praise for the successful raid, but right now he had other things on his mind.

"Drinks are on the house," Jenny said as he took a seat at the long counter. "Even the good stuff."

"Just a beer," he told her.

She poured and set the glass in front of him, then frowned. "What's wrong? You don't have hero face."

"I'm no hero. I did what I was supposed to do and this time the bad guys didn't win. End of story."

"You should be a little more excited than that."

Instead of answering, he pulled the jewelry box out of his pocket and passed it across to her. She opened it and gazed at the ring.

"Very nice. I'm impressed."

"She wasn't. Rachel passed."

"Ouch." Jenny closed the box. "I'm sorry."

"Is that it? Shouldn't you want to gloat? Maybe call a few other exes and have them in for a party? Carter finally got his."

Jenny untied her apron. "I'm taking a break, Jon," she yelled to the other bartender, then came around the counter and grabbed Carter's arm. When she'd guided him into the breakroom and closed the door, she turned on him.

"What are you talking about?" she asked. "What's going on? I've never wished bad things would happen to you."

"I know. Sorry. Just a knee-jerk reaction from the biggest jerk." He sank into a plastic chair and closed his eyes. "Why didn't I see it coming? Why did I think it would be okay? I'm the one who didn't believe in love or forever. I finally meet someone who makes me want to believe and now it's going to be okay? Who am I kidding?"

He hurt from the inside out. He hurt in ways he hadn't thought possible. He looked at Jenny. "Did I do this to you? Did I make you feel this crappy? Did I make you ache and bleed?"

She crouched in front of him. "It wasn't all that bad. I loved you, but not so much that I couldn't recover. I know it hurts now, but you'll get better. That old saying about time healing is true. The edges blur. Besides, aren't you jumping to conclusions? You caught Rachel off guard. Maybe she'll come around."

Not likely, he thought grimly, wishing he hadn't left his beer at the bar. This seemed as good a time as any to get drunk.

"Rachel isn't coming around. She isn't interested in being in love. It scares her." He explained how she'd lost her family and been left alone in the world.

"So her reaction isn't about you," Jenny said as she stood and pulled a plastic chair close to his. "She's doing it out of fear."

"I'd hoped she'd be motivated by something else. Something stronger than fear. I was wrong."

He'd known there was a risk, but he'd been stupid enough to think he could win. She was lost to him. He knew that and it left him empty.

"So you're just giving up?" Jenny asked.

He looked at her. "What should I do? Bully her into marrying me? Either she wants me or she doesn't."

"It's not that simple. Rachel obviously wants to be with you. She's been spending enough time with you. A case could be made that you changed the rules with no warning. Maybe you could give her a little time to catch up."

"And if she doesn't?"

"Then you're where you are now. But if you give up and walk away, there's no chance."

He leaned forward. His gut felt as if he'd taken a hit from a three-hundred-pound linebacker. "She either loves me or she doesn't. My wanting things to be different won't change that."

"You said she's dealing with her past. Is it possible she doesn't know what she feels? That she's only reacting? Give her time. Let her miss you. See what happens before you walk away."

He shrugged. "Sure." He could give Rachel all the time she needed and then some. What did it matter? He wasn't interested in being with anyone but her. Missing her, aching for her, would fill his days anyway.

Jenny smiled. "You could have a little faith in love."

"I have plenty of faith in love. It's Rachel's faith I'm questioning."

* * *

While Rachel didn't actually expect to hear from Carter, she still missed him over the next few days. She was torn between the need to see him and annoyance over what he'd done.

He could have given her a little warning. They'd gone from pretend dating to a proposal in an eighth of a second. He'd changed things so fast, she'd reacted without thinking. Without saying anything. She had a bad feeling she'd hurt him.

She wanted to tell herself that she hadn't—that Carter wasn't capable of deep emotions. Only that wasn't true. He didn't lie and he'd told her he loved her. When she thought about him saying that, she got all gooey inside. Like she wanted to give the world a hug. But then she thought about marriage and her whole body went cold.

Marriage was out of the question. Maybe it was her past. Maybe he was right and she did keep people at arm's length. So what? It was her right. All she knew was that she wasn't interested in forever.

But she hadn't meant to reject Carter like that. He'd proposed and she'd acted badly so the next step was up to her. Even without marriage, there was still the baby to consider.

She picked up the phone, then put it down. She had no idea what to say to him. Obviously they should talk, but about what?

She reached for the phone, but this time it rang. She snatched up the receiver.

"Hello?"

"Rachel! It's Nina. I'm cooking dinner on Friday night. Just family. I feel the need to have everyone I love around my table. Six o'clock. Say you'll be here."

"I..." She opened her mouth to refuse, then hesitated. Nina was going to be her baby's grandmother and the only grandparent. Sure, the night might be awkward, but better to get that awkwardness over now. Plus, Rachel wanted an opportunity to talk to Carter. "I'd love to."

"Good. I know you have to work, so don't worry about bringing anything. I'll see you then."

"I'm looking forward to it," she said, and meant it.

She arrived a few minutes early and found that nearly everyone else was already there. Although she'd braced herself for a cool greeting and lots of questions, no one acted as if anything were different.

"You're glowing," Merry said as she hugged Rachel. "I look like a cow when I'm pregnant, but I can see you're going to be one of those beautiful expectant mothers. That means I'll have to hate you, but I'll get over it."

Rachel smiled. "I'm sure the glow will pass."

"That's just not how my luck goes. What do you want to drink?" Merry asked the question as she guided Rachel into the kitchen. Rachel chose flavored water and continued chatting as she tried to see if Carter had arrived yet. She didn't spot him and was a little surprised by the rush of disappointment she felt. Okay, sure, she'd missed him, but it wasn't a big deal. It wasn't as if she were devastated by the fact that he was no longer in her life the way he had been. She was only interested in making things right so they could be friends again.

Nina carried a large tray into the kitchen. "Here it is," she said, then stopped when she saw Rachel. "Oh, good. You're here." The older woman set the tray down. "How are you feeling? Any symptoms yet? Are you getting enough rest? You have to eat, too. Lots of good, healthy food for you and the baby."

"I'm doing well," Rachel said, still startled that everyone was being so nice. She'd come prepared to tell her side of the story, but there didn't seem to be a story to tell. Was it possible that Carter hadn't said anything? She knew he was close to his family. Wouldn't he mention that he'd proposed and she'd refused?

Apparently not, she thought a half hour later as Nina urged them to sit down to dinner. She hadn't actually seen him yet. While the women had hung out in the kitchen, the guys had been in the family room watching the end of a college football game. She'd tried to think up an excuse to casually go in, but hadn't come up with one. Funny how before the proposal, she would have simply walked back and joined him. Now, that didn't feel right.

From what she could tell, he hadn't said a word about his proposal or her rejection—which was really nice of him and probably explained the sudden rapid beating of her heart when he walked into the dining room.

He looked good. Relaxed and handsome. She took in his features, as if she'd been hungry to see them again.

He glanced at her and nodded. "Hey, Rachel. How's it going?"

She blinked. How's it going? That was it?

She looked around the room, but no one seemed to notice anything was different between them. No one had realized she and Carter weren't what they had been before. Even though she didn't know exactly what that was.

She found herself sitting across from him, and that meant she couldn't avoid looking at him. When he caught her eye, he smiled, which should have been great, but wasn't. There was something missing in that smile. It was casual, meaningless, as if she wasn't special anymore. Until just now she hadn't appreciated how much she liked being special in Carter's world.

Dinner was the usual mix of great food and fast-paced conversation. Rachel relaxed, thinking that maybe everything was going to be all right, when Carter said, "I have a couple of announcements."

She tensed. While she couldn't believe he would tell his family this way and put her on the spot, she knew she'd reacted badly. Maybe in his mind, she deserved this. She ran over a list of reasons as to why she hadn't wanted to marry him and braced herself for the public humiliation.

Nina looked at her son. "A good announcement or a bad one? I'm an old woman. Don't break my heart."

He reached down the table and patted his mother's hand. "You always were a little dramatic."

Nina smiled. "I know. It's charming."

"It is." He released her, then addressed his family. "As you all know, I passed the test to be a detective awhile ago, but I never bothered to apply for the job. I liked what I was doing. I've decided it's time for me to move on. There's an opening coming up in a few weeks and I've put in my application. I've got a good shot at it."

Nina clapped her hands and beamed. "Oh, Carter, I've longed for this. Finally you won't be shot at so much."

"Way to go," Frank said and clapped him on the back.

Everyone else congratulated him, including Rachel, although she felt a little lost. A detective? Since when? She didn't even know he'd wanted to make a change. He hadn't said anything to her.

She could see why he wouldn't have in the past few

days, but what about before? He'd wanted to marry her? Shouldn't they have talked about a career shift for him?

Before she could figure out what it all meant, Carter cleared his throat. "There's something else."

Rachel felt all eyes suddenly turn in her direction. She swallowed hard. They thought he was going to say they were engaged.

Heat climbed up her cheeks. She looked at Carter, but he wasn't looking at her. Instead, he focused on his mother.

"Mama, you're an amazing woman. Truly. I'm lucky to have been your son. But it's time for me to have my own place."

"You have your own place," Shelly said. "Your own house."

Nina flicked her fingers at her daughter. "It's all right. Let your brother finish."

"I'm putting the house up for sale," he said. "I'm buying another one. It's about three miles away. Close enough for me to drop in, but far enough away so I can have my own life."

Conversation exploded.

"Did you know about this?" Merry asked Rachel. "You didn't tell me."

"I didn't know," Rachel said honestly, just as surprised as everyone else. She would never have thought Carter would want to be away from his family.

Nina looked at her son. Her eyes were bright with tears, but she blinked them away. "I understand," she told him. "You and Rachel need a chance to start your own lives together. This is a good thing." She raised her glass of wine. "To Carter and Rachel."

The rest of the family joined in. Rachel looked at

Carter and found, for the first time that evening, he was watching her. Did he expect her to say something? She couldn't. Not like this.

She tried to figure out what he was thinking, but couldn't do that, either. Nothing about this felt right, she thought, uncomfortable and not sure what to do to make things better.

Dinner finally ended. While Rachel had started the evening hoping to talk to Carter, now she just wanted to get out of the house. She felt out of place, as if she were a fraud. She hated that Carter's family still treated her as if she were one of their own when she obviously wasn't anymore.

She picked up several dinner plates, intent on carrying them into the kitchen, only to stop in the short hallway between the two rooms when she heard Carter talking to his mother.

"No, no," the other woman was saying. "You were so good together."

"It's all right," he said. "We tried to make things work out, but they're not going to. Not the way everyone wanted. It's no one's fault and I don't want you grilling her. Or anyone else. Rachel didn't do anything wrong."

"But you care about her. I can see it in the way you look at her. Tell me it's not different."

Rachel held her breath.

Carter stunned her by saying, "I love her, but sometimes love isn't enough."

"It has to be," his mother told him.

"It's not this time. We'll be friends and raise a baby together."

"But I thought you changed your job for Rachel. I thought you were moving for her."

"I'm doing it because it's time for me to move on."

"You're a good man," Nina said after a moment of silence. "I'm proud of you, Carter. Your father would have been proud of you, too."

Rachel stepped back into the dining room and set the plates on the table. What was she supposed to do now?

Rachel waited until Carter said he had to leave, then excused herself and followed him to his house.

"Can we talk?" she asked when she'd caught up with him.

"Sure." He pushed open the front door, then waited for her to enter first.

She walked into the pleasant room. Everything was familiar and yet nothing seemed right. She didn't belong here anymore.

He motioned to the sofa and took one of the chairs for himself.

"What's up?" he asked.

He seemed so casual, she thought, watching him watch her. As if none of this mattered. But it had to. He hadn't proposed lightly. He wouldn't. She'd turned him down and he'd moved on—she should be happy.

She tried to figure out what to say. How to explain something she didn't understand herself. She cared about him, cared deeply, but he didn't want to know that. What did caring matter when she couldn't say she loved him?

Because that's what he would want. He'd waited a long time to find the right woman and when he found her, he was going to expect her to give with her whole heart. Could she do that? Could she give him everything she had?

The question had barely formed when her chest got tight and the need to run burned through her.

"You never said anything about changing jobs," she said instead. "I didn't know."

"I've been thinking about it for a while," he admitted. "It's a good opportunity for me. Interesting, important work and I'll be a little safer. That's good for the baby."

She nodded slowly. "You're angry with me."

His dark gaze never left her face. "Not yet. I'm working up to anger. Get back to me in a couple of weeks and I'll let you know. Right now I still feel like roadkill."

"I'm sorry."

"Why? You told the truth. You couldn't do it and you said so. That beats the last two times when you pretended you could."

She flinched. "That's a little harsh."

"Maybe. I'm not in a position to judge. I fell in love for the first time in my life and I got dumped. I'm still bleeding, Rachel. What do you want from me?"

What did she? "I'm sorry," she whispered. "I never meant to hurt you."

"Too bad, because if that had been the plan, then hey, big win for you." He stood. "If you're done, I've got things to do."

She hated that she'd done this to him. She rose to her feet and stepped close enough to touch him.

"I'm sorry," she said again as she put her hands on his upper arms. "You have to believe me."

He looked down at her. "That's the hell of it, Rachel. I do believe you."

She could see the pain in his eyes and she'd been the

one to put it there. She hated that. Without thinking, she stood on tiptoe and pressed her mouth to his.

Familiar wanting rushed through her. He was warm and tempting and fifteen kinds of sexy.

This felt so right, she thought hazily as passion took over. She leaned in to him and parted her lips. But instead of responding, he stepped back.

"No, thanks," he told her. "Not my style."

"Wh-what?"

"I'm not going there with you. You've made it clear what you don't want from me, now I'm doing the same. We're just friends and I don't sleep with my friends."

But how could he deny their chemistry? They were so good together.

"You look surprised," he said, crossing his arms over his chest. "Don't be. I don't do stud-service and I'm not your pretend boyfriend anymore. I want it all, or I don't want any of it. All my life I'd blamed my troubles on women. The truth is, I created my own trouble by not being willing to step up to the plate. I'm not going to do that anymore. I'm taking responsibility and I'm taking charge. I'll be your friend, but it ends there."

She felt embarrassed and angry. His rejection cut her, yet she was aware enough to understand why he'd done it. A teeny, tiny part of her thought that maybe he was right.

"Fine," she said, doing her best to keep her voice from shaking. "We'll be friends. And parents."

"Sure."

There was something about the way he said the word. Something that really annoyed her.

"What?" she demanded. "You don't think I'm going to be a good mother."

"I have my doubts," he said, stunning her. "You're

afraid to care too much. Given your past, it's understandable to me. But is the kid going to care about your issues? I think a baby is only going to know that her mother doesn't love her and that's not right."

She glared at him. Her fingers itched to throw something, to lash out. "How dare you say that to me? You don't know anything about me."

"I know a whole lot about you. I know you're letting being afraid control your life. I know you walked away from something that could have been good because it's easier than going through the fire. Sometimes fire can burn the hell out of you and you're never the same, but sometimes it just gets rid of all the dead wood and you're left with something new and clean." He shrugged. "It was your call, Rachel, and you made it. Now we both live with it."

She trembled with rage and disappointment. It was truly over. There was nothing left to say, nothing left to save. So she did what made the most sense. She left.

Chapter 14

"It's not fair," Rachel said as she paced the length of the family room in Noelle's beautiful house. "He's being totally unreasonable. Now that he's figured out how he feels, I'm just supposed to fall in line. Well, excuse me if life isn't that convenient."

Crissy leaned back in the overstuffed sofa and sipped her wine. "You're right. What is it about guys? They manage to get it all together and suddenly the rest of us should pause and gasp in honor of that? So what if Carter loves you? You didn't ask him to care. You didn't pretend that he matters."

Rachel paused at the French doors and glanced at her friend. "He does matter. He's the father of my baby, so that has to count."

"Fine." Crissy shrugged. "So he gets points for mobility. Big whoop."

Rachel had a feeling Crissy was playing her a little—

backing her into an emotional corner so she was forced to defend Carter. She wasn't sure how she felt about that. Carter might be really annoying, but for the most part, he was a good guy.

Noelle waddled in with a tray of appetizers. She set them on the large coffee table, then sank into the chair by the sofa. "One of you is going to have to help me up later," she said with a sigh. "I'm getting too big to maneuver on my own."

"Absolutely," Crissy said. "I'm happy to lend a hand."

For a moment Rachel wondered what Crissy thought about both her friends being pregnant. Did it bother her to know they were keeping their children? She'd mentioned her guilt at taking the easy way out before. Did she also regret what she'd lost?

"What did I miss?" Noelle asked.

"Rachel is still pissed at Carter. He's such a jerk."

"He's not a jerk," Noelle said. "Honestly, the poor man proposed. Why does he have to go to prison for that?"

"He doesn't," Rachel said as she moved to the sofa and sat down. The mini quesadillas were calling to her. She grabbed a napkin and picked up one. "I appreciate what he's trying to do. What annoys me is his assumptions about me. As if by not wanting to marry him, there must be something wrong with me."

Noelle sighed. "He's hurt. He loves you. I couldn't understand what that meant before, but now, with Dev, I so get it. When I fell for Dev and was afraid he didn't love me back, I thought I was going to die. I couldn't imagine living through that much pain. It was horrible. Carter's hurt and he's lashing out. You have to give him a little room to deal with his pain."

"He can have all the room he wants," she grumbled. "He can have miles and miles."

"It's not that simple," Noelle said. "You're having his baby. That's going to connect you forever."

"I'm sure he's hating that." Rachel took a bite of the quesadilla.

"I still think he's being totally unreasonable," Crissy said. "Men are such a pain. Yes, he's had his great emotional revelation, but is it Rachel's fault that she doesn't love him back?"

"You can't force love," Noelle admitted. "It's just too bad you can't return his feelings. Then you could be a family."

Rachel knew her friends were being supportive and she was grateful for that, but she also felt a little judged. Crissy was trying to make a point and Noelle kept talking about Carter and what he'd done. In a perfect world, yes, she would have fallen madly in love and they could have lived happily ever after. But life wasn't perfect.

"I just can't," she said as she balled up her napkin and tossed it on the table. "I can't be what he wants me to be."

"Which is what?" Crissy asked. "What does he want from you?"

"He wants me to be…" Rachel paused. What had Carter asked for? Except for her to love him back and marry him, she couldn't think of anything. "A person who loves him. It's just not me."

"That's okay," Noelle said soothingly. "He'll find someone else."

Rachel spun to face her. "What?"

"Someone else," her friend repeated. "Now that Carter understands that he can fall in love with someone, he's going to want to do it again. I hope this time he can find someone to love him back."

Right. Because that was the mature and responsible thing to want. But that would mean that Carter would get married. Rachel would be like all his other exes—except she would have his baby. There she'd be, invited over at holidays like Jenny and a few select others. She'd bring the baby and they'd all fuss. Especially Carter's new wife, because she wouldn't want anyone to think she minded.

Eventually he would have other children. Children who would make him forget the one he had with Rachel.

"Stupid man," she muttered. "It's all *her* fault."

"Her who?" Crissy asked.

"That woman he married. She's awful."

Crissy sipped her wine again. "Are we talking about Carter's imaginary wife? Maybe you'll like her."

Rachel didn't respond. She was busy dealing with the uncomfortable realization that she didn't want Carter for herself, but she didn't want anyone else to have him, either. And that thought made her exactly the kind of person she hated.

"I'm sorry," she said as she stood. "I can't do this tonight. I have to go."

"Are you all right?" Noelle asked as she struggled to her feet. Crissy rose and helped her up. They both followed Rachel to the front door.

"I'm fine," Rachel said, wishing it were true. "I need some time to think. I'll be okay."

They both hugged her and made her promise to call. Finally she escaped and made her way to her car. But instead of driving home, she circled through different neighborhoods until she found herself at the mall.

It was a Friday night and the place was packed, mostly

with teenagers. Rachel wandered the first level, trying to interest herself in a new body lotion or maybe a soft pretzel. Instead, she found her attention shift to the kids passing by. Most of them were in groups, but she saw a few couples.

They were so intent on each other, she thought as she watched one girl melt into her boyfriend's embrace, then kiss him passionately in an alcove by the card store. She had never been like that in high school. Never that carefree or that willing to get involved. She'd held herself apart because it still hurt—every minute of every day she'd missed her family.

Someone should have taken her to counseling.

The thought was so unexpected, she stopped right there, forcing a family with two strollers to walk around her.

Counseling. Of course. She'd been twelve and she'd lost her entire family. Someone to talk to, someone who knew about grief, could have made a big difference. But no one had suggested it and she'd never thought to ask.

She started walking again, but she didn't see the stores. Instead she saw Brett, her first real boyfriend. He hadn't been surprised when she'd broken off their engagement. He admitted he'd been expecting it.

"You were never there," he said. "I hoped it would get better, but you were always somewhere else. I couldn't touch you."

She'd protested, saying they were both each other's first time. How much more touching could there be? But he hadn't meant physical contact. He'd meant something deeper and more significant.

She'd run then, because it was the right thing to do.

Because it was easy and what she knew. Ironically, she was still running.

Where would she run to next? How many times would she turn away from what she wanted because she was afraid?

But the fear was so real, she thought. So big. It was her world. It haunted her and when she tried to dismiss it, it reminded her of how much she had already lost. Could she survive more?

Rachel arrived home to find Crissy waiting for her.

"I can't stand this," her friend said from her seat at the top of the stairs. "I'm here to meddle, so brace yourself."

"I'm braced," Rachel said as she opened the front door. "Come on in."

Crissy followed her into the apartment and set her purse on the table by the door. "I know this is your decision," she said earnestly. "I've been telling myself this is your life and that you should be allowed to live it however you want."

"But?" Rachel asked, relieved to have someone to talk to.

"But you're going to make a mistake. I can feel it." Crissy walked up to her, put both hands on her shoulders and shook her gently. "What on earth is wrong with you?"

Rachel startled herself and most likely Crissy by bursting into tears. "I don't know. I'm so afraid."

Crissy led her to the sofa and sat next to her. "Oh, honey, I'm sorry. I didn't mean to make you cry. I'm sorry."

"Don't be. It's not your fault. It's me. I'm just not like other people. There's too much wrong with me."

Crissy pulled her close and rubbed her back. "Don't be

silly. You're one of the most normal people I know. We all have flaws. We all deal with crap. Don't beat yourself up for being human."

Rachel wiped her face. She felt emotionally spent and broken. "He's great," she said, still fighting tears. "I know that. He's caring and honest and good and sexy. He has a terrific family and don't all those articles say to judge a man by how he treats his mother? He's terrific with her and his sisters."

She struggled for breath, then gave up and let the tears win.

"Sounds good to me," Crissy said. "If I could face one more first date, I'd go for him myself."

Rachel gave a strangled laugh. "Please don't. Then I'd have to hate you."

"We don't want that." Crissy wiped her face. "Come on. What's the real problem? It isn't how great he is, because that's all a good thing. Talk about a fabulous gene pool. So what's really wrong?"

Rachel straightened and dug down for the honest response. "I can't do it. I can't love him as much as he wants me to."

Crissy gave her a slight smile. "So much material to work with in that sentence. I'll go with the obvious one first. As much as he wants? Is that what this is about?"

Rachel closed her eyes, then opened them. "As much as I want," she whispered.

"Okay. Good. Why not?"

She stiffened. "Why not? Because what happens if I do? What happens then? He could die."

Crissy blinked. "At the risk of being a bitch, we're all going to die. It's part of living. You're born, you live, you die. There's no getting around it."

"I'm not talking about later. When he's had a full life. I'm talking about now. I've already lost everything once. I can't do that again."

Crissy nodded. "Good point. What if he doesn't?"

"What do you mean?"

"What if he doesn't die? What if he lives a long, healthy life and dies in his sleep at a hundred and three? He's what, thirty? So you will have lost seventy-three years with him on the off chance he kicks the bucket early. Not a great trade-off."

"Seventy-three years with Carter," Rachel murmured. That was her definition of heaven. "I could do that."

"Okay, so it's not the actual dying," Crissy said. "It's him dying too soon. So how much is enough? If you knew he was only going to live until he was sixty—that's thirty years with him. Would that be enough?"

Rachel knew her friend was leading her somewhere, but she couldn't figure out where. "I'd want more, but yes, I'd take thirty years."

"Would ten be enough? Would you accept ten?"

The tears threatened. "I don't know. That would hurt."

Crissy drew in a breath. "What about the baby?" she asked in a low voice. "When will you decide it's safe to love your child?"

Rachel touched her stomach. "What do you mean? I already love my child."

"Do you? How can you know how long he or she is going to live? How can you live with that fear?"

She didn't know what to say.

"I don't have any answers," Crissy told her. "But here's my newsflash. I've always wanted to fall in love, but I've never allowed myself. I never thought I was good enough. I had to keep the punishment on because of what I'd done.

Thinking about you, knowing what you're going through, has caused me to question that. When is the punishment enough? When is it okay for me to be happy?"

Crissy shifted on the sofa and took one of Rachel's hands in her own. "You lost your whole family, your whole world. It was tragic. But a greater tragedy is that you survived only to become trapped in a fear so great you're afraid to live. Is this what your parents would have wanted? Would this make them happy? You go through the motions, but you don't feel any of it. I'm saying this because you're my friend and I love you. And because I'm afraid you're going to become one of those obsessive, psycho moms who make their kids live in a plastic bubble."

"I'd never do that," Rachel whispered through her tears. This was all too much. She wanted to go back to the way things were before. When she didn't have to hurt or wonder or feel.

Her breath caught. That's what it all came down to— feeling. Being willing to put it on the line.

"You think if something bad happens, you won't be able to deal with it," Crissy said softly. "My second news-flash is that you're not that twelve-year-old little girl anymore. You're a capable adult with a hell of a support system. We would all be there for you. You would never lose your home or your family. We go with you wherever you go. Trust us to be there and trust yourself to be strong."

Later, when Crissy had left, Rachel walked into her bedroom and pulled a battered wooden box out of the bottom drawer of her dresser. She sat on the floor and opened the lid.

Inside was all she had left of her parents and her baby brother. There were pictures, an old house key, their wed-

ding rings and the earrings her mother had been wearing that fateful night. Their passports, unused except for
the single stamp from their honeymoon trip to Italy. Her
brother's favorite toy car.

She flipped through the pictures, smiling at barely remembered Christmas mornings, tearing up at a candid
shot of her mother hugging her. Sometimes she could remember so much and at other times, everything blurred.

What would they think of her now? Would they be
proud or disappointed? Her parents had always said she
needed to do her best. If she'd done that, then they were
happy. She didn't have to be the best in the world, just
the best her.

The best her didn't live afraid all the time. The best
her believed and had faith. Crissy was right—Rachel
couldn't keep anyone from dying. It wasn't the death she
feared, it was her inability to cope with it. Her inability
to stay strong.

But she had been strong. She'd survived a devastating
loss. She'd grown up and made a life and now she was a
few months away from being a mother herself.

She turned to the next picture. It was of her parents.
They gazed at each other with such love in their eyes.
She smiled as she remembered how it felt to be around
them. Surrounded by love. Nurtured, cared for, protected.
Carter looked at her the same way. He made her feel safe
and cared for. He…

Rachel scrambled to her feet. Was she crazy? Carter
loved her. He was the best man she'd ever met and he
loved her. Did she really think she was going to get this
lucky again? Did she think she would find someone better? Crissy was right—they had a set amount of time on

this earth. No one knew how long, but to waste it because it was eventually going to end seemed really stupid.

She glanced at the clock. It was nearly midnight. Too late to call. Too late to...

"Forget it," she muttered as she ran out of her bedroom, grabbed her purse and her car keys, then flew out the door. She was done waiting. She'd already waited too long.

She made the drive across town in record time, then ran up to his front door and rang the bell over and over. She didn't let herself think that he might not be home, that he might already have found someone else. She wouldn't imagine trouble. She already had a lifetime of doing that.

The door opened and there he was. Sleepy and mussed and the most gorgeous man she'd ever seen.

"Rachel? Are you okay?"

"No." She pushed past him. "I'm not. I haven't been for a long time."

She refused to believe it was too late. If he loved her, then somehow she would convince him to give her a second chance. If he didn't... No, she wasn't going there.

He closed the door and faced her. "What's wrong?"

"Everything. I'm so scared all the time. It eats at me. I was thinking earlier that I probably should have gone into some kind of therapy after I lost my parents. Maybe I still should, I don't know. But what I do know is that event changed me. I was afraid to care too much about anything. If I didn't care, then it was okay if it was taken away. You were right. Crissy was right. I guess everyone was right but me."

"Rachel, it's okay."

She wanted to go to him, to touch him and hold him and have him want her, but she remembered their last conversation. No part-time anything. First she had to convince him that this was forever.

"It's like my dancing," she said, speaking quickly, needing to get it all out as fast as possible. "I took one teacher's word. What if she'd been having a bad day? She said I couldn't make it and I believed her. I let one person's opinion define my life. I stopped trying. I took classes, but they were just for me. I went to my fall-back plan and became a teacher. I love what I do and I'm really glad I'm doing it, but I wish I tried dancing a little more."

She stopped and drew in a breath. His dark eyes didn't tell her what he was thinking, but at least he hadn't thrown her out.

"I have plants," she said. "They're safe. I really want a dog, but I've been too scared. I say it's because I live in an apartment, but I could move. I haven't bought a house. Sure it would have been tough, financially, but my parents left me some money. I have the down payment. I've been so careful not to make mistakes or get hurt that I've missed the best parts of life. The messy, unpredictable, emotionally scary parts. I nearly missed you."

She took a step closer and placed her hand on his chest. "You are the most wonderful man. You are everything I could ever want and more. I have been horrible to you and I'm deeply sorry. I know I don't deserve a second chance, but I'm asking for one. I'm willing to do whatever you say to prove myself to you. Just please, please give me another chance."

She drew in a deep breath and spoke the words that she'd been hiding from for far too long. "I love you, Carter. I love you. I want to be with you. I want to have children with you and grow old with you. I don't care how long we have. Okay, yeah, the more time the better, but even if it's just for today, I want to be with you."

She waited, studying his face, hoping for the best. One corner of his mouth turned up and he held open his arms.

She rushed into them and held him as tightly as she could. He pulled her close.

"I love you," she told him.

"I love you, too."

"I'm glad. I'm sorry I was so stupid about everything."

"You had some things to work out."

"I still do, but maybe we can work on them together." She raised her head and looked at him. "I want to be someone you're proud of. Someone you can depend on, no matter what. I want to be the best part of your day."

"You already are."

"You're the best part of mine, too."

She stood in his embrace and felt the strength of him, the love.

He pressed his lips to her cheek, then whispered, "I have something of yours."

"What?"

He jerked his head to the left. She turned and saw the velvet jewelry box sitting on the coffee table.

"Marry me, Rachel," he said.

"Yes." She kissed him. "Yes, yes. Absolutely. Say when. Today? Tomorrow? I don't need a big wedding."

"Sure you do. It's a chick thing. We'll have it all. Flowers, a cake, whatever you want."

She smiled. "I have what I want. I have you."

* * * * *

SOME KIND OF
WONDERFUL

Sarah Morgan

To Dianne Moggy,
for making my dreams a reality
and for allowing her adorable dog Maple
to play a starring role in my O'Neil Brothers series.
Thank you.

Friendship is a sheltering tree

—Samuel Taylor Coleridge

Chapter 1

Zachary Flynn should never have been born.

His conception, as his mother was fond of telling him, had been the result of an excess of alcohol and a burst condom. She'd spent the first eight years of his life blaming him for everything from poverty to bed bugs. Who she'd blamed after that he had no idea because at the age of eight someone had asked questions about the recurring bruises and broken bones and he'd been sent to live with a foster family. As churchgoing, God-fearing Christians, they'd deserved better than a messed-up reject from a rough neighborhood of Boston who'd been raised to believe the only way to stop someone from screwing you was to screw them first. He'd had the distinction of being the first foster kid to snap the patience of these good, kind folk. After that he'd been handed from fam-

ily to family like a baton in a relay race, everyone eager
to pass him on.

He'd been on the fast track to a life on the wrong side
of the law when he'd discovered flying.

Twenty years later he still had a clear memory of the
exact moment everything had changed.

It had been an unbearably hot day at Camp Puffin,
the air in the forest thick with the scents of summer and
the hum of insects. Zach had committed mass murder
as he'd chased mosquitoes the size of small birds around
the airless cabin he'd shared with seven other kids. Seven
kids whose families cared enough to send them to camp
with enough food and gear to smooth the rough edges
of parting.

Zach had been given his place as part of a scholarship program and they'd made sure it was something he
didn't forget. He'd taken revenge for their endless taunt-
ing by dumping their stuff in a tide pool. Most of it had
been washed away and furious parents had demanded
the culprit be duly punished.

Zach couldn't imagine having a parent who gave a
damn, least of all about stolen candy and a few sweat-
shirts with fancy logos.

His punishment had been a date with Philip Law, the
director of Camp Puffin.

Zach, who viewed all authority with suspicion and
was never going to be comfortable around a man whose
name was "Law," had expected to be sent on his way.
He'd pretended not to care, but in truth he would have
endured being bitten by a thousand mosquitoes if it had
meant living on an island where the forest met the sea.
Anything was better than having to spend his days looking over his shoulder in the sweltering city and although

he wouldn't have admitted it, Puffin Island was a cool place. There was something about the clean air and the way the ocean melted into the horizon that made him feel less like killing his neighbor.

He'd stood, braced, ready for another door to slam shut in his face, practicing his "I don't give a fuck" look, but instead of telling him to pack up his things, Philip had driven him to the small airfield on the far side of the island.

Twelve-year-old Zach had slumped, sulky and rebellious, in the front of the Cessna, waiting for the ax to fall, wondering what was so bad that he had to be flown out of here and not take the crowded ferry like everyone else. Maybe Philip Law was planning to take him up high and then push him into the ocean.

Yeah, do it. Why not?

Who the hell would care?

He knew no one would miss him.

He wasn't even sure he'd miss himself.

As Philip had put his hands on the controls and taxied along the short runway, Zach had wondered whether he'd die when he hit the water or drown slowly. And then the small plane had lifted into the air and Zach, who had lived with fear all his life, had known a moment of breath-stealing terror closely followed by soaring excitement as the sparkling sea and the emerald green of the island shrank beneath him.

His stomach had swooped and his eyes had almost popped out of his head.

"Holy shit." He'd watched hungrily, dazzled by the complexity of the instrument panel, absorbing every move of Philip's hands, envious of the knowledge that gave them flight. He'd wanted that knowledge and skill more than he'd ever wanted anything in his life. In a blinding flash he realized there was a world outside the one he inhabited.

Years later Philip had told him that was the moment he'd known he'd made the right decision in offering what some might have viewed as a reward for bad behavior. He could have delivered a lecture, sanctions, even expulsion, but all that would have done was harden a boy who was already solid steel. At twelve years old, Zachary Flynn had seen more than most people saw in a lifetime. Authority slid off him, instructions and orders bounced back like a ball from concrete. Nothing penetrated.

Until they reached six thousand feet.

There, up in the clouds, the mask of indifference had slipped away, revealing an excitement too raw and real to be contained.

For Philip it had been a way of giving a jaded, disillusioned boy a glimpse of another life.

For Zach, it had been love at first flight.

They'd flown over the island of Vinalhaven and towards Bar Harbor, over forest, lakes and the glittering expanse of Penobscot Bay, where yachts peppered the ocean. Absorbed by a different view of a world that had so far delivered nothing but bitter blows, Zach had fought to stop himself from whooping like a little kid.

Look up, look up, he'd yelled inside his head as he saw cars the size of matchboxes winding along the noodle-thin coast road. *Look up and see who's bigger now.*

By the time they'd landed, his whole body had been shaking.

He'd felt like the king of the world.

"Oh, man—can we do it again? I want you to take me up again. I'll do anything." He'd all but begged and hadn't cared. Not even when he'd seen the look of satisfaction on Philip's face.

"You want to learn one day?"

Zach had dragged his palm over his sweaty brow, feeling like an addict shown a whole new way of getting a fix. "To fly? Yeah." What sort of a stupid question was that? Who the hell wouldn't want to? It was the coolest thing ever.

"Then stop dicking around." Philip had pinned him with his gaze. "Stop wasting your brain, stop living down to everyone's expectations and do something with your life."

Zach almost swallowed his tongue. He didn't know which had shocked him most. The fact that someone had noticed he had a brain, or that the camp director had used the word *dick*.

Confused, he'd responded in the only way he'd known. By attacking.

"I didn't ask for my life to suck. It's not like I walked into a place and ordered a supersized misery burger served with a side of crap."

"Just because someone serves you something, doesn't mean you have to eat it. People can dish it up and hand it to you, but you don't have to swallow it. Folks can tell you you're useless and nothing, and you can believe them or you can prove them wrong. What happened in the past wasn't your fault. What happens in the future is your decision. You can make good ones, or you can watch it all slip away and spend the rest of your life blaming everyone else for the things that happened to you."

He'd made it sound so easy, as if all Zach had to do was pull an Abercrombie sweatshirt over the scars and the cigarette burns to become one of the cool crowd.

Zach knew it didn't work that way. He could have dressed in Armani and it wouldn't have changed the facts. He came from nowhere and he was going nowhere.

Except now he wanted to get there by plane.

He'd stared ahead, mutinous, conflicted, the urge to kick and defend himself deeply ingrained. Against his will, his gaze had slid to the instrument panel of the Cessna and he'd almost purred with longing. He'd wanted to reach out, stroke and touch. He'd wanted to take her soaring high above the water and bank into the clouds. It was more than want. It was need.

And because he knew people, and loved flying, Philip had seen that need and understood it.

"I have an instructor qualification. I can teach you."

It was like holding out a freshly baked loaf to a starving man.

Zach had all but drooled, but years of mistrust had held him back. "What's the catch?"

Philip's gaze hadn't wavered. "Does there have to be a catch?"

"There's always a catch." The cynicism was entrenched, cold hard layers of *fuck you* protecting him from do-gooders who eventually gave up on him when "doing good" proved unrewarding. Zach didn't see why he should help anyone feel good about themselves when most of them went out of their way to make sure he knew he was worthless.

"The catch is that you have to clean up your act. No more skipping classes. It's a shame to waste a brain like yours. You come back here every summer and when the time is right, I'll teach you. And you can pay me."

There, right there, was the catch.

"I don't have money." But he'd get it. He was figuring out the best way of stealing what he needed without getting caught when Philip shook his head.

"I don't want your money. I want your commitment."

Zach had looked at him blankly. He had no idea what the word meant. "Sure. Whatever."

"I want you to help out at camp. Every summer for the whole summer. Start taking some responsibility."

Help out at camp?

It had taken a moment for the words to sink in and Zach reflected that it was just as well they were inside a plane or a million insects would have flown into his open mouth while he'd been gawping. He tried to imagine how Mr. and Mrs. More-Money-Than-Sense would react to the news that Zach would be helping.

"You're kidding me."

"I'm not kidding. And just in case you don't recognize it, I'm giving you something life hasn't given you before—a chance. Up to you whether you take it."

"So it's not going to cost me?" Life had taught Zach that good things didn't happen for free. In his experience, good things didn't happen at all. Had he been wrong about Philip? Maybe the smiling wife was a front. Maybe he liked young boys and was planning to fly Zach somewhere they wouldn't be caught.

Panic drenched him as various hideous scenarios played through his head, none of them worth the thrill of a plane ride.

One of the many disadvantages of being worthless was that when you disappeared, no one cared or asked questions.

Philip had looked at him steadily. "It's going to cost you. You're going to scrub out toilets and clean up boats until you're old enough to take on more responsibility.

After that you're going to train to be a camp counselor. You like the forest, so I'd suggest wilderness training. You'll learn survival skills. Not the sort you've learned so far, but how to live alongside nature. There's no catch, Zach. No one is trying to screw you over. I'm offering to teach you to fly, that's all. At your age my dad took me up. I wanted to do the same for you."

"Why?" The suspicion refused to die.

"Because everyone needs a break now and then, and no one needs it more than you."

The one thing he'd never been given in life was a break. Black eyes, swollen lips, broken bones—he'd been given all those things several times over, but this—this was something else.

For a horrible moment he'd thought he was going to break down right there and howl like a baby. It was years of practice at burying his feelings that saved him from humiliation.

"Right." His throat had felt swollen and thick, as if he'd been caught in the neck by an insect with a big fat stinger. "Whatever makes you feel good."

"There are rules."

Rules had never stopped him doing anything. Mostly he stepped over them. Sometimes he kicked them in the teeth, but they never got in his way. Noticing Philip's serious expression, he'd decided the least he could do was look as if he cared. "I'm listening."

"No more taking things that don't belong to you, no more being a badass. Flying a plane is serious business."

Flying. The word made his mouth dry and his heart pound.

The guy was serious. He really was offering to teach him to fly. He probably thought it would change his life or something, which meant here was another do-good jerk he was going to disappoint, but who cared?

Zach figured that wasn't his problem. To fly he would have promised anything.

How hard would it be to clean up his act?

So he had to stop stealing. Most of the kids here didn't have shit worth taking anyway. Zach stole to ward off boredom and because it was his way of hitting back at them, not because he wanted what they had. He wouldn't have been seen dead in a fancy sweatshirt.

"Sure." He'd kept his tone casual. "I guess I can do that."

And he had.

From that moment on, his life had a purpose and that purpose was flying.

Everything he did, he did for that one reason.

Math and physics had seemed pointless and boring taught in a classroom to thirty kids with glazed expressions, but math and physics applied to the science of flying gripped him. Hungry for knowledge, he'd studied it all and his brain had come alive.

But what he loved most of all was the plane.

Philip had taken him up every summer until he was finally old enough to learn. The first time he'd been allowed to take the controls his hands had shaken so much he'd been sure he was going to ditch the thing in the ocean.

When Philip had told him he was a natural he swelled with something he'd never felt before.

Pride.

The praise had fed him, nurtured him and ultimately freed him.

On the ground his life was a dead end with no way

out, but in the air he saw more than sunshine and fluffy clouds beyond the horizon. He saw a world without limits, full of possibilities.

He saw hope.

With the aircraft he achieved a depth of understanding he'd never reached with another human being.

A social worker had once told him the only thing he was good at was screwing up. Given that she'd caught him breaking into her office to make his own additions to the case file she had on him, he hadn't disagreed. He would even have considered it a fair summary of his talents. Until he'd put his hands on the controls of a plane. Then he'd known immediately there was something else he was good at.

From that moment on, flying was the only thing that mattered.

Flying satisfied his need for adventure and excitement and it leveled the field. Up in the air, he was equal to anyone. Not just equal, superior. Most times passengers didn't speak to the pilot so he did what he loved and some stupid fucker with more money than sense paid him to do it.

For the first time in his life, he'd pushed himself. Challenged himself.

He'd dragged all the information he could from Philip and thirsted for more. Even when Philip had taken him in and given him a home, he'd still thirsted. After spending his formative years trapped and helpless, something in him needed to be free. Why stay in Maine when there was a whole world out there waiting to be discovered?

He'd flown in places most pilots chose to avoid, places with more land than people, including remote parts of Alaska with no runway and enough ice to freeze a plane out of the sky, until finally he'd returned to the island that on a good day he almost regarded as home.

His reputation as a pilot was such that he'd immediately been offered a job by Maine Island Air, the company that flew freight and passengers around the islands.

Zach didn't want that life.

To him, flying was freedom. He didn't want his days dictated by someone else's schedule and demands and anyway, thanks to a stroke of luck and his instinct to live life closer to the edge than most people, he now owned his own plane.

So instead of taking the job, he'd used that sharp brain Philip had identified and noticed the number of superwealthy individuals who owned property around Penobscot Bay. Those people flew into Boston on their Citation or Gulfstream and then needed something private and personal to transport them onward to their beach house or yacht. They needed a pilot skilled enough to land anywhere, on land or sea.

For a fee that made him laugh out loud, Zach offered that service.

Personal?

Yeah, he made it personal. Hell, he offered bottles of chilled champagne and caviar on silver platters if that's what they wanted, although he didn't recommend it because with the crosswinds across the bay the one thing he couldn't guarantee was a bump-free ride.

It never ceased to amaze him how much people were willing to pay for the privilege of picking the time, the place and, most importantly of all, exclusivity. For one flight ferrying a rich banker and his family from their private jet to their private island, he made enough to ensure he didn't have to work for the next month.

It was robbery, but for once he was on the right side of the law.

He picked and chose the jobs he took and had sufficient funds to play with projects that interested him.

If all the people who had written him off could see him now, they'd choke on their good intentions.

Looking back, he always divided his life into two parts. Before flying and after flying. Before flying was a time he chose to forget, a time when his world had been small and terrifying with no escape. After flying—after flying was the world he chose to live in now, and it was a world he loved.

Zach smiled as he completed his preflight check.

It was a bright sunny summer morning in Maine and today the man bankrolling his lifestyle was Nik Zervakis, a Greek-American billionaire who was landing in Logan and wanted one of his female guests flown direct to Puffin Island. Which meant that in exchange for flying one rich pampered princess across the bay, Zach was going to make an obscene amount of money.

The businessman in him was satisfied.

The badass was laughing his head off.

"I want to fly this way for the rest of my life." Cocooned by the feather-soft leather seat of the Gulfstream, Brittany closed her eyes. "No more tedious queues, no more screaming toddlers wriggling in the seat next to me, no more lost baggage and no more trying not to breathe while strangers cough all over you. Push Lily out of the window, Nik, and marry me instead. We can make it work, I know we can. You own four properties—we don't even need to see each other. You can live in San Francisco. I can live in New York."

Bronzed, handsome and filthy rich, Nik Zervakis was scrolling through his emails with one hand while with the other he kept a possessive hold on Lily.

It made Brittany smile to see them together.

She was sharp enough to know that her own laughably brief experience of marriage colored her judgment and careful enough not to apply that judgment to others. Even she had to admit she'd never met two people more perfect for each other than Nik and Lily. And if a small part of her felt wistful, she chose to ignore it.

Lily almost hummed with contentment. "You love your independence."

"You're right, I do. And even a Greek-American billionaire with a private jet isn't going to persuade me to give it up. All the same—" She glanced around at luxury living and shook her head in disbelief. "You've won the lottery, Lil."

"I know." Her friend smiled up at the man who had swept her off her feet and he lowered his head and delivered a lingering kiss to her mouth.

Brittany was fascinated by the sight of the notoriously ruthless business tycoon softened to the consistency of butter by her sweet-natured friend. There was no doubt in her mind that they shared something deep and special.

"Hey, you need to watch out—you've turned into a pushover, Zervakis. If your competitors find out, your shares will plummet. Economies will shatter."

Without shifting his attention from Lily's mouth, Nik made a rude gesture in her direction and Brittany grinned.

"Don't mind me. You guys go ahead and make a baby right here and now. I'll look the other way."

Lily pulled away with a murmur of embarrassment. "Sorry."

"Don't apologize. It was decent of you to give me a lift. The good news is I'm getting off at this stop and the two of you can rip each other's clothes off all the way to New York."

"We're spending a few days in Boston first. Nik's meeting isn't until Tuesday, so if you need anything, call. Then we'll be in New York for a few days and I've arranged to meet up with Skylar." Lily touched her fingers to the necklace at her throat and her gaze slid briefly to Nik's. "We're going to her exhibition in London in December. Will you be there?"

Brittany knew that the necklace, one of Skylar's exclusive pieces, retailed for more than she'd earn in a year as an archaeologist.

She opened her mouth to remind her friend that not everyone had access to a private jet and a bottomless bank account, but then remembered that such a response was likely to illicit all sorts of generous offers from Lily and Nik, and they'd already done more than enough for her. "Not sure. I have some big decisions to make. Life plans." Which was a more impressive way of saying she didn't have a clue what she was going to do next. "But I'll be in touch. That's if you can stop kissing for long enough to pick up a text."

As the plane taxied to a stop, Lily eased herself out of Nik's possessive grasp and gathered together Brittany's belongings. "No, don't move. It's important that you don't use your hand. You have to rest that wrist. Doctor's orders."

"I'm not good with orders."

"We've been roommates all summer. I know exactly how bad you are with orders, but, Brittany, it was a nasty break. You fell awkwardly."

"Yeah, I know. So embarrassing. I'd kick myself, except with my current luck I'd probably break an ankle doing it."

Lily gave her a hug. "You're injured. You have to look after yourself."

"I can look after myself." Not for a moment did she reveal how much it cost her simply to drag her purse from under the seat and slide it over her shoulder. Her left shoulder. The movement felt awkward and unnatural. It wasn't until she'd lost the use of her right hand that she'd realized how much she depended on it. Apparently she didn't do much with the left side of her body.

Why hadn't she looked where she was going? She'd been on archaeological digs all over the world and never gotten so much as a scratch and now she had a broken wrist, and all because she'd been laughing so hard she'd fallen into the trench she'd been excavating moments earlier.

Living that one down was going to take her through to the next ice age.

Rolling her eyes, she reached for her backpack only to find Nik had already placed it on the seat.

"My staff will unload your case. Your onward flight is all arranged. If you encounter any problems, call my cell. I'll have my people sort it out."

My people.

She smiled at him, this man who ran a small empire and was responsible for the employment of so many. He was sophisticated and intelligent. She'd enjoyed spending time with him. If he hadn't fallen in love with her friend, she might have been tempted to sample more than the delights of his conversation. She was sure the hard, honed physique beneath the expensive clothes would be well worth exploring. But unlike Lily, she would have handed him back at the end of the encounter.

She wasn't interested in permanence, either in her relationships or where she lived. Better to move on, as humans had done for centuries.

She took the card he handed her. "Are you sure this flight to Puffin Island is all arranged? I can easily get a cab and take the ferry. It's what I usually do. Cram in with the rest of humanity."

"With a broken wrist? No." Nik was polite but firm. "A friend of mine owns a place in Bar Harbor and he has a pilot he uses for transfers to his yacht."

"Of course he does. Because how else would you get from your beach home to your yacht? It's a problem I've often pondered." She made a joke of it, and wondered if he even realized how different his world was from most people's. "Just as long as your pilot isn't expecting to drop me at *my* yacht. I do own a kayak, but I'm guessing that doesn't count."

Lily handed her the hat she'd tucked under the seat. "You have a beach house. Castaway Cottage. After everything you've told me about it, I'm determined that Nik and I are going to visit one day."

"I hope you do." Brittany wondered what Nik, who owned homes in San Francisco, New York, London and Greece, would make of her simple beach house and then shrugged away the thought. It was home and she loved it. And simple or not, it was worth a lot of money. She'd had numerous offers from people willing to pay for the privilege of living in the relative seclusion of Shell Bay on the much-sought-after Puffin Island.

But Brittany had never considered selling.

Castaway Cottage was special to her.

True, there had been times growing up when the community on Puffin Island had felt suffocating, but whenever she returned home after long absences she discovered how much she missed it. After the relentless summer heat of Greece it would be bliss to feel the cool breeze on her face and fall asleep listening to the crash of the surf. She wanted to taste lobster and pick blueberries. Most of all she wanted to see her two closest friends.

Emily was now living on the island and Skylar was only a short flight away in Manhattan.

"How will you manage?" Lily was still fussing. "How are you going to cook and care for yourself? You struggled when you tried to change midflight."

Halfway across the Atlantic Brittany had roused herself enough to use the sleek bathroom in the Gulfstream and change into clean shorts and a simple strap top. Lily, ever sensitive, had appeared and offered to brush and braid her hair. It drove Brittany crazy that she couldn't do it herself and she was forced to admit that Lily had a point.

How *was* she going to manage with just one hand? Cook? Shower?

For someone as independent as her, the next few weeks were going to be frustrating.

"I'll be fine. I can eat cereal from the packet with my left hand."

"Do you need me to come and stay for a while?" Lily's

warmth and generosity was one of the many reasons Brittany loved her. They'd been working together on the same project for several months in Greece, sharing a small airless bedroom. Brittany knew that, living in such close quarters, it was Lily's patience that had prevented irritation arising. And it was that sweet nature that had snared the notoriously tough Nik Zervakis, who had the sense to know when he'd struck gold and put an enormous diamond on Lily's finger before anyone else could.

"You need to start your new life. And if there's one thing there's plenty of on Puffin Island, it's help. My friend Emily is living in the cottage right now so I'll be fine. Go and have fun. But invite me to the wedding."

Lily's face lit up like a lightbulb. "Of course. We were thinking we might get married next summer in Greece. I want Nik's family to be there. I don't have family of my own so I've adopted his."

Brittany smiled. Of all the benefits that came from marrying a shockingly wealthy man, the thing her friend coveted most was not the size of his wallet or his powerful connections but his family.

"I might be there next summer," she said. "I haven't decided. My research post has finished so I need to think about next steps. And whatever step I take, I need to do it without breaking my wrist again. Stay in touch." She moved to the front of the plane. A small part of her envied her friend. Not the wealth, although money was always useful of course. No, what she envied was the connection Lily had with Nik. The closeness. Their relationship had been a whirlwind, but no one who saw them could possibly believe what they shared was anything other than deep, genuine and long lasting. Already their depth of understanding and mutual appreciation was rooted deep.

She'd never had that.

Even in her short, ill-fated marriage, she'd never had emotional intimacy.

Giving her friends a final farewell hug, she left the luxury of the plane and made her way to the Cessna seaplane that would take her direct to Puffin Island.

She was relieved to have been spared the ferry. At this time of year it would be crowded with day-trippers and summer visitors keen to enjoy all that Puffin Island had to offer. In recent years the island had attracted a colorful crowd—artists, musicians, wealthy folk looking for an exclusive retreat that still offered the trappings of civilization.

Brittany was happy to use Wi-Fi when it was available, but equally happy when it wasn't. To her, *luxury* was a word that could as easily be applied to a night sleeping in the desert under a canopy of stars as it could to a night in a five-star hotel sleeping in silk sheets. Luxury was the freedom to explore and indulge her adventurous spirit.

In pursuit of that adventure, she'd traveled the world. After leaving the United States, she'd moved to the UK and done her master's and then her doctorate. During her time she'd followed in the footsteps of Hiram Bingham and trekked the Inca trail to the lost city of Machu Picchu, joined excavations in Egypt and virtually adopted Greece as her second home. But Maine—Maine was her first home and always would be.

Her heart was here. Her roots. Her history.

As an archaeologist, she was someone who knew the importance of roots and history.

With a smile of anticipation, she pulled out her phone

and sent a quick text to Emily, who had been using Castaway Cottage over the summer.

I'm at Logan. Can't wait to catch up.

It was ironic that she'd offered Emily the sanctuary of the cottage when Emily was in trouble, and now Brittany was in trouble herself.

That turn of events had been unexpected.

Brittany slid her phone back into her pocket and glanced at her wrist. The plaster felt hot and heavy against her skin. The restriction of movement frustrated her. Still, it could be worse. It was nothing a few weeks of rest wouldn't heal, and it would give her time to work out what she wanted to do next. Should she apply for a tenure-track faculty job in the United States? Or maybe return to Cambridge where she'd spent so many happy years, or even Greece? She loved everything about the island of Crete. The history, the climate, the food, the people.

She'd spent the early part of the summer flirting with Spyros, a local archaeologist who had been part of the team from Athens. He'd made it clear he was up for more than flirtation, but at the time she'd chosen to keep their relationship platonic. Now she was wondering if that had been a mistake. She'd enjoyed their friendship. He was attractive and charming.

Maybe she should invite him over for a few weeks. Maybe she'd take their relationship a step beyond flirtation. No further, of course. She never went further.

She was pondering her options as she walked to the Cessna that was to be her transport to the island.

Usually when she returned home she took the *Captain*

Hook, the ferry that did the trip between Puffin Island and the mainland three times a day. She'd grown up listening to the boom of the horn and the clatter of cars as they drove off the ramp onto the road that led from the harbor. Once or twice over the years she'd used the services of Maine Island Air, the company that flew cargo, locals and tourists between the islands of Penobscot Bay. On those occasions she often found herself wedged between the mail and several grocery orders.

This experience was going to be different.

For once, she was arriving in style.

Imagining what the residents of Puffin Island would say when word got around that she'd arrived on a private plane, Brittany smiled to herself. Dan, who worked up at the airstrip, would tell his wife, Angie, who would mention it in Harbor Stores or the Ocean Club, the favorite watering hole of the locals. From there it would travel across the island faster than the wind blew. It was a joke on Puffin Island that gossip traveled faster than the internet. It was certainly more reliable. There were times when the lack of privacy drove her insane but other times when it had proved useful, like recently when the islanders had closed ranks to protect Emily from trouble.

She felt a rush of affection for them. True, they occasionally drove her crazy with their interfering ways, but there was no doubting the strength of the community.

Suddenly eager to get home, she hoisted her backpack onto her shoulder, dragged her single suitcase behind her and strolled the last few steps towards the plane, thinking that she wasn't dressed for such an upmarket mode of transport.

The pilot was probably more used to matching Louis Vuitton luggage than the tough outdoor gear she hauled around the world on her archaeological digs and she was pretty sure Manolo Blahnick would have cried if he'd seen her favored footwear. Her boots were scuffed and sturdy, built for hiking across rough, unforgiving terrain, although even they hadn't been able to prevent her falling in Greece.

Thanks to her carelessness she was facing a summer of inactivity. She had regular appointments at the hospital scheduled, all of which would require a tedious trip to the mainland. To be sure of regaining full mobility in her right wrist, they'd told her she needed to be patient.

As she walked up to the Cessna, the pilot appeared at the top of the steps.

Dark glasses shielded his eyes, but she felt a jolt of instant recognition followed by a strange flutter in her stomach and an alarming shake of her knees.

It had been ten years, but she would have known him anywhere.

The shoulders under the crisp white shirt were broader and thickened with hard muscle, the glossy black hair cropped shorter, but he had that same "don't fuck with me" attitude that had drawn her adventure-seeking eighteen-year-old self all those years before. A million times since then she'd wished she'd looked for another way of enjoying an adrenaline rush, like bungee jumping or white-water rafting.

Instead she'd gone after bad boy Zachary Flynn. On an island bursting with fresh fruit, he'd been the one bad apple.

In the first dizzying weeks of their relationship she'd thought there could be no bigger adventure than love. Her feelings for him had overwhelmed her and made her vulnerable, open and exposed. She'd spent the entire summer walking around the island on legs the consistency of jelly, her stomach clenched in nervous knots. Her ability to sleep had vanished along with her appetite. Overnight, her vision for her future had changed.

She'd had plans and ambitions, but for Zachary Flynn she'd thrown them all away. Her life and her future had taken a different shape. Faced with a choice, she'd chosen him. And when she'd given him everything, all of herself, he'd walked away with a shattering disregard for her and she'd crashed so hard she still had the bruises. She'd often thought the damage would have been less had she jumped from a plane without a parachute.

"One female passenger, and it's you." His handsome face was inscrutable. "What are the chances."

"Given that I live here, I'd say the chances are pretty high." She held herself together, whipped up the control and calm she'd mastered over the years. Despite the turmoil inside she refused to give him any clues about her emotions, nor did she need to study his face for clues as to how he was feeling. She already knew he felt nothing.

"I thought you were living in Greece. Rumor has it you're the female Indiana Jones."

She'd heard it all before, all the jokes about whips, hats, snakes and rolling boulders. Usually she made a flippant response, but not today.

He strolled onto the tarmac and lifted her case before she could stop him. The luggage label flipped over and caught his eye. "Dr. Forrest?" He studied it, and then her. "So you lived up to everyone's expectations."

His statement made her feel dull and boring, as if her whole life had been mapped out in front of her. Which of course it had, apart from a brief diversion when she'd met him.

"I studied archaeology because it was what I wanted to do. My choice was my own. And Puffin Island is my home. Always has been." And it had been her relationship with him that had driven her from it. She couldn't stand the sympathy, the pitying glances, the *I told you so*s every time she'd ventured into town. Stewing in her own mistake, it had been impossible to forget and move on while she was living on the island. "What are you doing here, Zach? Last thing I heard you were flying in the wilds of Alaska." And from time to time she'd hoped he had developed frostbite in certain vital parts of his anatomy.

Irritation and a touch of outrage merged with something that felt disturbingly close to panic.

He had no right to be here in her space, her part of the world.

She'd moved on, built a life. She had no wish to be forced to confront the path she hadn't taken.

"I'm flying people with more money than sense to the islands. Today that seems to be you."

"Would you have refused if you'd known?"

The corners of his beautiful mouth hinted at a smile. "I'd fly the devil if he paid me. I don't care who's in the passenger seat as long as the money is in my account." His drawl was deep and dark with hints of sophistication that disguised the truth about his background.

When she'd first met him he'd been damaged, bitter and rebellious. He'd cared for no one. Trusted no one.

She'd thought she could change all that. She'd made that classic mistake of thinking she could be the one to tame the wild in him.

Her brain had gone missing in action the day she'd decided to go after Zachary Flynn. To someone who had spent her life on a small island where she knew almost every face she saw in the street, he'd proved fascinating. She'd always striven to exceed people's expectations. Zach, it seemed, had lived to smash them into the ground.

He'd been the forbidden fruit. The boy every good girl avoided.

He was black to her white, dark to her light, hard to her soft.

Her one big mistake.

In a wild attempt to prove everyone wrong, she'd proved them right.

They'd warned that he'd break her heart and he had. And he'd done it in the most humiliating way possible.

She transferred her attention to the plane. "So this is what you do now?"

"If you mean I target people with too much money and help myself to some of it then yeah, this is what I do. And it seems I'm your ride." He removed his sunglasses and stood to one side. "Climb aboard, princess."

She didn't want to climb aboard. She wanted to run.

Panic nailed her feet to the ground, but pride drove her forward. If she turned away now he'd know it was because of him. And anyway, if she did that, how was she going to get to the island? In this case practicality had to take precedence over emotions. Alternative transport would be expensive and uncomfortable. Her wrist was already hurting and her head was fuzzy from a combination of lack of sleep and the long flight. The hospital had suggested she remain in Greece for another week to recuperate before traveling. Lily had insisted that private travel would make the journey a thousand times easier and Brittany had agreed.

The one thing she hadn't done was ask questions about her onward transfer to the island.

Why would she? It would never have crossed her mind the pilot could be Zach.

And how pathetic would she be if she let a joke marriage that had lasted barely five minutes affect her after a whole decade? She was bigger than that.

Telling herself it was only a twenty-minute hop at most and that Zach was going to be too busy flying the plane to take any notice of her, Brittany walked up the steps. She was careful to avoid eye contact. He was strikingly good-looking, but it was those eyes that had been her downfall. They were so dark they seemed black, the hard gleam radiating his deep suspicion of mankind. He'd had a way of watching her, his hooded gaze brooding and dangerous, as if daring her to stop wondering and fantasizing, and take the leap.

Never one to turn down a challenge, she'd taken the dare.

It had been like trying to tame a feral beast that was inevitably going to turn on her.

She brushed past him and felt the hard swell of his biceps brush against her bare arm. She jerked back, but not before a rush of awareness had burned through her body.

Her gaze slid to his shadowed jaw and from there to the hard lines of his mouth.

She still remembered how it had felt to be kissed by him, and remembering kicked her heart rate up a notch.

"Nice plane." Her voice was as cold as a Maine winter. "Did you steal it?"

Her question drew a flicker of a smile. "No, this time I was the one who was robbed. You have no idea what price they pin on this baby."

She wanted to ask how he could afford it, but didn't want to show that much interest, so instead she slid into one of the large leather seats. She wished now she'd chosen to wear something less casual than shorts. They were the practical choice for the life she led, and her favorite product was high-factor sunscreen. She'd learned that any makeup she applied was quickly sweated off in the heat, so she restricted herself to a lip balm that protected against the sun.

As a result, her selection of cosmetics remained mostly unused, but she was woman enough that if she'd known she was going to meet Zachary Flynn after a gap of ten years, she would have raided the makeup counter. Maybe even worn a dress and heels, though her wardrobe contained few examples of either. With enough advance warning she would have called Skylar, who had a talent for color and dressing people.

With the help of her friends, she would have planned the meeting carefully, deciding how she was going to handle it and what she was going to say so that she controlled every moment of the reunion. And she wouldn't have chosen to do it this way.

Knowing that he was studying her, Brittany resisted the temptation to shift in her seat.

Yeah, that's right, take a good look at what you gave up. Are you sorry now?

Finally she looked at him, looked into those flinty eyes framed by lashes as dark as coal. Her heart started to pound and her head spun. *Tired*, she thought. *I'm tired, that's all.* But she knew it wasn't the long flight or the time change that was responsible for the shift in her heart rate. It was seeing him. Panic ripped through her because she didn't want to feel anything and she was feeling— everything.

Damn him.

Damn every supersexy inch of him.

Maybe flying private wasn't so great after all. Right now she would even have embraced a bunch of screaming toddlers. Anything to dilute the tension. "So who are we waiting for? Am I your only passenger?"

"The rich don't share. I'm exclusively yours."

He'd never been exclusively hers, not even when he'd slid that cheap, hastily purchased gift-store ring onto her finger and spoken words that had almost jammed in his throat. Their marriage had been the shortest exclusive deal on record. He'd lasted ten days before walking out of her life. Brittany had been raised to believe that people kept their promises but had learned that words, at least when they were uttered by Zachary Flynn, were meaningless. It had been a devastating betrayal of her trust. Hadn't she believed in him when no one else had? Hadn't she defended and excused him? *He's had a bad childhood, it's not surprising he doesn't trust people when they've always let him down.* She'd said those things to anyone and everyone who would listen and ignored warnings and dire prophecies. She'd been a true friend to him and he'd cast that friendship aside as if it were nothing.

"Let's go. If I'm the only passenger, then there's nothing keeping us from taking off."

"Sit down and strap in. There's a strong crosswind today. You're going to be shaken up some."

She was already shaken up, and it had nothing to do with the crosswind.

Relieved it was a short flight, Brittany reached for the seat belt but he was there before her. Those strong fingers tangled with hers and she flattened herself to the seat.

"I can do it." Being helpless brought out the worst in

her and she snatched her good hand away just as he eased back, a gleam in his eyes.

"Still the same old Brittany. So who did you punch?"

"What do you mean?" She wasn't the same Brittany. The girl who had danced willingly into that reckless, short-lived marriage wasn't the same girl who had limped out.

"Unless you're wearing that cast for show, you've broken your wrist." He straightened his shoulders. Shoulders she'd once explored with her fingers and mouth. She knew he had a scar at the top of his right shoulder blade and another under his ribs on the left. He'd refused to discuss either. To her knowledge, apart from the social workers who had removed him from his abusive home, the only person who knew the details of his past was Philip Law and she suspected even he only knew a small part of the story. The rest Zach buried deep inside, allowing no one access. "Just wondered what happened to the other person. Knowing you, they came off worse."

"You don't know me." And she didn't want to think about how well he'd once known her. She didn't want to think about the way he'd touched her, kissed her and made her feel alive. "So why are you back in the area?" Brittany tried to remember what Nik had said about his friend. "You're living in Bar Harbor?"

"No. I have a client who has a place at Bar Harbor. I'm living on Puffin Island."

It was the worst news possible. "You're *living* here now?"

"Is that going to give you a problem?"

It was going to give her a big problem.

After their relationship had gone south, she'd retreated to Castaway Cottage and watched the sun rise and set

over beautiful Shell Bay. With the help of her grandmother, and later her friends, she'd pieced herself back
together. She'd traveled the world, but still regarded Puffin Island as her home.

Her home, not his.

Finding him here was like discovering a fly on your
food. It felt contaminated.

"We haven't seen each other in ten years, Zach. You're
not part of my life and I'm not part of yours. I don't give
a damn where you live."

As long as it's not on my island.

"You're sure?" His gaze was steady on hers. "Plenty
of women would be bearing a grudge."

"Because you walked out on me ten days after our
wedding?" She managed a laugh. "You did us both a
favor by ending it when you did. Instead of throwing
my whole life away, I threw away a few weeks. I don't
begrudge you a few weeks, Zach."

"It was a whole summer."

"I wasn't counting." She'd counted every day. Every
hour. "And talking of counting, my friend is paying you
big bucks to fly me to the island so let's do it. I'd hate
for him to fire you."

"I don't work for him, I work for myself. I decide when
I fly. I pick the jobs and the people." Something flickered
in his eyes. "Taking orders isn't one of my strengths. You
should know that."

She did know that. And she no longer cared enough
to make excuses for his bad behavior.

The details of his past were hazy, and that haze had
succeeded in fueling the rumors. Rumors of an abusive
childhood, of a life where the law turned up at the door
more often than the mailman, of a boy who had moved

from one place to another, never sticking. Those rumors had flown around the island and a few people who had never before locked their doors had started locking them whenever Zach had shown up as part of the scholarship program at Camp Puffin.

He'd come back every summer and stayed the whole time. As a result he became a familiar figure on the island.

His background had made him a suspect for every crime committed, something that had outraged teenage Brittany, who had a strong sense of justice and believed everyone was innocent until proven guilty. It had frustrated her that he'd been indifferent to people's unflattering assumptions.

Even when he'd finally moved in with Philip and Celia Law, he still hadn't been entirely free of suspicion.

"I'm tired," she croaked. "It's been a long journey, so why don't you do whatever it is you do to make this thing fly and take me to Puffin Island."

For a brief, unsettling moment she thought he was going to say something else. Then he handed her a headset, turned and strolled to the pilot's seat, casual and relaxed.

Brittany tried to relax, too.

The sooner he took the controls, the sooner this whole awkward encounter would be over.

Except that now her life was in his hands. As someone who liked to be in control of her own destiny, it didn't feel good. It was hard to forget what he'd done with her heart when she'd trusted him with that.

She remembered overhearing Philip telling her grandmother that Zach was the most gifted pilot he'd ever taught, but that his brilliance could easily slip over the line into reckless and wild. He was fearless, or maybe it was just that an unspeakable childhood had set his bar for fear higher than most people's.

Exhausted, her wrist throbbing, Brittany swallowed. She knew all about reckless and wild. She'd been both those things when she'd been with him.

Watching him slide into the pilot's seat, she felt her heart bump hard against her ribs.

He'd said he'd fly the devil as long as he was paid, but she knew the devil was already in the plane.

And he had his hands on the controls.

Chapter 2

"I should have warned you." Emily hauled Brittany's suitcase into the cottage, maneuvering it over the blue-and-white-striped rug that welcomed visitors to the beach hideaway. The colors had faded over the years but the familiarity of it was as soothing as hot soup on a cold day.

"How could you have warned me?"

"Sky and I saw him a few weeks ago. We decided as you weren't here you didn't need to know. We assumed he'd be long gone before you came home. If you hadn't broken your wrist, you wouldn't have known."

"Don't you believe it. This is Puffin Island. I would have heard about it the moment I stepped off the ferry. There are no secrets in this place. Although somehow I missed the fact you've moved out of the cottage. Tell me the details."

"Later. Let's unload the car first."

Brittany walked through to the kitchen. The sun flooded in from the garden, bouncing light across the room. For a moment she saw her grandmother, standing in front of the stove, humming as she stirred and tasted.

One blink and the image vanished, but the ache in her chest remained.

Everything looked the same. The jars of brightly colored sea glass collected on trips to the beach, the hurricane lamp and strangely shaped piece of driftwood Brittany had found washed up on the shore as a child. Everything was as it should be, each piece part of the jigsaw that created a picture of her childhood.

The only gap was the one left by her grandmother.

She missed her all the time, but never more so than now. *He's back, Grams, and I don't know what to do.*

Emily followed her into the room. "I put your case in the bedroom. It weighs a ton. Please tell me it's not full of Bronze Age weapons."

"That case contains my life. A bit sad that I can cram it all into one suitcase." But she knew her grandmother wouldn't have agreed. *People, experiences, those are the things of real value, Brittany.*

She slumped on the kitchen chair, exhausted from the journey and the stress of keeping up the pretense of indifference in front of Zach. The worst thing was that she didn't want it to be pretense. She wanted to feel indifference and it worried her that she didn't.

How could seeing a man who had walked out on her without a backward glance make her feel weak at the knees? "Do you know what's crazy about all this? I'm over him. I really am. I know people say that, but I mean it. So why am I feeling like this?" She ran her hand over her face and Emily walked across and gave her a hug.

"Anyone would be unsettled to meet their ex after such a long time, especially after the relationship ended the way yours did. And on top of that you're jet-lagged and in pain. What you're feeling is totally normal. Don't overthink it, Brittany."

"I'm not." It was a lie and both of them knew it. "My relationship with him was the one big failure of my life and I hate failing. Seeing him back here is like finding someone spray painted 'you screwed up' on a wall."

"If you'd given us more notice we could have killed him and hidden his body before you arrived home."

"How did you even recognize him? You never met him."

"The first thing you did when you arrived at college was stick a picture of him on your wall and ask us to decorate it."

"I remember. I met my two best friends because of him. I suppose I should be grateful."

"I was responsible for the warts on his nose. The three of us stared at his face every night for three months. Skylar gave him a skin condition with her paints and you pushed pins into him. By the time you stopped crying yourself to sleep he had multiple piercings that weren't of his choosing. It was kind of a shock to come face-to-face with him and not see a face riddled full of holes. And it's a memorable face. Not hard to see why you fell for him."

"Take a good look. His face won't be so memorable once I've rearranged those perfect features. It's amazing how much damage a girl can do with a plaster cast." Brittany closed her eyes briefly, trying to calm the pool of emotion simmering inside her, but even with her eyes shut all she saw were strong features and dark masculinity. "Thanks for the ride. I should have called a cab but

I couldn't face handling the questions Pete would throw at me. Did I drag you away from something important?"

"No. And whatever I was doing would have been less important than meeting my best friend at the airport after a long flight. Wait there." Emily vanished to the car and returned moments later with her arms loaded up with bags. "I stocked up at the store after I got your text. I assumed you wouldn't have anything in so I bought the basics."

"As long as the basics include soda, I'm happy." Brittany eyed the bags gratefully, hoping they were full of food that didn't require two hands to prepare. "You're a friend in a million."

"So are you." Emily piled the bags on the table. "I can't ever repay you for letting me use this place. You saved me. And Lizzy. We owe you so much."

"You don't owe me anything. And talking of friends, I'm guessing Ryan knows Zach is back?"

"Yes." Emily pushed milk and cheese into the fridge. "Like I said, you weren't here and it's not as if Zach has a habit of sticking around."

"You're talking to the woman he married and then left less than two weeks after so I know exactly how long he generally sticks around." It annoyed her that she felt so unsettled. So what if he was back? She'd hurt and healed. It was in the past. And although the past fascinated her so much she'd made it her career, that fascination didn't extend to her own history.

"Are you mad with us for not telling you?"

"I'm so churned up inside I don't know what I'm feeling." Brittany sighed and shook her head. "No, of course I'm not mad. In your position I wouldn't have told me, either."

"It seemed like the right decision at the time, but it seems like the wrong one now."

"Yeah, well, I know all about that, too. I married Zach thinking it was the right decision and look how that turned out."

Emily was still unloading food. "Did you eat on the flight? I can cook you something. I bought eggs, and a fresh loaf from the bakery."

"Thanks, but I'm not hungry." She felt as if her stomach was doing gymnastics.

"You have to eat something." Emily handed her a bag. "Here. Blueberry muffins I baked fresh this morning."

"Seriously?" Brittany peered into the bag and sniffed. "Since when do you cook?"

"Since I inherited a six-year-old girl. I have also learned to braid hair, make pasta necklaces and fix torn fairy wings. And before you accuse me of gender bias, I should tell you I'm also skilled at making pirate maps complete with tea stains and authentically burned edges, and last weekend I bought her a bow and arrow. A child's version, obviously."

Brittany felt a flash of guilt. "I haven't even asked how you're both doing. Your life went to hell and I wasn't here and now I *am* here I'm talking about myself. I'm the most selfish friend in the world. Skylar updated me on your recent crisis. The journalist? Bastard. Why would they go after a child?"

"Because the whereabouts of the daughter of a dead movie star are apparently of public interest."

Brittany nibbled the corner of the muffin. "So they came here and tried to trick the islanders into revealing information."

"Which they didn't, of course, because the islanders were amazing. Ryan was amazing." Emily's cheeks turned a deep shade of rose and Brittany looked at her closely.

"I can't believe you're saying that. The first night you arrived you left me a message saying you were on the first ferry out of here. You were threatening to head somewhere landlocked like Wyoming or Nebraska. I know you hate the sea. What happened?"

"I didn't hate it as much as I thought I would."

"There's something different about you."

"This red shirt is new. Sky chose it."

"It's flattering. Better than your usual black. But that's not what I'm seeing. You mentioned you had something to tell me. So tell me."

"Today is about you, not me."

"I need to be distracted from the pain in my wrist and my compelling need to kill my ex. Talk. And I want detail, including the brilliant sex I'm fairly sure you're getting."

Emily gave a choked laugh. "What makes you think that?"

"You're glowing and happy. You've lost that white, pinched look you always had when you were with miserable Neil. I didn't see it immediately, mostly because I was focused on escaping from Zach, but you've changed."

"That's ridiculous. It's just a shirt."

"I'm not talking about the shirt. Your hair is different. A little shorter and you're wearing it loose."

"There's a new hairdresser up at the harbor. Her name is Hanna. Lisa and I wanted to give her some business, that's all."

"She's good. Maybe I'll book myself in. I believe in supporting new businesses on the island." Brittany studied her friend. "You look happy. I'm relieved. I was worried. I felt helpless being so far away when you were going through hell. And Sky was stuck in Manhattan with the soon-to-be senator who suffered a sense-of-humor failure at birth. I didn't know what to do, so I called Ryan."

"I'm glad you did."

"I didn't give him details, just asked him to keep an eye on you." Contemplating her friend's dreamy expression, Brittany laughed. "I'm guessing he kept a very, very close eye on you. Next time I need to be more specific in my brief. I asked him to support you, not seduce you. Not that there's anything wrong with comfort sex and I'm sure Ryan was very good at that side of things."

Emily placed fruit in the bowl in the center of the table. "It's a bit more than comfort sex."

"How much more?"

"We like each other."

"Of course. You went to bed with him. You'd never go to bed with a man you didn't like."

"Love." Emily stumbled over the word. "I love him. He loves me. And if there was a seduction, it was mutual."

Brittany hid her surprise. "Love terrifies you." And she understood why. She, like Skylar, knew all of Emily's secrets. "It always has."

"Yes. But that was before Ryan."

"Well—wow." Brittany felt warmth burn out the chill inside her. Love wasn't something that had worked out for her, nor had it worked out for her parents, but it was great seeing it work out for her friends, especially Emily who had avoided that emotion since childhood. "Seems like we have a *lot* of catching up to do. We should invite

Sky for the weekend. Bottle of chilled wine, pajamas and full confessions all round. It will be just like old times."

"Sounds good."

Brittany watched as her friend pushed her hair back—hair she'd habitually worn secured to the back of her head but which now swung loose around her shoulders. "So is Ryan the reason you're no longer living in my cottage?"

"He asked us to move in with him. We're living in Harbor House."

"His old family home? I love that place. The high ceilings, the views—it's incredible. So this isn't just love, it's serious." She caught sight of the ring on Emily's finger for the first time and gasped. "Is that—? Holy crap, Em. How could I not have noticed that? And why didn't you wave it under my nose?"

"Because you have enough to think about and anyway, it's all been very sudden—"

"But if you know, then why wait, right?" She grabbed Emily's hand and took a closer look and felt her eyes fill. "Em, oh, Em!" She hugged her friend with her good arm and felt tears spill onto her cheeks. "I'm so happy for you both. Two of my favorite people getting married and to each other! I expect to be invited every Thanksgiving and Christmas. This calls for a major celebration."

"I wasn't going to mention it yet. I thought it might be tactless with Zach back on the island."

"Just because my own love life is in a coma and I'm tripping over my ex, doesn't mean I can't be thrilled for my friend. And I *am* thrilled." She released Emily and wiped her hand over her cheek. "Look at me. I'm a sentimental mess. Where did he find that ring?"

"We went to Boston for the weekend."

Examining the glittering stone, Brittany felt something stir inside her. Zach hadn't given her a ring. At the time she hadn't cared. Their impulsive wedding had seemed the ultimate in romantic gestures and she'd told herself that Zachary Flynn wasn't the sort of man to buy a girl a diamond. It had taken her a while to realize it was just another sign that he couldn't be tamed. She'd tried to create a bond with a man who didn't understand the meaning of the word.

Letting go of Emily's hand, she reminded herself that a diamond wouldn't have sealed a relationship that was already cracked beyond repair.

"So if you've moved into Harbor House, where is Ryan's grandmother living?" Agnes Cooper had been her grandmother's closest friend. "Much as I love her, having her as a housemate would be seriously restrictive. No spontaneous sex on the kitchen table."

"Agnes has already moved into one of the retirement cottages."

"Leaving you free to have sex anywhere you like. Well—" Pondering, Brittany sat back in her chair and picked up her soda. "Everything changes. I turn my back for five minutes and my childless, water-hating friend has a child and is living by the water. And in love."

"Not just living by the water. I've learned to swim."

Knowing her friend's phobia of the water and the reasons for it, Brittany choked on her drink. "You went into the water voluntarily?"

"Ryan taught me. I don't love it, but I don't panic. And talking of panic—" Emily helped herself to a tiny piece of muffin. "You didn't know Zach would be flying you today?"

"No. The whole thing was arranged by a friend." Brittany lowered her drink. "Do we know why he's here?"

"Zach? No. Ryan hadn't heard from him in a while and then suddenly he showed up at the Ocean Club a couple of months ago. He owns his own plane and he hires himself out for megabucks which, Ryan says, basically means he gets paid a year's salary for doing a week's work."

"Sounds like Zach."

Emily hesitated. "He isn't entirely mercenary. When Lizzy was sick and needed to go to the hospital on the mainland, he was the one who flew me. No one else would do it because the weather was so wild. It was scary and he was—"

"Reckless?"

"I was going to say brave. And skilled." Emily sent her an awkward glance. "I felt disloyal getting in the plane with him."

"No need. It was a long time ago. I don't have any feelings for him." At least, none she was going to admit to. "And if Lizzy was sick, he should have flown you for free."

"He did."

"Oh." That news jarred with the negative images she was nurturing in her mind. "Well, that's—great. Doesn't sound like Zach, but I still think it's great."

"I guess he charges so much the rest of the time he can afford to be generous occasionally."

"The second part of that sentence doesn't sound like him at all."

The Zach she'd known hadn't wanted to give anything to a society who had given him nothing.

"I've heard that sometimes he'll fly for Maine Island Air if they're overbooked. That's why he flew Sky that day. It depends on his mood."

"Now that *does* sound like him. A moody opportunist." Keeping her voice casual, Brittany stood up. "I'm grateful for the ride, but now you need to get back to Ryan and Lizzy." *And stop talking about Zach.*

"I'll stay and help. It isn't going to be easy with your wrist in a cast."

"No. I want you to go and have wild monkey sex and make up for all those years you were stuck with boring Neil."

"I'm getting that you didn't like Neil."

"He wasn't right for you." Brittany started to help Emily unpack the last of the shopping, but with one hand it wasn't easy. "Let me pay you. My wallet is in my backpack." She glanced across the bags towards her case. "Must still be in your car."

"I don't want your money, but I don't think your backpack is in my car. Are you sure you brought it with you?"

"I had it with me on the flight over. I was so damn desperate to get away from Zach I must have left it on the plane. Crap. It has everything. My passport and my purse. Which means I have no money." Annoyed, Brittany paced across the kitchen. "How could I have been so careless?"

"You're tired, in pain and you met your ex-husband for the first time in years. I'd say you had reason to be distracted. I'll fetch it."

"You've done enough. I'll sort it out tomorrow."

"What if he brings it over?"

The thought unnerved her more than she wanted it to. "He won't. He'll probably hand the bag to Ryan."

"How did he react when he saw you were his passenger?"

"He didn't, but Zach isn't exactly big on showing his feelings." And she'd wanted him to. Once upon a time, she'd wanted him to say those three little words. How many nights had she spent waiting, hoping? "Probably because he didn't feel anything."

"I don't believe that." Emily looked worried. "I don't want to leave you on your own."

"I'm fine." Her smile was bright, swift and totally false. "It was a bit of a shock seeing him, but only because I haven't thought about Zachary Flynn in years. Hearts heal. Bruised feelings heal. And in a way he did me a favor."

"You mean by making your first time unforgettable?"

Brittany felt her whole body heat. "No, I do not mean that. I mean by walking out on me, leaving me free to take up my college place. Can you imagine what my life would have been if he hadn't left me? I wouldn't have done any of the things I've done. Thanks for the lift, Em, but now I need to go to bed and sleep off that journey."

Emily gave her a long look. "You're not going to cry, are you?"

"Are you kidding? The only time I cry is when I'm peeling onions and I can't do that one-handed."

"In that case I'll see you tomorrow." Emily picked up her purse and her keys. "Ryan is treating Lizzy to breakfast at the Ocean Club. Ten o'clock. Join us?"

Her wrist throbbed and her head throbbed. Worse still was the way she felt inside. Wounds, long covered, lay exposed and smarting. She felt weak and vulnerable and she hated feeling that way. "I'll be sleeping."

Emily refused to budge. "You won't. You'll be waking up early and grumpy with jet lag. We'll fix that with coffee. I'll drive over here just before ten."

"You don't give up, do you?"

"I know you're hurting and I'm not going to let you

hurt alone. For now you need sleep, but on the weekend we're going to talk about this. Things always seem better when the three of us are together."

Friends. They laughed with you through the good times and hugged you during the bad. They cheered your successes and bandaged the wounds from falls.

Men came and went from her life, but her friends always had her back.

It made her feel better knowing that. "Thanks for the lift and the shopping. I'll see you at breakfast, but I'll walk. It will do me good. Now go back to your man and your child."

"And my dog."

"*Dog?* Who are you and what have you done with my friend?"

Emily smiled. "Agnes can't cope with Cocoa so we've inherited her. Lizzy is thrilled."

"Man, child, dog and swimming." Brittany shook her head in disbelief. "I've been away too long."

Zach strolled into the busy bar of the Ocean Club and dumped the backpack on the seat next to Ryan, who was deep in conversation with Alec Hunter.

"Can you drop that off next time you're passing?"

"Passing where?"

"Castaway Cottage."

Ryan raised his eyebrows. "Do I look like I work for FedEx? And since when does anyone 'pass' Castaway Cottage? The clue is in the name. It's at the end of the road to nowhere."

"You've been passing it often enough the last month so that you can have sex with the pretty blonde who moved in with the kid who looks like Goldilocks."

"Has someone installed a webcam I don't know about?"

Alec suppressed a yawn. "This is Puffin Island. The most secure place in the whole of the North America. If a caterpillar lifts its head, people can tell you how high. The reason we don't have an island newspaper is because there is nothing anyone could write that the population don't already know." Pushing a beer towards Zach, he said, "Sit down. We bought you a drink in case you joined us." After a moment's hesitation, Zach slid into the vacant seat.

The summer after he'd turned sixteen, he hadn't returned to Boston. Instead, Philip and Celia had taken him in with the approval of the authorities. For months, Zach had lived on a knife edge, waiting for them to tell him they'd made a mistake and that other plans had been made for him, but they never did. Instead of throwing him out, they'd given him a key to their home.

Carrying that key, he'd felt like a fake and a fraud. He knew a hundred different ways to break into a house. He didn't need a key.

Philip had arranged for him to attend the local school and it was there he'd met Ryan.

His closest brush with happiness had been on the days he'd been sucked into Ryan's noisy, disorganized family life.

"How's Rachel? I saw her with Jared."

"Who my little sister dates is her business."

Zach eyed Ryan's fingers, white on the bottle, and knew how hard he was struggling not to make it his business. Knowing that Ryan had all but raised his younger sister after the death of their parents, the protective streak didn't surprise him.

"You could do her hair at the wedding." Knowing

that humor always worked better than sympathy, he went with that. "You always were good with bows and braids."

Ryan shot him a black look. "She's not marrying the guy."

Alec stretched out his legs, a gleam of humor in his eyes. "So it's just sex?"

Ryan cursed softly and ran his hand over the back of his neck. "Why do I feel this way? I'm not her father."

"You care," Alec said mildly, "and caring is the first step towards psychological trauma. Buckle up. It's going to get worse before it gets better."

And sometimes, Zach thought, it never got better.

Sometimes, the trauma was so great you learned how to stop caring.

Ryan drained his beer and looked at Zach. "So how did you end up with Brittany's backpack?"

"She left it in my plane. Your blonde friend gave Brittany a lift home but they managed to leave the backpack." And he'd stared at it for the best part of thirty minutes, weighing up his options, annoyed that he'd been so distracted by seeing her again he hadn't noticed it. "She's back."

"Brittany? Yeah, I know. As you say, I'm having sex with the friend who gave her a lift whose name, by the way, is Emily. For the sake of accuracy I should tell you that her hair is more caramel than blond and we've never actually had sex in Castaway Cottage. Her choice, not mine." Ryan jerked his head towards the beer. "Drink. Given that you just flew your ex-wife in, I'm guessing you're going to need several of these. Or maybe something stronger."

Something stronger sounded tempting, but Zach didn't

want to fight the crowd at the bar. "How do you know I flew her in?"

"Same reason you knew I was having sex with the woman living in her cottage. Nothing travels faster than gossip, especially when it's juicy. And because I'm a man and have no tact or sensitivity, I'm going to ask the question everyone wants to ask. How hard did she punch you?"

Zach reached for the beer. "There was no physical contact." He didn't mention the solid thump in his gut that had come from seeing her again. "It was a civilized encounter."

"Civilized?" Ryan's brows rose. "That doesn't sound like Brittany, especially since the last time she saw you was when you walked out days after your wedding."

"Thanks for the reminder."

Knowing how protective the islanders were of Brittany and how suspicious they were of him, Zach hadn't expected a warm welcome on his return to the island, but Ryan had immediately invited him for a drink at the Ocean Club, sending a clear message to the locals that whatever had happened in the past had no bearing on the present. "For that she didn't black your eye? Are you sure you picked up the right passenger? Fierce brunette who once shot me in the butt with an arrow? I've got money on her taking a swing at you within five minutes of laying eyes on you."

Zach gave a grim smile. "Pay up. Seems like she didn't care enough to take a swing at me."

But it was true he'd expected a greater response from her.

Guilt, an unfamiliar emotion, nagged at him like an old wound.

He'd broken hearts before, right along with rules and property, and it had never bothered him until Brittany.

Unlike everyone else he'd ever met in his life, she'd believed in him.

Turned out living up to someone's expectations had been more of a pressure than living down to them. He knew he'd done her a favor by disappointing her sooner rather than later, but he should have found a less brutal way of doing it.

"Ten years is a long time," Alec said easily. "You were both young. It's history, long forgotten."

Ryan finished his drink. "That's a strange statement from someone who makes a living ensuring history isn't forgotten."

Alec Hunter, a naval historian, had carved out a successful career as a TV presenter and explorer. "That's different. I'm talking about relationship history."

"So am I." Ryan shrugged. "In my experience women don't forget. They nurture the mad and then produce it when you least expect it. Either way, you're doomed, Zach."

"She wasn't mad," Zach said flatly. "She was indifferent."

She'd sat with casual poise, those endless legs bronzed from the Greek sun, her response to seeing him again approaching boredom.

Why should that bother him?

Alec finished his beer. "Last time I checked, archaeologists didn't earn enough to fly private. How could she afford your services?"

Zach thought about the phone call from the Greek offices of ZervaCo. "Seems she's keeping rich company these days."

Ryan gestured across the bar for Tom to bring them more drinks. "You're not exactly struggling yourself."

"My bank account is healthy enough, although I'm a long way off from owning a Gulfstream."

"Would you want to?"

"No." Zach took a mouthful of beer. "It has to be landed on a strip of tarmac."

"Whereas you'd rather land where no sane man would ever venture. So if the reunion was civilized, what's stopping you from delivering the backpack yourself?"

Evading the question, Zach looked across the crowded bar and caught the eye of a young woman who'd been watching him since he'd walked in.

She gave him a shy smile and he immediately looked away.

All his relationships were short-term but he couldn't contemplate even short-term while his ex-wife was jammed in his head.

And shy didn't work for him. He made it a rule not to let himself touch anything breakable or vulnerable.

"I haven't set foot in Castaway Cottage for over a decade." Not since that day Kathleen Forrest had gone to the mainland with her knitting friends, leaving her granddaughter alone in the secluded house on the beach.

The first thing Brittany had done was phone Zach and invite him over.

He'd figured that if the good girl wanted to try her hand at being bad it wasn't his business to talk her out of it.

Remembering what had happened next brought sweat to his forehead. It had been the beginning of a long vacation for his judgment.

He was doing better these days, but barely a day

passed without him encountering someone who wanted to punch him for past offenses.

He'd assumed today was Brittany's turn and no one, least of all himself, would argue that he didn't deserve a hell of a punch for what he'd done to her.

He'd weighed that fact carefully before returning to the island, then decided that since she mostly spent her time traveling and had all the support of the islanders, he was the one who would suffer. Despite his relationship with Philip and his friendship with Ryan, most of the locals still viewed him with suspicion. He figured he'd earned that and anyway, he was used to being on the receiving end of disappointment and disapproval. It didn't bother him. He didn't live his life to please others. He did what felt right to him. Made choices that felt right to him. As long as he could live with himself, that was all that mattered.

But in the end it hadn't been hatred or anger he'd seen in her eyes.

It had been—nothing.

His ex-wife really didn't give a damn that he was occupying her space.

In which case he should just return the bag and have done with it.

She needed it. He had it. It was as simple as that.

Maybe then the two of them could make a go of living side by side.

With a rough curse he snatched up the backpack, ignoring Ryan's curious look.

"I'll take it over there in the morning."

"Why not now?"

"Long flight. She'll be asleep." And there was no way

he wanted to risk seeing her in her pajamas or, worse, naked.

He'd knock on the door, hand it over and leave. No words needed to be exchanged. No emotions, although if she wanted to yell at him he would stand there and take it. He wouldn't even defend himself because how did you defend the indefensible? But in any case, it was clear Brittany no longer had any feelings she wanted to express.

She wasn't looking for closure.

The door between them had been closed a long time.

Chapter 3

Castaway Cottage had stood at the edge of the curve of sand known as Shell Bay for over half a century. Built of clapboard and surrounded by a pretty coastal garden, it had been purchased by Brittany's grandparents just after their marriage.

Brittany's mother, Linda, had been born there and spent the next twenty years longing to escape the confines of island life. At that time the sole economy of the island, like so many in the area, had been fishing. It wasn't until years later that a wealthy Bostonian had discovered the island by chance on a sailing trip and proceeded to build a home. Others had followed and, together with tax breaks encouraging people to live and work there, the fortunes and population of the island had been boosted. But for Linda, life had been all about the lobster and the never-ending cycle of worry that went with the business.

Marriage had been a way out. Brittany's father had worked as an engineer for an oil company and was often away, leaving Linda alone on an island she couldn't wait to escape.

Brittany was ten when her parents had divorced. Her mother had immediately remarried and moved south to Florida. Brittany, settled on the island, had stayed with her grandmother.

Occasionally her mother would visit, more to confirm her life choices than to spend time with her daughter. Her father she'd rarely seen. Wrapped in the warm cocoon of her grandmother's love, Brittany had barely noticed their absence. She'd grown up knowing that families came in different shapes and sizes, and the island community was so small and close-knit, she'd taken for granted the support of a wider group of people who knew and loved her. She'd been taught to swim by Kathleen, her grandmother, but it had been John Harris, the harbormaster, who had settled her down on the edge of the quay one day and shown her how to tie a bowline. John was the first to take her sailing and Dave Brown, who had lobstered the waters around Puffin Island for three decades, had been the one to teach her about the business that had been a mainstay of the island's economy for longer than anyone could remember. Along with other islanders, she'd spent time helping him get ready for the season. She'd scraped the buoys, pressure washed the hull of his boat and painted the side where the surface had chipped from hauling traps. In return he'd taken her out on the water. From him she'd learned about hydraulic haulers and bottom sounders, that the temperature of the water changes with the seasons and that lobsters migrate from shallow waters to deeper ones. And from her grandmother she'd learned how to cook the lobster in a fish kettle and eat it fresh, dripping with butter. Raising a child on Puffin Island was a communal activity, especially during the long winters when so much of the time was spent indoors, often without power. Brittany had understood that the fortunes of the island were linked with the waters that surrounded it, and she also understood why people were working to change that.

A thriving island needed people, and people needed work.

Some of the older islanders resented the large influx of visitors that swelled the population over the summer months, many of them wealthy Northeasterners from Boston, New York and Philadelphia, but most accepted them as necessary for the survival of the community.

It wasn't until her late teens that the warm embrace of the community began to feel more like constriction and interest became intrusion. Instead of feeling soothed by island life she'd felt smothered, unable to breathe without at least ten people knowing the depth of each breath she took. She'd started to wonder what it would be like to live in a place where the whole population didn't know what you had on your report card.

And then she'd fallen in love with Zachary Flynn.

Zachary Flynn.

With a groan, Brittany rolled over and opened her eyes, remembering the events of the night before. It hadn't been a dream. He was really here, invading her home.

Outside dawn had barely broken and a quick check of her phone told her it was only 6:00 a.m.

Thanks to the time change, her body thought it was already after midday and as a result she was awake. Exhausted, but definitely awake.

After Emily had left the night before, she'd stumbled up the stairs and collapsed onto the bed, too tired to undress let alone wrap her mind around the problem of Zach. She hadn't even bothered sliding into the bed her friend had made up with clean sheets. Instead she'd covered herself with the pretty patchwork quilt lovingly stitched by her grandmother as another layer of protection against the cold months and taken refuge in sleep.

Now, with sleep evading her and the gradual dawn lighting the gunmetal gray of the sea, she had no choice but to think about the events of the day before.

Her head still heavy from the journey and the time change, she sat up and scooped her hair away from her face.

The quilt lay on the floor by the bed where she'd kicked it during the night. Probably a result of dreaming about Zach.

Crap.

When she'd made her decision to return home to heal, she hadn't planned on finding him here. If she'd known, she would have stayed in Greece. In a moment of wild panic she contemplated flying back to Europe but dismissed the idea instantly. If she left now he'd know she was running away. And she didn't run from anything. Her grandmother had taught her that.

You stood and faced things. You dealt with them.

So how should she deal with this?

Indifference. That was the way to go.

Whenever she saw him, which hopefully would be infrequently, she'd pretend indifference. She'd deal with this situation with quiet dignity.

How hard could it be?

Through the open windows she could hear the rhythmic crash of the surf on the rocks, and the pretty muslin curtains billowed in the breeze. Not for the first time she was grateful that Castaway Cottage was away from the main hub of the island. It meant that he would have no reason to come here.

She flopped onto her back and stared up at the same ceiling she'd stared at growing up.

No matter how conflicted her emotions about Zach, it felt good to be home.

And Castaway Cottage wasn't just home, it was a haven. Despite the fact she was alone in the house, the feeling of security wrapped itself around her.

How many times had she lain here, listening to her grandmother clattering beneath her in the kitchen? She'd sung as she'd cooked, humming to herself as she'd whipped up pancakes to go with blueberries freshly harvested from the bushes outside the cottage door.

Pushing aside the pang of sadness, Brittany gave herself a little longer in bed, and then sat up.

Self-pity wasn't going to help and as her grandmother wasn't there to kick her butt, she'd kick her own.

But first she had to find a way of managing everyday tasks with a broken wrist, starting with a shower.

After that, she'd walk across the fields to the Ocean Club and meet Emily and Ryan for breakfast. The sea air would wake her up.

Turned out that undressing with her wrist in a plaster cast wasn't easy.

Inside the bathroom she pulled her T-shirt over her head and lost her balance. Steadying herself against the wall, she dropped it on the floor, followed by her shorts and underwear. Who would have thought that stripping one-handed could be so hard? Or that taking a shower while trying to keep her cast dry required something close to gymnastics. Making a mental note to buy more shampoo on her trip to the harbor, she was congratulating herself on how well she'd managed and was about to reach for a towel when she noticed something on the floor of the bathroom.

And screamed.

Zach had knocked on the door, prowled around the house and had reached the conclusion Brittany wasn't home when he heard the scream. It was like something from the most gruesome horror movie and it froze his blood.

Cursing under his breath, he vaulted over the fence and used skills he wasn't supposed to have to open her back door.

It took him a matter of seconds, and he wondered not for the first time why islanders were so lax about their security. She might as well have left the door open with a notice saying All Welcome.

His heart was pumping, his hands clammy as he anticipated what he might find.

Fire?

A masked intruder?

For Brittany to be scared it must be something truly threatening.

He strode through the kitchen, noticing with a frown that it looked as if an intruder had been having a party. A couple of unwashed dishes were stacked on the counter and the table was covered in bags. Following the direction of the scream, he took the stairs two at a time and reached her in under a minute.

She was flattened against the wall of the shower,

naked and shivering. Her body was gleaming wet, droplets of water clinging to the rosy tip of her breasts.

"Christ." Distracted by the lean lines of her glorious body, Zach banged his head on the low door frame and saw stars. He remembered too late that he'd done the same thing the last time he'd set foot in Castaway Cottage.

She'd been naked then, too. At the time he'd taken the blow to the head as punishment for his sins, which had been considerable.

This time the sin was all in his head, but the pain was real enough.

Her gaze connected with his as she finally registered the identity of her rescuer.

"Zach! What the hell are you doing here?"

"You screamed." It took effort, but he hauled his gaze up to her eyes. "What's wrong?"

Shivering, she pointed to the corner of the bathroom. "That."

He turned his head from smooth, golden limbs and raw temptation and saw the thong on the floor. He'd seen more substantial dental floss. Heat uncurled inside him. "You dropped your underwear?" And then something moved and he saw the problem. An intruder, but the not the sort he'd been expecting. "It's a spider."

"I know what it is." She spoke through her teeth. "Get rid of it. Please."

If he hadn't been trying to will his libido into sudden death, he would have laughed. He'd never met a woman more capable of looking after herself than Brittany. If a man had broken into her house, she probably would have knocked him unconscious with the nearest heavy object, but a large insect left her quivering and helpless.

Forgetting his intention not to look at her again, he shifted his gaze back to her. "So it's still spiders." He noticed that her hair was longer. Or maybe it just seemed that way because it was wet. It lay over one shoulder in a dark heavy mass, leaving the other bare. "You always were scared of them. Nothing else. Just spiders."

"If you don't stop talking and catch the damn thing it will run away and then I'll have to move out because there isn't room in this house for both of us."

It wouldn't make any difference if he looked away because the image of Brittany's naked body was imprinted on his mind.

He wasn't quite sure how he'd managed to end up in a small, steamy bathroom with his naked ex-wife but he was sure he deserved every moment of the punishment.

That brief glance had been enough to show him that she'd lost the angular lines of girlhood, the awkwardness of inhabiting a body that developed at its own time and pace. It had been right here in this house that he'd taught her what her body could do, used his skill and experience to extend her education into areas not covered by school.

As in everything, she'd proved a quick study.

She'd been an eager pupil, lying on the bed with her hair spilling over her naked body, doing everything he'd demanded of her and more.

If he'd been filling out her report card, he would have given her top grades.

Her reward had been a broken heart.

He dragged his eyes from sun-kissed skin and lean muscle and focused on the spider. To be fair it was too big to fit comfortably under a teacup, which he knew to be the favored way of dealing with anything born with more than four legs. "Probably thinks it's a good place to raise a family."

"You're not funny. *Please* get rid of it."

The fact that she hadn't even reached for a towel told him how freaked out she was.

For his own sake, he grabbed the nearest towel, threw it to her and dealt with the spider.

When he returned to the bathroom, she was still in the same place, the towel clutched to her chest with her good hand.

Turned out it was a hand towel, and she didn't seem to realize that clutching it across her breasts left most of the lower half of her bare. Or maybe her priorities were elsewhere.

Her teeth were chattering. "Is it dead?"

"No." There were plenty of humans he would happily have flattened under his boot, but when it came to animals and insects he preferred a more sympathetic approach. "Didn't see the point in killing it. I relocated it somewhere it might be more welcome and comfortable."

"That means it's going to find its way back into the house." She took a step back, and he turned his head, desperately searching for a bigger towel.

"Last time I looked, spiders didn't come equipped with GPS. They don't have spiders in Greece?"

"Not ones that size. Or maybe I managed to avoid them." Distracted, she pushed damp hair back from her face. "What are you doing here anyway?"

Finally, now the crisis was averted, she was registering exactly who had come to her rescue. He had a feeling that up until that point he could have been anyone. "You left your backpack. Thought you might need it."

"But how did you get in? I locked the doors—" Her

voice faded and her eyes widened. "You *broke* in? Why would you break in?"

"You screamed."

And he was trying not to examine the reason he'd felt the fierce need to protect something that wasn't even his to protect.

She stared at him, lips parted, breathing shallow. "Right." Her mouth closed and she swallowed hard. "I guess I should be grateful breaking and entering is still one of your party tricks."

It had been years since he'd used anything other than a key to open a door, but he knew there were many who would have shared her assumption. Usually it didn't bother him. People could believe what they wanted to believe; the only difference was that in the past she'd been the first one to defend him.

He could hardly blame her for recalibrating her expectations.

And if part of him was unsettled by how quickly he'd been driven to gain access to a locked property once she'd screamed, he ignored it. He'd believed her to be in trouble. Any man would have done the same.

Silence, tense and awkward, spread between them.

Her body was lightly tanned, the bronze glow of her shoulders intersected by paler strap marks. The uneven marks told him she'd gained that color while doing the job she loved, not by lying on a beach, soaking up the sun.

Now that the spider had gone, there was nothing between them but the past and the electricity that shimmered and crackled in the air. The way she stayed flattened to the bathroom wall made him wonder if she saw him as a threat worse than the spider.

She lifted a shaky hand to her damp hair. "I'm grateful for the whole knight-in-shining-armor routine. You said you came to return my bag. Where is it?"

"Kitchen." And he knew she wasn't grateful. She was livid that she'd needed help and that he'd been the one to give it.

"Thanks. Do I need to count the money?"

It was a question she never would have asked before, and he stared at her for a long moment, watching the flush build in her cheeks.

Although that was one crime he wasn't guilty of, he knew he was guilty of plenty of others so he didn't bother defending himself.

Instead, he looked at the clothes strewn haphazardly on the floor of the bathroom where she'd obviously struggled to strip them off. He was no detective, but it seemed to him that she'd slept in the clothes she'd traveled in.

Dragging his eyes from the thong, he eyed her plaster cast. "You having trouble managing with that thing on your arm?"

"No. No trouble."

It was her right hand. She was right-handed. It had to be a problem, but he guessed she would rather have faced another spider than admit to him that she was struggling.

He glanced from the mess on the floor to the cast on her wrist and told himself it wasn't his business.

"You've got people you can call if you need help?"

"I don't need help. Goodbye, Zach."

His legs refused to move. "You need to think about getting a new bolt on your back door." The cottage was isolated. Her nearest neighbor was a mile away. The thought sent his tension levels rocketing.

"My lock is fine. This is Puffin Island."

"Last time I looked there was nothing stopping the criminal element stepping aboard the ferry."

"I guess you're proof of that."

Zach's eyes met hers. He'd always assumed that his less-than-clean-cut past had been part of the attraction for her, at least initially. At the time it had amused him that a few nasty secrets had the upside of making him more interesting to the opposite sex. He'd milked it for all it was worth. Why wouldn't he? If the gutter had a silver lining, then he figured he might as well wrap himself in it.

Those days were long behind him, but clearly not forgotten. Not by him and not by the residents of Puffin Island. And, it seemed, not by his ex-wife.

With a brief nod, he turned and walked out of the house, this time leaving by the front door.

If she chose not to buy a better lock for the back door, that was her business. At any rate, he was willing to lay bets that there wasn't a decent lock to be had in any of the stores since he'd landed back on the island.

"Holy crap, he saw me naked. Could it *be* any more humiliating?" Brittany lay on her back on the bed, talking to Skylar on the phone.

"He heard you scream and broke in to save you. That's so romantic."

"It's not romantic, it's the sign of a misspent youth. Would *you* know how to break through a door without damaging the lock?"

"No, but we all have different skills and you're missing the most important point. All these years you thought he didn't care, but he obviously does."

"I don't know how you draw that conclusion."

"He thought you were in trouble, Brit! You screamed and he came. A knight in shining armor."

"He was wearing black jeans." An old pair of Levi's and a black T-shirt that had fitted him perfectly, molding to every contour of his muscular frame. "He looked like a ninja not a knight."

"Yum."

"Not yum! I don't want him."

Sky chuckled. "You mean you don't *want* to want him."

Remembering the sizzle of awareness when their eyes had met, Brittany bit her lip. "Why did this have to happen? Why did he have to pick this moment to come back here?"

"It's fate."

"I hate it when you say that."

"Finish the story. You saw the spider, screamed and then he appeared. And you weren't wearing anything at all. Not even a teeny tiny thong?"

"I was wearing a teeny tiny thong fifteen minutes before he arrived. It was on the floor." She heard a sound and frowned. "Are you laughing?"

"I might be. Look, maybe he didn't notice."

"He noticed. He smacked his head into the door frame."

"Oh, poor him. That must have hurt. I always said that door was too low. I can't walk into that bathroom in heels."

Brittany gave a murmur of exasperation. "Whose side are you on?"

"Yours, of course, but I do sympathize that he banged his head and I'm not going to be angry with him for looking out for you. So he saw you naked—then what?"

"He threw me a towel and got rid of the spider." With those big, calloused hands that could break down a door or the defenses of a woman with equal ease.

"Well, there you go. The actions of a perfect gentleman."

"It was a hand towel. And I can think of lots of different ways of describing Zachary Flynn, but 'perfect gentleman' isn't one of them."

"Did he, or did he not, get rid of the spider?"

"He did, but—"

"And he came back to check you were okay?"

"Yes, but—"

"It wasn't his fault the closest thing was a hand towel. So then what? You stood there looking at each other and all you were wearing was a plaster cast. That must have been awkward."

"It was a little more than awkward." And hadn't been made less so by the fact the incident had played out on the same stage as their intense affair. They'd had sex in that bathroom. They'd had sex in almost every room of the house.

"Just awkward? Not sexy? He didn't push you up against the wall and press his heated body against yours?"

"No! And you need to rein in your imagination." And she needed to rein in hers.

"Can't do that, I need it for my job."

"So keep it for your art and don't get creative with my sex life, especially not where Zach is concerned."

"I always thought he'd be the kind of guy to take what he wanted without asking permission."

"I think we've already established he didn't want me." And it shouldn't bother her. It really shouldn't bother her.

"It must have been hard for him to commit to someone, given he'd been alone all his life."

"You sound as if you'd like to adopt him."

"Now you mention it, he's like one of those stray dogs who have been badly treated and no one ever wants to give a home to because they're afraid of being bitten."

"Not every stray dog can be tamed."

"Agreed. So what happened after he'd performed epic spider removal? He left?"

"Right after I virtually accused him of stealing from my purse."

"You didn't! Brit? Why would you do that?"

"Because—because—I don't know." She was upset with herself. "I was feeling vulnerable. And he *had* just broken into my house."

"To save you! Do you want to know what I think?"

"No."

"I think seeing him really messed with your head and you wanted to see the worst in him."

"Of course it messed with my head. I was naked! And I have no idea what I'm going to say next time I see him."

"You say 'thank you for removing my spider.' What are you doing this morning?"

"I'm supposed to be meeting Em for breakfast. She's in love."

"I know. Can you believe it? And Ryan is gorgeous. How come we never met him when we came to stay?"

"Bad timing, I guess. Up until four years ago, he was always traveling. How do I handle the fact that Zach is here?"

"How do you think you should handle it?"

She went through the options. "Anger would imply I

still care, happy would be too hard to play, so I was going with indifference."

"Indifference sounds perfect to me."

"But he saw me naked."

Sky laughed. "Honey, it's not the first time."

Chapter 4

Brittany took the prettiest route to the harbor and the Ocean Club, walking up the coast path and then cutting across the fields that skirted the wooded interior of the island.

With the sun shining and the air filled with the scent of grass and wildflowers, it was impossible to feel anything other than pleased to be home.

The spectacular coastline of Maine matched anything she'd seen in the Mediterranean. From the lush, emerald perfection of Acadia National Park to the granite islands inhabited only by puffins and cormorants, Penobscot Bay was a wild, unspoiled paradise.

From high up on the bluff she could see fishing boats bobbing in the sheltered harbor and yachts and windjammers dotted across the bay.

It took her a little over an hour to walk to the Ocean

Club. She arrived to find Ryan and Emily already sitting on the deck along with Lizzy, Emily's six-year-old niece who was now living with her. The little girl was clutching a wooden boat to her chest and the moment she saw Brittany she moved closer to Emily.

Brittany watched as her friend scooped the child onto her lap and murmured words of reassurance.

She knew how hard the past few months must have been for Lizzy, but she also knew how hard it had been for her friend who had always vowed never to have children.

"That boat," she said slowly, "looks *exactly* like the *Captain Hook*. Can I take a look? Where did you get it?"

Lizzy hesitated and then handed it across the table. "John made it for me."

"He did? I've never known him to make anything like this for anyone before." She turned it in her hands and read the words on the side. "The *Captain Lizzy*. This is beautiful. You're lucky. John must think you're very special to have made you this."

"It floats."

"You'll have to show me." She handed the boat back. "John taught me to sail when I was your age."

"I'm learning. Ryan is teaching me."

Brittany had known Ryan Cooper her whole life. She'd spent her summers with his sister Helen at Camp Puffin and babysat his younger sister, Rachel, to earn money.

She greeted him with a quick kiss on the cheek and then settled down in the vacant seat.

"Good to have you home." Ryan tilted his chair back and reached for Emily's hand. "I hear you've already seen Zach and the two of you managed to keep it civilized. You didn't kill him."

Civilized?

There was nothing civilized about the chemistry between them. Never had been. Being with Zach had been the most dizzying and exciting time of her life.

Until he'd dumped her.

"Why would I kill him? It doesn't bother me whether he's here or not." Ignoring Emily's raised eyebrows, she sat back while Kirsti delivered food and drinks to the table.

"A special welcome home, Brittany! Fresh blueberries, our homemade cinnamon-and-honey granola, Greek yogurt in case you're missing Crete, coffee and pancakes. I'm pretty sure they don't make those in Greece. And I added a side of bacon to your order because I know it's your favorite. Enjoy."

Brittany's stomach purred. Apart from a mouthful of the muffin Emily had produced, she hadn't eaten since the flight. "If I eat this I'll be the size of a small yacht."

"You're tired. Fuel will help that. And diet soda isn't fuel." Kirsti gave her a knowing look and Brittany returned it with a sheepish grin.

"It was my breakfast of choice in Greece."

Kirsti shuddered. "I know nothing about Greek history but I'm fairly sure that isn't part of the traditional Mediterranean diet. Eat your granola."

As she walked away, Brittany glanced around the crowded terrace. "Business is good? I don't see many empty seats."

"Business is good." Ryan reached across and rescued the soft toy Lizzy had dropped.

Looking at the plush puffin, Brittany knew instantly where it had come from. "Rachel had a million of those when she was little."

"Because she kept losing them and couldn't sleep without one."

Knowing that Ryan's experience of raising his younger siblings had left him with a thirst for a child-free existence, Brittany was surprised by the change in him. "How is Alec? Is he in London at the moment?"

"No, he's back. Had a drink with him last night. Zach joined us." Ryan picked up his coffee. "He has your backpack. He's going to return it."

"He already did." Not wanting to dwell on the fact she'd screamed like a baby and then stood in front of him naked, Brittany picked up her spoon and dug it into the granola and yogurt. "There's no need to look so worried. Our relationship was over a long time ago. I can barely remember it."

Ryan gave her a steady look but said nothing and she felt a rush of gratitude.

He'd been a good friend to her.

In those few initial weeks after Zach had deserted her, he'd been the one to pick up the pieces.

With his help and the help of her friends and grandmother, she'd healed.

And gradually she'd forced herself to accept the truth.

Zach had never loved her.

He wasn't capable of it. He wasn't capable of intimacy or sharing or any of the things that went hand in hand with love.

Brittany looked down at her plate and realized she'd eaten the food without noticing it. "Maybe I was hungrier than I thought." She looked up just as Ryan reached out and stroked Emily's cheek with his fingers.

They shared a look that reminded Brittany of Nik and Lily.

Everyone was in love, she thought numbly. Everyone was holding hands and exchanging long looks.

Unsettled, she finished her coffee and stood up. "Thanks for breakfast. I need to pick up a few things at the harbor. See you later."

She walked out of the Ocean Club, enjoying the view of the bay. After the sweltering heat of Greece in August she was grateful for the sea breeze. High above, the gulls circled, hopeful of an impromptu meal delivered by careless tourists.

The *Captain Hook* was leaving on its late-morning trip to the mainland, its squat bulk and red paint making it instantly recognizable. Knowing that this was the busiest time of the year for John, the harbormaster, she didn't pause to talk to him and was surprised when he came striding across to her.

"Hi, John! I saw the boat you made Lizzy. It's beautiful! It's good to see you after— Oh." She staggered as he pulled her into a giant bear hug. She'd known him since before she could walk, but this was the first time she could ever remember him hugging her. "That's nice." The words were muffled against his shoulder and then he released her, his eyes fierce.

"You've been away too long. I hope this time you'll stay awhile. No more of those flying visits."

"I was working, John. I was on a dig in Greece, and before that I was studying."

"I know. Oxford and Cambridge. *Doctor* Forrest. The night Ryan and Alec told us, we all raised a glass up at the Ocean Club."

"You did?" Surprised and touched, Brittany felt a rush of affection for the islanders.

"We always knew you'd do great things. Kathleen

would have been proud of you." His voice was gruff. "And all I can say is I'm sorry. A good girl like you deserves better."

Confused, Brittany looked at him blankly. "Er—better than what?"

"Better than coming home with so many achievements to celebrate and finding that cheating ex-husband of yours living on your island."

Her stomach lurched.

"He didn't cheat, John, and it's not my island. He has a perfect right to be here."

"You were here first. And you're local. You belong here."

As a child it had both fascinated and offended her principles that people had to "earn" the right to be accepted on Puffin Island. As far as she was concerned, people had a right to come and go as they pleased and the place would be all the better for the variety.

"There's room for both of us."

"I hear he was the one who flew you from the mainland."

It was inevitable that the manner of her arrival would have been the subject of local gossip, but still the thought of it grated over her skin like sandpaper. "He did."

"That must have shaken you up some."

She chose to deliberately misunderstand. "Not at all. The weather was smooth and Zach is an excellent pilot." He'd been a lousy excuse for a friend and an even worse husband but she didn't intend to discuss that with anyone, no matter how much they probed and how much she loved them. She tried to turn the conversation. "How are you, John?"

"I'm good, considering. Must have been awkward for

you, seeing him again. By my calculation you haven't laid eyes on the man since he left you all those years ago."

"That's why it wasn't awkward. It was so long ago I barely remember it. I appreciate how much you all care, but no one needs to worry about me. Good to see you, John. I have to pick up a few things from Harbor Stores before I go back to the cottage." She extracted herself from the inquisition, crossed the road and bumped into Hilda, who had been a close friend of her grandmother's.

"Hilda!" Genuinely pleased to see her, she gave the old lady a warm hug. "How are you doing? I hear Agnes has moved near you. I bet the two of you never stop talking."

"Talking with friends is one of life's pleasures, especially now that my hips won't let me rush anywhere. Can't even run away from a handsome man, not that there are too many chasing me these days." Hilda patted her arm. "And on that topic, I just want you to know we're all watching him so you don't need to worry."

"Watching him?"

"After the way he treated you last time—" Hilda gave her a fierce look that would have repelled the most determined invader. "If he puts a foot out of line, we're going to deal with him. There are some who have forgiven him everything because he flew that child to the hospital when no one else would, but as far as I'm concerned, he still has to prove himself. And if you ask me, Ryan should be a bit more careful in picking his friends."

There was no need to ask who she was talking about and Brittany sighed. "Hilda—"

"Don't you worry yourself. You live your life and leave it to us. We've got your back, honey."

"I'm trying to live my life, Hilda, but people keep—"

"Caring." Hilda patted her hand. "It's the least we can

do. Protecting our own is one of the perks of island life. Welcome home, pumpkin. Your grandmother would be proud."

Feeling eight years old, Brittany gave a weak smile. "Thanks, Hilda. You take care now. And please don't worry about me. It was a long time ago and I have no feelings for him." She fled and took refuge inside Harbor Stores.

Holy crap.

No wonder so many people left and moved to the mainland. If it carried on like this, she'd be joining them.

If there was one thing she hated it was pity. She'd all but drowned in it after Zach had left her. And what did Hilda mean when she said they were watching him?

She had visions of the islanders setting up a roster to monitor the exact movements of her ex-husband. If it hadn't been so frustrating it would be funny.

Dropping soap into her basket, she glanced into the street to check no one she knew was about to come into the store.

"Well, if it isn't Brittany Forrest Flynn."

Recognizing the female voice, Brittany closed her eyes.

She should have stayed in bed.

Pinning a smile on her face, she turned. "It's just Forrest these days. I dropped the Flynn."

"No one would blame you for that, seeing as he dropped you first."

Definitely should have stayed in bed.

"Hello, Mel. How are you?"

"Better than you, I should think." Mel Parker, who had been at school with her and now ran Harbor Stores with her parents, eyed her wrist. "I heard you were injured.

I'm guessing that's what happens when you do a dangerous job. I saw *Raiders of the Lost Ark* a while back. And *Lara Croft*. Looks like an exciting way to earn a living, archaeology. And dangerous."

"Well, those are both movies, obviously, and movies remove most of the boring parts. Weeks of people excavating the same piece of earth and finding nothing doesn't make for gripping viewing."

"But you broke your wrist." Mel looked at Brittany's cast in awe and admiration and Brittany decided she'd better spell out the detail or the next time she came into town she'd be hearing stories about how she'd been chased by natives with a massive boulder rolling towards her.

"I was talking to someone and tripped." In fact she'd been laughing so hard at one of Spyros's jokes, she hadn't looked where she was putting her feet. "I fell into the trench."

Mel's eyes went round. "That sounds awful. Were there snakes?"

"No. No snakes. And no angry natives." Just Spy, also laughing so hard that it had taken him a moment to realize she'd actually broken something. "Sorry to disappoint. And anyway, I don't mind snakes. Just spiders."

"We were all real sorry to hear the news."

"That's kind of you, Mel, but it will heal."

"I wasn't talking about *that* news. I was talking about Zachary." The girl's voice lowered and she glanced around the empty store, even though both of them knew that a store crowded with people wouldn't have stopped her gossiping.

Deciding it was time to move this reunion on, Brittany

dropped several cans of tomatoes that she didn't need into her basket. "Everything is fine, Mel."

"Can't see how it can be fine when you're living with your cheating ex under your nose."

Brittany frowned. "He didn't cheat."

Why did everyone keep saying that?

"Oh, that's right, he just upped and left. I guess that's almost worse." Clearly not in any hurry to return to the demands of her job, Mel pondered the severity of the crime. "Mom always says that when a man leaves you for another woman, then all it means is he met someone he liked more and you weren't right for each other, but when a man leaves you for no one in particular, it means he didn't like being with you enough to stay. That's got to hurt."

Brittany contemplated swinging her good arm and decided she didn't want to be arrested on her first proper day back on the island. "Or it means we were both too young to be married."

"You *were* young." Mel leaned against the aisle, settling in for a long chat. "And to think we were all jealous, because you were the one who caught his eye. We all wanted Zach to be our first. Who wouldn't? The man was sex on a stick. I still remember the rumors about just how good he was in the bedroom." She looked at Brittany expectantly, clearly waiting for confirmation and juicy details.

"Nice meeting up with you again, Mel." She snatched toothpaste and shampoo without looking at the brand and headed to the checkout.

"I'll ring those up for you." Suddenly efficient, Mel walked behind the counter. "Zach comes in here sometimes so if you're looking to avoid him, just send me a text and I can warn you if he's here. You won't want to be anywhere near the man."

"I don't need warning and I'm not trying to avoid him. I'm just trying to live my life." And that was turning out to be a thousand times harder than she'd expected. She was tempted to abandon her purchases and run. "But thank you for caring."

"Thought it might be awkward, what with you making such a giant fool of yourself and all. Throwing in college, marrying the man. You always were a romantic, and so in love with him. Which just goes to prove that even smart people can be stupid when it comes to love."

"I don't think—"

"If it were me, I might have forgiven the fact he hadn't bought me a ring." Mel bagged up the purchases. "I'm not sure I'd have been so forgiving if a man had left me after my wedding night."

Great. No doubt the whole island had been speculating that Brittany Forrest was bad in bed.

"It wasn't my wedding night."

"Oh, that's right, he waited ten nights." She gave Brittany a knowing look and Brittany waited for her to voice the implication hovering in the air.

Ten nights to see if she would improve and when she hadn't, he'd walked.

Was that what they were all saying?

It horrified her to think of people talking about it and speculating about something so personal.

"I appreciate your concern and deep interest in my life, Mel, but it was a long time ago."

"He's still sexy as hell, though. And now he has money. No one knows exactly how he came by it, of course, but who cares?" Mel sighed and stared dreamily out the window, her feelings for Zach visible on her face.

Brittany frowned. "I would care, but I don't think for a moment that he—"

"The way he flew that little girl through that storm when she was sick and no one else would? There's a touch of a hero inside him. I've always said that what he needs is the right woman." It was obvious she thought she might be that woman. "I mean, he's single and all, and I'm guessing you're not interested." She eyed Brittany closely, looking for visual signs of inner trauma, and Brittany held her gaze and her temper.

"I'm not interested, Mel. He's all yours. I moved on a long time ago."

But it seemed no one else had.

Apparently it wasn't just with Zach that she had to keep up the pretense that she didn't care, it was with most of the island.

"If you change your mind about me texting you when he's in town, just let me know. He's living over at Camp Puffin, but I expect you already know that."

No, she hadn't known that. She hadn't got as far as wondering where he was living.

As long as it wasn't next door to her, she didn't care.

She was already exhausted and she'd been home less than twenty-four hours.

Ignoring Brittany's silence, Mel decided this was information that needed to be disclosed. "Seems Philip Law is helping him out again, like he always does. Zach showed up here a couple of months ago, bold as brass. Flew his plane in, didn't explain himself to anyone."

"Why would he need to explain? He's like a son to them."

"Molly Noakes told me they hadn't heard from him in months. Then one day he just shows up like he has a perfect right to be here."

"He does have a perfect right to be here. Puffin Island isn't private."

"Folks were speculating on why he was back. Last thing we all heard, he was flying in Alaska. And now he has his own plane." Mel leaned forward and lowered her voice. "I heard a rumor he might have stolen it, but I'm guessing not."

Brittany stared at the girl who had sat across from her in the classroom and paid more attention to the boys than the teacher. "I'm guessing you're right."

She ignored the niggle of guilt that came from knowing she'd also wondered how he'd come to own a plane.

"He's flying people with money. *Real* money. Charging a fortune. If you'd waited to divorce him, you might be a rich woman now. Could have bought yourself that diamond ring he never gave you."

Brittany had studied weapons through the ages and found none more effective for inducing pain than the barb of the female tongue.

"Thanks, Mel. Great to see you again."

Get me out of here.

Desperate to escape before any more locals came in to do their shopping and gossip, she strode through the store, her eyes fixed on the exit.

The doors slid open at her approach and she quickened her pace, her strides just short of running.

Determined not to catch anyone's eye she kept her head down.

And collided with the solid wall of muscle that was Zach.

Chapter 5

Groceries tumbled out of the bag and Zach caught Brittany's shoulders and steadied her. He felt the smoothness of bare skin, and breathed in the faint smell of summer roses. Heat ripped through him.

He was no stranger to sexual attraction, on the contrary, it formed the basis for every relationship he'd ever had, but nothing came close to the desire he felt for this woman.

He half expected to see flames licking around his ankles.

In the circumstances his response was beyond inappropriate.

He tried to work out what had happened to send her almost sprinting out of the store. It was true that shopping bored the hell out of him and he felt like running whenever he had to buy groceries, but he assumed it had to be more than that. She'd been so desperate to escape, she'd slammed right into him.

He tried to let her go, but his hands refused to cooperate with his brain. Instead he tightened his grip and stroked his thumbs soothingly over her bare arms. "What happened?"

She gave a soft gasp of dismay as she registered who was holding her and immediately stepped back.

"Sorry about that. Didn't see you."

He was about to demand the reason for her rapid exit when Mel appeared from the front of the store, her mouth gleaming with a coat of freshly applied lipstick.

Whenever he appeared, so did the makeup.

On one occasion he'd seen her crouched behind the counter, using her phone as a mirror as she'd checked her reflection.

Her barely concealed infatuation didn't bother Zach, who believed a person's feelings were their own. He'd done nothing to encourage her and as far as he was concerned his responsibility ended there. He'd been careful never to give Mel a single reason to think it was worth her while depleting the world's makeup stores in his honor. If she wanted to go to the trouble, that was her choice.

And today she'd definitely made that choice.

"Well, that was quite the reunion." She was giggling and fluttering lashes weighed down by a thick layer of mascara. Watching the effort Mel took made him glad he wasn't a woman. As far as he could see, the number of hours spent applying and then removing makeup could amount to a whole year over the course of a lifetime.

He knew he was looking at the reason Brittany had run. Gossip was Mel's favorite hobby and judging from the expression on her face, he'd been the subject.

He had no interest in whether his actions pleased or displeased others, but he knew it would bother Brittany.

Without looking at him, she bent to rescue cans, shampoo and toothpaste from the bag she'd dropped, an endeavor hampered by the fact she only had use of one hand.

He stooped to help her, brushed against her and saw her scoot away.

"I can manage."

He saw Mel's eyes narrow as she registered the tension and put her own spin on it.

"I'll help," she cooed and stooped, too, an elaborately choreographed maneuver that gave him an eyeful of carefully constructed cleavage contained by a froth of black lace as unsubtle as the red lipstick.

Zach, who was as shallow as the next guy, wondered why all that voluptuous flesh on display failed to distract him from Brittany.

She was wearing her usual trademark cutoffs and a bright top that showed the contrasting strap of her sports bra. Her outfit displayed limbs that were toned, strong and golden.

He wondered if she was wearing a thong under those shorts and then decided he was better off not knowing. He dragged his eyes from the taut curve of her butt to her hair, which fell in a thick braid between her shoulder blades.

The color on her cheeks was natural and there was no gloss on her lips, yet of the two women there was no doubt in his mind who was the sexier.

He clenched his jaw, wondering why Brittany's soft, bare lips should be so much more kissable than Mel's glossy pout.

Ten years and a whole lot of bad feeling lay between

them, but still all he wanted to do was shove her back against the wall and bury himself in her.

Tension made his voice rough. "How are you getting home?"

She straightened, clutching the bag awkwardly with her good arm. "I'm walking."

"That bag won't survive. I'll give you a ride."

Mel clearly had her own ideas about that. "No need to go out of your way, Zach. I'll give her another bag. All part of the service. You just wait right there, Brittany." She vanished to do whatever she had to do to keep the two of them apart and Zach looked down at Brittany and raised his eyebrows in question.

"It's your call. Do you want to go another round with her?"

"Is that a serious question?" She spoke between her teeth and he almost smiled because he suspected he was the lesser of two evils, which was a refreshing change for a man who usually found himself the greater of the two.

"I should probably warn you that at least ten locals currently have eyes on us, including Rita Fisher. She spreads gossip like butter on dinner rolls. You climb into my car and you know what they'll be saying."

"I don't care if the whole damn island is lining up for front-row seats for whatever it is we're supposed to be doing," she said. "Get me out of here."

They made it to the SUV he'd left unlocked and there was still no sign of Mel.

Brittany shot in so fast she almost scratched the paint-work and he gave a faint smile as he strolled around the car and slid into the driver's seat.

"So it's not just spiders. Never thought you'd be afraid of Mel."

"I'm not afraid, but I don't want to kill her on my first day home. I'll alienate the islanders."

He'd lived that way his whole life and she must have been thinking the same thing because she sent him a glance and sighed.

"I didn't mean—"

"I know what you meant."

"It's been a hard morning, that's all. I'm a little tired of people sympathizing with me."

"They're all sorry about your wrist."

"It has nothing to do with my wrist." She muttered the words under her breath but he caught them anyway and wondered why it hadn't occurred to him that his presence would cause her a problem.

"They've said something to you?"

"No." She answered a little too quickly and he wondered for the millionth time in his life why people couldn't just attend to their own business and leave others alone.

I don't care what anyone thinks. I want you to be the first, Zach. Do anything. All of it.

The memory came from nowhere and messed with his concentration.

He gave himself a mental shake, trying to delete the image of her naked. He wished he hadn't broken into her cottage when he'd heard her scream. He should have called the emergency services and gotten the hell out of there. Then he wouldn't have seen her wet and gleaming from the shower.

"What are you waiting for? Drive, or I'll push you out and drive myself." She spoke through her teeth and he snapped back into the present and glanced at her face.

"I'll drive, but you need to smile or we'll have the law on us."

"Why would the law care whether I'm smiling?"

"Because the good people of Puffin Island will want to be reassured that you came with me of your own free will and that I didn't kidnap you with the intention of taking you back to my lair so that I can do bad things to you." The engine roared to life. "Again."

"Again?"

"They've never forgiven me for corrupting you the first time around."

Her gaze held his for a fraction of a second longer than was necessary and he knew she was remembering exactly what he'd done to her in the dark of her bedroom that first night.

He remembered it, too. Every stroke. Every gasp. The softness of her. The addictive combination of eager and innocent. The breathless exploration of untouched flesh. She'd given and he'd taken. All of it. Everything she'd offered, without hesitation or conscience. Back then he'd seen life as black-and-white, good and bad. She'd said yes and he'd seen no reason to hold back.

It was only with the benefit of maturity he'd begun to see the world in shades of gray.

Almost incinerated by a rush of sexual heat, he shifted in his seat.

He might have thought he was the only one suffering if it hadn't been for the slight change in her breathing.

Their eyes held and they shared a look that said a thousand times more than words.

Then she turned away and fixed her eyes on the road.

"There was no corruption, just choice. Mine. Let's go."

He drove away from the busy hub of the harbor and

took the forest road that wound upwards through the center of the island. In places the road narrowed to the width of one car and in the winter it was usually impassable except by snowmobile.

It was one of Zach's favorite places. Over a thousand acres of rolling mixed forest, interspersed with rustic trails peppered by roots and rocks, hidden ponds and streams gushing full with silvery water. Here pine, spruce, fir and white cedar grew together along with bunchberry and lowbush blueberry. Summer tourists rarely ventured into the interior of the island unless they were the adventurous type, preferring instead to spend their time on the beaches near the harbor or sailing in the sparkling waters of Penobscot Bay. As far as Zach was concerned, they were missing the best part of the island, but as the peace of the forest was part of the reason he loved it, he wasn't about to broadcast its charms.

He took the bridge over Heron Pond and then steered left down the unmarked track that led down to Shell Bay. A squirrel bounded across the road in front of him and he stepped sharply on the brakes.

He heard the hiss of indrawn breath and turned to look at Brittany.

"You're in pain? You taking anything for it?"

"I don't like swallowing drugs. I'll be fine."

"You don't look fine. You're the color of an oyster."

"You're comparing me to smelly shellfish? You always did know how to compliment a girl." She watched as the squirrel darted up a tree. "You'll put a spider outside and do an emergency stop for an animal, but I bet if that had been one of the islanders, you would have run right over them."

"Depends on the islander. There are a few I'll slow

down for. So what happened to your wrist? You were demonstrating weapons? Accident with a newly discovered Greek ax?"

"Nothing so glamorous. I wasn't looking where I was putting my feet and fell down a hole I'd been excavating a few minutes earlier."

One of the things he'd always liked about her was her ability to laugh at herself.

"Anything interesting in the hole?"

"A few things. Cretan arrowheads. Ceramic fragments."

"But your expertise is weapons?"

She frowned slightly, as if surprised that he knew that. "Bronze Age weapons. Aegean Bronze Age, although I dabbled in Celtic for a while." She settled her wrist carefully on her lap. "Most of the weapons that dominated Europe until the Middle Ages—swords, battle-axes, shields—originated in Crete. The place is an archaeologist's paradise."

"Which explains why you were there, but not how you managed to hitch a ride in a billionaire's jet."

"He's a friend."

He wanted to ask how much of a friend, and then reminded himself that he'd given up the right to care when he'd walked out on her. "You're planning on going back?"

"No. The project is wrapping up. They've run out of funding and my research post has ended so I need to plan what to do next."

That had always been one of the fundamental differences between them. She'd been planning for the future while he'd been trying to survive the moment.

"So you're staying for the rest of the summer?" He kept his eyes forward and his tone casual.

"As long as I'm not going to be grilled by the islanders every time I take a trip into town. What is *wrong* with them? It was years ago. Why would something that happened years ago be a problem?"

Because I behaved like a total bastard and you should be punching me.

It puzzled him that she didn't have more to say about the past. Clearly the islanders were puzzled, too.

"They're protective. They're probably thinking it's awkward for you. We were married."

She laughed. "Seriously? You call that married?"

He kept his speed steady. "It was legal."

"So was the divorce. Ten days barely counts. If our marriage was a consumer purchase, we would have been entitled to a refund, no questions asked. And anyway, I was the one who proposed to you, remember?"

He remembered all of it.

He gripped the wheel so tightly his knuckles whitened. "Didn't make it less legal."

"But you weren't engaged, in any sense of the word. Tell me, Zach—" she turned to look at him "—did you *feel* married?"

Yeah, he'd felt married. That was the problem. He'd felt horribly, irrevocably married and the panic had almost choked him. He, who had rarely spent an entire night with a woman, had found himself facing a lifetime of nights.

He'd lain awake in the dark, suffocating under the smothering weight of her expectations, wondering how the hell to undo what he'd done. Of all the bad situations in which he'd found himself, that had been one of the most terrifying.

"I knew I was married."

She looked at him for a long moment and then shrugged. "Well, either way, it's water under the bridge."

"I guess so." He tried not to think about the previous winter when the river up near Heron Pond had swollen and burst its banks, taking the bridge with it. The damage had been serious. If the same thing happened in their relationship, they'd be in trouble.

"Why would we be bothered by something that happened so long ago? I don't get it. It's like asking if I still think about a meal that poisoned me at college. Move on, people. I have and I know you have."

So he'd been no worse than an episode of food poisoning?

He looked at her hands, bare of rings and jewelry. "You didn't marry again?"

"No. You?"

"No. Once was enough." He realized how that sounded and cursed under his breath. "I meant because I wasn't good at it. I hurt you."

"Briefly. Didn't hurt much more than my wrist and at least I didn't have to put my heart in a plaster cast." She suppressed a yawn. "So you're staying up at Camp Puffin?"

She was behaving as if he was a casual school friend she hadn't seen in a while. As if he hadn't been her first lover. As if they'd never lain naked in her bed, exploring every inch of each other's bodies while thunder crashed above the cottage. The one thing there had never been a shortage of in his life was sex, but he still remembered every single thing he'd done with Brittany.

Ego aside, he wouldn't have thought she would have forgotten it, either.

Or maybe her sex life had been so active since then she could no longer remember that first time.

He wondered whether it was the rich Greek who had wiped her memory of their time together.

He tried to push that thought out of his head. "I've been living in the old beach cabin at Hawker's Point."

"Seagull's Nest?"

"Yeah. It's been exposed to a bit too much wind and weather. When it rains there's as much water inside as out. I've been fixing that."

"You always were good with your hands." She spoke without thinking and then caught his eye and gave a faint smile. "That wasn't what I meant, but that, too. And you don't need to look at me like that. We're not teenagers, Zach. We can both agree the sex was good. It's just a shame we didn't leave it at that. Tell me about Philip. I heard about his arthritis. That must be tough on him. He's used to being so active and I know how much he loves Camp Puffin and the kids. It's been his life. How is he doing?" She moved the conversation forward smoothly, but nothing, not even her cool tone, could dampen the sizzle of awareness that heated the atmosphere in the car.

"The place is getting to be too much for him. Winters are the worst. He's trying to cut back, but he's not good at it and there isn't anyone to take over." And that was something else that bothered him. He felt something he'd never felt before.

A sense of obligation.

The word made him shift in his seat, but nothing so simple could ease a discomfort that had its origins deep inside him. Never in his life had he ever felt he owed anyone anything. Until Philip.

He'd never known his father and had never been interested in finding a substitute, but of all the authority figures he'd met in his time, Philip had come closest to fulfilling that role.

It was Philip who had taught him to fly. Philip who had ignored the dire predictions of the social workers and everyone else who had ever come in contact with Zachary Flynn, and taken him in.

Without Philip Law, he wouldn't have the life he had now. It was very possible that he wouldn't have a life at all. Instead he could have died in a gutter, another sad story that people read and felt bad about for one minute before returning to their own comfortable, insulated lives.

"You're helping him out? You're going to stay awhile?" There was nothing in her voice that suggested she cared either way.

"I help when he needs me." He didn't elaborate on the detail of that help. "And I'll stay as long as it feels right. I guess that's a decision that's going to bother some people."

Judging from her lack of reaction, Brittany wasn't one of those people.

"You don't care what they think. You never did." She sat up straighter as they left the cover of the forest and drove down the track that led to Shell Bay. "Emily tells me you were the one who flew her and Lizzy to the hospital when no one else would. Why did you do that?"

"Because no one else would."

There was a long, drawn-out silence and then she stirred. "I appreciate you helping my friend. Will you do me one more favor? Next time you shop in Harbor Stores, make it clear you and I were over a long time ago. I can't face having a one-on-one with Mel every time I go in to buy a bunch of bananas."

"It wouldn't matter whether you and I were over and done or not. I would never touch Mel." He pulled up outside Castaway Cottage and watched for a moment as the surf crashed over the rocks that guarded the peaceful curve of Shell Bay.

It was the prettiest part of the island, away from the tourist spots and all the favorite meeting places for the islanders. Here the sky merged into the sea and the only sound was the rush of the waves and the call of the gulls. The only place he'd rather be was up in the air looking down on it.

His moment of quiet contemplation was disturbed by a few choice words from the seat next to him.

"Holy crap, is that what I think it is?"

He turned his head to see what had shaken her out of her mood of calm indifference and saw the large blue earthenware pot placed in the center of her front porch.

"Looks like a casserole."

"I can see that," she muttered, "but what is it doing on my porch?"

Zach studied it in silence, absorbing the implications. Knowing exactly what a casserole signified among the islanders, he stirred. "Unless you ordered takeout, I'd say someone thinks you're in deep trouble."

Brittany slid from the car and approached the casserole as if it were a dangerous device that might explode in her face.

Seriously, after everything she'd been through so far that morning, now *this*?

Everywhere she went she was confronting sympathy and pity and it made her squirm.

She could imagine the islanders talking behind closed

doors, watching her as she walked around the island, waiting for her to fall apart.

They'd probably called a town meeting to discuss how they were going to support her.

She heard the car door slam and the solid crunch of Zach's footsteps on the path as he approached.

Why couldn't he have just driven away?

She'd wanted him to drop her off and leave so she could stop this insane happy act she was putting on, first with the islanders and now Zach. She felt drained. Keeping up the pretense of indifference was exhausting and she wasn't entirely sure she wasn't overdoing it with her singsong voice and bright smile. She felt like a circus performer trying to get a laugh from a crowd of kids who didn't want to be there.

All she really wanted to do was kick something. Hard. Starting with Zach. And the longer he hung around, the greater the chances of it happening.

Instead, she studied the large pot with dismay. "I've never seen a casserole that size. It would feed a family of twenty. If I'd been inside the house and opened the door I would have fallen over it and broken my other wrist."

"Any idea who left it there?"

"No, but it's someone who has no idea how impossible it is to lift a heavy casserole dish when you only have one working wrist." She rubbed her forehead with the fingertips of her good hand. "I know people mean well and I'm grateful, really I am, but—" She was an object of pity and she hated that. "How am I meant to get it inside? Drag it? Hell, Zach. I've been back less than twenty-four hours and already I'm ready to leave."

"It's island life." His tone was neutral. "Someone out

there figured it was going to be hard for you to cook with one hand. It was intended as a kind gesture."

Brittany stared at it miserably. Yes, it was kind but it was also a whole lot of other things. On Puffin Island, a casserole wasn't just a meal, it was a symbol of solidarity, support and sympathy provided in moments of crisis.

She knew it.

He knew it.

She wondered if the casserole was in sympathy for the broken wrist or the return of Zachary Flynn.

He lifted the lid and sniffed. "Beef, I think. Smells good."

"That's not the point and you're not funny."

"I wasn't being funny, I was being practical. Want me to heat it up for you? Chances are that I'm the reason you've been given this delicious-looking meal, so the least I can do is help."

She didn't want him heating it up. Enough of her was already heated up just by seeing him.

There was something ironic about being offered help by the man who, in all probability, was the reason for the casserole in the first place.

If there was one thing she hated more than being pitied by the locals, it was the idea that Zach might think she was still bleeding inside.

"I can manage."

"Yeah? That's a lot of casserole for one person." His eyes gleamed. "Even a person in need of serious sympathy."

"You think the volume is in direct relation to the degree of misery I'm supposed to be feeling? Extreme comfort eating?"

"I don't know, but you can't eat this by yourself. You'll

need to freeze some of it and that won't be easy with your wrist in a cast." Without waiting for her response, he took the key from her hand. The brush of his fingers sent a jolt of electricity running through her and she snatched her hand back.

There was a brief question in his eyes and then he turned away, his handsome face inscrutable. "I'll carry this inside for you."

Brittany tried to drag air into lungs that had forgotten how to work.

Despite her efforts not to, she must have made a sound because she saw him freeze, hesitate and turn fractionally, as if he wasn't sure whether or not to look at her.

For a brief moment the sun hit his profile, spotlighting features that were almost absurdly masculine. If he'd been so inclined he could have had a career modeling rugged outdoor menswear. He would have been the kind of model staring unsmiling from the flanks of Mount Everest, wearing arctic clothing and an inch of stubble on his strong jaw. His face was near perfect and at first glance his body was, too.

But she knew that underneath the black jeans and the shirt that molded lovingly to hard muscle, he bore scars, each one of them a brutal reminder of a life no child should have to live.

Seeing those scars had hurt her heart.

Despite her parents' divorce, her own childhood had been happy. It had appalled her to discover the reality of his, and offended her sense of justice.

She'd wanted to give him everything he'd never had. She'd wanted to give him the love she knew he deserved, believed he needed and thought he wanted, and then been confused and hurt when he'd rejected her sympathetic attempts to encourage him to talk through his experiences.

Zachary Flynn talked about nothing.

Revealed nothing.

Staring at his retreating shoulders, a sick feeling churned her stomach. He walked with the lethal grace of a predator, unusually light on his feet for such a powerfully built man. In all the years she'd known him, she'd rarely seen him smile. He'd ranged from inscrutable to brooding, his mood on occasion bordering on the dark. There were people on the island who gave him a wide berth, but no matter how black his mood, Brittany had never felt threatened. Despite the violence that had been shown to him, or perhaps because of it, she'd never seen him display those tendencies towards anyone else.

On the contrary, she'd seen him behave with exceptional gentleness towards anything weaker or more vulnerable.

Their relationship had been the most intense physical experience of her life. She would occasionally pretend she was just seeing it through teenage eyes but she knew that wasn't true. The truth was that no relationship since had come close to evoking the feelings she'd felt with Zach, and acknowledging that brought her close to despair.

She wished it had.

She didn't want to feel this way.

And she certainly didn't want his help with the casserole. What she really wanted to do was push his head inside and drown him in it.

Ignoring the little voice that told her she should just black his eye and tell him to get the hell out of her life, Brittany was about to follow him inside when she saw the note that had been left under the casserole.

She picked it up and followed him into the house, relieved to discover that her pulse rate and breathing were almost back to normal. As a teenager she'd spent half her time in a state of hyperventilation whenever he was around so it was nice to know she'd taken a few forward steps. "There's a note, but no signature."

He placed the casserole on the counter without looking at her. "What does it say?"

"'Sorry for your troubles.'" To compensate for her embarrassing slip, she tried to make a joke of it. "Which troubles? My wrist or my ex-husband?"

His brief glance told her he knew exactly what his touch had done to her. "I guess you can take it any way you want to take it. Doesn't matter. What matters is that if you divide this up into portions, you'll be fed for the next week."

"Unless the casserole is from Mel, in which case it's poisoned and I'll be dead by five o'clock."

"Why would she want to poison you?"

"She thinks I'm competition for your affections. I tried telling her there's nothing about you that interests me, but judging from the layers of lipstick, she didn't believe me." She moved around the kitchen, careful to keep her distance, wanting him to leave and not knowing how to engineer it without revealing more than she already had. It wasn't just the effect he had on her that bothered her. Having him here, in her home, made her think of that night.

There'd been a storm, which wasn't unusual for an island often in the line of fire from Mother Nature.

With black clouds sending a menacing gloom over the sky, Kathleen had taken the last ferry across to the mainland for her theatre trip with Hilda, Agnes and other members of the island's women's group.

Standing on top of the bluff, Brittany had waited for the deep boom of the horn and watched as the ferry had moved into the bay before making the call. Her palms had been clammy, her heart racing the whole time because she knew she was inviting danger into her home.

Most people locked their doors when they saw Zachary Flynn coming.

She'd opened hers.

The moment he'd set one scuffed boot over her threshold she'd known her life would never be the same.

Shaking off the memory she turned to find him watching her. Those smoldering dark eyes were fixed intently on her face, revealing thoughts and emotions that matched hers.

"I'm not interested in Mel." His deep voice had a husky, rough quality that she'd always found fascinating. It was that voice that had urged her over the edge that first time.

Let go and relax, I know it's your first time but you don't have to be shy. I'm going to make it good for you.

He'd made good on his promise. Over and over again.

Her face heating with the memory, she turned away. "Wouldn't bother me either way. That's your business."

"There's nothing you want to say to me?"

"What could I possibly want to say to you? Thanks for carrying the casserole. Just leave it there. I can manage."

He eyed the dirty dishes in the sink. "Must be hard keeping the place neat with one hand. Need some help?"

"No, thanks, and I can manage perfectly well with one hand."

It wasn't true, but she wanted him out of the house.

Having him there whipped up memories she'd worked hard to suppress. And they were hot, sexy memories, not the miserable ones she would have chosen as a shield to keep him at a distance.

Instead of seeing the empty bed on their "honeymoon," she kept seeing him naked, that lean, hard body stretched out next to hers as he'd encouraged her to give him everything he demanded.

"I'll be fine. I'm not hungry right now. I had breakfast with Ryan and Emily. Still digesting. I don't mean to be rude, but I have work to do." Her laptop sat on the table, providing the perfect excuse. "I need to check my emails and update my archaeology blog. I don't want to keep you from flying another billionaire to his yacht."

He didn't move, and something about the stillness of his body unnerved her. It was as if he was waiting for something.

Forcing herself to look at him, she turned her head and her eyes locked with the glittering black of his.

The first time he'd made love to her he'd insisted she keep her eyes open. He'd wanted to see what she was feeling, he'd told her, he'd wanted to know if he was hurting her or turning her on. Staring into those dark eyes had been just as responsible for her sensual meltdown as the slow thrust of his body. He'd controlled the whole thing, every movement, every touch and kiss. At that moment she'd truly believed there was no force on the planet strong enough to pull them apart. She'd thought they'd be together forever, that he was as much hers as she was his.

Her wake-up call had been all the more brutal for that delusion.

It was clear to her now that sexual attraction wasn't dulled by negative past experience. If so, then her body should have repelled him. Instead she felt inexorably drawn to the dark, dangerous appeal of the man who had broken her heart.

It took a physical effort not to slide her hand into the silky strands of dark hair that flopped over his forehead. She wanted to pull his head down to hers and lock her mouth to his, wanted to feel the skilled stroke of his tongue as he seduced her mouth with his.

Instead she curled her fingers into her palms, feeling the heat of his gaze.

She had no idea how much time passed. No idea whether it was seconds or minutes, but finally he turned and walked to the door.

Only when she heard it shut behind him did she let her smile slip.

She flopped onto the chair, groaned and closed her eyes.

One thing she knew for certain—

It was going to take more than a casserole to fix her feelings.

Chapter 6

Zach lounged on the deck, nursing a whiskey. The chair was tilted back, his legs resting on the top of the railing, as he stared at the ocean and listened to the plaintive cry of the seagulls. The water churned and boiled, lashing the rocks at the far side of the bay. The sky was black and angry. It suited his mood perfectly.

"You're drinking Jack Daniels, which makes me think you've had a hell of a day. Nursing spoiled rich folk?" Philip's voice came from behind him and Zach turned.

"I flew a bunch of bankers up to Moosehead Lake. They're white-water rafting on the Kennebec River, staying up there tonight and I'm flying them back tomorrow. That's if they don't drown in the meantime."

"You'll lose money if they drown."

"No I won't. I made them pay in advance." He swung his legs down. "I'm guessing you don't want whiskey, but there's beer in the fridge. Help yourself."

Philip did that and joined him. "I heard you saw Brittany."

Zach watched as a couple of seagulls swooped low over the bay. "I'm not even going to ask how you know that."

"Hard to keep anything a secret around here. Rumor has it the two of you drove off together looking cozy." Philip pulled on a sweater and Zach frowned.

"Are you cold? Do you want to go inside?"

"No. I want to spend some time looking at the ocean, something I don't do often enough seeing as I live right by it. Don't fuss. Celia does enough of that."

Celia was Philip's wife and had been for thirty-five years.

It humbled Zach. He couldn't imagine the level of trust and connection that came along with spending that length of time with another person. It was something he'd never experienced. And he knew that was his fault. A psychologist might have said it was because his trust had been betrayed at a young age, but Zach couldn't remember ever trusting anyone. Especially not psychologists.

"You're mistaking me with someone else. I don't care what happens to you."

Philip grinned and rested his feet on the splintered railing where Zach's had been a moment earlier. "That's right, you're just a big, tough guy with no feelings. I keep forgetting. My bad. On the other hand you're out here drinking whiskey, which means you're not as relaxed as you're pretending. Want to talk about it?"

"No."

"You never do." Philip took a mouthful of beer. "Bound to unsettle a man, though, seeing his ex-wife. I've known

Brittany her whole life. She always was a little firecracker."

"Is this conversation going somewhere?"

"Just saying she used to be a hell of a girl."

"Your point being?"

"You haven't seen her in ten years."

"I know when I last saw her."

She'd been asleep, her hair trespassing on to his pillow, her lips still curved in the smile he'd put there the night before.

He hadn't hung around to see what her face looked like when he'd wiped the smile away. Making women hate him was his special gift.

"It's a long time to not see a person. You've both changed." Philip glanced at him. "I should imagine she had plenty to say after all that time. Must have been some reunion."

Zach was starting to think he should have sold tickets.

"Sorry to disappoint everyone, but it was uneventful. The ground didn't shake and no blood was drawn. Maybe there should have been. If I'd needed medical attention, maybe that would have kept the islanders off my back. The sight of my carcass by the harbor would have made a few people's day, I'm sure." Zach wondered why everyone still took such an interest in his life. "Sadly for them, she was civilized. Polite."

Philip nursed his beer and stared thoughtfully at the churning ocean. "That bad?"

"Civilized is bad?"

"I'd say so. When a woman is polite and civilized, I worry. Celia has a polite smile that has me checking out the exits."

Knowing Celia, Zach didn't argue. "Maybe, but Brittany and I were together for a little over five minutes. In this case it meant she didn't care enough to be mad."

"Oh, she cared. Cared enough to throw it all in, marry you and go wherever you wanted her to go."

"And spend a lifetime regretting what she gave up."

"You don't know that."

"Cambridge, Oxford, PhD, Dr. Forrest—you think I could have competed with that?"

"So you looked her up."

Caught, Zach had no choice but to admit it. "Once." More than once, but that he wasn't admitting. And he didn't need to. He had no doubt Philip knew.

"She's done well, no doubt about it, but Brittany would have done well at anything she'd tried. She's that sort of person."

"I'm pretty sure she wouldn't have done well living with some loser who spent his life kicking the system."

Philip raised his eyebrows. "Sometimes the system needs kicking, and last time I looked you were doing well enough for yourself."

"Yeah, I'm transformed. A shining example of what a man can do with his life."

"I happen to think that's true." Ignoring the sarcasm, Philip finished his beer. "Which is why I'm hoping that you're not going to run off just because she's back. There are a couple of kids on the scholarship program I'd like you to meet. I can tell you their stories if you like."

"I don't need to hear the stories." He already knew them all. They'd be like his, only each would have its own variation. They'd look at him with hard eyes, waiting for him to let them down the same way everyone else in their lives had. "I've got some spare time this week. Want me to take them up?"

"That would be great. They always love it. And we could use some help with Starlight Adventure. Overnight in the forest is your area of expertise. Or you could just hang out in the camp and look cool. That's usually enough to impress."

"Your sense of humor always was one of the best things about you."

"I think so." Philip swatted an insect. "We're doing good things here. *You're* doing good things. Did you tell Brittany that you—"

"No. And I don't intend to." He frowned. "Shit, Philip, what is this? Make Zachary Feel Good About Himself Day?"

"Don't you already feel good about yourself? Because you should."

"That's crap."

"Not from where I'm sitting. I think you deserve some credit, that's all."

He finished his drink. "I get all the credit I need."

"I had an email from Todd Richards." Philip's voice was casual. "Medical school. Can you believe that?"

"Yes. He'll be a hell of a doctor." Zach rose to his feet. "You really think she's nursing a mad?"

"Brittany? You know her better than me."

He did. And none of it fitted what he knew. "If she's nursing a mad why is she so calm? She was calm when I flew her here and calm today when I gave her a lift home from the store. She was more upset with Mel than she was with me."

"Pride? All those islanders who warned her you were trouble were able to say 'I told you so' and, worse, they gave her sympathy."

"She was the injured party. She deserved sympathy."

"It's the last thing Brittany would have wanted."

Zach gave a humorless laugh. "That's a shame because they left a casserole big enough to feed the entire population of Maine on her doorstep this morning."

Philip winced. "I'm willing to bet she hated that."

"You'd win the bet." Zach thought about the sentiments behind the casserole. "They're all watching her, waiting for her to freak out because I'm living here."

"It will settle down. By tomorrow you'll be yesterday's news."

"I've never understood why someone else's life is of so much interest. It's none of their damn business."

"On an island, everything is everyone's damn business. That's the way it works. They mean well. They want to offer support."

"Which she hates, because she prefers to be independent." He wondered how long it would take before her control snapped. "I don't know how you stand it."

"There's good as well as bad." Philip gave a faint smile. "And either I'm having a bad dream or you're back living here."

"You're having a bad dream. But that's nothing compared to the nightmares the islanders are having." It almost made him smile to think about it. "I swear most of them have been double locking their doors since I came home. I'm waiting for the law to knock."

"I'm the only Law around here." There was a brief pause. "You called it home."

"What?"

"Home. You said they'd been locking their doors since you came back home."

Zach felt a strange pressure in his chest. "Slip of the tongue."

"Right. Well, if your tongue ever felt like slipping again, it would make Celia feel good to hear you say that. You know we've always wanted you to think of this as your home."

"Never could figure out why. You worked with a hundred kids more housebroken than I was. I didn't deserve what you both gave me." It was the closest he could get to a thank-you. After years of hiding everything and trying not to feel, he found it hard to identify emotions. Even harder to put words to those emotions.

"There were plenty of things that happened in your life that you didn't deserve. Living with us wasn't one of them." There was a brief pause. "Camp Puffin is getting too much for me."

It felt as if a hand had reached inside Zach's chest and squeezed his heart.

"I know." And knowing made him feel ill. He knew how much this place meant to Philip. Knew how much he needed it.

"The hospital wants to run a few more tests, but whatever those tests say the result will be the same. I need to do less. I can't be as actively involved as I have been. I'm going to need more help running this place."

"You wouldn't be short of interested people."

"Camp Puffin has been as much a part of my life as my home and family. There's only one person I want to hand it to."

Hearing something in his tone, Zach glanced at Philip and saw something he hadn't expected to see.

Love. He saw love, and he knew that with love came expectations and following swiftly on from that, disappointment.

His mouth dried. Panic thudded into him. "No."

This time the emotions were stronger. They came at him like a powerful crosswind, buffeting him off course so that he leaned on the railings to steady himself.

Next to him, Philip stirred. "Why not? You don't have to do much more than you're doing now."

"The difference is that you'll rely on me and you know that's a mistake." Discomfort and guilt made him irritable. "You know I'd let you down."

"Why would you let me down?"

"It's what I do best."

"That's not how I see it. Not how Celia sees it, either."

"Then maybe the two of you aren't looking hard enough."

"Don't sweat it. Just wanted to run it past you, that's all. So what are you going to do about Brittany?" Philip's tone was mild, the transition smooth, and Zach took a moment and breathed, relieved to be off the hook.

"Nothing. What would I do?"

"You could start by talking about what happened."

"What would be the point of that? It happened. Talking about it doesn't change anything."

"Might change the way she feels about it if she understood. You could give her an explanation. Talk it through."

"What would be the point of that?"

"The two of you had something special. Maybe you shouldn't throw that away."

"You're ten years too late with that advice."

"Would it have changed anything if I'd given it to you then?"

Zach thought about the way he'd felt. He'd married in a haze of panic, saw the hope and expectations in Brittany's eyes as he slid that cheap ring on her finger, and wanted to run the whole time. "No."

"So you don't care about her at all."

"I didn't say that."

"Poor girl. All alone in that cottage with no neighbors."

Zach set his jaw. "She's the most independent woman I've ever met, and she loves that cottage."

"I know, but she can't go next door if she has a problem. Must be hard managing with one arm in a cast, and being Brittany, she wouldn't admit it to anyone. She'll just struggle along."

The thought of her struggling made Zach uncomfortable. "She seemed just fine to me." He tried to forget the disaster in the bathroom and the mess in the kitchen.

She'd just come off a long flight.

She wasn't the tidiest person.

Didn't mean she was struggling.

Philip stood up slowly and straightened gingerly, rubbing his joints. "Can't be easy managing one-handed. I'm guessing she's in a bit of trouble. You going to turn your back on that?"

"Yeah, I am."

"Why?"

Zach felt a rush of irritation. "For a start, because she wouldn't want my help. I offered to heat the casserole for her lunch and she all but pushed me out the door. You don't have to worry about her. I've never met a woman more capable than Brittany."

"Which is why she won't ask for help even when she needs it."

Remembering the oyster-pale skin and the dark shadows under her eyes, Zach shifted uncomfortably.

"She might want your help, if it was the right sort. When does she go to the hospital?"

"How would I know? We didn't exactly sit down and swap schedules." He hadn't asked. Hadn't thought about any of it. All his energies had been focused on not flattening her to the backseat of his car and doing all the bad things people were no doubt predicting he was already doing to her. It was the first time in his life he could remember wanting to live up to their expectations.

"So you don't have a plan?"

"I have a plan. My plan is to stay the hell away from her."

"That's one way. Another way would be to make amends. She's going to need transportation to the hospital and she can't drive. Taking the ferry and a cab will cost her. You could fly her direct."

Zach didn't consider himself an expert on relationships, but he was fairly sure that a free flight wasn't going to compensate for a broken marriage. "One of her friends will take her. Emily or maybe Ryan."

"Emily has her hands full with Lizzy and there is no way Brittany would ask Ryan. This is peak month for the Ocean Club. The place is bursting at the seams every day. And then there's the fact you're the one with the plane."

Zach looked at him in exasperation. "You seriously think I should offer to fly my ex-wife to her next hospital appointment?"

"Makes perfect sense to me. You could land right next to the hospital."

"Why would I do that?"

"Out of the goodness of your heart. Because you owe her."

Zach gave a humorless laugh. "I don't have a heart. And she'll say no."

"Then at least you've made the offer. Ask her. If the past really means nothing to her, if she's as indifferent to you as you think she is, she'll probably say yes."

"And if she doesn't?"

Philip put his empty beer bottle down on the table. "Then I'd say you've got something worth exploring."

"I don't think so. Even I have a problem with screwing the same person's life up twice."

Brittany had intended to spend the afternoon writing her blog and exploring ideas for her future, but after ten minutes of staring at her laptop screen without seeing it, she gave up. Her head felt fuzzy from jet lag. Her thoughts were full of Zach and she needed to clear her brain before she could work, so she took the sandy path that led directly from the cottage to the beach.

A couple with two young children was flying a kite near the water's edge. Shaped like a dragon, it dived towards the sand and soared skyward again in a blaze of color, its tail flapping in the wind.

Brittany watched for a while and then walked to the rocks at the far end of the beach. Protecting her wrist, she clambered out of reach of the sea and chose a flat boulder as a seat. From here she could see the granite outcrop where the puffins nested and one of the boat tours hovering close by. She recognized the boat and knew it was skippered by Doug, famous locally for managing to cram the maximum number of tourists onto each trip.

He was one of the many islanders who had found alternative ways to supplement the fishing business. On Puffin Island, they'd been luckier than some of the smaller islands in the bay. The varied and beautiful landscape and sheltered natural harbors made it a favorite not only for people looking for a weekend retreat from the city, but also for the sailing community, all of whom created a demand for restaurants and other services the locals were only too happy to provide.

Despite the swell of summer visitors, Shell Bay was never crowded. Day-trippers chose to stay on the beaches closer to the ferry and locals were too busy trying to tempt money out of the summer visitors to have much time to enjoy the pleasures of their own island.

The sea air cleared her head and she returned to the cottage, cut herself a slice of cheese and wrestled with the loaf of bread Emily had delivered the day before. With one hand, the end result was an uneven wedge that definitely could have provided a useful prop for an Indiana Jones movie.

The casserole was in the fridge, a constant reminder that her ex-husband had moved back to the island and she was considered to be in dire need of sympathy.

Muttering under her breath, she reached for her phone and sent a text to Skylar.

Are you busy this weekend? I have a casserole.

The reply came moments later.

You cooked? Are you sick?

Brittany grinned and texted back.

Don't ask. Just eat.

There was a brief pause.

I'll bring the wine. Tell Em to get a babysitter.

Feeling instantly better, Brittany flipped open her laptop and nibbled the cheese while she checked her emails.

There was a message from Spyros, her colleague from Greece, asking if she'd contact him.

She checked the time, decided he'd still be awake and called.

Moments later his face was on the screen and she felt her mood lift.

"Hey, you—how's your day going? Tripped up any more innocent archaeologists? I'm guessing it's the only way you can get a woman."

"I was nowhere near you at the time."

"You made me laugh. My concentration lapsed. And I'm paying the price."

"Does it hurt?"

"Like hell. A reminder that next time I need to look where I'm stepping. I got your message. You can't manage without me? You want me to fly back so you can drop grapes in my mouth?"

"We found something." His voice was deep and rich, his Greek accent more pronounced than usual. "I thought you'd like to see it."

She felt the rush of excitement that came with every new find. "You found it after I left? Do you have it? Show me."

He held it up to the camera and she narrowed her eyes. "Closer." She paused and studied the screen. "Could be obsidian. Hard to tell from here. Want to send it to me so I can take a closer look?" They both knew objects couldn't be removed from the country where they were found and Spyros smiled, showing a flash of white teeth in a bronzed, handsome face.

"I think the Greek government might object. And US Customs might not be thrilled, either. It's sharp."

"Yeah, well, obsidian was useful for weapons because it made great knife blades. Naturally occurring black volcanic glass—it was their equivalent of using a broken bottle. Anything else?"

"Nothing that would interest you. Pottery fragments."

"You're right. Boring. Pottery is Lily's area."

"It's not interesting enough for Lily, and anyway she's living the high life with her billionaire."

"She is. And they're perfect together. You should have seen them, Spy. So cute." Brittany sat back in her chair. "When do you go back to Athens? Is the university letting you stay until the end of August?"

"Yes. What about you? What are your plans?"

Her immediate plan was to get through the next few weeks without killing her ex-husband.

After that?

She was about to confess that she didn't have a clue what she was going to do with her life when she heard a knock at the door. "Hold on, Spy—" Hoping it wasn't another casserole, she sprinted to the door and opened it.

Zach stood there, dark eyes hooded, powerful thighs encased in the same black jeans he'd worn the day before. He radiated masculine vitality and seeing him rocked her in a way she didn't want to be rocked.

His gaze connected with hers and sent a thousand volts of electricity through her body.

Her response annoyed her and fried the mellow feeling she'd had talking to Spy.

"What can I do for you?" Worn-out with the effort of

projecting happiness, she went for crisp and businesslike but what effect that had on him she had no idea. Zach didn't share his thoughts and feelings with anyone. Not even her. If he had, she might have known he was thinking of leaving so soon after their wedding.

One of the hardest things to cope with afterwards was the realization that while she'd been dreaming of the future, he'd been dreaming of escape.

"We need to talk."

"I can't imagine what we have to talk about and I'm on video chat with someone right now, so—"

"I'll wait." He stepped inside the house before she could think of a reason to close the door in his face.

"Right. Well, you'll have to excuse me." She walked back into the kitchen, more rattled than she wanted to admit. "Spy, I have to go. Great to talk to you. And I definitely think it's obsidian."

Like Zach's eyes. The same volcanic black, sharp enough to slice like a blade.

It was a comparison she wished had escaped her.

For years Zach had been no more than a slightly uncomfortable memory, like a small stone rubbing inside her shoe.

She didn't want him to take up space in her head. There wasn't room for him anywhere in her life.

There certainly wasn't room in the small pretty kitchen of Castaway Cottage.

Zach topped six feet and his shoulders were broad and strong. She felt crowded and didn't like the feeling. What was he doing here and why would he choose to knock on her door after so many years had passed since he'd walked out of it?

"Something wrong, *agape mou*?" Spy's voice was smooth and deep and carried through the house.

Knowing that Zach was listening, Brittany felt tension ripple through her. "No, everything is fine, but I need to go. Speak to you soon, Spy." She ended the call, turned and met Zach's gaze. "Well? What did you want to talk about?

"Boyfriend?"

"Work colleague, although it's no business of yours what our relationship is. You lost the right to question me on my love life the day you walked out and left a note on the pillow." She snapped out the words before she could stop herself and then clenched her teeth together.

Damn, damn and double damn.

He didn't move. "I shouldn't have done that."

"Are you apologizing for leaving me?"

"No." His gaze held hers, dark and hypnotic. "I'm apologizing for the way I did it. I should have done it face-to-face."

So he didn't regret leaving her.

She was right back there, eighteen years old and bathed in humiliation. "Good to have cleared that up. Is that all you came to say? Because I'm busy."

"I didn't come to say that. I came because I thought you might need help."

"Why would I need your help?"

"You've injured your right wrist. You're struggling."

"Excuse me? I'm doing just fine and even if I wasn't—" she gaped at him, confused and exasperated "—am I supposed to believe you've suddenly morphed into this caring, sharing guy?"

A muscle flickered in his jaw. "I'm offering to help you."

She breathed deeply, wishing she'd paid more attention at her meditation class in college. "Goodbye, Zach. Close the door on your way out. And don't knock on it again. Or enter my house through any other means." Only with him would she have needed to add that qualifier. Maybe she'd get that lock he'd suggested. If only to keep him on the other side of her door.

"Your next hospital appointment is Tuesday?" He eyed the letter she'd left on the counter and she snatched it up.

"That is none of your business."

"I'll fly you there."

She blinked. Her ex-husband was offering to take her to the hospital for them to check her broken wrist? As far as she could see that turned a crappy trip into a double-crappy trip.

"I can't afford your services. Or do jilted wives get a special rate?"

He held her gaze and when he spoke his voice was devoid of emotion. "There's no charge."

"No, thanks." Flustered, she jabbed her fingers into her hair. "Look, you said you wanted to talk, so go ahead and say what you want to say and then leave."

"Not me. You."

Confused, she stared at him. "I don't need to talk."

"Are you sure? Because I don't see water flowing under that bridge."

Heat spread across her skin and misery seeped into her bones. "Believe it or not I know when I want to have a conversation. I don't. So you can just—"

"You never used to bottle things up. You used to come right out and say whatever was on your mind. It was one of the things I liked about you."

The breath left her lungs in a whoosh.

He'd never said he'd liked anything about her. He'd never complimented her or used smooth words.

At the time she'd told herself it didn't matter that he wasn't able to express his feelings.

It was only after he'd left her that she'd realized the reason he hadn't expressed himself was because he hadn't felt the things she'd wanted him to feel. She'd imagined his feelings to suit her own needs, but in reality they hadn't existed.

It was bitterly ironic that the first time he said something personal to her was ten years after they'd broken up. And even more ironic that he'd used her own emotional transparency against her.

"There is nothing I want to say."

"I walked out on you ten days into our marriage." His gaze was steady. "Most women would have plenty to say about that."

"I know what happened, Zach. I was there." *In pieces. Broken.* "And I had plenty to say at the time. Unfortunately you weren't there to hear it."

"I'm here now."

"And now I don't care."

"Seems to me that if you didn't care, you'd be accepting my offer of a lift to the hospital."

"Maybe I prefer to take a cab and go on the ferry."

His gaze held hers. "Yeah, that makes total sense. Why accept a twenty-minute journey when you could make it last four hours? The offer stays open. If you change your mind, call me."

"Goodbye, Zach."

She closed the door after him and stomped around the kitchen, crashing plates as she cleared the mess.

She'd spent so long putting the whole thing behind

her. Moving on. She'd rationalized it and learned from it. On a good day she could look back on it with humor. The bad days she ignored. Either way, it was in her past.

But now he'd shoved it into her present.

He'd ripped off all the new layers she'd built over the hurt. It was like demolishing a building right down to the foundations.

And what the hell was it all about?

Why was he offering to fly her to the hospital?

Confused and unsettled, she paced the kitchen and back again, trying to find the calm she so desperately needed. Instead her insides churned and boiled like the ocean threatening a storm.

She had no idea what to do with all the emotions inside her.

As far as she could see, there was only one way to fix this and it wasn't a casserole.

She needed emergency help from her friends.

Chapter 7

"Are these Greek olives?" Skylar reached out slender fingers and popped one in her mouth. "Mmm. Kalamata. So good. There's a tiny deli near my workshop that sells them marinated in garlic and oregano. I'm addicted. How many jars did you bring home?"

"Four, including that one." Hampered by having only one hand, Brittany handed the wine to Emily. The arrival of her friends had relieved some of the tension that had threatened to explode inside her. "You'll have to open this, it's one of the many tasks that are near impossible one-handed."

"Not being able to open a bottle of wine by yourself constitutes a life crisis." Skylar tilted her head. "If you clamp it between your thighs, you should be able to twist off the cap with your good hand."

"I can think of better things to clamp between my

thighs. And it's simpler to ask Emily. What are friends for if not to open wine?"

"To help you drink it." Skylar held out her glass. "Fill it up. I need it after the week I've had. Richard is stressed out. Understandable given that the elections are only a few months away. It's going to be very close. It makes him short-tempered so I'm walking on eggshells most of the time." Something in her tone set off alarm bells in Brittany's head.

She glanced at Emily who gave a brief shake of her head and filled the glasses.

Making a mental note to quiz Emily later, Brittany let Sky's remark go without further comment. "So what's new in the world of Tempest Designs?"

"My whole life is focused on my exhibition in December." Sky slid off her pumps and flexed her toes. "It will feel weird being in London so close to Christmas."

"You and Richard can turn it into a romantic break."

"He's not sure he can make it. If he wins, he'll be busy. And it's the holidays of course."

"But it's your big moment." Emily put her glass down slowly. "Surely he wants to be there."

"I wouldn't mind that much if he couldn't make it. He'll spend the whole time on the phone anyway and he's not at his best when he isn't the center of attention." Skylar turned her head and sniffed. "Something smells good. What are you feeding us?"

"Casserole of unknown origin." Brittany wondered if she was the only one who felt uneasy about Sky's relationship with Richard Everson. "Getting it into the oven required a feat of dexterity I'm glad you didn't witness, but one of you is going to have to lift it out because I'm not cuddling it now that it's hot."

"Talking of cuddling things that are hot, tell us about Zach."

"Nothing to tell."

"You invited me for the weekend so we could talk about nothing?"

Emily frowned. "She doesn't have to talk about it if she doesn't want to."

"Yes, she does." Sky leaned forward, an impish look in her eyes. "Have you talked to him since he saw you naked?"

Emily's eyes widened. "He saw you naked?"

Sky reached for another olive, the bracelets on her wrist jangling. "He heard her scream and rescued her. It was romantic."

Brittany sat down, enjoying the soothing warmth of the kitchen and the company of her friends. "Breaking and entering is not romantic." Knowing she wasn't going to get away with anything less than a full account of the happenings of the past few days, she surrendered to the inevitable and told the whole story.

Emily sipped her wine. "I hope you accepted his offer to fly you to the hospital."

"I didn't. Nor did I accept his suggestion that we talk."

"Why?" Skylar leaned forward. "Why turn down a golden opportunity to fry his firm, muscular butt?"

"Because it's in the past. I've moved on."

"Are you sure? Because no one would blame you if you hadn't. The man is hotter than hell in a heat wave." Skylar caught Emily's eye and shrugged defensively. "What? It's true! He is superhot. In a very bad-boy, dissolute, don't-turn-your-back-on-the-silver sort of way, of course. If it were me, I'd be tempted to rip his clothes off and find out if the sex is as good as ever."

Brittany thought about the moody black eyes and that lethally sexy body. Those strong, competent hands brushing over her underwear. "I'm not tempted."

"Of course she isn't," Emily said stoutly. "Brittany is smart. She has far more sense than to make the same mistake twice."

Skylar raised an eyebrow expectantly and Brittany sighed.

"Fine, I find him sexy—" she snapped out the words, more irritated with herself than with them "—but it makes no difference because I am not sleeping with my ex. I wouldn't put myself through that. Oh, hell, why did I ever come back here?"

"Because you need rest and recuperation and this is the perfect place."

"Not when it's been contaminated by your ex-husband. I've never felt less rested in my life."

"So to summarize," Emily said slowly, "you thought you felt nothing, you wanted to feel nothing, then you saw him and you felt something."

Skylar helped herself to another olive. "She felt a whole lot of something she didn't want to feel."

Brittany slumped in her chair and stared gloomily at her wine. "I don't know what I felt, but none of it was good."

"You need to explore those feelings."

"No, she doesn't!" The suggestion seemed to trouble Emily. "I think she needs to let it go. It's bound to feel a little weird and uncomfortable seeing him after all this time, but if she *ignores* those feelings, they'll fade."

"Ignoring feelings is dangerous. They have a way of growing and damaging your insides. Better to let it out. It's cathartic." Skylar picked up the wine bottle and emptied it into Brittany's glass. "There's another in the fridge. Move your butt, Em."

"We should eat the casserole before we open the next bottle. And it might not be cathartic." Emily stood up. "It could just open old wounds and then she'll be upset all over again. I don't see what there is to be gained."

"For a start, she'd enjoy some spectacular off-the-scale sex."

"I'm sitting right here," Brittany muttered. "You could include me in the conversation. And your imagination is in overdrive."

Sky grinned. "You were the one who told us the sex was amazing. I was so envious I wanted to poke you in the eye with a stick. At that point in my life I'd only been on the receiving end of awkward teenage fumbling, but you'd had the real thing. Mature guy who knew everything about sex. He must have been the perfect first time. And second time."

Brittany felt as if she'd been fried in hot oil. "I can hardly remember. I probably exaggerated to impress you."

"Lying has never been part of our friendship."

Emily gave a sigh of exasperation. "She was eighteen. It was her first time. She's turned it into something big in her mind, that's all."

The corner of Sky's mouth dimpled with wicked humor. "Was it big? Because any moment now I'm going to leave Richard and try it for myself."

Emily rolled her eyes. "Eat another olive, Sky. Do anything except talk."

"I'm just trying to establish the facts, that's all. I grew up in a house full of lawyers. I can't help myself. So Dr. Forrest—" Sky adopted a formal tone "—you need to remember you are under oath. Was sex with Zachary Flynn the best you've ever had in your life?"

"Maybe." It was something she tried not to think about because the good feelings were all mixed up with the bad, but both her friends were looking at her and she sighed. "Yes."

Skylar glanced triumphantly at Emily. "Your witness."

Emily shook her head and walked to the fridge for the second bottle of wine. "You're encouraging her to have sex with a man she hates."

"Emotion doesn't need to play a part. She should enjoy all that superior skill and experience without worrying about the rest of it. All hormones and no heart."

"Not going to happen." Brittany held out her glass. "I'm not interested and neither is he. There are no feelings on either side."

"Are you sure about that? He broke into your house to save you. Those aren't the actions of a guy who has no feelings."

Brittany gave Emily a desperate look. "Can you stop her talking?"

"No. And I actually agree with her about that part." Emily's voice was soft as she topped up the glasses. "I think he cares, Brit."

Brittany shook her head. "To most men a gesture of caring would be a bunch of flowers or a box of chocolates. To Zachary Flynn it's a bit of B and E."

"Did he break a window?"

"No."

"A lock?"

She shifted in her seat. "No."

"Then how did he get in?"

"I didn't ask. I don't want to know."

"Well, you should." Worried, Emily glanced at the kitchen door. "It means the cottage isn't secure. If he can get in, so can someone else."

Brittany rubbed her fingers over her forehead. "He said the same thing, but it's nonsense. Not everyone has his skills."

"So you keep telling us." Sky gave a dirty laugh. "Which brings us back to the original conversation."

"Stop talking and eat." Emily removed the casserole from the oven. "I can't believe someone made this for you. The islanders are so kind. I'll never forget the way they protected Lizzy when that awful journalist was trying to find her." She set the casserole in the middle of the table and lifted the lid. "Smells amazing. Wine and herbs. *Boeuf bourguignon?*"

Skylar stood up, too, and headed for the drawers nearest to the door. Both girls had spent so much time here over the years that they moved around the kitchen as confidently as Brittany. "This is one of the many things I love about Puffin Island. If you mooch around the harbor looking brokenhearted you could eat free for the whole month. No cooking." It was a well-known fact that Sky, despite being astonishingly creative in so many different ways, hated cooking. Today her contribution was to find napkins, twist them into pretty shapes and light a candle she found at the back of a drawer. Intercepting their glances, she shrugged. "What? I know we're all girls, but I don't see why every meal can't be beautifully presented. We deserve a romantic atmosphere."

"You sound like Kathleen. She always insisted we sat down at the table with napkins. No TV dinners or eating on the run." Emily served rice and ladled the casserole into bowls. "I miss her."

Brittany felt the pang of loss. "Me, too. I could do with having her here to kick my butt right now." And to hug her and tell her everything would be all right. "It's a sad truth that kicking your own butt is nowhere near as effective as someone else doing it."

"Don't worry, we're here to kick it for you." Skylar returned to her seat and raised her glass. "To Kathleen, who was as wise as she was wonderful. And who would want you to do what feels right, even if that meant having sex with Zach."

"I'm not having sex with my ex-husband. For a start it would be more than he deserves and secondly that would make me stupid twice."

"Was it stupid the first time?"

"Yes." Brittany took a sip of wine and stared through the window, watching as the last of the evening sun sent a golden glow over the garden. "He was too damaged, too messed up, to ever trust anyone. He treated every human being he met with anger and suspicion. Maybe that was understandable in the circumstances, but it didn't make a great foundation for a relationship and you can't build a solid, lasting structure without foundations. A relationship is a structure, isn't it? It's something you build together." She stared into the distance, thinking about what had gone wrong. "I was flattered that he was even interested in me. Everyone warned me, but I didn't listen. I thought we had something special, and in a way maybe we did, but it still wasn't enough. You can't have a relationship without trust and intimacy, and Zach didn't know anything about either of those things."

Emily picked up her fork. "You still have feelings, don't you? In which case you're right to be careful."

"Where's the fun in being careful?" Skylar ate hungrily. "I don't want to be bed bound at ninety with arthritic hips, regretting all the sex I didn't have. I want to be able to lie there with a smile on my face thinking, *man, that was good*. I think you should throw caution to the wind and have wild monkey sex with him."

"It isn't going to happen. I'd rather drop a hair drier in the bath while I'm standing in it. My plan is to ignore the feelings and hope they go away." Brittany ate a few mouthfuls. "This is good."

"It is. I'm trying to work out what's in it—" Emily dissected the food on her plate. "And even if you're planning on ignoring those feelings, you can still let Zach fly you to the hospital. It would be the perfect opportunity to prove to him once and for all that you're not hiding anything. Think of it this way. The journey will be quick and free."

"Nothing in life is free. Zach was the one who taught me that."

And she wondered what the price was going to be this time.

Chapter 8

Of all the planes he'd flown since that first flight with Philip, the Cessna Caravan was his favorite. As a bush pilot, he'd flown at both ends of the temperature spectrum, first in Australia where he'd spent a short time flying for a company that served remote Aboriginal communities, then in Alaska where the sheer versatility and performance of the aircraft had enabled him to fly across 92,000 square miles of isolated Arctic wilderness that included the oil-rich Prudhoe Bay. He'd flown everyone from physician's assistants on search-and-rescue missions, to a school volleyball team competing in a high school athletic program. They all had one thing in common. They needed a skilled pilot and a reliable plane that could land anywhere.

When it had come to setting up his own business, Zach had known which plane he wanted. He'd chosen the Amphibian so that he could land on any terrain, and opted for an interior luxurious enough to satisfy the pickiest billionaire.

Philip Law had taught him many things, one of which was the importance of a thorough preflight check.

Given that flying was still the single thing he loved most in the world, he figured it made sense to make sure the plane wasn't likely to fall out of the sky.

He started at the nose of the aircraft, checking the battery and fuel control unit. The sun beat down on him and he wiped his forearm across his brow before moving on to the exhaust stack, the P3 pneumatic bleed air lines and the orange cockpit heat hoses. In this aircraft the engine-fire detection loop went around the exhaust stack and the P3 bleed air lines, so he made sure there were no cracks in the exhaust or loose connections that were likely to trigger the engine fire light and set off ear-splitting alarms in the cockpit.

He moved through his checks, swift but thorough, and gave the cowling door a gentle punch with his fist to make sure it wasn't going to pop open after takeoff.

Because he was on top of the aircraft, he saw the car approach and pull up.

A glimpse of rich gold in the driver's seat told him Emily was driving and he watched as the two women hugged, displaying an emotional connection far outside the scope of his own experience. The visible demonstration of affection did nothing to warm the cold, dark place inside him.

He had no doubt that their friendship was deep and genuine. He also knew that true friendship required trust and a leap of faith, which was why his relationships only ever skimmed the surface.

It wasn't just that he didn't trust anyone. He knew he couldn't be trusted.

And Brittany knew that, too.

She'd handed him her heart, and he'd dropped it.

He watched as she stepped out of the car.

Her hair shone in the sunlight and an oversize pair of dark glasses covered her eyes. She'd replaced her trademark shorts with a pair of skinny jeans and her favorite hiking boots with pretty canvas flats.

Wondering what the hell had possessed him to offer to fly her to the mainland, Zach turned back to the aircraft, finished his check and then joined her on the tarmac.

"Philip gave me the message that you'd changed your mind." And he'd done it with a knowing look that Zach had chosen to ignore.

"I decided you were right." She adjusted the glasses on her nose. "There was no reason at all for me to turn down your kind offer."

It hadn't been a kind offer. It had been a— What had it been?

A salve to his guilt?

He had no idea, but he was beginning to wish he'd kept his mouth shut.

As she stepped towards the plane, he caught the light scent of her perfume. His senses spun and desire ripped through him. As someone who rarely had a problem controlling his feelings, it was irritating to discover that lusting after someone wasn't something you could turn off.

He gritted his teeth, pushed down the surge of awareness and watched as Brittany strolled around the plane and then stood with her hands on her hips and her head tilted to one side. "Is this a good moment to tell you that the nose is crooked?"

The sunlight added polish to her hair and her skin, and the breeze played with a loose strand, whipping it across her face.

She was arresting rather than pretty, her body honed to an impressive level of fitness from a life spent outdoors. But what really drew him wasn't the dip of her waist or the curve of her mouth, it was the energy that pulsed from her, the sense of optimism that sent a thousand volts of positivity into the surrounding air. She was the type of person who assumed the toast would always land buttered-side up. He'd heard her described as "the girl next door" and had never really understood that because she was nothing like the neighbors he'd had growing up.

All he knew was that she was sexy as hell.

He wanted to bury himself in her. He wanted to take her, right there and then, like the animal he was fairly sure he was.

Instead he reached for a cloth and wiped his hands, focusing on the small things to try to distract from the feelings that were driving him crazy. "That's normal." His voice was surprisingly level given the fact that his willpower was stretched to breaking point. "The engine is canted down three degrees and to the right five degrees. Helps minimize propeller effects during power-ups."

He prayed she wasn't going to start talking to him about thrust or propulsion or he'd be in serious trouble.

The corner of her mouth dimpled into a smile. "I have no idea what any of that means."

"Do you want me to explain?"

"No. This is your domain. I've never been a nervous flyer but if I knew the details, that might change. We should probably go, shouldn't we? I don't want to be late for my appointment." She was talking a little too fast, the fingers on her good hand fiddling with the strap of her purse.

Recognizing the gesture, Zach frowned. He saw the same thing in passengers used to flying first-class in a jumbo jet, where most of the time they forgot they were even in the air. A small plane was a different experience and, for some, an unnerving one. "You don't need to be anxious."

"Why would I be anxious? You don't scare me, Zach. You never did."

He watched her for a long moment, absorbing the implications behind her answer. "I was talking about the plane."

"Oh." She captured a wayward strand of hair and tucked it behind her ear, exposing the streak of pink on her cheek. "The answer is still no. I'm fine. I know you're a good pilot. And it's not as if it's my first time."

He wished she hadn't used those exact words.

He remembered her first time.

Judging from the deepening color in her cheeks, she did, too.

She mumbled something unintelligible and then turned and climbed the steps into the plane leaving him wondering if it was safe to be standing this close to a tank of aviation fuel.

The way he was feeling right now, the aircraft was likely to ignite.

He followed her up the steps and saw her fumbling to fasten the belt without damaging her injured wrist. Her teeth were clamped on her lip as she focused on getting it done. She didn't want his help and he didn't want to give it.

He didn't trust himself to be that close to her.

He was sure that both of them were relieved when the belt clicked home.

Wordless, he handed her a headset and settled himself in the cockpit, grateful for the routines and discipline that distracted him from the woman seated behind him.

The takeoff was smooth and the flight short and uneventful.

Once in the air, Zach forgot about his passenger. For a short flight like this one he chose not to switch on the autopilot, preferring to hand-fly the airplane. That strategy had kept him alive in icy conditions in Alaska, where he'd discovered the autopilot could mask cues. He listened to the airplane, drew on training, experience and sheer gut instinct. And he loved every moment. That part had never changed. His love for flying hadn't reduced since that first time Philip had taken him up. If anything, it had deepened.

Twenty minutes later, he landed and checked on his passenger, only to find her asleep.

"Brittany." He said her name, got no response and braced his hands on the arms of her seat. "Brittany." This time he said it louder and she stirred, her eyes opening slowly, as if her eyelids were too heavy to lift.

Her eyes were bronze, flecked with gold lights, and they were focused on him. The look in them was one he remembered. It was the way she'd always looked at him in those first moments of waking.

Trusting.

The look was gone in an instant.

"Get away." She pushed at his chest with her good hand. "You're invading my personal space."

"Yeah, well, there was no waking you." He straightened, telling himself it was a good thing the trust had gone.

Expecting people to let you down was a much safer way to live a life.

"I have jet lag, that's all." She reached for her purse. "Will you be here when I come back?"

"You think I'm planning on leaving you stranded?"

"Wouldn't be the first time."

Defenseless against that accusation, Zach simply looked at her. "I'll be here. Do you want me to come with you?"

"No, thank you. What will you do while you wait? Do you have someone else to fly?"

"Just you. Today is quiet." He'd made sure he kept the day clear, just in case she'd changed her mind about accepting his offer. The fact that he'd turned down a potentially lucrative job flying a family to their lodge up in the mountains was information he didn't intend to share. He'd told himself he owed her this favor. "I have things I can do."

It was a long time before Brittany reappeared, and when she did she looked irritated and visibly upset.

After several hours of trying to cure an acute case of sexual arousal by working on the plane, Zach's mood wasn't the sunniest, either.

"How was it?"

"I was hoping he'd say the plaster could come off in a couple of weeks, but he seems to think it needs to stay on a while longer if I want to regain full function of my wrist and not have problems in the future." And she was obviously deeply unhappy about that decision.

"What did they say at the hospital in Greece? You had surgery?"

"Yes. They decided it was necessary because I'm

young and need full movement of my wrist." She climbed into the airplane and slumped into the nearest seat. "I'm starting to wish I'd paid more attention to where I was putting my feet."

"What happened? You tripped and put your hand out to save yourself?"

"Yes. I wish I'd fallen on my face. At least I would have had two hands to work with. It's driving me crazy. I'm bored out of my skull and I've only been home a few days."

"What do you need to do that you can't do at the moment?"

"Everything. I can't even take my kayak out, which is one of the things I love doing when I'm home. I can't ride my bike." She frowned. "Actually maybe I could ride my bike. I don't need two hands for that, right?"

He suspected this might be one of those instances where she wasn't really asking for his opinion. "The trails are uneven. If you fall, it's going to take longer to heal."

"So what am I expected to do for the next month? Just sit around watching TV? I'll die of boredom. And why did I never learn to do things with my left hand? I burned scrambled eggs this morning. How can anyone burn scrambled eggs?"

"Plenty of folk do that when they have both hands in use." Risking his life, he reached forward to help her with her seat belt, and the backs of his fingers brushed against her abdomen. She tensed and her eyes met his.

In that brief unguarded moment he saw everything she was hiding. All the emotions simmering right there just beneath the surface.

And he knew she wasn't indifferent.

Knew that everything he'd seen since he'd flown her to the island that first day had been an act.

"Brittany—"

"I'm really tired and it hasn't been a great day so far. If it's all right with you, I'd like to go home now." Her voice was husky and she turned her head away, staring out the window.

He stared at her profile, seeing the clenched jaw and the glaze of misery in those golden eyes.

Knowing that he was the last person who should criticize someone for trying to hide their feelings he straightened and returned to the front of the airplane.

He'd disciplined himself right from the start never to allow emotions access to the cockpit. He flew with his head and his instincts engaged, knowing that plenty of accidents had occurred when the pilot was distracted.

He told himself that today was no different.

He might have dropped Brittany ten days into their marriage, but he wasn't about to dump her into the ocean.

And if she was upset, well, she had her friends to talk to.

She didn't need him.

Why the hell hadn't she taken the ferry?

Her head ached and her wrist throbbed, but the feeling that bothered her most of all was the butterfly flutter of awareness in her stomach that refused to die.

It was a feeling she associated with her teenage years, along with the heady excitement of first love and the shivery recklessness that was part of youth.

She didn't expect to feel it now, years later, when she was older and supposedly wiser.

Too wise to be distracted by a strikingly handsome

face and a body made of hard honed muscle and sinuous strength.

Remembering Sky's suggestion that they should just have sex, she ran her good hand over her face and closed her eyes.

The more she tried not to think about it, the more she found herself thinking of nothing else. She could imagine herself sliding her hands under his shirt, tracing skin pulled taut over the brutal swell of hard muscle. She could feel the coarseness of chest hair grazing her naked flesh, the graze of his jaw as he dragged his mouth down her body. She could feel the slow stroke of his hands, the skill of his mouth...

Shit.

She opened her eyes.

She wasn't going to feel any of that.

She wasn't going to be the sort of woman who repeated her mistakes.

He'd been her first lover. She'd been eager, but clueless, following his lead in everything. It had felt like the biggest adventure of her life. She'd had relationships since, but nothing that had matched the physical intimacy she'd shared with Zach.

What would it be like now?

With a groan, she opened her eyes and stared out the window.

That was one question she was never going to be able to answer.

No way.

She wasn't going there.

The moment they landed, she ripped off the headset, dived into her bag for her phone and called Emily.

The call went to voice mail and she decided to wait a few minutes and call back instead of leaving a message.

Zach strolled out of the cockpit. "Something wrong?"

"No. But I'm supposed to be calling Emily when we land, and her phone is going to voice mail."

"I'll take you home." He gave her a long look that made her wonder if somewhere on his sophisticated instrument panel was a device that scanned her thoughts.

Presumably not, or the aircraft would have been filled with ringing alarms and flashing red lights.

"I'll get a cab." She fumbled with her seat belt, stood up and caught her foot in the strap of her purse in her haste to get away from him. Without her right hand to save her she would have fallen, but Zach shot out his arm and caught her around the waist.

She fell against him, her good hand planted in the middle of his chest and her thighs pressed against the hardness of his.

It was as if fate were trying to torture her.

She heard him mutter something under his breath, felt the strength of his arm and the warmth and pressure of his hand on the dip of her waist. In that instant there was no space between them. With anyone else she would have laughed it off as nothing more than an embarrassingly clumsy moment, but Zach wasn't just anyone and she was a million miles from laughing. It was impossible not to notice that her body fitted against his perfectly. They molded together as if they'd been designed to custom fit and she felt a dizzy excitement she'd only ever felt when she was near him. Desire ran through her like liquid fire, sexual heat so intense she was afraid she might burn up right there and then. If the fuel tanks were full, it was likely she'd take the airplane with her. She had no idea how something so wrong could feel so right.

"Sorry. Clumsy seems to be my middle name." Without meeting his eyes, she eased away from him and stooped to pick up her bag. Her legs were liquid. So were her insides.

She didn't dare look at him. She didn't need to know if he was feeling what she was feeling.

What she needed was to get out of here as fast as possible.

She called Emily again as she walked down the steps to the tarmac, the phone almost slipping from her fingers as she willed her friend to answer.

Pick up, pick up, pick up.

The phone went to voice mail again.

"My car is parked here." His tone was level. If he'd felt what she had felt, then he wasn't showing it. "I just need a few minutes and then I'll take you."

"No need. I'll call Pete." Pete drove one of the island cabs and Brittany had known him since she was a child.

"The ferry just docked. Pete will be busy. I can get you home faster."

There was no logical reason why a woman who was supposedly indifferent to him would refuse.

Ten minutes, she told herself. Ten minutes, and she wouldn't invite him in.

"Thanks. I'll wait by the car while you do whatever it is you need to do."

She waited, bathed in sunshine and her own sinful thoughts.

When he finally joined her, she noticed that he'd slid on sunglasses.

She did the same.

She didn't look at him.

He didn't look at her.

Neither of them spoke during the short journey to Shell Bay, but the silence created more tension than words would have done.

By the time Zach pulled up outside her cottage, Brittany was contemplating plunging fully clothed into the Atlantic to cool off.

"Goodbye, Zach. Thank you." She was out of the car the moment it stopped, running for the sanctuary of Castaway Cottage.

Zach gripped the wheel. Ahead of him waves crashed onto the rocks that guarded the soft curve of Shell Bay, and to his right lay the cottage.

And Brittany.

She'd closed the door in his face, and that was after she'd done just about everything to try to avoid being in the car with him.

Ignoring the part of his brain that said this was a bad idea, he walked up to the door of the cottage. He didn't bother knocking because he knew she wouldn't answer. Instead he took a chance that she hadn't locked the door.

She hadn't, and he stepped into the hall just as she emerged from the kitchen to investigate the noise.

Her eyes widened. "More breaking and entering?"

"You can't break through something that isn't locked." In the back of his mind he knew he needed to address her lax approach to security, but right now he had other things on his mind.

"What do you want, Zach?"

"I want you to say whatever it is that's on your mind

instead of behaving as if you're auditioning for cheerleader of the year."

The faint flicker in her eyes told him he'd scored a direct hit. "I don't have anything on my mind. What could I possibly have to say to you after all this time?"

"Plenty, I would have thought, given the note I left on your pillow." He still remembered lying awake in a blind panic and then scrabbling in her bag to find a pen, something to write with. He couldn't remember exactly which words he'd used, but he knew they weren't Shakespeare.

"The message in the note was clear enough."

"And you don't have anything you want to say about it?"

"I had plenty I could have said to you at the time, but that was ten years ago. I don't have feelings about something that happened so long ago."

"I don't believe you. I'd say you have plenty of feelings. In fact I'd say you have so many feelings you don't know what to do with them." He saw the brief flash of her eyes, shards of anger that dazzled before she masked it.

"You should go now, Zach."

Zach decided that he hated polite conversation almost as much as he hated cocktails and social media.

"I'm not leaving until we've dealt with this." He moved closer to her and Brittany backed away until her shoulders made contact with the wall.

"It's ironic that when I wanted you to stay, you couldn't wait to leave, and now when I can't wait for you to leave, it's impossible to get rid of you."

For some bizarre reason it made him feel better to hear her finally speaking the truth. "I know I deserve that."

"Oh, you deserve a hell of a lot more than that, Zach. You want me to tell you how I really feel? Right now I hate you." Her eyes blazed and her chest rose and fell. "I hate you and I want you to get the hell out of my house."

He was standing so close he could almost feel the heat coming from her.

Their relationship had always been intensely physical. Long stretches of simmering promise interspersed with wild moments of sexual oblivion.

"You don't hate me. I think you *want* to hate me, but you don't and that's driving you crazy." He cupped her jaw, lifting her face to his. "You hate the fact you still feel something." He could feel the softness of her skin and the rapid pounding of her pulse beneath his fingers.

"What I feel is regret that I ever got involved with you in the first place. Goodbye, Zach."

If he'd been paying attention to the words he would have left, but there were other forces at work. Deeper, darker forces that sparked something on an elemental level.

"You don't feel anything?" He caged her, planting an arm on either side of her to prevent her escape.

"That's right. Sorry if that bruises your ego, and now you need to—"

He flattened her to the wall and brought his mouth down on hers. The feel of her lips brought a groan to the back of his throat. She tasted soft and sweet, like strawberries dipped in sugar. And then the sweetness turned darker, more wicked and the explosion of heat consumed him. He'd expected to prove a point, but ended up slaking a hunger, filling a need.

Sex was a skill of his. He'd learned all the moves, knew how to touch, how to give maximum pleasure to his partner. He treated sex like an athletic workout, a sequence of calculated physical moves culminating in mutual satisfaction. For Zach, there was never an emotional element. He was well aware that there were women who had wanted him to fall in love with them. Women who had hoped to be the one to cure him of whatever defect stopped him from truly engaging with another human being. They'd never succeeded.

As a young child he'd learned to switch off feelings and then as an adult had discovered he had no idea how to switch them on again.

He'd married Brittany because it had felt like the right thing to do, and he had swiftly discovered that it wasn't.

Like everyone else, she'd wanted something he wasn't capable of giving. Disappointing people, letting them down, had been a feature of his life. Up until the point where he had married Brittany, it had never bothered him. He figured that people's expectations were their own and if they chose to pin them on him, then it wasn't his fault if their worst predictions came true. With Brittany, it had been different. Her naive and unquestioning belief in him had almost suffocated him.

He'd known from the start that he was going to let her down.

That part had been inevitable.

This, he thought, as he focused all his expertise on her mouth, this was all he'd ever been capable of giving.

He waited for her to slap his face, or at least push him away, do any of the things he'd been waiting for her to do since the day he'd flown her back to the island. Part of him would even have welcomed it. He'd take real honest emotion any day over this bland coating of indifference she'd painted over her feelings. He wanted her anger as if fury might be a salve for his own guilt.

What he got was her desire, as raw and real as his own.

Her mouth opened under his, and he felt the moist tip of her tongue touch his in erotic invitation.

The kiss rocketed out of control so fast it almost unbalanced him. It should have been all about technique, a less-than-subtle way of proving a point, but somehow Brittany had shifted the balance of power. Her arms came up and locked around his neck, her head angled to one side as she pressed against him.

Never in a million years would he have described himself as sensitive or gentle, but he usually made an attempt to keep things one step up from animal, if only because reading his partner's physical needs was one of his skills.

Not this time.

This time his response was primal and overwhelming. He devoured her mouth, flattened her back against the wall and cupped her breast in his hand. He felt her nipple peak under the deliberate brush of his fingers, felt the race of her heart against his palm and the movement of her chest as she pressed against him.

She moaned against his mouth and he clamped his hand behind her head and held her there, trapped, captive, locking her against him in an exchange of sparks, fire and raw lust.

He felt her good hand go to the front of his shirt and drag him closer still, until every part of them was touching and the only thing separating them was a thin layer of clothing.

Still it wasn't enough.

He planted his hand against the wall to steady himself, using the other to haul her close so that her lean body was welded against the hardness of his. Her response was to hook her leg around his waist and drive the soft parts of herself against the thickened length of him. Only the fabric of his jeans and hers stopped him being inside her.

"Holy shit." He felt the restless grind of her hips and anchored them with his hands. He was hard and throbbing, his breaths coming in ragged pants as he felt her fingers go to the snap of his jeans.

That blatant move cut through any doubts he might have had.

She fumbled, moaned in frustration and he slid his hand from her breast to her jeans, stripping them off with a speed that would have raised eyebrows in some circles. Removing clothes had never given him problems. He might not have a college degree, but he knew a thousand ways to get a woman naked.

He pushed her jeans down her thighs and lifted her. Without detaching her mouth from his, she kicked off the trousers and wrapped her legs around his waist, supple as a gymnast.

Supporting her with one arm, freeing himself was more of a problem but he managed it, dealt with the ribbon of cotton that masqueraded as her underwear and provided the final barrier between them, and felt the delicious heat of delicate flesh.

Her mouth was hot on his, her legs wrapped so tightly around him that for the first time in his life he almost forgot the condom he always carried. He was seconds away from breaking a lifetime rule when some deeply ingrained sense of self-preservation made him dig it out of his pocket.

He paused long enough to ensure there would be at least one consequence he wouldn't have to face and then lowered his forehead to hers. Their gazes locked. Her breath came in rapid pants and her eyes, those rich, tiger-gold eyes that challenged him at every turn, were bright with need.

"Yes." She murmured the word against his mouth. "God, yes."

He felt her angle her body to his and then he thrust and there was nothing but the heat.

He felt her stretch, her body welcoming the invasion of his. She tensed slightly, slick and tight against the solid fullness of his erection, and he closed his hands around her thighs, holding himself still, giving her time to adjust. Held like this, she was helpless. *His.* He'd discovered sex earlier than most and for years it had been the only place where he had control. He had an armory of moves at his disposal, and he'd learned to use them.

As a result, bed was the one place in the world where he managed to please a woman.

Her gasp turned to a sob and he swallowed it, licking into her mouth as he drove deeper, surging into her until they were joined so deeply, he could feel every tiny ripple and movement of her body. Desire consumed him, hot waves of pleasure swamping thought and reason. Neither of them paused to question whether it was a good idea. Neither of them hesitated or tried to pull back. It was a raw, primitive and utterly basic slaking of sexual need.

He felt her hand slide into his hair while the other, the one restricted by the cast, lay useless against his shoulder. He felt the urgency of her mouth on his as he surged into her with slow, relentless rhythm designed to drive them both insane.

He clamped the smooth curve of her bottom, and felt her hand slide to the hard muscle of his shoulder. If she'd had long nails he would have been lacerated, and still they kissed, crazily, frantically, as if it were the only way of sustaining life. They kissed right the way through to the screaming peak of pleasure that slammed into them with the force of an express train. Feeling her tighten around him like a silken vice, Zach groaned deep in his throat and gave himself up to the wild pulsating force of his own release.

It took a moment for his head to clear and for him to emerge from the dizzying fog of arousal.

He lowered her but didn't release her, and she didn't release him, either. Her good hand stayed on his shoulder for support while the other lay limp by her side.

She struggled for breath, her head turned away from him.

Finally his brain cleared and he realized two things: that he was still fully clothed and that she was naked from the waist down. At some point he'd managed to rip her thong and it lay on the floor, a seductive wisp and an accusation. Destruction of property. Another crime to add to the many.

He wondered if he could plead insanity.

Words were never his strong point, and right now he didn't have a clue which ones to use or which order to use them in.

"Brittany—"

"Sex and screwing up," she said. "The two things you were always good at." Her eyes lifted to his and he felt a rush of emotion he couldn't identify.

He'd wanted the truth and she'd given it to him, but somehow hearing it didn't bring him the relief he'd anticipated.

"And flying." His voice sounded raw. "Don't forget flying."

"Damn you." She pushed at his chest with her good hand. "Damn you, Zach. I— You have to leave."

He wondered how the hell she expected him to leave when he'd managed to create a situation a thousand times more complicated than the one he'd hoped to fix. "No."

"I'm begging you."

He was about to refuse again when he saw the glisten of moisture in her eyes. It floored him more than a punch from her fist would have done.

He'd made plenty of women cry in his time. It was another thing he was good at. What he wasn't good at was fixing it, usually because fixing it required some sort of promise he wasn't prepared to make. Because he never made promises, he figured he was free to walk away without a stain on his conscience.

Except that one time of course, when he hadn't just made a promise, he'd made it in public in a way that was legal and binding.

His entire body was tense.

Over the years he'd wondered about her reaction to what he'd done.

He'd imagined her storming with anger and punching holes in the wall.

The one thing he hadn't allowed himself to imagine was her crying.

It was something he'd never seen. He'd seen her furious, those tiger eyes sending lightning shards of anger towards the source of her annoyance, and he'd seen her doubled over in helpless laughter.

He'd never seen this.

He lifted his hand to pull her close but he had no words of comfort for this situation.

How did you comfort someone when you were the cause of their misery?

All he could do was remove himself, but his legs refused to take him in any direction, not even towards the exit.

"Don't cry." His teeth were gritted and his entire body ached with the willpower required to not touch her. "Hell, Brittany, hit me. Yell at me. Anything, but don't cry."

"Get out, Zach." Her voice cracked. "Get the hell out of here."

And finally, perhaps because of her tone or maybe because the moisture in her eyes was brimming like a river about to burst its banks, his body unfroze itself and his legs obliged long enough to walk him through her door.

Chapter 9

"Ryan wanted to change it to granite or soapstone, but I love this butcher's block." Emily ran her hand over the counter and Skylar nodded.

"I love it, too. It's a little stained in places but that's because it's a natural material. And each mark tells a story."

"I'm a little worried the story it's going to tell about me is that I shouldn't be allowed in the kitchen. What do you think, Brittany?"

Brittany was staring over the garden, watching the last of the evening light fade away. Her stomach felt hollow and she felt physically sick.

"Brittany?"

"Sorry?" She blinked and realized both her friends were staring at her. "What?"

"We were talking about the kitchen. What do you think of the counters?"

"I—" She couldn't think of anything except Zach, the midnight black of his eyes as he'd held her gaze and surged into her. The heat of his mouth on hers as they'd shared every breath. "I think you should do whatever feels right to you."

Or maybe not.

Sex with Zach had felt utterly right at the time and utterly wrong five minutes later.

For years he'd been a mistake in her past and now he was right back in her present.

"Is something wrong? You're very distracted." Emily stirred the chowder. "I called you twice yesterday and you didn't answer. I was about to drive over when you texted."

"I was catching up on some things, that's all. I did some reading, answered some emails—" Sat on the beach, stared at the sea, wondered what the hell it was about Zachary Flynn that drove her to do crazy things. What was she going to say next time she saw him? Their relationship had been complicated before, but nothing compared to now. "I put my phone down somewhere and couldn't find it." The thought of what Emily might have found had she driven over made Brittany vow never to let her phone out of her sight again. "Were you calling for a reason?"

"Ryan was giving Lizzy a sailing lesson and I was going to ask you to the Ocean Club for dinner. I wanted to hear what happened at the hospital."

"It was uneventful. I have to keep the cast on a while longer. Which means I'm doomed to be bored and cross for the rest of the summer."

Bored, cross and sexually frustrated.

"You could help Lisa at Summer Scoop. Her business has really picked up over the last couple of weeks. Sky, there's a fresh loaf from The Beach Bakery in that bag. Can you slice it?" Flustered, Emily checked the chowder again and then turned her attention back to Brittany. "Is that why you're upset? Because you were hoping the cast would come off?"

"I'm not upset. I'm just impatient. You know me."

Unfortunately they did know her, which was why neither was prepared to accept that explanation.

Skylar sliced fresh bread into chunks. "Is Zach the reason you're upset? Did something happen when he flew you to the hospital?"

Before Brittany could reply, the door opened and Ryan walked into the kitchen.

"Do you need any help with the food?"

"What's that supposed to mean?" Emily's face was pink from standing over the stove, wisps of hair falling around her face. "I may not be an experienced cook but I can follow a recipe." She glanced nervously at the pan. "At least I think I can."

"It smells delicious and that was a genuine offer of assistance, not veiled concern." Ryan strolled across the room and wrapped his arms around his fiancée. "Don't turn into one of those women who imagine things that aren't there."

Skylar cleared her throat pointedly. "You're in a room with three women and hot liquid. Think before you generalize based on gender or we might add certain delicate parts of you to the chowder."

Wincing, Ryan kissed Emily and then released her, hands raised. "Hey, I'm as simple as I look. All I want is food." Dodging Skylar, he reached for the bread. "We can start with this. The three of us are dying of starvation."

"The three of you?" Emily tasted the chowder. "Lizzy is supposed to be asleep."

"She is asleep. I checked her ten minutes ago." Ryan found some plates for the bread. "Zach is here."

Brittany felt her insides turn over. Those were the three words she least wanted to hear. "Zach?" Her voice didn't sound like her own. "Why is he here?"

"Because I invited him."

"You—? Why would you do that?" Emily stared at Ryan, appalled, and he raised his eyebrows.

"Because he's our friend," he said slowly, "and as our friend, he's welcome in our home."

"But—" Emily shot Brittany an agonized look. "I'm *so* sorry. I had no idea he'd be here or I would have warned you."

"Why does she need warning?" Ryan looked baffled. "He flew her here on her first day, drove her home from the store the other day, flew her to the hospital and back—I assumed everything was cool between you guys."

"Oh, *Ryan*!" Emily looked at him reproachfully and he looked at her blankly.

"What? If there's a problem here, then you need to spell it out."

"For a start it would have been nice to have known I was catering for six, not five."

"Whenever you cook you always make enough for the entire island but you're right, I should have mentioned it. I would have done but I just happened to bump into Zach a few hours ago." Ryan put the bread and the plates down on the table, then walked over to her, cupped her face in his hands and kissed her. "Forgive me."

Emily melted, murmured a few words that the others couldn't hear, and then eased away. "It's not me you should be asking for forgiveness, it's Brittany. This is awkward, Ryan."

Ryan smoothed Emily's hair back from her face with a gentle hand and then glanced at Brittany. "Is it awkward? Am I in trouble?"

Brittany managed a smile. "Of course not. It's fine."

"There. I told you. They've been divorced for a decade. They've both moved on. Is this ready? I'll carry it through. It's heavy." Ryan reached for the chowder. "You can bring the bread and bowls, Sky."

Skylar waited until he'd walked through the door and shook her head. "Men," she said slowly as she juggled the bread and the bowls. "*Utterly* clueless."

"I'm not arguing with that, but in this case he's right. I've moved on." Keen to avoid a conversation, Brittany grabbed the bread. "I'll take that before you drop it." She didn't know which was more stressful, facing her friends or facing Zach.

How should she handle it?

Did she smile and pretend nothing had happened?

Did she just ignore the whole thing?

Deciding she might as well get it over with, she walked through to the dining room and almost fell over Cocoa, Ryan's spaniel, who was running around, excited at having so many visitors in the house.

"Sit." Ryan placed the chowder in the center of the table and glared at the dog. "Do *not* jump up."

Ignoring him, Cocoa wagged her tail hard, almost vibrating with the effort not to jump and put her paws on his legs.

The distraction gave Brittany a moment to compose herself.

Zach was lounging in tense, brooding silence at the far end of the table.

Even without looking she was aware of him, as if her body had some sort of internal radar that sent off signals whenever he was nearby.

Deciding that the longer she left it, the worse it would be, she glanced at him and acknowledged his presence with a brief nod.

Those volcanic dark eyes focused on her for a brief moment and she felt as if she'd been fried alive. Dark lashes shielded his expression and his slim, sensual mouth was unsmiling.

Remembering everything he could do with that mouth made heat rush from her toes to her neck.

Last time she'd seen him, he'd been stripping her naked in less time than it took most people to switch on their phone. And she would have done the same to him if she hadn't been a fumbling wreck. Fortunately, he'd had enough skills for both of them, which was why they now found themselves in this embarrassing situation.

The level of physical intimacy contrasted starkly with the emotional distance between them.

Awkward? No, it wasn't awkward. It was so much more than awkward, there wasn't a word for it.

She deposited the bread on the table.

What should she say?

She wanted to leave, but that would stimulate questions she didn't want to answer. It would also potentially create a problem between Ryan and Emily and she didn't want to be the cause of friction.

She slid into the only vacant chair, wishing it wasn't so close to Zach.

Alec and Ryan were locked in an argument about one

of the yachts moored in the marina and Emily was busy
ladling creamy chowder into the deep bowls. The atmosphere was warm and relaxed, laughter and conversation
flowing around her. Brittany was aware of nothing except
the pounding of her heart and the incredible stillness of
the man seated at the end of the table.

She couldn't breathe.

Couldn't think.

She kept her eyes down, reminding herself that these
were her friends. Four friends and one ex-lover.

Except he was no longer an ex.

Brittany's studied contemplation of the table was disturbed by a clatter and a gasp as Emily stepped forward
to pass a bowl and almost fell over Cocoa.

Ryan's hand shot out and he caught the bowl with one
hand and Emily with the other. "She isn't used to having so many people in the house at once. I'll put her in
the kitchen."

"No." Finally Zach spoke and he snapped his fingers
gently to attract the dog's attention. "Come."

He'd said the same thing to her, Brittany thought.
Right in the middle of the most mind-blowing sex of
her life, he'd said the same thing. And she'd obeyed without hesitation.

Apparently Cocoa was equally seduced by his charms.
Or maybe she was equally lacking in willpower. Sensing
an ally, the dog went to him instantly, pressed her face
to his palm and looked up at him hopefully.

Zach smiled at her.

Brittany felt the breath jam in her throat.

He smiled so rarely that when he did, she found it impossible to look away.

"You need to calm down or someone is going to fall

over you." He spoke quietly to the dog, his tone gentle. "You stay here with me."

Cocoa pressed closer to him and the moment he tried to withdraw his hand she nudged him, so he continued to stroke her ears with gentle, casual rubs of those long, strong fingers.

Brittany's heart started to pound a little harder.

He'd always been good with animals. Animals and vulnerable people.

Ryan looked amused. "From now on you're in charge of animal taming."

Zach's fingers continued to stroke and soothe. "She's tame enough."

"She's usually pretty good." Emily carried on serving the chowder. "She gets overexcited sometimes, that's all."

Who wouldn't? Keeping that thought to herself, Brittany reached for the bowl Emily handed her. If Zach were stroking *her* like that, she'd be overexcited, too.

Heat spread through her body and pooled in her pelvis.

That first time they'd had sex, he'd been so careful with her. So gentle.

Her mouth felt dry and her mind woolly.

"I was speaking to Rachel today." Ryan picked up his spoon. "She said they could do with help up at the camp. They've lost a couple of counselors and one instructor who had a wilderness first-aid certificate."

"Can't they recruit?" Alec gave an appreciative sniff. "Smells good, Emily."

"Too late in the season to recruit. They're managing to cover water sports, but they lost their archery instructor last week and they're short of people to help with outdoor adventure activities."

Brittany was only half listening. She kept reliving the

moment Zach had slid his hand into her hair and stared down into her eyes.

Her breathing grew shallow.

She couldn't take her eyes off his hand, hypnotized by the slow stroke of his fingers as he calmed the dog.

Cocoa was in a coma of ecstasy.

Brittany dragged her eyes from his fingers but only made it as far as his biceps. Unsettled, she forced herself to look up and collided with the heat of his gaze.

She waited for him to look away, but he didn't. He kept looking at her until her heartbeat was like a pounding drum and it felt as if all the air had been sucked from the room.

Through a fog of desire she could hear Ryan's voice, but not the words.

Then she heard her name and realized everyone was staring at her.

Everyone except Zach, who finally turned his attention to Emily's chowder. He picked up his spoon in one hand while with the other he continued to gently soothe Cocoa.

He was calm and relaxed whereas she was a simmering ball of tension.

Aware that she'd missed an entire conversation, she tried to focus. "Sorry, what were you saying?"

"That you could have taught archery if you hadn't broken your wrist. This chowder is delicious." Ryan smiled at Emily, an intimate glance that briefly excluded everyone around the table.

"Thanks. It was Kathleen's recipe. Brittany gave it to me." Emily looked across at her and frowned. "You're not eating. Something wrong with your appetite or are you just scared of my cooking?"

Brittany blinked. "I— Neither. I was watching Cocoa." She ignored Skylar's raised eyebrows. "So what happened to the camp staff? It's unusual to lose people this late in the summer season. Usually if they're going to drop out they do it early on."

Ryan reached for his beer. "Family emergency in one case, illness in another. Why don't you call Philip? You often helped out in the past and you have all the qualifications."

It wasn't her ability to do the job that worried her. It was the fact that spending time at Camp Puffin would increase the likelihood that she'd bump into Zach and she wasn't sure how she felt about that. "I can't teach archery with one hand."

"Do you have to demonstrate? You can push and pull the kids into position. Use your good hand." Ryan pushed the bread towards Zach. "Do you want me to take Cocoa? Is she bothering you?"

"No. She's fine."

She was more than fine, Brittany thought. Cocoa was in doggy heaven.

"Zach, you know more about what's going on at the camp than I do." Ryan cleared his bowl. "You should be trying to persuade Brittany to help out."

Zach put his spoon down slowly. "I believe people should make their own decisions."

He didn't want her there.

It was clear in his tone and his body language.

He might as well have told her bluntly to stay away.

"I loved camp." Skylar's cheery voice cut through the tension. "The alternative was spending the summers at home playing mock trials with my brothers so I talked my parents into letting me stay the whole summer. It was at camp that I first made jewelry. Right there and then I knew what I wanted to be."

Alec glanced up from his food, his gaze lingering on Sky's silver-blond hair. "Ballerina? Fairy princess?"

Sky's eyes flashed. "Artist." She spoke through her teeth. "I wanted to be an artist, although for your information, ballet is a seriously athletic sport and definitely not for wimps. Did you want to be something else when you were younger or was 'asshat' always your goal?"

"That's not a career," Ryan said mildly but neither was paying attention.

Knowing how easygoing Skylar was, Brittany was puzzled by the tension pulsing between her and Alec. They seemed to have temporarily forgotten everyone else in the room.

Alec's gaze was fixed on Sky's face. "For about two terms in junior school I wanted to be a submarine captain. After that, an academic."

Sky gave him a witchy smile and reached for another piece of bread. "Professor Asshat." She turned back to her food, missing the appreciative gleam in Alec's eyes.

"You were telling us about camp, Sky," Emily said hastily. "You spent your whole time painting and making jewelry?"

Hearing Emily's conciliatory tone, Brittany concluded this wasn't the first time Alec and Sky had clashed.

"I found a camp that focused on art and spent most of the time covered in paint or up to my elbows in clay. Bliss."

Alec took a last long look at that shiny waterfall of blond hair and then turned his attention back to his food. "You don't seem the type to relish being messy."

Sky put her spoon down with a clatter. "You think

you know me but you don't and, by the way, someone with your reputed brain power should know better than to judge on appearances."

Alec carried on eating. "Like it or not, our unconscious minds take the available data and shape our perceptions."

"And your unconscious mind has decided I'm a fairy princess? Based on what? The color of my hair? Carry on making comments like that and you really will be unconscious." Sky caught Emily's eye and subsided. "This chowder really is delicious, Em." She was about to say something else when her phone rang. She checked the caller ID and immediately her spirit and energy evaporated. "Sorry, I know we have a 'no phones at the table' rule, but I need to take this. It's Richard." She mumbled the words and stood up, almost knocking the chair over in her haste. Mumbling apologies, she shot out of the room.

Alec's gaze followed her to the door. "Who," he said slowly, "is Richard?"

"Her asshat boyfriend," Ryan said cheerfully. "You handled that well, Al. Your charm is second only to your tact. I can see why you're in such demand as a dinner guest. And why you're single."

"He's the perfect guest." Emily served seconds of chowder. "But you have Sky all wrong, Alec. She's not the person you seem to think she is."

Alec stirred. "I'm single because, having sampled the alternative, that's the way I prefer to live my life. And I don't think about Skylar at all."

"So her boyfriend calls and she answers no matter where or when?" Ryan frowned. "Doesn't seem like Sky."

"Richard is stressed about the campaign. Sky is being supportive." Emily swiftly sprang to Sky's defense but

Brittany knew they were thinking the same thing—that with Richard Everson, Sky was a different person.

Ryan wisely changed the subject and soon they were engaged in a lively discussion on how they'd spent their summers during childhood.

Zach was the only one who didn't participate.

Brittany knew that camp for him had been an escape, not a luxury.

The links with the university and the marine center meant that they attracted a mix of children from different backgrounds. Camp Puffin offered a few sponsored places so that kids from the cities had a chance to learn more about the outdoors.

Zach had been one of those.

Ryan glanced at her. "So what do you think, Brittany? Would you consider helping in some capacity? You used to love it."

Her brief moment of respite was over and the focus was back on her.

Camp was intimately entwined with her relationship with Zach. Their relationship had begun while she'd been helping out there.

"It's not a bad idea." Emily reached for her drink. "You're bored, Brit. And you loved working with the kids. Why not do it?"

Her reason for not doing it was seated close to her.

His gaze connected briefly with hers. Those devil-black eyes gave no hint as to what was going on in his head, but she knew instinctively that he wanted her to help out at Camp Puffin as much as she wanted to be there.

She stood up abruptly. "I'll clear the plates."

Skylar reappeared at that moment. She made no reference to the call. "I'll help."

"And I need to prepare dessert. No—" Emily held up her hand as Ryan started to stand "—tonight is on me. You can do the whole thing next time."

The three girls vanished into the kitchen.

Zach pushed back from the table and rose to his feet. "Thanks for dinner."

Ryan frowned. "Where are you going?"

"Back to my cabin. I shouldn't have come." Next to him, Cocoa gave a whimper of protest and he stooped to give her a last stroke. She pressed into his hand adoringly, apparently the only female in the world who didn't sense that he was a bucket load of trouble.

"Dinner isn't finished yet. Sit down." Ryan pushed another beer towards him and Zach straightened and shook his head.

"I appreciate the sentiment but it's awkward for you, me being here—"

"I said, sit down." Ryan's tone was polite layered over steel. "You're not going anywhere. It will upset Cocoa and it will upset me."

Zach thought about all the things Ryan didn't know. "Look, you and Brittany have been friends a long time and—"

"You and I have been friends a long time, too. Which is why I'm offering you another beer and a seat at my table."

"Best to sit," Alec said mildly. "You know he never gives up. It's one of his more annoying traits."

Ryan raised his eyebrows. "I have annoying traits?"

"You want a list?" Alec drained his beer. "Because I could put that together for you, with references."

Zach felt as if a heavy weight were crushing him. "It's Emily's table, too."

"Which is another reason you're not leaving. After all the hours she spent in the kitchen, she'd be offended."

"Maybe not." He wondered if Brittany had told her friend what had happened. "Seems to me she's in an impossible position. I don't want to be the one causing friction."

"The friction seems to be between Sky and Alec, and if Brittany has a problem with you being here, then she needs to get over it," Ryan said pleasantly. "You were the one who flew Lizzy and Emily to the hospital that night. And you were the one who bothered to pick up the phone and tell me what had happened. You were a good friend to both of us. And let's not forget I was best man at your wedding."

If Zach could have found a way of forgetting, he would have done. "The wedding I screwed up."

"I share the blame for that. You tried to run and I wouldn't let you."

"Another time you've been put in a difficult position because of me."

Ryan shrugged. "Relationships are messy things. You don't have the monopoly on screwing things up. Alec here will support me on that one."

Alec stretched out his legs. "I will. The happiest part of my marriage was the divorce."

"Sit down, Zach." Ryan jerked his head towards the chair. "While you're drinking that beer, tell me more about Cessna capabilities. I'm thinking of expanding next summer and offering skippered yacht holidays. We already have the *Alice Rose*, but at the moment if people want to charter her they have the hassle of a ferry trip. I'm thinking you could fly them direct to her and land on the water. Joint venture. Are you interested?"

"In working with you?" Zach curbed his natural desire to run from anything that looked remotely like a commitment and cautiously sank back down. "I might be."

"Good. I'll play with some ideas and then we'll talk again."

Zach eyed the kitchen door, which had remained firmly closed. "Are you sure you don't want me to leave? Seems to me dessert is taking a while longer than it should."

"It's always the same when the three of them are together. They're probably just talking."

Zach felt heat spread through his body. He suspected he knew exactly what they were talking about.

"I had *no idea* Ryan had invited him for dinner," Emily hissed behind the closed kitchen door. "We agreed we'd invite our friends. I just didn't think—"

"It's fine." Brittany stacked the dishwasher. Usually she was a clear, methodical thinker, but since Zach had come back into her life, that skill seemed to have deserted her.

"Yes, it's fine," Skylar echoed brightly. She still hadn't mentioned the phone call that had required her to leave the room. "After all, they're both civilized people and anyway, Brittany has been pretending to be indifferent so this is a perfect way to prove it. Isn't that right, Brit?"

"Yeah, that's right. I—actually no, that's not right." Giving up the pretense, Brittany plopped onto the kitchen chair. "Things are—complicated."

Emily abandoned the dirty plates and gave her a worried look. "Has something else happened?"

"You could say that."

"Another spider? Something else? You finally lost control?"

Brittany gave a moan and covered her face with her hands. "Yes."

"No one is going to blame you for that. So you shouted at him. You shouldn't feel bad about it," Skylar said stoutly. "It will have done him no harm to find out how you really feel. There's certainly no reason to be avoiding him. You can hold your head up high. He's the one who should be hiding in the kitchen."

"I didn't just shout at him."

"You punched him? Nobody is going to blame you for that, either. What you need is dessert. What are we having, Em?"

"Ice cream."

"Perfect. It will cool her down. Just give her the tub and a spoon."

"I didn't punch him." Brittany rubbed her fingers over her forehead. "I had screaming sex with him."

Silence descended over the kitchen. Skylar stared at her and then turned to look at Emily, who was also mute.

"Stop gaping at each other," Brittany muttered. "It happened. I can't change that. But I have to work out what to do next."

"But—why?" Skylar sounded faint. "How—how did you get from 'I have no feelings for you' to screaming sex?"

"Well, for a start because you told her to!" Emily glanced at Sky in exasperation. "*You* told her she should have sex with him to see if it was still as good as she remembered."

"I didn't mean for her to *actually* do it! It was the wine talking!"

"We're never giving you wine again." Emily looked at Brittany. "Where? *When?*"

"He gave me a ride home after my trip to the hospital."

"That explains why you didn't call me."

"I did, but your phone kept going to voice mail."

"You're kidding." Emily groaned. "Lisa called me to tell me what a great week she'd had at Summer Scoop."

"So in fact this is all *your* fault." Skylar closed the dishwasher. "Our friend was in trouble and you were talking about ice cream? You need to reevaluate your priorities."

"I didn't know that was going to be the exact moment she called. Why didn't you leave a message?"

"Because I didn't know how long you'd be and I didn't know how to refuse his offer without looking as if I cared."

"So he dropped you home and then what?"

"He followed me into the house."

Sky blinked. "He forced you?"

Brittany glanced towards the door. "No! Look—we should get back out there—"

"So basically it was a wild-animal moment. No romance or emotional bullshit. No bunches of roses or singing cherubs. Just mind-blowing sex." Sky grinned. "That's not so hard to understand. The man is in crazy shape."

Emily closed her eyes. "Sky—"

"What? I know you're blind to every man but Ryan, but you should take a closer look. I don't know which I prefer, his pecs or his abs. And the way he calms Cocoa does something indescribable to my insides. Did you see his hands? It's all so quiet and understated. I love that. And I love a man who is kind to animals. Did he use a condom?"

"Skylar!" Emily glanced nervously towards the door.

Brittany felt heat rush into her cheeks. "Yes."

"Wow. He carries one in his pocket just in case his rampant sex drive overwhelms him in the middle of Main Street. Good to know."

Emily intervened. "He protected her. That's all that matters. Now can we—"

"So he followed you into the house and the next thing you were ripping each other's clothes off." Sky gave a slow smile. "Mmm. That is *so* hot. Definitely time to fetch that ice cream, Em."

Emily kept one eye on the door. "This is *definitely* not the time or the place for this conversation. I'm supposed to be sorting out dessert. If we don't go back in there soon, Ryan will come looking for us." She pulled open the freezer and dug out a tub of blueberry ice cream emblazoned with the Summer Scoop logo. "I hope everyone likes blueberry. Fetch some bowls, Sky."

"In a minute. She still hasn't answered the most important question—was it or wasn't it?"

"What?"

"As good as you remembered."

Brittany stared blindly out the window. "It was nothing like I remembered."

"That's to be expected." Emily opened the tub of ice cream. "You were very young and you're probably seeing the past through rose-tinted glasses."

"I think she's saying it was better," Sky murmured. "Get her a bigger bowl, Em. She might need to push her whole heated self into the ice cream. And I guess Zach might want the option of licking it off."

"Better still, I might just push you in there," Emily muttered. "Cause of death, ice-cream inhalation."

Sky was still looking at Brittany. "It's all falling into place. The fact that you had wild sex with your ex explains the smoldering glances and the suppressed tension around the table."

"I'm not smoldering. And there was no tension."

"Honey, that look you gave him could have lit a candle without a match and I could have sliced the tension with the bread knife. But I'm starting to understand why you don't want to help out at Camp Puffin. You're right. It would be crazy to throw yourself in his path again given that you have no willpower. We'll get you out of it."

And that was the sensible thing, of course. The easiest way. So why did she feel a twinge of regret?

She always loved her summers at Camp Puffin. There were plenty of things she'd enjoyed that had nothing to do with Zach. Building camps in the forest, surrounded by the smell of pine. Kayaking in the bay beyond the camp, toasting marshmallows over a campfire and scaring each other to death with spooky stories as night fell. Starlight Adventure had been one of her favorite nights of the year, an overnight camp deep in the forest. And friendship. Talking late into the night with her friend Helen, Ryan's other sister, and creeping into each other's cabins after dark for feasting and fun.

The summer she'd worked as a counselor had been happy, too. So happy, that for a short time she'd toyed with the idea of training to be a teacher.

Helping out at the camp would have been the perfect way to occupy her time over the next few weeks. Even though she didn't have the use of both hands, she would have been able to improvise and find ways of making herself useful.

Only one thing was stopping her from phoning Philip Law and volunteering her services.

Zach.

"We need to go or they'll send out a search party." Emily smoothed her hair and opened the kitchen door.

It was like a Shakespearean farce, Brittany thought.

"So what do you think?" Ryan took the ice cream from Emily. "Will you help Philip out for a few weeks, Brit?"

"Ryan, how can she with her wrist in plaster?" Armed with new information, Emily immediately leaped in to defend her. "Be practical."

Sky nodded. "Em's right. It's out of the question."

Brittany felt a rush of love for her friends. No matter what the situation, they always had her back.

There was a pause while they both waited for Brittany to confirm that there was no way she'd be doing it.

She looked down at the ice cream, slowly melting in her bowl. It was the way she felt when she was with Zach. One look and her insides melted into a puddle.

But that was her problem to deal with.

Why should she stay away from a place that had played an important part in her life, just because of something that had happened ten years ago?

And as for what had happened yesterday, well, that was just sex.

This time she wasn't going to make the mistake of dressing it up with roses and hearts in her brain.

"I'll do it," she said firmly. "I'll help out at camp."

"But—" Skylar looked startled. "Brit, you can't possibly do it with your wrist in plaster. Everyone understands that."

"There will be plenty of things I can do. I want to do it. I'm going to do it. Unless Zach has a problem with that?"

Zach's gaze locked on hers.

Brittany felt her heart start to pound.

He was wondering what she was doing. Probably thinking to himself that she was attaching meaning to what had happened. Perhaps even wondering if her decision to help out at camp was driven by a desire to get closer to him.

The thought of him reaching that conclusion made her squirm.

She wanted to tell him he had no reason to worry. She wanted to assure him she was no longer a naive, dreamy teenager. That she knew his feelings didn't go deeper than sexual attraction.

She wanted to tell him all that but she couldn't with their friends looking on, waiting for his response.

Finally he stirred, reaching for his spoon with the same economy of movement that characterized everything he did.

"No." He spoke slowly and deliberately. "I don't have a problem."

Back home, Zach stripped off his shirt and was about to do the same with his jeans when he heard a light tap on the cabin door.

People rarely knocked on his door. His cabin was far beyond the edge of the camp and off-limits. Although he helped out during the day with activities when it suited his schedule, he didn't have direct responsibility for any of the children. He'd only ever had two people knock, and each time it had been an emergency and the person had been looking for Philip, so he crossed the room in three strides and dragged open the door, anticipating trouble.

Trouble faced him, but not in the shape he'd expected.

"Hi." Brittany stood there, thumbs tucked into the pockets of her cargo pants, her shiny dark hair illuminated by the wash of light from the cabin. Her gaze slid from his face to his bare chest and then away. "I know it's late, but do you have a minute? I thought we should talk."

Talk?

He wondered what it said about him that talking was never the first thing that came to mind when he was face-to-face with her.

"I seem to remember I already suggested that and you didn't have anything to say."

Instead they'd found other ways to communicate. Ways that were now lodged in his head, disturbing his concentration and his sleep.

The corner of her mouth tilted into a faint smile. "I have things to say now, unless this is a bad time…" Her voice tailed off and her gaze slid from his bare chest to the snap of his jeans that wasn't completely fastened and then to the cabin behind him. "You're busy. You have company and I didn't think—which was stupid of me—and it's none of my business who you—sorry—" Flustered, she backed away and he took one look at her face and realized she thought he was with a woman.

He wondered what she'd say if she knew he'd never brought a woman back here.

He should have let her leave, but not doing the things he should have done had been a trademark of his life, so he pushed the door open a little wider, letting her see the interior of the cabin.

"I don't have company."

"Are you sure?"

"You think I don't know when I have a woman in my bed?" His blunt response brought a flush to her cheeks.

"I—" She glanced from the cabin to his face. "In that case, can I come in?"

The cabin was small and rustic. It was big enough for one to live in comfortably. Two, if they didn't mind an intimate atmosphere.

Given what had happened last time they'd been alone together, Zach decided not to take the risk.

"We can talk on the deck." He snatched up his shirt from the back of the chair and saw her frown.

"Why the deck? It's fine by me if you haven't made the bed or something. I don't care if the place is a mess."

"It's not a mess. I'm methodical. Comes from being a pilot. Routines keep me alive."

"So why can't we—oh, never mind." Sparks danced between them like the crackle and pop of a bonfire.

"It isn't that I don't want to invite you in," he lied. "I feel like fresh air, that's all."

Deciding that the more layers between them the better, he pulled his shirt on over his head, noticing that she kept her eyes fixed on the room behind him.

"I always loved this cabin. It's romantic." She spoke without thinking and then looked at him and gave an awkward laugh. "Except not right now, of course. We didn't do romantic, did we?"

He didn't want to think about what they'd done. And he definitely didn't want to think about all the possibilities of the cabin. "What did you want to talk about?"

As if he didn't know.

As if it wasn't obvious.

Restless, she paced to the edge of the deck. Occasionally when the sea was rough, the waves hurled spray over the broad planks and anyone standing on them, but tonight the sea rolled in quietly, licking the shore in slow, sleepy waves.

She leaned on the railing and stared down into the inky depths. Then she took a deep breath and turned to look at him.

"I want to forget what happened. And if the only way of forgetting is to talk about it first, then let's talk."

This was the Brittany he remembered. Frank, honest and straightforward in her approach to a problem. Lies didn't suit her.

And they didn't suit him. "You want to talk about what happened? I've always found you sexy as hell and you didn't exactly seem in a hurry to stop me," he said roughly. "That's what happened."

There was a gleam of wry humor in her eyes. "I meant what happened ten years ago, not what happened the other night. We don't communicate well, do we?"

He couldn't argue with that.

It was like a game of catch, and each of them kept missing the ball.

"You want to talk about what happened back then?" His mouth was dry. "Go ahead. Say what you want to say." After what he'd done, he owed her that much.

"When Ryan asked me about helping at camp, my first instinct was to say no. I thought it would be awkward for both of us. And then I realized that saying no would mean missing out on something I love. Camp was part of my life. Some of my happiest memories come from the time I spent here. I'd like to help, and the only thing stopping me from doing that is you." She pushed her hands into the pockets of her cargoes. "We're both adults, Zach. It was a long time ago. I just want to forget it and move on."

Braced for a litany of his own deficiencies, Zach stared at her. "That's it?"

"Yes. It was a long time ago. Was I upset? Yes, I was. The worst part was that I thought we were friends and the fact that you'd just leave like that without talking to me—" she bit her lip "—well, that was the saddest thing of all. But I got over it. I want to work here. I want to spend some time at the camp, and I don't want it to be awkward. Tonight, with our friends, it felt awkward. And I don't want that. It makes it difficult for everyone." She drew in a breath. "I think we should both forget it and start again. Can we do that?" She stood like a little warrior, her eyes fierce and her head tilted slightly to one side as she waited for his response.

"Are we forgetting our marriage or what happened the other night?"

"Definitely the first, and probably the second, too. That would be the sensible move. And this time round we're going to be sensible. We don't have youth as an excuse for doing crazy stuff anymore."

Zach wondered what she'd say if he confessed she was the one woman he'd never forgotten.

Except for Brittany, his relationships had all looked the same.

The only thing the women he'd met had in common was that he'd disappointed each and every one.

He wondered how much she'd told her friends when they'd all vanished to the kitchen.

"Ryan invited me for a drink and to discuss the changes he was making to the house. I didn't know dinner was included and I didn't know he had a houseful of guests."

"Not guests," Brittany murmured, "just us."

And that was the difference between them, he thought. She took the friendship for granted, and assumed she'd always be welcome. She'd grown up with these people, their lives interwoven like the fronds of seaweed on the seabed. The Forrest family was rooted on Puffin Island, as was Ryan's family, the Coopers. They wandered in and out of each other's houses, sharing conversation and hospitality. Friendship, so easy and natural to her, still seemed alien to him. He didn't trust it not to explode in his face.

"Do your friends know you're here now?"

"No."

"I expect they warned you to stay away from me."

Instead of denying it, she nodded. "Emily did, but she's almost as cautious about relationships as you are. Sky had already told me to have sex with you, but I think she was a little surprised to discover how quickly I took her advice."

He swore under his breath and raked his fingers through his hair. "You told them?"

"We talk about things." She was up front and honest. "If I hadn't told them, they would have guessed. They're my closest friends. I trust them."

And that was another difference between them.

What did he know about trust?

About as much as he knew about the sort of friendship she was describing.

He couldn't imagine revealing such intimate details to another person. He'd never revealed anything, confessed anything or confided in anyone. He didn't see the point of giving someone ammunition they could use against you when they managed to find plenty without help.

And never in a million years would he have discussed his sex life with anyone.

"I can't believe you did that."

She leaned on the railing and stared out at the sea, darkened to an oily black under a midnight sky. "When I was young I used to love this place almost as much as Castaway Cottage. Did you know Philip was offered a huge sum of money by a developer for the land? The same person who wanted to buy my place?"

"Yes."

"Of course you do." She traced her finger over the smooth wood of the railing. "You stayed in touch?"

"He was better at it than I was."

She nodded in understanding. "Sometimes when you're busy living your life, home seems very far away. How involved with the camp are you?"

He could have told her the exact extent of his involvement but that would have meant revealing information he made a point of not sharing.

"I help out when they need it."

She gave a crooked smile. "You knew every path through the forest. You could name every tree and every berry."

"I liked being outdoors. It made sense to me."

"Philip tells me the sponsorship money has increased. That's good. I still remember those kids who came from the city for the first time. They arrived here not knowing the difference between an oak and a pine and by the time they left they could build a camp in the forest and cook their own food."

"I was one of those kids. It's an important education.

Connecting kids with the outdoors." For him it had been more than that. It had been life changing and it had triggered his interest in nature and the wilder areas of the planet.

"Philip tells me the Marine Center is involved."

"They run sessions on coastal ecology and the marine environment. He's thinking of adding in archaeology."

"Good plan." She nodded. "I ran an archaeology club for local kids when I was in Cambridge. It was four times oversubscribed. Everyone wants to be Indiana Jones."

"You should talk to him."

"Which brings me back to my reason for being here. Do you mind if I spend time here over the next few weeks? I don't want it to feel awkward."

"It isn't awkward." It was other things, though. It was tense and arousing.

And it was dangerous.

Her gaze met his, direct and honest. "So we're cool?"

Cool wasn't the word Zach would use to describe the heat coursing through his body but he managed a nod.

"Yeah. We're cool."

And he knew that this time he was the one telling the lies.

Chapter 10

Brittany was up at dawn the next morning and found Philip Law in the catering barn where the children ate their meals. Breakfast had ended and the barn echoed with laughter and conversation as the kids left in their groups for their first activity, following the colored signs that marked the tracks through this section of the forest.

It was an idyllic location for a summer camp, a curve of land where the forest met the ocean and the sharp scent of pine mingled with the fresh sea air.

Reliving happy memories, she strolled across to Philip, who was in conversation with one of the other camp directors.

"Brittany." Philip gave her a warm greeting, exchanged a few pleasantries and then got straight down to business. "How is the wrist? Would it survive a few archery lessons?"

"Yes, as long as you don't expect me to demonstrate." She accepted the coffee someone handed her with a smile of thanks, and then rolled her eyes as a few drops sloshed onto the floor. "Oops. Maybe archery is a little ambitious as I can't even get a mug to my mouth without spilling it."

"Anything you can do would be great. We have a lively, inquisitive group this year. They need to be kept busy."

Brittany put her mug down on the nearest empty table and straddled a chair. "Zach mentioned that you're thinking of running an archaeology activity." She saw the surprise on his face. "You're surprised we had a conversation? Did you think I would have buried his body so deep he'd turn to oil before anyone found him?"

"No. But I thought you'd have a few things to say."

"I did, and I said them." She retrieved her mug and sipped her coffee, trying to think about anything other than Zach. "So—archaeology. Tell me what you're thinking. A talk in the barn or a session out in the woods digging?"

"Both? The focus of this place is always the outdoors and the environment, how we can preserve it and what it teaches us. Do you remember when we saw each other in the Ocean Club a few summers ago?"

"That time when Ryan was developing the apartments and we had to yell to be heard above the drilling and banging?" She put the mug back down. "I remember."

"You were full of enthusiasm about a summer camp you'd led at Cambridge."

"That was a day camp, not residential. They came for a week and helped on-site."

"There are a few children here this week who I think

would be interested. We can try it. If it's popular, we'll plan a full program for next year. I contacted the university back in the spring to see if they could spare someone. They couldn't, but now you're here and your credentials are impressive."

"Kids don't care whether you have a PhD."

"But they're going to care that you've been on digs all over the world. Didn't you do an excavation in Egypt?"

"Years ago. Since then it's been mostly the Mediterranean." She took another sip of coffee. "I can definitely put something together, especially as we're starting right at the beginning." Her spirits lifted. Maybe the rest of the summer wouldn't be such a washout after all. "How old are the kids in my group?"

"Seven to twelve."

"And how long would I have them for?"

"Mornings for a week? Start with that. See how it goes. In the afternoon they can choose between water sports and coastal ecology. If it works out, you can do the same next week with a different group. Then write me a report with your recommendations for next year. I know you won't be here, but give me something I can take to the university."

"I can do that." She felt a rush of excitement and energy that had been missing since she'd stepped off the plane. "When do you want me to start?"

Philip glanced down at her shorts and hiking boots. "Now? Why don't I show you round, introduce you to a few of the team and we can take it from there. What equipment would you need?"

"They'll learn more if they're hands-on. It would be fun to do some actual digging, mark out a site. You'll need to find me somewhere we can dig—" She pondered. "Can you get me a couple of masonry trowels? That flat type that they use to spread cement? I have a couple in my bag but a few more would be good. And I'll buy a few toothbrushes next time I'm in the store."

"We have toothbrushes. You want them all to clean their teeth before they smile at you?"

"No. I want to teach them that sometimes excavation requires cleaning up what you find, and that archaeologists often improvise when they're looking for the right tool for the job. Talking of improvising—" she glanced over her shoulder "—can I take a few spoons from the kitchen?"

"Help yourself." Philip rose to his feet. "I presume that's not so you can eat dessert?"

"You can dig with a spoon." She picked up the small backpack she'd brought with her with some of her equipment and walked with him out of the barn. "What exactly is Zach's role here?"

Philip gave her a cautious look. "He didn't tell you?"

"No. I know he's living in Seagull's Nest."

"He—" Philip paused. "He helps with the sponsorship program."

"Tapping his rich contacts for money?"

"Something like that." His answer somewhere between vague and evasive, Philip led her towards a group of eight children sitting in a circle. "These are the Seagulls. Seagulls, meet Dr. Forrest."

With no time to give any more thought to Philip's answer, she dropped her backpack down and joined them in the circle. "Call me Brittany. I was a Seagull when I was your age. It's the best group."

* * *

Zach leaned against the tree, watching. She was friendly and natural with the children, answering their questions and engaging them in conversation.

Camp had been part of her summer routine growing up and the year she turned eighteen, the summer they finally got together, she'd helped out with the younger children. She'd taken groups kayaking, taught archery and forest skills, and they'd loved her.

It seemed nothing had changed.

Within minutes of Philip's introduction, they were bombarding her with questions. All except Travis Whitelaw. Travis had barely spoken since he'd arrived at camp a week earlier. He was part of the sponsorship program and Zach knew Philip was concerned.

Not that the boy was disruptive. He wasn't. But he said nothing and made no attempt to integrate with the group.

When it came to activities he did what needed to be done and nothing more.

At Philip's request, Zach had taken him up in the Cessna, but even that hadn't induced Travis to talk.

Zach knew social workers were involved and he felt a pang of sympathy for the boy who trusted no one.

He knew exactly how that felt.

Brittany had obviously noticed the boy at the edge of the group, too, because she delved into her bag and handed something over, trying to draw him in.

She included Travis even when he made no effort to include himself.

Zach eased upright. Even as a teenager she'd sought out the kids who were on their own; the awkward, the homesick, the unpopular.

That was how she'd first got talking to him.

He'd hovered, silent and detached on the edge of the group, observing a life that wasn't his. It was like looking through the window into a party to which you weren't invited.

Brittany had ignored the fact he was older and pretty much a social leper. She'd talked to him as if he was someone worth knowing. To begin with he'd assumed he was being patronized. Then he'd noticed that she was the same way with everyone. Friendly and interested. Confident.

Realizing that any moment now he was going to be caught staring, Zach was about to walk away and return to the woodshop where a group of older children had spent the week constructing a raft, when Brittany glanced up and saw him.

It was too late to move. Too late to pretend he hadn't been watching her.

The sounds of the forest faded away, as did the laughter of the children and the sounds of excited chatter.

There was only her.

And he saw something he'd never seen in her eyes before. Uncertainty and confusion.

She didn't know what their relationship was anymore.

And he couldn't help her because he didn't know, either.

Brittany watched as Zach walked away. That brief wordless exchange had unsettled her.

Shaken, she focused her attention on the kids who were bursting with questions.

"So you're like a detective?" asked one girl sitting cross-legged, peering through glasses as thick as bottles. "You're looking for clues about what happened a long time ago?"

"That's right. Clues and answers. We're asking ourselves how an ancient community survived. We want to know how they lived, what they made and what they ate. Sometimes the answers are buried in the ground, so we have to dig to find them."

A girl who wore her hair in neat braids stuck her hand up. "My mom doesn't like me to get dirty."

"Well, you don't do it in your party dress." Brittany decided not to mention the time Spy had called her late in the evening about something they'd found and Brittany had gone there straight from a restaurant in a minidress. By the time she left the site her legs had been muddy and her dress ruined, but the find had been worth the sacrifice. "Of course that's another reason archaeology is the greatest thing ever—" she rocked back on her heels "—it's the perfect excuse to get dirty."

One of the boys perked up. "How do you know where to dig?"

"Survey, mapping and excavation."

"Are you allowed to dig anywhere? My dad went mad when I dug up his potatoes."

Brittany grinned. "There are laws that protect the land, and in every country they're different. That's why we have national parks, to protect them, so no one can ever build on them. Before builders can build on a site, there has to be an archaeological survey."

"So you might find treasure and then you'd be rich?"

"There are laws that protect archaeological artifacts from being removed from a country. Whatever you find in a country has to stay there. Here in the US whatever you find belongs to the person who owns the land."

"What do they do with it?"

"If it's valuable, they might choose to give it to a museum."

They fired questions at her. What was the most valuable thing she'd ever found? How far had she traveled? Did she have a whip like Indiana Jones? Had she seen the pyramids in Egypt?

At one point Philip Law came and sat on the edge of the group and Brittany saw the pleasure in his face as he witnessed the enthusiasm of the children.

She tried to find a way of explaining what she did in a way that would mean something to them. "When I used to come to camp, I kept a journal. Do you still do that?"

Two of the girls nodded. "We write it in the evening, after dinner and before campfire."

"Archaeology is a bit like keeping a journal, only it's a journal of human history. That's why archaeologists don't like artifacts to be removed from a site before they've seen it, because it isn't just what we find that tells us about the past, it's where we find it. Context. Do you know that word?"

She talked, expanded, watched their faces to see when she was getting too complicated.

One of the boys crept a little closer. "Have you ever found a dinosaur?"

"I've never found a dinosaur. Archaeologists don't actually look for dinosaurs, but sometimes they might find one by accident."

"I'd like to look for dinosaurs."

"Then you need to study paleontology. Paleontologists are interested in the remains of plants and animals, whereas archaeologists are interested in humans and how they lived." She answered their questions patiently and then Philip joined in. He suggested they mock up a site so that Brittany could give them a taste of what it meant to "dig."

The morning passed quickly. The children were engaged, their excitement infectious and motivational. All except Travis. He said nothing. Even when Brittany made deliberate attempts to include him, he responded with the bare minimum.

Everyone had a story, she knew that. As an archaeologist she focused on the stories of those living in the past, but that didn't mean she didn't have an interest in people living in the present.

There was no doubt in her mind that she needed more information if she was to stand any chance of drawing him into the group.

The children had gone and Zach was sawing planks to the required length as a favor to Philip, when he realized he wasn't alone.

He glanced up and saw Brittany leaning against the door frame watching him.

Given that he'd spent a good ten minutes watching her earlier that morning he wasn't in a position to complain but this time he kept the eye contact brief. It was a bad idea to use a tool that could remove his fingers and look at Brittany at the same time.

"Something I can do for you?"

"Yes." She eased away from the door and strolled towards him. "I wanted to talk to you about Travis."

"Can't help you with that." He measured the wood and marked it. "You need to speak to Philip."

"I intend to." She helped him steady the plank. "I remember the summer I made a canoe. It used to be one of my favorite activities until it came to put it on the water. I was always terrified it would sink. He reminds me of you, by the way."

"Philip?"

"Travis. He sits on the edge, as if that's the only place he feels safe. He doesn't trust anyone. You were the same."

He could feel her looking at him as he positioned the plank carefully. "I thought we weren't talking about the past?"

"I'm interested in what makes people behave the way they do."

"Maybe you should have done psychology not archaeology."

"There's some overlap. It's my job to ask questions."

"But not personal questions."

"No, not personal questions." She ran her finger along the grain of the wood. "Do you ever think about it? About what happened between us?"

"We both know what happened. You felt sorry for me so you paid me attention." He lined up the wood and picked up the saw. "You were hot, so I screwed you. I wanted to carry on screwing you so I went along with the whole marriage thing without thinking it through. End of story." His summary was crude, brutal and fundamentally inaccurate but he was going for effect rather than accuracy.

"You think I felt sorry for you?"

"Didn't you?"

"No! I mean—" she frowned and searched for the right words "—I was sorry that you'd had a difficult life, but that had nothing to do with what happened between us."

"Are you sure about that?"

"Yes." Exasperation crept into her voice. "Is that really what you think it was? Everything we shared—everything we had—you think that was pity?"

"I never knew what it was."

"Why did you think I was interested in you, Zach?"

"Because you wanted to know about sex and you're the sort who always turns to an expert when they want to learn something. It's the way your brain works." It was the reason that made the most sense to him. That and her teenage urge to rebel against everyone's expectations.

She gave a soft laugh. "The sex was part of it, I'm not denying that."

"Only part of it?"

"Hey, you're good but not *that* good."

He flicked her a glance and she blushed.

"Okay, maybe you *are* that good, but for the record arrogance isn't attractive so your sex appeal has just diminished considerably."

He didn't want to think about sex, not right now when she was standing right in front of him with that silky dark hair caught in a careless braid that hung down her back. She was casually dressed, but she'd never looked sexier. He wanted to strip her naked in two moves and drive himself into that lithe softness.

He kept his hands on the saw. "It's not arrogance, it's about knowing yourself. Sex and screwing up. You said it yourself. The two things I was good at."

"I was upset when I said that. It wasn't true."

"Aside from the fact you missed out flying, it was true." He wondered if the conversation was bothering her as much as it bothered him. "Even now when I walk into Harbor Stores, I'm always under observation."

"That's because Mel wants to get inside your pants."

The way she said it made him smile. "We both know how much that would thrill her parents. They don't want me touching anything that belongs to them."

"You're wrong, Zach. Maybe that was how it was when you were younger, but to be fair you were a little scary. You were this brooding, silent, Heathcliff type."

"Is this conversation going somewhere? I need to finish this. I'm flying a CEO and his family to their lodge in Bar Harbor later this afternoon."

"You pretend you don't care about anything, but I know that isn't true. I know you care."

"I don't need anyone's approval."

"I know. You're just a big tough guy who does his own thing." She gave a crooked smile. "Maybe you could use some of your carpentry skills to remove that big chip on your shoulder. And while you're at it, chop down some of those barriers you've built so that you can get out of your own way."

He finished with the plank and laid it on the floor with the others. "Are you about done?"

"No. You still haven't told me what you know about Travis."

"What makes you think I know anything?"

"Because you always know twice as much about everything as you let on. I want to know what's going on in the boy's head. He's not joining in. I don't think the other kids are being mean or excluding him." She bit her lip and frowned thoughtfully. "Maybe he isn't interested. Maybe archaeology isn't his idea of fun."

Zach picked up the last piece of wood. "Or maybe he doesn't know how to have fun. Maybe his life so far has been all about surviving and making it through the next hour."

There was consternation in her eyes. "Do you think that's it?"

He suspected he'd barely scratched the surface. It was times like this when he was reminded of the enormous gulf in their life experience. "It's a guess."

"Was that what it was like for you?"

He'd never talked about it. Not even to Philip, although he knew the man probably had a file a mile thick on him in his office. Zach had never seen it and wouldn't have wanted to.

"We were talking about Travis."

"I know, but I thought—" She broke off and drew a breath. "I thought maybe this once we could talk about you."

"Why? So you can understand me?" He sawed through the last plank and added it to the others. "Has it ever occurred to you that I don't need you to understand me?"

"Has it ever occurred to you that your life might be happier if you stopped pushing people away?"

He stilled. "Is that a general comment or a specific one?"

She pushed her hair away from her face, flustered. "General," she said quickly. "I wasn't suggesting—" Her eyes met his and the air temperature rose around them.

"Good," he said roughly. "Because we agreed we weren't going there."

"I know! I don't want to go there."

He watched her mouth move, seeing the way she wrapped her lips around the lie and wondered why neither of them was mentioning the obvious.

That they'd already gone there.

It was too late to wish it hadn't happened, because it had.

His gaze held hers for a long moment and then she dropped the piece of wood she'd been holding in her hands, turned and walked out of the barn.

Sarah Morgan

It was too late to wash it free; it happened; he was

94.91

His gaze held hers for a long moment, then she
dropped the piece of speed she'd been holding in her
hands, turned and walked out of the barn.

Chapter 11

Brittany threw herself into camp life. As well as running
an archaeology activity, or Mini Dig, as she named it, she
helped out on and around the beach. For many of the children, camp was the end of their summer and soon they'd
be back home and into the new school year. Some would
be seniors, all would have learned something different over
the summer months and hopefully left Camp Puffin having made new friends. The knowledge that the end was
in sight made those final days all the more precious. The
camp continued over the fall months in a leaner version,
directed towards school groups who used it as part of the
biology or geography syllabus, and teachers who signed
up for wilderness training. Philip was keen to add archaeology and Brittany was still exploring the options for that.

  She formed a habit of rising early so she could walk to
the camp. There were two routes from her cottage. One

curved around the rocky coast, and the other cut through the forest. Either way, it was a long walk but she loved being outdoors and enjoyed the exercise. In Greece the summer months were too hot to allow for long walks, but here on the island the combination of sun and sea breeze made for perfect hiking conditions. When the weather was bad and the fog settled over the ocean, she zipped up her raincoat and stayed under the protection of the trees.

She loved the seasons in Maine, even the long winter. During the freezing winter months the nature of the island changed, but if anything she loved it more. As an unbridged island they relied on the ferry. The service was scaled down in the winter and sometimes didn't run at all if the weather was too wild. As a result the community relied on each other, watched out for each other and created a web of support.

Although Brittany didn't love being the object of pity, she did enjoy the community spirit.

Winters for her had meant cozy evenings indoors with her grandmother and friends, playing cards, games or chatting over a meal while snow fell outside the window. She'd done her homework on the scrubbed kitchen table to the sounds of bubbling on the stove as Kathleen had cooked their supper. Her grandmother had prepared warming casseroles and homemade soup from vegetables she'd grown herself and stored in the freezer. Sometimes the snow had been so deep they'd had to dig their way out of the cottage, and sometimes they'd endured ice storms and long power outages. Kathleen had kept the cottage well stocked and treated every obstacle as an adventure.

Being back at camp reminded her of those times.

As the days passed, her wrist ached less and when Zach flew her over to the mainland for another checkup, this time the news was better. The doctor told her that the bones appeared to be healing well and the plaster could be removed on her next visit.

"And the first thing I'm going to do," she told Zach as they prepared the kayaks for an afternoon of water sports, "is swim in the sea."

"Happy to throw you in anytime. Just say the word."

"You did that once before."

"Yeah. You were spitting mad."

"Because I was still wearing my clothes!"

"Not for long. Seem to remember I helped you out of those wet things pretty quickly."

She remembered it, too. She remembered all of it. "Very generous of you."

"There are no limits to the sacrifices I'm prepared to make to get a woman naked. Push that kayak farther up the beach or it's going to end up halfway across the Atlantic."

"I know as much about kayaks as you."

She pretended to be annoyed, but the truth was that working with Zach had proved easier than she'd anticipated. Of course there were days when he wasn't around. Days when he disappeared to fly people with more money than she could imagine to remote parts of the state or up to Canada. But the rest of the time he pulled his weight in the camp, helping out wherever he was needed. There was a quiet strength about him, a self-assurance and confidence that meant the camp counselors often turned to him for advice. And so did the children.

Except for Travis.

He turned to no one.

Each week of camp ended with Starlight Adventure,

and Brittany was hoping that this particular activity might give her the opportunity to spend time with Travis.

The day before the overnight camp, she dropped into Harbor Stores to buy a selection of snacks for the hike through the forest. Today there were no issues with the weather, not even a hint of the fog that so often plagued this part of Maine in August. The bright sunny weather had brought a flood of summer visitors and the store was busy. Grateful to be able to avoid a conversation with Mel, she got in line behind a family loaded down with beach gear and two excited children, paid for her purchases, and then strolled out into the sunshine.

Main Street was busy, a mix of locals and tourists, all keen to make the most of the last days of summer.

On impulse, she took a detour via Summer Scoop, the ice-cream store that Emily had been trying to turn around over the summer.

One look at the line told her that her friend had done a good job.

She stood patiently, admiring the murals on the walls that Sky had painted along with some of the locals. The fresh paint and cheerful decor was proof that when things were tough, the islanders pulled together.

"Brittany! What can I get you?" Lisa beamed at her from across the counter, her smile yet more evidence of the turnaround in the fortunes of her business.

"You're busy."

"Insanely busy. I could cry with relief. I sold more ice cream this morning than I did in the whole first week of July. And it's all because of Emily. She's a genius. Scoop of the day is Salted Caramel Crunch."

"Scoop of the day?"

"Emily's idea. I promote a flavor. Larger scoop, lower price."

Conscious that the line was building up behind her, Brittany nodded. "Salted Caramel Crunch sounds good."

"Make it two." Zach's voice came from behind her and she felt delicious warmth spread to every corner of her body.

She was fairly sure the warmth reached her face, which was an embarrassing turn of events for a woman who'd believed she'd left her blushing days behind in her teens. Because she didn't want him to see how flushed she was, she took her time turning around.

"You're expecting me to buy you an ice cream, Flynn? I'm a penniless archaeologist." She cast what she hoped passed for a casual glance over her shoulder and her mouth dried. Now it wasn't just warmth, it was heat. The way he was looking at her made her feel as if she might need to call the paramedics.

911 dispatch, what seems to be the problem?

Well, there's this guy...

"I've got this." He handed over a bill, and took both ice creams. "I'm interested to know how you were planning on eating ice cream and carrying that bag when you only have one hand."

"I admit I hadn't thought it through. Ice cream finds a way." And in any case, if Zachary Flynn had the same effect on the ice cream that he had on her, her salted caramel would be in a puddle around her feet in seconds.

The intense pull of lust was entirely inappropriate for their surroundings. They were standing in a crush of small, eager children.

Reading her mind, Zach gave a faint smile, led the

way through the throng of children and parents, and held the door open for her.

She brushed past him, wondering why she should find such an old-fashioned gesture sexy when she'd been opening her own doors for most of her life.

Outside the sun dazzled, and she put her bag down and took her ice cream from him.

"Thanks. Do you realize this is the first meal you've ever bought me?" Trying to act normally, she licked around the edges, catching the sweet melting drips with the edge of her tongue.

"I bought you dinner when we were dating." He broke off as Hilda approached and Brittany saw his shoulders tense.

"Good morning, pumpkin. How's that wrist of yours behaving?" Hilda beamed at Brittany and gave Zach a speculative look. "I hear you broke into Kathleen's cottage."

Zach was still. "Yes, ma'am."

Brittany waited for him to explain that he'd heard her scream, but he didn't. He said nothing and she felt a rush of exasperation.

"He was helping me out, Hilda."

"I know. Emily told me all about it. She was round helping Agnes adjust some curtains the other day." Hilda nodded approval and patted Zach on the arm. "Good to know you're looking out for our girl. You have strong muscles and I like a man with strong muscles. My Bill was the same. We had a lot of fun in the bedroom."

Brittany didn't look at Zach. "Hilda—"

"What? Sex isn't just for the young, you know. The only difference is that we oldies aren't allowed to talk about it. You need to eat your ice cream before it melts."

She gave his arm a final squeeze. "And fix that lock for her. If anyone knows how to make that cottage secure, it's you."

"Yes, ma'am." Not by the flicker of an eyelash did Zach show any reaction to the oblique reference to his murky past.

As Hilda wandered off to her next conversation, Brittany closed her eyes. "Sorry. If it's any consolation, I think you've been given the seal of approval. Not sure if that's a good thing or a bad thing."

"She cares about you. They all care about you." He finished his ice cream. "And she's right that your lock needs fixing. I'm going to deal with that."

"There's nothing wrong with that lock."

"I gained entry into your property in under five seconds."

"That's because you have special skills."

He turned his head briefly and there was a sardonic gleam in his eyes.

She knew his mind wasn't on his housebreaking skills and neither was hers.

Sweltering under the heat of her own thoughts, she licked at her melting ice cream. "And for the record, you never bought me dinner, Flynn." She moved farther away from the line that was now trailing out the door and down the street. "And, let's be honest, we didn't date. We hung out and had lots of sex."

"And then got married."

She kept her voice light. "Put like that it's hard to see how it went so wrong."

"Are you saying I owe you dinner, Dr. Forrest?" He spoke slowly, in that rough masculine voice that had always made her nerve endings tingle.

"You don't owe me anything. But I now owe *you* a Salted Caramel Crunch ice cream. I don't want to be in debt, not even for carbs and sugar."

He smiled at her.

Her heart thudded and she felt a rush of excitement and awareness that only ever happened when she was with him.

His smile turned speculative and his gaze dropped slowly to her mouth. Neither of them spoke, but they didn't need to. She knew, *she just knew*, that they were thinking the same thing.

And those thoughts had nothing to do with Salted Caramel Crunch ice cream.

As a teenager she'd spent far too much time staring at his mouth and when she wasn't staring at it, she'd been kissing it. If ever a man's mouth had been designed for that task, it was Zach's, and if anything, his knowledge of what to do with that mouth had increased.

The struggle not to touch him was killing her and she suspected it was killing him, too.

She wanted to rest her mouth against him and breathe him in. She wanted to strip him naked and explore every inch of his body, discover the changes in him. Not a quick slaking of mutual lust like that time in her hallway, but a long, slow, intimate discovery.

"Zach—"

"No." His voice was thickened, and he dragged his gaze from her mouth with visible reluctance. "No."

"But—"

"We're not doing that again. I won't hurt you again."

Emotion hit her like a rogue wave, burying her in memories. It was all there, the excitement, the hope and the bitter misery.

The two of them stood alone, an island in a sea of tourists.

People flowed past them, laughing and chatting as they strolled along Main Street, dipping in and out of Surf and Swim, and enjoying the quaint charm of the village.

Zach lifted his hand and gently removed a blob of ice cream from the corner of her mouth. "It's the right decision. You know that."

She didn't know that.

All she knew was that she was burning up inside.

To try to break the atmosphere of intimacy, she breathed deeply and looked towards the harbor where the *Captain Hook* was docking. "I bought provisions for Starlight Adventure. Managed to get in and out of Harbor Stores without an interrogation from Mel."

There was a tense silence. "You're going on that trip?" There was no missing the lack of enthusiasm in his voice.

"I know I'm not exactly an extra pair of hands, but I tell great campfire stories and I can help if any of the kids are scared in the forest at night. But I'll be delegating spider-removal duty to someone else."

"I'll be available for spider duty."

Awareness shivered across her skin and seeped deep into her soul. He was badass, a little dangerous and insanely hot. Looking at him made her dizzy, as if she'd smacked her head on a hard object. Her brain, which had served her perfectly well for most of her life except the parts when she'd been with him, stalled. For a few seconds the only words she heard were *I'm available*, and then the implications of his words sank in. "You're going on the Starlight Adventure?"

Now she understood why he'd greeted the news that she was going with so little enthusiasm.

"I help when I can. I teach basic wilderness survival skills."

A fact that raised his hot factor another few notches. "So we'll be spending the night in the forest together."

His gaze didn't shift from hers. "Us, a camp director, four other counselors and eighteen kids."

That should have killed the rush of lust but it didn't. She still wanted to press her mouth to his and kiss him until they were both starved of air. She wanted to slide her fingers into his glossy dark hair and strip off the T-shirt that fitted so snugly over all that hard muscle.

"Philip didn't mention you'd be going."

"No." Zach's tone was short. "I don't suppose he did."

"He probably didn't think it was relevant, as we've been working together anyway." Or perhaps he was meddling. Would he do that? No, Philip was camp director, not Cupid. But suddenly it all seemed too complicated. Swamped with feelings she didn't understand, she stepped away. "I'd better go. I'll see you back at camp."

"Wait." He cursed softly. "How are you getting there?"

"I was going to call Pete."

"I'll take you."

It was obvious from the grim set of his jaw he would rather have stuck pins in himself.

"Forget it." Pride took precedence over convenience. "I know it's a nuisance for everyone having to help me out all the time. I can do this myself."

"You think that's what's going on here?" He planted his arm against the wall of a shop behind her, caging her so that she couldn't walk away. "You think you're a nuisance?"

His mouth was close to hers, his eyes dark pools of sexual promise.

"Zach—"

"Yeah, I'm finding this tough. You are, too. But that doesn't mean you need to take a cab. We're adults. Just because the feelings are there, doesn't mean we have to do anything about them. We can make a choice, and that's what we're doing."

His arm was next to her cheek, her lips a breath away from the brutal swell of his biceps. All she had to do was turn her head. "So what was the other night?"

"Random sex." His voice was low and rough around the edges. "It's not going to happen again."

"Do you often have random sex with people? Because I don't."

His eyes darkened to a dangerous shade of black. "I don't want to know about your sex life."

"Good, because I don't intend to talk about it." And suddenly the whole thing seemed ridiculous. Of all the men she'd met in her life, the only one who made her feel this way was her ex-husband.

There was no justice.

He eased away from her. "Get in the car, Brittany. I'll take you back to camp."

"Thanks. And, by the way, I don't like possessive men."

A smile flickered at the corner of his mouth. "And I don't like smart-ass women."

"So we're fine, then. Nothing to worry about."

Chapter 12

Zach finished loading life jackets and canoes on to the trailer.

One of the camp directors would be driving the gear up to Heron Pond so that it would be waiting for them when they arrived. Each of the children would carry a small backpack with waterproof clothing, lunch and a drink.

Excitement hummed in the air and the children were talking, swapping stories of their camp adventures so far. All except Travis, who lurked close by, slightly apart from the other children, making no connection with anyone.

One look told Zach that for Travis, Starlight Adventure was more torture than treat and he didn't need to read the boy's file to know what was going on. It was all there, written on Travis's face and the way he responded to the world.

He cloaked himself in desperate layers of "I don't care" and Zach knew all about that. He'd worn the same layers. He knew that caring made you hurt more and that withdrawing was the only way to protect yourself. He'd done the same thing.

As a barrier against cruelty he'd learned to shut off his feelings. He'd been so good at it that he no longer knew how to access that part of himself. When he'd been with Brittany the first time he'd tried to force himself to feel, but the only emotion that rose to the surface had been panic.

It seemed that the techniques he'd used to survive were irreversible and he'd long since given up trying.

He wondered if it would be the same way for Travis or whether he was still young enough to be prepared to give trust one last go.

Careful to keep his distance, he kept his voice casual as he talked to the boy. "Hey, did you remember your bug dope?"

Travis gave a brief nod. His gaze skidded warily to Zach and then away again as if he was checking the exits.

Zach recognized the gesture and it made him feel sick.

"I could use some help here. This stuff weighs a ton." He could have lifted it one-handed, but he wanted to pull the boy in from the margins. He wanted him to know there were people he could trust. That the world wasn't a black pit waiting to suck you in and swallow you whole.

Travis hesitated, then stepped forward and loaded the oars onto the trailer.

He didn't look at Zach, as if not making eye contact somehow reduced the risk.

"Heron Pond is a cool place." Zach talked as if the conversation wasn't all on one side, keeping the topic easy and neutral. "First thing in the morning it's so still it's like looking at glass. Throw a stone in there and you can see the ripples spread halfway across the water. But you're going to need that bug dope. There are insects so big they could swallow you whole without chewing."

There was a spark of something in the boy's eyes. Interest?

"Did I hear someone say bug dope?" Brittany strolled up to them, a baseball cap embroidered with *Camp Puffin* jammed onto her head. "You haven't seen bugs until you've dug in Egypt. First thing you do when you wake up in the morning is check your boots for scorpions."

Travis sent her a cautious look. "No shit."

She ignored the language. "At night we used ultraviolet torches to check for them. There's a compound in the exoskeleton of scorpions that causes them to glow in UV light. It means we can see where they are. They show up as a ghostly green color. Fluorescent. Remind me to show you a picture."

"Gross." But he looked fascinated.

"Truly gross." She tightened the straps of her backpack. "And you don't want to be bitten by one of those suckers."

"Would you die?"

"No, but it would hurt like a—" She broke off and grinned. "It would hurt *a lot*."

Travis was about to ask something else when a few of the children hovering nearby decided they wanted to hear more about scorpions, too.

As they drew closer, Travis retreated.

Zach saw it happen.

Brittany saw it, too. "Hey, more scorpion tales later, folks. Right now we have a hike ahead of us." She walked over to Travis. "I hate to admit this in front of Zach, but this backpack is too heavy for me to manage with my wrist in a cast. You look pretty strong—" she eyed Travis's skinny frame "—would you carry a couple of things for me? You'd be my hero."

The boy stared at her. The idea of being anyone's hero was clearly an alien concept. "I guess. If you can't manage."

"I don't want to load you down."

"I can handle it." He swung his backpack off his back and as he did so his T shirt rode up, exposing a livid scar on his stomach.

Zach saw Brittany's eyes narrow and then she was delving into her own backpack, carrying on as if nothing had happened. "If you could carry my sweater and raincoat that would be great," she said casually. "You better walk up front with me. I'm going to need that sweater if it gets cool."

She could just as easily have hollered for it, but she obviously wanted to keep the boy close and Zach approved of that decision.

After the brief interest triggered by the scorpion talk, Travis had reverted to his usual blank self. He showed no emotion. Not relief, not excitement, not even boredom.

It was as if someone had switched him off.

Jason, one of the camp directors, was in charge of leading the trip and Steph, one of the counselors, was the one designated to drive the gear up to Heron Pond and prepare for their arrival.

Three other counselors joined the trip, including Rachel, Ryan's sister who taught at the local school and helped at the camp during her summers.

While Rachel took a group of the younger children

and played games as they walked, identifying trees and plants, Zach noticed that Travis stayed close to Brittany.

She chatted to him about the various expeditions she'd been on over the years, knowing instinctively which stories were likely to hold the attentions of a teenage boy. Listening to the conversation, Zach started to form a picture of the life she'd led in the decade they'd been apart. It was a three-hour trek through the woods to Heron Pond and by the time they approached their camp he'd learned that she preferred Cambridge to Oxford, that her favorite food in Greece had been baklava and that she'd once fallen off a camel in Egypt.

"The worst thing about camels?" She smacked an insect from her arm with her palm. "The smell. Ever seen that scene in Indiana Jones where the girl sprays the elephant with her perfume? I wanted to do that with the camel but having already fallen off when the stupid thing stood up, I needed both hands to hold on."

Travis almost smiled. "You said real archaeology was nothing like that movie."

"It isn't, but that part made perfect sense to me."

"Did you see the pyramids?"

"Yeah. They're cool if you can dodge the tourists. Because we were working with the university, we had a private tour." She talked about the thrill of watching a sunset over the desert and of almost collapsing on the walk up to Machu Picchu. "Eight thousand feet above sea level. Breathing is a challenge and a couple of people in my group had altitude sickness, but it was stunning. I'll never forget it."

But most of the time she talked about Greece. About blue skies and transparent water and how the whole place was an archaeological nirvana. To pass the time she taught Travis a few words of Greek.

Zach couldn't stop watching her. He loved the way she used her hands when she talked, and sensed her frustration when her movements were restricted by the cast on her wrist. She told every story with energy and enthusiasm, until he almost felt like flying over the Atlantic just to visit some of the places she described.

The smart girl had grown into a strong, independent woman and if anything the attraction was even greater than it had been when they'd been together in the past.

Her anecdotes made a long trek through the forest feel like five minutes.

When they finally arrived, they ate lunch and then took the canoes out on the pond. There was much squealing as they waited for the boats to leak or sink and even greater satisfaction when they didn't. They raced in teams, then dragged the canoes onto the banks and swam in the clear sparkling water, jumping in from the dock.

It was lighthearted, innocent fun and by the time they gathered around the campfire, everyone was tired.

This part Zach would happily have avoided, but two of the younger children had decided he was the key to staying alive in the big scary woods and had latched themselves on to him like ticks. As he settled down for campfire, they sat next to him, so close that their legs pressed against his.

Suffocated, he'd glanced across at Brittany but she simply grinned at him and carried on handing out marshmallows.

He turned to the little girl on his right who had welded herself like superglue to his side. "You all right?"

"I want to go home. I'm scared of the forest."

In his experience, there was a range of things in life worth being scared of, but the forest wasn't one of them. He racked his brains for her name. "Which part scares you, Grace?"

"The dark." It was a nervous whisper. "And not knowing whether what's out there is going to come and get you."

Zach felt a twinge of sympathy. He'd felt that fear himself, although never related to the forest. "The dark isn't going to hurt you. And you know what's out there. Trees, plants, and the birds and animals that live in them. This is their home and they're not too interested in you as long as you treat their home with respect. And you're going to be tucked up cozy and warm in your cabin tonight."

"Will you be there?" Her head turned towards him and he noticed that one of the red ribbons in her hair had worked its way loose.

It made him think of all the times he'd hung out at Ryan's house, teasing him mercilessly every time Rachel had plopped herself onto his lap to have her hair braided.

Observing Ryan had made him relieved he didn't have a little sister.

There was no way he would have wanted the responsibility of caring for another person in the home he'd inhabited. It would have been like dropping a dormouse into a nest of vipers.

"You're losing your ribbon. Let me fix that for you." Leaning towards her, he retied the ribbon. "You don't need to worry, Grace. I'm not in your cabin, but you have Rachel and Stephanie. And I'll be close by."

The camp up at the pond consisted of a yurt and several basic cabins. The children slept six to a cabin with two counselors and the yurt was used as a staff room and indoor camp if the weather changed. Because technically he was "extra" on this trip, Zach got to sleep in the yurt.

Judging from the expression on her face, Grace wished he was going to be sleeping in the cabin with her. "Do you believe in monsters?"

Zach stared at the fire and wondered how the hell he was supposed to answer that. He believed in the sort of monster who tried to break through a barricaded door, fueled by rage and alcohol. He'd come face-to-face with that one. Memories darkened his thoughts and then he felt Grace press closer.

"Zach?"

Sucked back into the present he reminded himself that this was about her, not him. "You mean the sort of monster that hides under the bed and comes out in the night? No. There are no monsters in this forest, Grace. Just animals that think of this place as their home. As long we leave them to get on with their lives, it will be fine."

"What if something comes when it's dark and we're all asleep?"

"Then you holler and I'll be right there."

"Do you promise?"

Responsibility pressed down on him. He knew all about broken promises, but he also knew how it felt to be scared. "I promise." His mouth was dry. "And now you need to try and relax and have fun because this is your last night at camp." Most of the children would be heading home the next day. For them, this final campfire was the perfect end to an idyllic summer.

Zach glanced across at Brittany, who was laughing at something Rachel had said. Her laughter was so infectious he found himself smiling, too, even though he had no idea what she'd found so amusing.

How did it feel to be that trusting? To leave that door unlocked and believe that the person entering would do you no harm?

She held nothing back. Her emotions were open and accessible to everyone. Including him. She opened the door wide and let everyone in whereas he kept the door between him and the rest of the world closed and firmly bolted.

And that lock inside him was the only one he'd never been able to break.

Brittany lay in her cabin, wide-awake.

Around her the children were all sleeping peacefully, even little Grace Green who'd been stuck to Zach like a Band-Aid during campfire.

He'd been so patient with her.

Thinking about it made her feel hot and bothered, and Brittany turned over in her bunk, unable to settle. Animals and vulnerable children. The two things he always had time for. Which proved that the seemingly impenetrable steel surface protected a soft inner layer rich with kindness and humanity.

She lay there, staring up at the ceiling, thinking about the contrasts. He gave the impression of being remote and inaccessible, and yet there hadn't been a single moment of the trek through the forest when he'd lost sight of Travis. Nor had there been a single moment at the campfire when he hadn't been watching out for little Grace.

The thought turned her insides to marshmallow.

Giving up on sleep, Brittany slipped out of her bunk, pushed her feet into her hiking boots, pulled a sweater over her pajamas and picked up a flashlight.

Closing the door carefully behind her, she walked a

little way into the forest, breathing in the scent of pine and the cool night air.

She'd traveled the world, but there was nowhere like Puffin Island.

Unlike Grace, the forest didn't scare her and never had. She'd walked here with her grandmother as a child. In the summer they'd hunted for berries and in the winter they'd collected armfuls of pinecones and taken then back to the warmth of the cottage and used them as decorations. They'd piled them in bowls and hung them from the Christmas tree.

The forest had been standing for hundreds of years and she closed her eyes and let the sounds of the night settle her, trying not to think about Zach. Instead she thought about the people who had walked the trails before her.

How had they endured the winters? Had they loved, laughed and cried for their children?

A hand closed over her shoulder and she almost died of fright.

Heart pounding, she turned. "Zach? Are you trying to kill me?"

His fingers were warm and strong through the fabric of her sweater. "What are you doing out here in the middle of the night?"

"I couldn't sleep."

"Why?"

I was thinking about you. "I had stuff on my mind. And it's not the middle of the night. Just past midnight. And now it's my turn to ask you the same question. What are you doing out here?"

"Walking." The fact that he was wearing his jeans and boots told her that, unlike her, he hadn't yet gone to bed.

She remembered on several of the occasions they'd

spent the whole night together, waking to find him wide-awake and staring into the darkness. And another occasion, more vivid in her memory, when he'd had a nightmare.

"Do you still have bad dreams?" The question left her lips before she could stop it and he released his grip on her shoulder.

"You should go back to bed."

Which meant that he did, but didn't want to talk about it. Which came as no surprise of course. He never talked about any of it.

At the time she'd thought that was fine. That a person had a right to their own privacy. She'd been too young to understand how privacy was connected to intimacy.

Would it have been different if they'd met for the first time now?

Sadness settled over her like mist.

"I'm not ready to sleep. I'm going to sit by the pond for a while. Good night, Zach." She walked away, and heard him curse softly and follow her, his feet crunching on the forest path.

"I don't suppose there's any point in telling you not to walk in the forest on your own?"

"None at all." Part of her wanted him to walk away and another part of her was pleased that he hadn't, all of which she took as evidence that her brain was as mixed up as her insides. "I've slept under the stars plenty of times, Zach. I can handle the woods on my own island."

"Wearing pajamas?"

"They cover my legs so I'm not going to get bitten. And I don't need a guard dog so feel free to do whatever it was you were planning on doing when you started your evening stroll."

"I was taking a walk." And he continued that walk alongside her, keeping pace with her until they reached the dock.

She felt a rush of frustration. "I've told you, I don't need protecting."

"Who says I'm here to protect you? Maybe I just like spending time with you."

Her heart lurched in her chest and her legs went so weak she plopped down on the cool planks of the dock, wondering what it was about him that turned her insides to mush. "Oh. I— Well, okay, then."

Because he didn't often say things like that, when he did it had enormous impact.

She was overwhelmed by an almost uncontrollable urge to abandon caution and kiss him.

Would he push her away?

It wasn't as if they hadn't already taken a step down that path.

It wasn't as if—

Unsettled by the complexity of her feelings, she gave a little shiver and because he missed nothing, he noticed. "You're cold."

She waited for him to suggest going back to the cabin, but instead he shrugged out of his jacket and draped it around her shoulders. She was cocooned by warmth, enveloped by Zach. The jacket smelled good. It smelled like him and after five seconds of inhaling his subtle masculine scent she was heated like bread in a toaster.

"Now *you'll* be cold."

"I won't. Compared to Alaska, this is balmy." He sat down next to her, his arm brushing against hers. "You always did love the outdoors. Did you sleep under the stars on digs?"

She tried to forget the coat, his nearness and the ridiculous hammering of her heart.

"Sometimes. Usually under canvas. This summer in Crete, Lily and I shared an apartment, which sounds like luxury until I tell you I've eaten burgers that were bigger than our bedroom." She snuggled deeper inside the jacket, listening to the rush of the wind through the trees and trying not to think about the fact that Zach was sitting right there, right next to her, within touching distance. "Summer is almost over. I can never decide which is my favorite season. I love the fall colors, but I look forward to winter because there's no better feeling than crunching through fresh white snow or dragging your sled to the top of East Crag and sliding down into the soft snow at the bottom. Then after a few weeks of bitter cold and ice and maybe a couple of power outages, the novelty wears off and I remember how endless winter seems. Then I long for spring when the snow melts and the rivers swell and the air is filled with the promise of summer. Then summer comes and the sun shines and for a while I think summer is my favorite season, until I'm stuck in Harbor Stores behind a line of tourists being poked in the back with a fishing net. Which is your favorite season?" Surely he'd tell her that? It wasn't a personal question. Just a simple exchange of likes and dislikes.

When he didn't answer she turned her head and found him looking at her with that dark, intense gaze that always made her stomach drop. It was as if he looked deep inside a person, never trusting what lay on the surface. For a man who guarded his own innermost thoughts as fiercely as a vault in a bank, he was remarkably adept at reading others.

"Winter," he said roughly. "I guess mine is winter."

"Which is presumably why you chose to live in Alaska?"

"Alaska is one of the least densely populated places on the planet, which made it custom designed for me."

"Because there's more wildlife than people and you don't love people?"

"I judge them on a case-by-case basis, but it's true that on the whole I find wildlife easier to understand."

"So you picked lonely places so that it was just you and the polar bears?"

"Not many polar bears, and they're mostly up by the Wrangel Islands and the North Slope. You're more likely to meet a grizzly or a black bear."

"As you can probably tell, I don't know much about Alaska."

"Plenty of folks don't, even though it's the largest state."

She stretched out her legs. "What did you do out there? Who did you fly and where did you fly them?"

"A mix of people. Locals, businesspeople, oil folk and the school hockey team. And I took them wherever they wanted to go. The bush planes are a lifeline for many of those rural communities."

"Sounds dangerous."

"Not really, but when it was dangerous the danger always came from predictable sources—the wildlife and the weather. Life there has an appealing simplicity. If something is trying to eat you, you don't let it. If the weather doesn't want you to fly, you don't fly."

"But knowing you, you flew anyway."

He gave a soft laugh. "Occasionally."

"Do you miss it?"

"Sometimes. But even in the summer Puffin Island offers plenty of places to escape the crowds."

"Philip is pleased you're back. You're like a son to him." The moment the words left her mouth she sensed the change in him and cursed herself for carelessly wandering into the realms of personal. Swiftly, she changed the subject. "I sometimes miss Greece."

"Have you decided what you're going to do once that plaster cast is off your wrist?"

"No. I thought of applying for a tenure-track faculty position here in the US, or possibly returning to the UK. I don't know." And that was unusual for her. She always knew. She was used to having a clear goal and concentrating her efforts on going after it. "I'm not ready to leave the island yet. I think I might be having a midlife crisis."

"In your twenties?" There was a hint of amusement in his voice and she pulled up her legs and wrapped her arms around her knees. The cast felt awkward and unyielding and she gave up and shifted her position until she was comfortable.

"You're laughing at me, but I've always known exactly what I wanted to do. Every job I did, every path I took, was all part of my plan. I wanted to get my degree, then my PhD, I wanted to walk the Inca Trail and spend time in Greece because the whole place is like a museum, or maybe a Minoan theme park." She grinned, thinking how her professors would wince at the description. "Either way, I always knew what the next goal was. Until now. For the first time in my life I don't know what I want to do. I assumed coming back here would be a short, temporary thing. A brief visit while I recuperated and before I went off to do the next thing on my list."

"And?"

"And I don't have anything on my list that feels better than being here. And that's scary. It's the first time in my life I haven't known what I wanted. What I need."

Except when it came to him.

She knew she needed him.

There was a soft splash as a bird skimmed the water and Zach stirred.

"Maybe what you need is time to heal. That's why you came home, isn't it?"

"Mostly, but not entirely. I can only go so long without coming here. I get sort of itchy. No matter where I live, this place is still home." She struggled to describe the feeling. "I need a fix of all the things I love about Puffin Island. I soak it up, absorb it, then take it with me somewhere else. That's what I do. I should be applying for things now, but every time I sit down at the laptop and look at what's out there, there's nothing that grabs me. Nothing that feels worth leaving Castaway Cottage. I love it here. I'd forgotten how much. Listen—" She tilted her head and listened to a haunting, melodic cry from the far side of the pond. "Do you hear that?"

"Loons. They're calling to each other. It's an eerie sound." His leg brushed lightly against hers. "I guess it's their equivalent of texting. They're good parents, did you know that? They carry their young on their backs, protecting them."

His words brought a lump to her throat. From the little she knew, his own experience of childhood had been vastly different.

"John Harris used to bring Helen Cooper and me up here and we'd camp out by the water and watch them. I used to read with a flashlight and he'd tell me off for attracting insects. As long as it wasn't spiders, I didn't care. All I wanted to do was read about all these other places that existed beyond the shores of Puffin Island. It fascinated me that tourists were desperate to come here and we were all desperate to leave."

"I guess we all want what we don't have. That's human nature."

They sat in silence, listening to the soft lap of water against the dock.

"I used to dream about the world beyond Puffin Island. I read Robinson Crusoe and wanted to be shipwrecked. Then I discovered Jane Austen and wanted to live in an English country house complete with staff and to travel everywhere by horse-drawn carriage."

"Not the most reliable mode of transport."

"True. And in reality I would have been one of the servants, which would not have been fun. What did you dream about?" Her casual question was met with silence.

He stared into the darkness towards the call of the loons. "There wasn't much room in my life for dreams." The stillness of his features made her shiver.

Feeling it, he turned to her. "Still cold? Zip up the coat."

"I should be giving it back to you."

"I'm fine." He rose to his feet. "Stand up."

She did as he ordered and tried to zip the jacket herself, but with one hand it was impossible and Zach reached down and nudged her fingers out of the way. His head was lowered towards hers and she could see the rough shadow of his jaw and the molten black of his eyes. In the semidarkness his face was all hard lines and dangerous edges.

He was close. *So close.* If she leaned forward just a little, she'd be kissing him.

With sure fingers he eased the zip upwards, the movement drawing them closer still.

"This must be a whole new experience for you, Zachary Flynn." Her voice sounded croaky. "Dressing a woman instead of undressing her."

He paused for a fraction of a second, then zipped the jacket all the way up to her throat with careful hands. "I can manage it if I focus." The backs of his fingers brushed her jaw gently and lingered. "You were good with Travis today."

She wondered why such a simple gesture could have her nerve endings jumping. "He didn't really talk to me."

"But he listened. That's a start. You're a kind person, Brittany."

"So are you. You were good with little Grace. Patient."

He let his hands drop. "No reason not to be. Plenty of folk are scared of the forest."

"Before she went to sleep I heard her telling her friend that you told her the forest is home to the animals and they just want to get on with their lives. You made more progress with her than I did with Travis."

"He stayed close to you. Talked a bit. Listened a lot. I'd call that progress."

"But he didn't talk about anything personal. I was hoping he might." Because the urge to kiss Zach was almost overwhelming, she turned her head and stared across the water. "I can't bear that his default is not to trust anyone."

"When you're used to living that way, it's hard to change." He paused. "And sometimes it's not wise."

"How can it not be wise?"

There was a long pulsing silence. "Because," he said slowly, "sometimes not trusting is what keeps you safe."

She didn't move. Didn't breathe.

She knew, without even a flicker of doubt, that he was talking from experience.

He hadn't felt safe?

She turned to look at him but his eyes were as unfathomable as the darkest depths of the ocean. "Zach—"

"Do you want to sit down a little longer or walk?"

Neither. She felt like a child, peeping through the keyhole of a door, unable to form a complete picture of what was on the other side. She wanted to know more. She *needed* to know more. She wanted to ask him what was behind that remark, but he'd already revealed more than he ever had before and he took a step back, his body language making it clear that he considered the conversation at an end.

Retreating, she thought desperately. Always retreating.

She wanted to dig for the truth as she did in her job, but her training had also taught her the value of patience. As an archaeologist she knew that the past had to be uncovered layer by layer, the ground persuaded to yield buried secrets to the world. Too much haste and impatience and you risked damaging what was there and losing it forever.

Zach didn't want to talk about his past and because she didn't want to risk saying the wrong thing and driving him away, she didn't push.

Instead, she walked to the end of the dock.

"Be careful." His voice vibrated through the darkness, low and deep. "Some of the planks are uneven and you only have one working wrist."

"I'll be fine. My wrist was a silly accident, that's all. I was laughing at something a friend said and I wasn't looking where I was putting my feet."

"Was the 'friend' that guy you were talking to the

other night?" The roughness of his tone almost made
her miss her step.

"Yes. His name is Spyros. Dr. Spyros Nicolaides." She
stood at the end of the dock, trying to still the questions
in her head. Who? What? Why? At what age had Zach
not felt safe? How had he protected himself? "We call
him Spy. He's Greek." She closed her eyes and breathed
in the scent and sounds of the forest.

She felt his arm brush against hers as he stood next
to her.

"Did you have sex with him?" The question startled
her as much as his rough tone.

"Zach—"

"Sorry. Don't answer that question." His voice was raw
and she turned her head to look at him, confused and off
balance. She was still trying to work out the meaning behind his words when he curved his hand around the nape
of her neck and drew her face towards his in a possessive gesture. She was locked between the strength of his
hand and the desire in his eyes and in that single moment
she was aware of every detail of him. The thickness of
those lashes, the spectacular lines of his bone structure
and the hard pressure of his thighs against hers. She felt
the warmth of his breath brush against her lips and gave
a low moan of anticipation.

There was a moment of exquisite torture when she
thought he might pull back, but then his mouth touched
hers and he kissed her, opening her mouth with his. There
was none of the primal desperation of their last encounter. His kiss was skilled and gentle, a slow, deliberate
exploration, a relentless pursuit of pleasure, but her response was as powerful as ever. She fell, tumbling into
the whirlpool of heady excitement, lost in every breath-

stealing, heart-stopping moment of that incredible kiss. Never in all her life had she felt the same wild rush of excitement that came from kissing Zach. Pleasure was thick and sweet. Need became desperation, desire an agonizing ache low in her pelvis.

And he knew.

He knew what he was doing to her.

She felt his fingers tighten on her head as his mouth moved over hers with knowing expertise and erotic purpose.

A moment before she'd been cold, but it was impossible to feel cold as each melting slide of his tongue sent heat shimmering across her skin. She lifted her hand to his face, felt the roughness of his jaw against her palm.

This, she thought. This they'd always had.

It seemed impossible that a simple kiss could make her feel so much, until you remembered that this was Zachary Flynn, who knew how to kiss a girl until the flesh melted from her bones. And because she knew his skills weren't limited to kissing, she wanted more. So much more.

"Zach—" She tried to shift her body against his, but he eased back slowly.

"You're cold." His body was no longer touching hers but his hand was still locked behind her head, as if he was letting her go by degrees and couldn't quite manage the final part.

"That's why you kissed me?" Her voice was a whisper, lost in the rush of the breeze over the pond. "I thought you didn't want to. I thought— I don't understand what's going on here."

"Nothing is going on."

But she wanted it to. And she knew he did, too. She

could feel the tension in him. Knew that if she pressed herself close to him, she'd find him hard and ready. Once again she felt a rush of frustration that this had to be so complicated.

And still she felt the firm pressure of his hand, holding her. All it would take was a small movement on his part to bring their mouths back into contact.

"Have you wondered what would have happened if we'd met for the first time now?"

The pressure of his fingers increased. "Nothing would have happened."

"Yes, it would. And because I'm no longer an idealistic teenager, I wouldn't have pushed for more and scared the hell out of you." She heard the harsh rasp of his breathing and carried on. "I wouldn't have got so serious so fast. I'm not really interested in serious relationships anymore."

"That's because you married some loser who didn't treat you well."

"No. I married someone I didn't understand." Guilt stabbed at her, sliding between her ribs like the blade of a knife. "And it was over before I had a chance to figure any of it out."

"Probably a good thing. You found a job you loved and traveled the world, none of which you would have done if you'd stayed married to me."

"If we'd met for the first time now, all our baggage would be with other people."

Unsmiling, he drew the pad of his thumb slowly over her cheek. "And?"

She tried to ignore the pounding of her heart. "And I'd make you an offer you couldn't refuse. And before you freak out, I should tell you it would involve both of us naked and nothing more. Nothing deeper. No dreams and no promises. Just the moment." She felt his fingers tighten on the back of her head and there was a fierce gleam in his eyes.

"You'd make the same mistake twice? I thought you were supposed to be smart."

"You want the same thing, Zach. I know you do."

"What do you want me to say? That I can't look at you without wanting to nail you to the nearest flat surface? Of course I do." His voice was husky, and still his thumb stroked across her cheek in a motion that fell somewhere between soothing and seductive. "You're still the sexiest woman I've ever laid eyes on."

Her stomach lurched. "Even in my pajamas with bits of the forest stuck in my hair?"

A smile played at the corners of his mouth. "Especially that way. But it makes no difference. We're not going to do this, Brit. Last time I was selfish. I thought maybe if I pretended to be the way everyone else was, I could have the things they had. But you can't fake it. I can't fake it. I've never got close to a woman. I don't know how. I can give physically, but emotionally I don't feel anything. That isn't ever going to change."

She was the one who had been selfish, not him. She'd been so crazy about him, been so desperate for it to work, she hadn't stopped to wonder whether what was right for her would be right for him.

"How do you know it won't change?"

"I know." His voice was flat. "I learned to switch my emotions off a long time ago and I can't switch them back on."

"Because if you don't feel, you can't be hurt."

His hand dropped and his gaze held hers in the semi-darkness. "I don't spend time analyzing the reasons."

"But you do feel, Zach. You *have* made connections." It was desperately important to her that he see that. "Friendships. You have Philip and Celia, Ryan and Alec. They care about you. Even Hilda! Plenty of people care about you. I know they're not your family and maybe it's because I was raised on this island, but I always knew growing up that family was more than your parents. Friends are just a different type of family. Em and Sky—they're as much family as my grandmother was. When I look back over the things I've done in my life, it's the people I remember as much as the places. I love knowing that there are people who have my back, and I have theirs. I'd do anything for my friends. That's why I gave Em and Sky a key to the cottage."

He gave a grunt. "They don't need a damn key. They could have just pushed extra hard on the door to gain entry."

She ignored that. "The key was symbolic. Castaway Cottage is a special place for all of us. And they're not just my friends, they're your friends, too. Emily will never forget that you were the one who flew her and Lizzy to the hospital when no one else would."

"I'm on probation. They're ready to kill me if I hurt you again."

"That's not going to happen."

"No. It's not. And you should go to bed."

She hesitated, the emotional side of her wanting to argue, the rational side telling her to do what he ordered.

"First I need to ask you something." Something that she'd always wondered. "Why did you go through with the wedding? Because Ryan forced you to show up?"

"No." There was a long pause. "Because part of me wanted to be that guy."

"What guy?"

"The guy you thought I was." Finally, he released her. "Now go to bed, Brittany." And perhaps because he knew one of them needed to make the decision, he turned and strode away, leaving her staring after him, wearing his coat, her heart aching and her head full of questions.

you are. You are? Cried Brittany. He released her.
Now go to bed, Brittany. And perhaps she would worry
one of them need discuss the . . . desperately looked and
strode away, leaving her silent in after improved giving. His
felt her heart raising another acid inhibitions.

Chapter 13

When Zach looked back on his life, a life littered with examples of things he shouldn't have done, a fair proportion of his regrets involved Brittany.

He shouldn't have had sex with her when she was eighteen and too naive to know he was trouble. He shouldn't have married her and he shouldn't have left her ten days later.

When she'd returned to the island, he should have kept his distance. He shouldn't have had sex with her that night in her cottage and he definitely shouldn't have followed her to the pond the night before and kissed her.

That kiss had destroyed all hope of sleep and he'd lain awake listening to the ghostly sounds of the loons on the far side of the pond, trying with no success to will his body into slumber. He'd contemplated a cold swim in the water, but decided in the end that there was no point.

There was only one activity that was going to relieve his current frustration and that was strictly off-limits.

All he had to offer a woman was a satisfying sex life and a whole lot of emotional frustration and misery, and he wasn't prepared to serve that up to Brittany a second time.

He rose early, packed up his things and kept his distance as the other counselors gathered the group together for breakfast around the fire. Breakfast was followed by a morning swimming and canoeing in the pond.

Brittany was directing activities from the bank, wearing her favorite cargoes with a long-sleeve cotton shirt. Underneath the smile, her eyes looked tired and Zach could see she hadn't slept any better than he had.

He wished he could leave behind the conversation of the night before, but it clung to him like a burr clings to a sweater.

Have you wondered what would have happened if we'd met for the first time now?

He didn't need to wonder. He knew.

He would have stripped off those cargoes and kept her in bed until neither of them had the energy to crawl to the door. He would have explored every part of her firm, athletic body and then done it again and again. It didn't help that he knew how physical she was. Her sexual appetites matched his, and knowing that did nothing for his internal cooling system.

Hot and frustrated, he turned away and focused on something else. Usually the forest was his favorite place, but now he was looking forward to getting back to his cabin, away from Brittany's swinging braid and infectious energy.

Because walking behind her would have meant trying

not to stare at the swing of her hips, he chose to walk in front and led the way as they hiked back down the forest trail towards Camp Puffin.

Pushing the pace, he arrived back at camp a few minutes ahead of the others and immediately sensed a problem.

The area that was normally thronging with activity was eerily quiet and he glanced towards the catering barn and saw Callie, one of the counselors, guarding the door.

White-faced with anxiety, she waved at him frantically and he walked across to her.

"Problem?"

She cast a nervous look over his shoulder. "There's a dog prowling around the camp. Looks like someone dumped him in the forest and he broke loose. There's wire still attached to his neck. No one knows who owns him, but the chief of police is on his way. In the meantime Philip told all the kids to stay in the barn. You should bring your group here, too." As she finished speaking Zach saw the dog, a muscular bulldog breed, emerge from the trees, snarling and shaking his head as he tried to free himself from the wire. It didn't take an expert to know the animal was crazed with pain and fear.

Zach was about to radio Rachel and the rest of the group to warn them to stay back until the situation was handled when he saw a flash of red at the edge of the forest, and there was Grace, slightly ahead of the group because she'd been trying to catch up with him, her ribbons unraveling in her blond hair.

She saw him a split second before she saw the dog.

And froze. She opened her mouth to scream, but fortunately her lungs wouldn't work.

The dog saw her, lowered its head and started to growl,

a deep-throated, menacing sound that would have sent chills down the spine of the most confident child.

And Grace Green certainly wasn't that.

Zach knew fear when he saw it. He'd seen the same look in his eyes every time he'd looked in the mirror during the first eight years of his life.

Ignoring the frantic warnings of the counselor next to him, Zach strode across the clearing towards Grace.

"Stand still, Grace." He pitched his tone to a level he hoped would reassure her and not unsettle the dog. "Don't move. He doesn't want to hurt you. He's got a wire round his neck that's making him angry. It's not about you. He doesn't want to hurt you. He's just telling you he's in pain. And we're going to fix that. Stand still. That's it. Good girl. I've got this."

As he drew closer Zach could see dried blood matting the dog's fur and felt a rush of anger.

The dog snarled a warning. Zach chose to ignore it.

There had been moments in his past when he probably would have made the same sound himself.

"You're mad and you don't trust me. I know, and I don't blame you. Who did this to you?" He kept his tone low and measured and his movements smooth and unhurried as he put himself between the dog and the child. "We need to get that wire off your neck because it's digging in and making you sore. And you need to stop growling at Grace because you're scaring her. And we both know you don't want to scare her. You don't want to hurt anyone, except maybe the person who did this to you. And I wouldn't mind going a few rounds with them myself."

He kept talking, taking it as a positive sign that the dog didn't attack. Instead the animal backed up a few steps, growling deep in his throat. Then he shook his head angrily, sending blood and saliva flying through the air.

Zach kept talking. "You're probably wondering if I'm another bully like the one who dumped you in the forest, but I'm telling you I'm not. I know that thing must hurt like a b—" At the last minute he remembered Grace. "A lot. It must hurt a lot. But I'm going to take it off and make you more comfortable. And you're going to let me do that."

He saw Travis reach Grace. Saw the boy clock the situation in an instant.

"Stay right there, Travis." He kept his voice at the same easy pitch. "Stay near Grace for me. She's uneasy around the dog. Grace, you stay with Travis. He's going to take care of you. Whatever you do, don't run."

He saw Grace step closer to Travis and slide her hand into his. He saw Travis hesitate, shock and uncertainty on his face, more freaked out by the little girl holding his hand and trusting him than he was by the angry dog.

Anger was familiar.

Trust wasn't.

Zach was willing to bet no one had trusted him with anything before.

Out of the corner of his eye he saw Caleb Cook, the island's police chief, arrive and park his cruiser a safe distance from the barn.

The dog's growling intensified and Zach lifted his hand as a signal to Caleb to keep back.

Dimly aware that Brittany was approaching down the trail, he dropped to his haunches in front of the dog. "It's turning into a circus around here. You don't want to hurt anyone, do you? You just need someone to take this thing off."

The dog snarled, clearly ready to argue with that analysis of the situation.

"Who put it there? Who did that to you?" Zach slowly reached out a hand to the dog. The animal bared its teeth but didn't bite as Zach tried to gently maneuver his fingers under the wire. It proved impossible. Whoever had put it there hadn't intended it to be taken off. They'd intended the animal to die in the forest, helpless and alone.

Anger ripped through him and the dog must have sensed the shift in his emotions because he snarled and turned his head. For a moment it looked as if he was about to bury his teeth into Zach's arm. He snapped wildly and Caleb took a step towards them, but Zach sent him a look warning him to stay back.

"You've been pulling at it. That's why it's got so tight." He stroked the dog's head, gently soothing him. Then he slowly reached into his back pocket and pulled out a pair of cutters he kept with him whenever he went into the forest. "Hold still. If you move I'll either lose a finger or cut your throat and we don't want either of those things to happen."

Zach knew he only had one shot at it and he didn't hesitate. He slid the clippers under the wire and cut before the dog had a chance to protest at this apparent assault. The wire dropped to the floor and the dog yelped and shook himself, as if checking he really was free.

"It's gone." Zach kept talking to the dog in the same even tone, kept stroking him gently as he rose slowly to his feet. "I don't like the look of that wound so I'm going to put you in my car and take you to the vet."

The dog gave a whimper and sniffed his hand but he didn't run off.

"Yeah, that's right. Friend, not foe. I bet you haven't had many friends in your life, have you?"

He knew how that felt, too.

Knew how it felt to be so scared you didn't know who the hell you could trust.

Caleb moved closer. "If you pick him up, chances are he'll bite you."

"I don't think so, but I'll take my chances. He only snapped at me because I hurt him trying to get the wire off. He was trying to protect himself." Zach pushed the cutters back in his pocket, his fingers slippery with the dog's blood. "You're not going to punish him for acting in self-defense, are you, Officer?"

Caleb gave a faint smile. "It's your flesh. I got a call saying the dog was dangerous. If he's a stray, we can't leave him here. We need to trace the owner."

"That's your job. Trace the owner, and when you find him I hope you'll press charges. The dog would have starved if he hadn't broken free." Banking down the anger, Zach stroked the dog gently. "I'm going to take him over to the animal center and get that wound checked out."

"And then what?" Caleb frowned as his radio crackled.

"I don't know, but I'll work something out. You go and deal with whatever crisis is going on. I've got this." Zach carried the dog to his car, put him in the backseat and closed the door firmly. The truth was he had no clue what he was going to do with the dog, but it couldn't be left injured and angry in a camp full of children and the alternative wasn't an option.

Why the hell should a perfectly healthy dog be destroyed just because some idiot didn't see a place for him?

As someone who had always known that if he'd been

a kitten he would have been drowned in the river at birth, destroying a living thing for the convenience of others didn't sit well with Zach.

He wiped his hands on an old rag he kept in the car, closed the door on the dog and walked back to where Grace was standing. Obeying his orders to the letter, she hadn't moved a muscle and was still clutching Travis's hand.

"He t-tried to bite you."

"Because I hurt him taking the wire off. I don't blame him for that, do you?" Zach hunkered down in front of her. "Are you okay, Grace?"

She gave a tiny nod. "I was scared."

"You were great." He spoke firmly and saw the beginnings of a smile. "You stood still. It was the right thing to do."

"I've never met an angry dog before and that dog was *very* angry."

A little crowd had gathered around but Zach ignored them and focused on Grace. He took it as a good sign that Travis was still letting her grip his hand. "That would have been my first thought, too, but I've learned over the years that the emotion you see on the outside isn't always the same as the one on the inside."

Grace looked puzzled. "What do you mean?"

Zach picked his words carefully. He considered this a more important lesson than anything she'd learned out in the forest. "On the outside that dog was angry, but on the inside he was scared. A thousand times more scared than you. He was hurting and all alone. Someone left him there to die by himself in a horrible way and he was trying to stay alive. To survive. That's a natural instinct. I'm not going to blame him for that, are you?" He glanced briefly at Travis and saw he was still, his face the color of bone. Zach knew that look. He wondered what the boy had been forced to do to protect himself.

"Someone wanted him to *die*?" Grace's eyes filled. "Is that going to happen?"

"No, it's not. Not now."

"How do you know?"

"Because I'm going to see to it that it doesn't."

"What will happen to him? Will they punish him for nearly biting you? Will he be all right?" Anxiety flowed along with the questions.

"He's going to be fine, and no." Zach rose to his feet. "No one is going to punish him. It might take a while, but we're going to teach him that some people can be trusted. That not everyone is like the person who did this to him."

"He won't have to go back there?" Travis's question was so quiet it was barely audible. "You're not going to send him back?"

"No. I wouldn't send him back somewhere he's abused."

Travis licked his lips. "Not even if it's his home?"

Zach wished they weren't surrounded by people.

This was the conversation he knew Philip had been hoping Travis might have for weeks and this was neither the time nor the place.

"Home should be a place where he feels safe." He held Travis's gaze. "No one should feel threatened, or scared, in their own home."

"But what will happen to him? Where will he go?" Travis was holding Grace's hand as tightly as she was holding his. "I mean it's not like he's a baby or cute or anything. Who would want him?" His voice was hoarse and scratchy and Zach felt as if someone had reached into his chest and squeezed his heart.

"Plenty of folks would want him. Good folks, although it might take him a while to understand that they're good. Travis, why don't you take Grace to Philip. He'll want to know she's all right. Go and talk to Philip. Tell him the whole story." He spoke firmly and saw the boy nod slowly.

"Okay. I guess I'll do that. If you think it's the right thing."

A glimmer of trust right there in those words.

"I know it's the right thing."

Just a step, but hopefully enough of a step to begin the journey out of the hell Travis was living in.

"I'm going to say goodbye now because I'm taking the dog to the vet. You take care of yourself, Grace. I know you live on the island, so I expect I'll see you around."

She gave him a wobbly smile. "I'm coming back to camp next year. Will you be here?"

Unlike Brittany he'd never planned his life further than the next few days. "Maybe."

"I hope you are." She hesitated and then let go of Travis's hand, stepped forward and hugged Zach, her skinny arms squeezing tightly. "You're the *best*."

Zach froze. He could count on the fingers of one hand the number of times he'd been hugged in his life. He stood for a moment, his hand hovering in the air, and then lowered it to her skinny shoulder and gave her a reassuring squeeze.

Grace released him, muttered more jumbled thanks and then ran off to join the rest of the group who were gathering near the barn.

Travis followed more slowly and Zach pulled out his phone and sent Philip a quick text.

Then he felt someone touch his arm and turned to find Brittany standing next to him.

"Well, another heroic rescue on Puffin Island. You're

making a habit of it and Grace's dad is one of the town's selectmen so I'm guessing you might even find yourself on the agenda of the next town meeting. Who knows, you might even reach hero status."

Feeling as uncomfortable as if he'd just fallen in a thorn bush, Zach slid the phone back into his pocket. "For taking a wire off a dog? I happened to get to him first, that's all."

"And we're all relieved about that." Her mouth tilted into a smile of self-mockery. "That animal was crazy with pain and he had all my sympathy, but I wouldn't have risked giving him my fingers as well. You are now officially known as the dog whisperer." She glanced towards Zach's car. "We need to get him to the vet. I can't drive, so you'll have to do that part and I'll sit with Jaws."

Zach raised an eyebrow. "Jaws?"

"I call it the way I see it. And from what I've seen so far, it's a reasonable name. Those teeth were horribly close to sinking into your arm, Flynn."

"Knowing that, you're still happy to sit with him?"

"Yes, but don't ever rescue a tarantula because I'm not sitting next to one of those, even for you." She stepped away to tell Rachel her plans and then walked towards his car.

Zach stared after her, his feelings mixed up.

He'd been doing everything he could to put distance between them, trying to protect her from himself.

Thanks to the dog, that plan had gone out the window.

The dog lay with his head on his paws, watching her warily.

"I only have one good hand," Brittany told him, "so if you bite that, I'm in trouble and frankly so are you.

And if you bite the other one you'll break your teeth on the cast. I've never seen you before. Do you recognize him, Zach?"

"No." Zach turned the car and drove away from the camp. A steady line of cars was building in the opposite direction as parents arrived to pick up their children. "Someone probably brought him over on the ferry and abandoned him."

And the story could have had an ugly ending had Zach not intervened.

She knew it would take her a while to forget the sight of him putting himself between the little girl and the dog.

There was a smudge of dirt on his cheek and his hands were dusty.

She thought of those hands, sure and gentle as he'd handled the dog. "I don't know why anyone would abandon him. He's pretty cute."

Zach caught her eye in the mirror. "We both know this dog is as ugly as sin. He has nine chins."

"Maybe, but he's still cute. And I don't notice his chins because I'm looking at his eyes. He has nice eyes."

"You have a thing for damaged creatures."

"This from a man who almost got himself bitten taking the wire off the dog's neck." And he hadn't hesitated. He'd put the dog's comfort in front of his own safety. "And everything you said to Travis—that was nice work."

"We were talking about the dog."

"We both know neither of you were talking about the dog. I hope he opens up to Philip. You texted him?"

"Yes. The boy showed up at his office."

It didn't surprise her that he said no more than that.

Zach didn't gossip. He didn't chat. He respected Travis's right to keep whatever secrets he wanted to keep, while nudging open a door so that he could reveal them if he wanted to.

What secrets was Zach keeping?

Thinking about that, she slid out of the car and reached for the dog, but Zach was there before her.

"He's heavy, and you already have one damaged wrist." He lifted the dog carefully and Brittany saw the dog give his hand a swift lick.

Her heart kicked against her chest.

"Can you believe that? He's already in love with you. Are you sure it's a he and not a she?" She was rewarded with one of those lightning-quick smiles that made her feel as if she'd touched a live wire.

It had always been the same between them and ten years had done nothing to dilute the strength of the attraction. She didn't need to wonder if he felt it, too, because she knew he did.

She wondered if he was the reason she'd never become deeply involved with a man. She'd had relationships, satisfying relationships, but she'd never replicated the crazy chemistry she had with him.

It wasn't youth or inexperience that had been responsible for those feelings that had swept her away in her teens.

It was Zach himself.

Her head spinning as if she'd just stepped off a merry-go-round, she followed him into the clinic where they were met by Sara, the vet nurse, who also ran the small animal sanctuary on the island.

"Zach!" It was obvious from the pink that gathered in her cheeks that she was a Zachary Flynn supporter. "Chief Cook called, so we knew to expect you. Go right on in. Dr. Brent is waiting for you. Hi, Brittany. Good to see you."

"Hi, Sara." They'd been at school together, a couple of years apart. Brittany remembered Sara as a gentle girl who had excelled at biology and taken the class fish home every summer. "How long have you been working here?"

"Since the start of the summer. Dr. Brent gave me the job. It's great to be back on the island." She stroked her hand over the dog's head and said, "Oh, aren't you adorable. What happened to you?" Jaws grunted gratefully at the contact and slobbered on her hand.

"Did you say Dr. Brent?" Zach shifted the wriggling dog. "What happened to Dr. Tanner?"

"Got a job over in Portland. Small animal practice. Dr. Brent is very good." Her mouth tightened when she saw the wound on the dog's neck. "Wire? If I found the person who did that I'd inject him with something that would keep him down for a week. Does he have a home?"

"None that he's going back to." Zach's mouth was grim and Sara nodded in agreement.

"You can't take him while you're flying all over the place and he shouldn't be near children until we know more about his temperament, so do you want him to stay in the shelter until we can find someone to adopt him?"

Brittany looked at the ugly, slobbering dog and felt a pang. Even she had to admit that his appeal wasn't immediately obvious. He was the sort of dog most people would walk past on their way to a cute spaniel or a sturdy Lab. "You think someone will take him?"

"Why not? There's someone for everyone, right? At least that's what Gran tells me when I moan about still being single." Ignoring the slobber and the risk to her life, Sara took Jaws from Zach and gave a tut of disapproval. "You've no flesh on your bones. We're going to have to do something about that. You're going to be eating gourmet food as soon as Dr. Brent has taken a look at you."

Zach and Brittany followed Sara through to the surgery where the island vet, Gabe Brent, treated the wound and gave Jaws a thorough going-over. When they walked out an hour later, a bandaged and drugged-up Jaws had taken up temporary residence with Sara, and Zach was considerably poorer.

Reeling from the cost, Brittany pulled open the car door. "Holy crap, I paid less than that for my rent in Greece. Why didn't I train as a vet? Do you want me to pay half or are you going to sell one wing of the Cessna?"

"I'll manage. Are you going back to camp or do you want a ride home?"

"Home, but you don't need to drive me. If you could just drop me on the corner of Main and South, I'll walk from there." She slid into the passenger seat. She still hadn't touched on their conversation of the night before even though she wanted to. She wanted to know more. She wanted to ask him what he'd meant when he'd said that sometimes not trusting kept you safe. But she knew that Main Street in the middle of the day wasn't the time to broach a subject Zach rarely touched. "You're not going to offer to adopt Jaws?"

"No. That dog needs love and attention to feel secure. He deserves a stable home. I can't give him that."

"Why?"

"You know why. *Love, stability* and *security* aren't words that appear in my vocabulary. If they were, we'd still be married." He pulled into the flow of traffic and she felt her heart bump.

Was that true? Would they still be married?

"Jaws will be gutted," she said casually. "It was love at first sight."

"It was gratitude. If you'd cut that wire off his neck, he would have bonded with you."

"If I'd cut that wire off his neck, I'd have two damaged wrists by now. You showed some serious animal magic there, Flynn."

"Being kind to animals isn't magic."

"It is when you do it. You have this quiet way about you—" She frowned as she tried to put her observations into words. "It's as if animals know that they're safe with you."

"They are safe with me."

She saw the Warrens' barn out of the corner of her eye and turned to look at him. "You were supposed to be dropping me back there."

"I'll drop you at your door."

"I was planning on walking. Do you ever listen to anyone?"

"Depends on whether they're saying something I want to hear. Do you ever stop arguing?"

"Depends. I enjoy a good argument. It wakes my brain up." Smiling, she sat back and let herself enjoy the view, trying not to think about the powerful length of his thigh only inches from hers or the conversation they weren't having. "It's hot today. That last half hour through the forest was sweaty. It's at times like this I hate having this cast on my arm. Actually that's not true. I hate having it on my arm the whole time."

"When does it come off?"

"With luck at the next appointment."

"I'll fly you there."

Last time she'd argued. This time she didn't want to.

She told herself it was because it made sense to accept his offer, but knew it was really because she enjoyed spending time with him. "Thank you. I appreciate that. And when I get home, the first thing I'm going to do is swim in the sea."

She hoped the freezing waters of the bay would cool her down because nothing else was working.

A week later Zach delivered a group of bankers on a corporate team-building exercise to their exclusive lodge on the banks of the Kennebec River and then flew back to the island.

He'd taken on more flying jobs than usual recently. He figured that the less time he spent on Puffin Island, the less likely he was to bump into Brittany.

She was still spending most of her time up at the camp, despite the fact that the last of the children had now left.

Encouraged by Philip, she was pulling together plans for the following year and liaising with the university. Sometimes, when he was passing, he heard her laugh coming from Philip's office, that rich, infectious giggle that always made him want to smile, too.

That was just one of the many reasons he'd decided to spend more time in the air.

It was his bad luck that a storm had been forecast, the result of which would mean spending more time at the camp.

To delay his arrival, he stopped at the vet's practice to check on Jaws.

"He's doing so well!" A delighted Sara led him through to the kennels at the back of the practice that led onto open fields and farmland so the dogs had room to run around.

Zach watched as Jaws pounced on a squeaky toy. "You bought him that?"

"No, Brittany brought it a few days ago. He loves it."

"She's been visiting?"

"She's been coming by every day. She didn't mention it?" Sara looked surprised. "I guess she forgot or something. She spends at least an hour with him and yesterday when we were crazy busy, she took him for a walk, although I think she ended up carrying him most of the way. Can't have been easy with one arm in a cast."

Zach absorbed the news that Brittany had been visiting the dog. "How's he healing?"

"It's all looking good. Gabe is pleased with him. I had a couple of people in here wanting to adopt a dog, but so far no one that's right for Jaws. One couple seemed interested, but I said no."

Zach wondered what sort of couple would be interested in an ugly dog with an uncertain history. In his experience that wasn't a résumé that was likely to get you snapped up into a loving home. "I'm guessing you're not going to get that many offers. Would have been less work for you if you'd said yes to them."

"Not really, because if it doesn't work out, the dog is back here again in a few weeks and each time that happens his trust takes a bit more of a knocking until finally you've got a dog that won't trust anyone. That's not going to happen on my watch. When I meet someone I think is right, I'll go through the checking procedure and if they pass, I'll let them take him. Until then, he stays here with me."

Zach found her dedication touching. "Sounds like you should run a dating agency."

She shook her head and gave him a quick smile. "I'm

no good with humans. I don't understand them. Just animals."

He looked at her for a moment, this slender girl with a bright smile and dark hollows under her eyes. Everyone had a story, he thought. Everyone.

"It must be pretty quiet round here. Do you miss the city?"

"Never." The way she kept her eyes down made him think she'd had very specific reasons for leaving.

He frowned. "Sara—"

"Oh, look at that! He's seen you. He knows you're the one who saved him."

It was true that right at that moment Jaws spotted Zach and decided to declare his undying love by hurling himself across the pen.

Zach winced and crouched down. "Easy now. Don't do yourself more damage."

Jaws howled and looked at him adoringly.

"He loves you," Sara said delightedly. "He thinks you're the one. Just so we're clear, I'd let you adopt him if you wanted to."

Zach felt a flicker of alarm. "Then maybe you're not such a great judge of character after all. I'd be the wrong home for him. He's already had one bad owner. He doesn't need another."

"What makes you think you'd be a bad owner? I think you'd be the perfect owner." Sara studied him for a moment and then smiled. "But you can't adopt a pet unless you really want to, and you don't want to, so that's fine. If you change your mind, let me know. I'd approve you in a heartbeat. In the meantime if you want to come and walk him with Brittany, she usually comes around seven in the morning on her way to camp."

Zach wondered why she was telling him that. "If she's already walking him, then I don't need to."

"I thought you might enjoy doing it together, seeing as you both brought him in and you used to— I mean you seemed to be— But what do I know? Forget I said anything. I match animals with humans, not humans with humans. I don't know anything about relationships." Blushing, Sara blew a kiss to Jaws and walked back towards the clinic leaving Zach to wonder how many of the islanders were speculating about his relationship with Brittany.

Before going back to his cabin, he stopped at Harbor Stores to pick up some milk. As an afterthought he scooped up some beer.

Dawn Parker was manning the checkout and she assessed his purchases with tight-lipped disapproval. "Guess you're lining your stomach with one before drinking the other."

Zach could have told her that the milk was for his coffee and he kept the beer in case Philip stopped by, but he figured that what he did with his purchases after he bought them was his business so he handed over the money and kept silent.

"You should know that my Mel is seeing that nice Carter Ashford, so if you've got any ideas in that direction, you can forget them. He's got a college degree and he's sensible."

It crossed Zach's mind that if Carter Ashford was dating Mel he couldn't be that sensible, but he filed that thought along with all the others he had no intention of expressing.

He was about to bag up the milk and attempt to navigate his way through the fog of disapproval when he heard someone calling his name. He turned, and saw little Grace Green running towards him across the store, followed by a powerfully built man who was obviously her father.

"That's him, Daddy. That's *him*."

Anticipating trouble, Dawn Parker stiffened. "If you have a problem you should take it outside. I don't want any—oh—" She blinked as Grace threw her arms around Zach and squeezed tightly.

"Zach—I mean, Mr. Flynn—this is my dad. I've been telling him all about you. How you saved me and how you told that poor dog he wasn't to bite me."

Dawn, who had clearly been on the verge of dialing the emergency services, watched with her eyes popping out of her head. "Well, I don't—"

Ignoring her, Zach hunkered down in front of the child. "That dog? Sara is caring for him in the Animal Rescue Center. I saw him just now. His favorite toy is a squeaky bone. Once we cut that nasty wire off his neck and gave him some attention, he was just fine." It was important to him that she knew the dog wasn't vicious. That his behavior had been the result of fear. "You should drop in and see him, Grace. He'd be pleased to see you." He gave her a smile, then rose to his feet and found his hand grasped tightly by Grace's father.

"I'm Michael Green. Gracie told me what happened. Can't thank you enough for looking out for her."

Zach discovered that attention of any sort, even positive, made him uncomfortable. "She wasn't in any risk."

"That's not what Caleb told me. He said you put yourself right between my girl and that dog and that you almost lost your hand doing it."

"The dog had been badly treated. He was scared, not vicious. And Grace was brave and stood her ground."

Grace's shoulders straightened. "I stood right where you told me to stand and didn't move a muscle."

"That's right, you did." Zach gathered up his purchases. "It's good to see you, Grace. Sir." He nodded to Grace's father and made for the door, wondering what Dawn Parker would make of that exchange.

She was the type who put people into compartments, as if she were stocking the shelves of her store. He could imagine her roaming the aisles, searching for a suitable place to shelve him. No doubt her preference until now would have been to tuck him in a dark corner along with gasoline or fireworks, probably under a big label saying "handle with care."

Now she was confused.

He smiled. No doubt she'd still find a reason to shelve him along with the dangerous goods.

Noticing the blackening sky, Zach drove back to camp and went in search of Philip.

He was in his office, but so was Brittany, seated on his desk among the half-empty mugs and the untidy piles of paper.

She was wearing a simple T-shirt and a pair of denim cutoffs that showed off her athletic shape.

Drowning in desire, Zach found it impossible not to look at her.

All he wanted to do was throw her over his shoulder, take her deep into the forest and have sex with her until she could no longer walk straight, but that wasn't what worried him most. What almost had him running for the door was the realization that she was virtually the only person whose company he preferred to his own.

She threw him one of her blinding smiles. Philip said something by way of a greeting, but Zach couldn't hear through the roaring in his ears.

He thought his reaction should have been obvious but apparently it wasn't because they carried on their conversation, which left him with nothing to do but simmer in the heat he'd created himself.

Restless, frustrated, he strolled to the window of Philip's office and tried distracting himself with the view, but it was impossible to concentrate on anything when Brittany was in the room so he gave up and let himself look.

She was one of those people who wore every emotion on her face. When she was angry or frustrated, her eyes flashed. When she was amused she laughed, and it was such an infectious laugh that it usually had everyone around her laughing, too. Today, she seemed irritated as she sat on the edge of his desk, her legs swinging. "I spoke to three different people in the department and so far I can't find anyone interested in running an archaeological activity."

Philip pushed his glasses up his nose. "I'm grateful to you for trying."

"I'm going to keep trying. It's a great idea. It was fun and the children loved it. I can't imagine why the department wouldn't want to take that on. They could get some of the undergraduates involved."

She never gave up, Zach thought. Whatever she did, she attacked it with the full force of her personality.

He was acknowledging just how much trouble he was in, when she glanced towards him.

"Am I in your way? Did you want something?"

Yes, he wanted her. He wanted her so badly it was

driving him crazy and he knew he had to get out of there before he did something that couldn't be undone.

"It can wait." Sexual frustration made his tone harder than he'd intended and he saw her eyebrows lift.

"Hey, if there's a problem, Flynn, just say so. Don't give me passive-aggressive."

Passive? There was nothing passive about his feelings.

He strolled towards the door, his fingers digging into his palms. She had no idea, *no idea*, what it was costing him to keep his distance. "I said it can wait."

"By the way, Zach—" Philip's voice cut through the swirling clouds of lust in his brain "—I forwarded you an email from Todd earlier. Take a look. You'll be pleased."

"Good to know." He couldn't think about anything while Brittany was in the room.

"Zach!" Her voice rang with frustration. "Why are you leaving? There's no need—"

He met her gaze, and saw her puzzled look melt under the fiery heat of sexual chemistry. The brief exchange was so intimate, so deeply personal, he was surprised Philip didn't cover his eyes.

Her eyes widened as she registered the reason for his tension.

In under a second she went from confident to deliciously confused.

"Right." Her voice was a raw croak. "Well, okay. If you're sure. Although I was pretty much done here anyway. Philip and I were just thinking through some options, that's all."

He was thinking through options, too.

Option one, tell Philip he was needed in the camp, lock the door and take Brittany right here on the desk without bothering to strip off her clothes.

Option two, take Brittany back to his cabin, strip her naked and have sex in every position known to man and a few known only to him.

Option three—

"Zach?"

Disturbed from a vision that was close to porno-graphic, he stirred. "What?"

Her cheeks were a hot pink. "What did you want?"

"Nothing." *Everything.*

But one thing held him back.

He was the kind of trouble no woman needed in her life a second time, especially Brittany.

Chapter 14

Go straight home. Straight home. Call Pete, take a cab. Do it now.

You are not going to follow Zach to his cabin. That would be stupid.

There was going to be a storm. The sensible thing would be to get home before it hit.

Brittany stood with her phone in her hand and her finger hovering over the call button.

Then she frowned.

They were both adults and both unattached. And they both wanted the same thing.

She'd seen the look in his eyes. If Philip hadn't been in the room, that would have been it. It was a wonder they hadn't set fire to all the stacks of paper on Philip's desk.

Heart pounding, she dropped her phone into her bag.

Dusk was falling over the forest. Already it was cooler

in the evenings, as if fall was trying to nudge summer to one side and take center stage.

She walked across the clearing, exchanged a few words with a couple of the camp staff who were restocking the cabins to be ready for the training week, and took the path that led past the beach and along the bay towards Zach's cabin.

The sky was stormy, with black clouds threatening rain.

Nerves fluttered like butterflies in the pit of her stomach and she snatched in a breath.

She was an adult and she was making an adult decision. There was no reason to be nervous.

All the same, she hesitated before walking up to his door.

She knocked and waited, her heart in her mouth.

He'd tell her to go away.

He'd tell her it wasn't wise, or sensible, to get involved a second time.

And she'd tell him—

She frowned and knocked again, but it seemed she wasn't going to be able to tell him anything because there was no answer.

As she turned away she heard a soft splash and walked to the end of the deck.

He was the only person in the sea, cutting through the water with smooth, powerful strokes as he swam from one side of the bay to the other.

She watched him without noticing the passage of time, absorbed by masculine power and sheer athletic ability.

The sea had to be cold, but he kept up the relentless rhythm and she kept watching until finally he swam back towards the cabin and hauled himself onto the deck.

Water streamed off his broad shoulders and turned his hair sleek and inky dark. He cleared his face with his hand, reached for a towel and noticed her.

The way he stilled made her think of a sleek, dangerous jungle cat.

His gaze met hers. "Is something wrong?"

"Yes." She pushed her hands into the pockets of her cargoes, nerves dancing in her belly and mingling with sexual awareness. When he reached for his sweats she shook her head. "Don't bother getting dressed. I'm just going to undress you again so you might as well save me time."

His hand froze in midair. "Brittany—"

"I'm tired of pretending, Zach. I'm tired of feeling this way and not doing anything about it. And don't tell me you don't feel it, too, because I know you'd be lying. We almost had sex in front of Philip back there, and that's not good. There's a reason you're taking a long dip in the cold sea, and I doubt it's all down to an interest in physical fitness."

His movements slow and steady, he looped the towel around his neck. "As I said the other night, you're a smart girl. And you're thinking of making the same mistake twice?"

"Being with you wasn't a mistake." She spoke softly, her voice just audible over the soft rush of the sea as it hit the sand. "Marrying you might have been, but not the rest of it. And the marriage part was my fault. I pushed you."

"I could have said no."

"It doesn't matter. None of it matters. It's history. If we'd met for the first time a few weeks ago, we'd both have baggage, but it wouldn't be with each other. The past isn't relevant. That was then and this is now. I'm not eighteen anymore, Zach. I know what I want."

Somehow they'd moved towards each other, and now he was standing right in front of her. His height and the width of his shoulders almost blocked the glowing circle of the moon but there was still enough light for her to see the rigid tension in his jaw.

"I'll hurt you. I'll screw up and break your heart. It's what I do."

"That isn't going to happen. And I don't think it's *my* heart you're worried about. I think it's your own." She put her hand on his chest and felt the steady beat of his heart under her palm. A quick glance might have suggested his body was perfect, all smooth, taut lines and curving muscle. A closer look revealed imperfections, scars she knew were there, but that he'd always refused to talk about.

She'd told herself that his past was his business. That if he didn't want to talk, that was his decision. She'd told herself that everyone had a right to their secrets.

But what if he simply hadn't trusted her enough to talk?

Guilt settled over her and she had a flash of self-insight almost too uncomfortable to examine.

She should have kept asking.

She should have—

"What's wrong?" His voice was rough and he lifted his hand and cupped her cheek. "Changing your mind? Are you afraid? Because you should be."

Ten years ago she would have assumed that comment was about her, but now she knew better. Now she knew it was about him.

"I'm not afraid, but I think you are. I think you're

afraid to let anyone close because that gives them the power to hurt you. But I'm not going to hurt you. I'd never hurt you."

Sounds of laughter floated towards them on the breeze and she realized there were people on the far side of the beach.

Zach closed his hand around her wrist and for a moment she thought he was going to push her away.

For a breath-stealing moment they stood there, locked together.

Then he led her into the cabin and kicked the door shut behind them.

Zach had spent every moment of the past few days trying not to think about her. When he did, he spent the time listing a hundred reasons why this was a bad idea.

In the end he'd resorted to hard physical exercise in an attempt to relieve the simmering sexual tension that blocked any hope of rest or peace.

And now here she was, in his cabin, with a smile on her lips and promise in her eyes.

All he had to do was take what she was offering.

The selfish side of him, the side that allowed him to focus on his own needs to the exclusion of others, the side that had developed from a need to survive, just wanted to ease the ache in the most basic way known to man and to hell with the consequences. Any consequences would be hers, not his. If she wanted to play with fire, why not hand her the match?

But he couldn't.

And deep down he knew she was right. It wasn't about her, it was about him.

He *was* afraid. Not of being hurt, but of discovering that even with Brittany, he still couldn't feel.

That one brief occasion in her cottage had been easy enough to discount. It had been all about hot sex and nothing else. But this—this was different.

"Why are you here?" Forming the words felt difficult because life had taught him to greedily snatch the good moments wherever you could find them. And one of them was standing right in front of him. "You need to leave right now." Before the bad side of him overwhelmed the small part of him that was decent.

"I'm not leaving, Zach." Her voice was a smoky, soft invitation and he clenched his jaw and kept his hands by his sides.

"You don't want to do this."

Her eyes were clear and honest. "Why don't you let me worry about my feelings and you worry about yours?"

"I don't have feelings." His voice sounded strange. Thickened. "That's what I'm trying to tell you. I don't feel anything. I never do." He didn't understand why she didn't see the danger, the futility, of getting involved with him again.

"I know." Her hand came up to his face and she touched him gently, soothingly, which didn't make sense to him because he knew that if she had any sense she would be backing away.

The window was open and he could smell the scents of late summer and the salty air. He could hear the rhythmic rush of the sea and the call of the gulls.

He could hear the beating of his heart and feel the throb of blood in his veins.

"And knowing that, you still want this?"

She nodded. "I think you should stop worrying about

not feeling and just be with me. It's just us, Zach. We've done this before."

But before he'd only ever cared about pleasing himself and his partner.

He'd never wanted anything more.

Now, for the first time in his life, he resented the hollow emptiness inside him that had kept him safe for so long.

He wanted to fill it with her, he wanted to warm himself on her and thaw out the ice-cold center that had somehow become part of who he was.

He wanted to feel.

But because he knew he couldn't, the pressure grew. "You should take better care of yourself. You need to leave."

"If you want me to leave, I'll leave, but first I'm going to ask you the same question I asked you the other night in the forest. The one you didn't answer. If we'd met for the first time a few weeks ago, what would we be doing now?"

That was easy. "We'd be having sex without coming up for air and—" He sucked in a breath as she pulled her top over her head and slid her cargoes over her hips. All woman, she stepped out of them and stood in front of him in nothing more than silk and lace.

He couldn't see or hear past the roaring of lust in his head. "What the hell are you doing? You said you were going to leave."

"I said I'd leave if that was what you wanted. It isn't." She pushed her clothes away with the toe of her bare foot and his mouth dried.

"I told you—"

"You told me that sex is nothing more than a physical

workout for you. You can't feel. I know. I heard you. So let's share a physical workout. Exercise is good for you, it's a medically proven fact and I'd rather have a naked marathon with you than pump iron in the gym. And, Zach, you're going to feel *something*—" She gave him a smile that made it impossible for him to think.

Up until the point where he'd met Brittany, his life had been about taking care of himself when no one else would, keeping himself safe and alive. Other people's feelings had come low on his agenda, mostly because he'd grown up knowing that he was the only person looking out for himself. His connection with women had been on one level only, a physical one. The only time he'd broken that rule had been Brittany and even though he knew she hadn't really loved him, he knew he'd hurt her and he'd regretted it.

But she gave him no opportunity for more argument because she stepped forward and he felt the silken brush of her skin against his and breathed in the scent of her hair.

He was still fighting the crashing waves of lust when he felt her fingers on the waistband of his damp board shorts.

"You can't—"

"I can, and you should stop talking now." Her voice husky, she dragged the shorts down and slid to her knees.

"Brittany—" Her name jammed in his throat and his vision blurred as she took him in her mouth.

When they'd been together the first time, he'd been the one to lead the way on everything. He'd nudged her out of her comfort zone, although *nudge* was perhaps too gentle a word for what he'd done. The moment she'd turned eighteen, he'd considered it his duty to teach her

everything she didn't already know, which had turned out
to be a lot. She'd been gutsy and independent, but sexually inexperienced. He'd given her an intensive course
and plenty of practice, making no concessions to shyness
and embarrassment.

Apparently she'd left shyness behind.

He felt the warm heat of her soft mouth slide over him
and his mind shut down. He knew that if she carried on
it would be over in five minutes and nothing that felt this
good should be over that fast.

Finding willpower he didn't know he had, he eased
away from her, hauled her to her feet and powered her
back to the bed, catching her as she lost her balance.

Careful to protect her wrist, he lowered her to the bed.

"I want to feel something." His tone was raw. "I want
to—"

"I know—" she drew his head down to hers "—I know
you do. And it will happen. We just have to be patient.
And in the meantime if you could do that thing you do,
that would be great because you're killing me here."

He breathed her name against her mouth, feeling her
soft lips part under the pressure of his. He kissed her
slowly, skillfully, taking his time. Then he eased away,
stripped off the last of her clothes and slid his hands
over warm skin and secret places until she was moan-
ing under him.

"You don't have to take it slowly." Her voice was
desperate and she slid her leg over his hips and arched
against him. "I need you—I need you to—"

"Not yet." He wanted to take it slowly. Maybe if he
took his time, if he savored every moment—and he did
that, exploring every part of her, starting with the curve
of her neck, then her shoulder and lower to the peak of

her breasts. When she writhed and shifted, he flattened her to the bed, trapping her with his weight.

He felt her push against his shoulder with her good hand but he kept her pinned beneath him as he explored her with his mouth. He felt her nipple harden under the slow stroke of his tongue and heard her breathing grow shallow. The taste of her skin was like a drug, and he tasted and licked, his hunger for her building. It burned through him, ravenous, insatiable, and he knew she felt the same way because she squirmed under him, the supple lift of her body an explicit invitation.

Through the clouds of dizzying pleasure he could hear her saying his name, over and over again, until the soft pleas became sobs and the movement of her hips against him became almost frantic.

Still he held her down, ignoring his almost all-consuming need for her, willing himself to feel something other than blazing sexual heat.

Her body had changed, her breasts deliciously rounded and her thighs lean and strong from long hours spent outdoors. He explored those changes with his mouth and the tips of his fingers, touching her skin, breathing in the scent of her, tracing every soft feminine inch with his tongue.

When he finally stroked his hand between her legs, she moaned, and when his fingers slid skillfully into that vulnerable part of her, she parted her legs.

He slid his mouth over her hip and lower to the inside of her thigh, then traced her with his tongue. This, he knew how to do. He knew exactly how to touch her and with each gentle glide and flick he drove her closer and closer to the edge. He could feel every ripple and tremor of her flesh and he responded until she was writhing under him. He felt her hand on his shoulder and knew what she wanted but he wasn't ready to give it to her. Wasn't ready to give up hope that being with her could break that lock inside him.

Through the heat of his own desire he heard her saying his name over and over again, telling him how much she wanted him, how she couldn't wait any longer, how he was killing her, but still he drew out the torture.

Finally, when he decided it wasn't fair on her, he eased himself up from her body and reached for the condom he was never without.

She shifted under him, her fingers biting into the muscle of his back and he slid his hand under her, reining in the urge to thrust deep. Instead he lowered his forehead to hers, held her gaze and entered her slowly. He felt her nails dig hard into him and saw her lips part in a soft gasp as he joined them intimately. It cost him, but he kept his movements slow and gentle, easing into her by degrees as he felt the warm, feminine yielding of her body.

When he was buried deep he lowered his mouth to hers and spread slow, lingering kisses across her mouth and then her jaw as he gave her time to grow accustomed to him.

Her hand slid into his hair, and she brushed her mouth against his. "You're safe," she whispered, "you're safe. You can let go, Zach. You can trust me."

He moved with long, slow, breath-stealing strokes, building the rhythm and shifting position so that every controlled surge created a perfect, delicious friction, watching as a soft flush highlighted her cheeks and her eyes glowed with heat.

"Zach, Zach—" She whispered his name, slid her arm around his neck and dragged his head down to hers, licking into his mouth as he drove into her with erotic precision. Her gaze stayed locked on his, open, trusting, sharing everything.

The pleasure built and multiplied until it was no longer in his power to hold back physically. Zach took her mouth and sent them both flying into a perfect storm of sexual excitement. He felt her come, felt her body rippling around his and dragging him to the same place.

Physically, it was about the most perfect sexual experience of his life.

He curled her into his arms, holding her against him, listening to the sound of the ocean mingling with the pounding of rain through the open window and thinking that if this was all it could ever be, then maybe it would be enough.

She snuggled closer. "I love this cabin. It's so cozy. You don't get lonely, out here away from everything?"

"I love it."

She slid her arm around him so that each part of her was touching a part of him. "The other night when we were in the woods, talking about Travis, you said that it might be possible for some people to change. To learn to trust. You're not one of those people, are you?" When her question was met with silence, she took a deep breath. "You never trusted me, did you? And because my default is to trust people up until the point where they let me down, it never occurred to me that you wouldn't. We were coming at our relationship from completely different places and I didn't understand that."

There was another long silence, broken only by the sound of the ocean through the open window.

"I was closer to you than I'd ever been to anyone."

"You never talked to me. And you didn't sleep. At

night you just lay there, awake. Then when it was light you'd fall asleep for a few hours."

"I'd taught myself to stay awake. To me, monsters weren't nameless, faceless creatures that lurked under the bed. They had a face and a name and they lived in my house." It was something he'd never talked about, but he told himself that if he couldn't open up in other ways, then at least he could give her this. "Night was the most dangerous time. I moved furniture and blocked the door, but I still had to be vigilant. And when he was drunk he was twice as strong as when he was sober."

It was something he had never revealed.

All social workers had got from him had been silence.

Even Philip didn't know all the details.

Saying it aloud felt strange, like stripping off your clothes and standing naked in front of a room of strangers.

Part of him wanted to snatch the words back, but it was too late.

Brittany propped herself up on her elbow.

"Your father?"

His mouth was dry. "My stepfather."

"What about your mom?"

He thought about his mother, vicious, mean and utterly unsuited to be left in charge of anything, let alone another human being. "She stayed out of the way."

"She didn't try and protect you?"

"And put herself in the line of fire?" Why the hell had he started this conversation? Zach sat up in the bed, remembering now why he kept that part of his past carefully locked away. It leaked, ugly and thick as tar, contaminating all that was good about his life. "Why would she do that?"

"Because that's what parents are supposed to do." Brittany sat up, too, sitting shoulder to shoulder with him. "They're supposed to protect you."

"Protect?" He ran his hand over his face, finding the word almost laughable in the context of a conversation about his mother. "Whatever parenting manual you got that from, I can tell you my mother hadn't read it." Running from his thoughts and the conversation, he sprang from the bed and snatched up his jeans, pulling them on roughly. What had possessed him to talk about this?

He should have kept silent.

He should have— "I need to get out of here. I'm sorry, but I need to walk."

"It's raining."

"I don't care. I need some air."

"Then I'll come with you." She was out of the bed, too, pulling on her clothes. "Wait for me. We'll go together."

"You don't understand, I don't want to talk about this anymore." It was the growl of a wounded animal and Brittany stilled but didn't back off.

"Then we won't talk." Her voice was kind and calm. "I'll just walk with you."

"Why? What's the point?" He felt her hand on his arm. Gentle.

"Because a friend doesn't leave a friend alone when they're hurting. And you're hurting."

"Brittany—"

She slid her arms around him and hugged him tightly, then let him go before he could push her away. "Let's go. I love the rain."

"You don't have a coat."

She shrugged. "My skin is waterproof."

His pulse rate was slower, his breathing more steady. The panic receded like the tide.

"I'm sorry." He ran his hand over his face. "Shit, I'm sorry."

"You don't ever have to apologize."

"After what I did to you?" He gave a bitter laugh. "I could apologize for a month and it still wouldn't wipe out what I did."

She shook her head. "I'm the one who should be apologizing. For being naive, blind, selfish—I should have tried to get you to talk to me back then."

"I wouldn't have done it. I never have." Realizing that his legs were shaking, he sat back down on the edge of the bed, embarrassed by the weakness. "What's your earliest memory?"

She hesitated and then sat down next to him. "I was four. I was on the beach with my grandmother, digging in the sand. I remember crying because it started to rain and we had to run back to the cottage. I didn't want to leave. I wanted to stay and dig."

There was a pounding in his head. "My stepfather moved in when I was three. That's my earliest memory. I don't remember a single day of my childhood when I wasn't scared."

There was a moment of silence and then he felt her press against him, as if she wanted to wrap his body with hers like a soothing bandage around a wound.

"Zach—"

"I couldn't stop it happening, so I tried to detach myself from it. I switched my mind off, pretended it was happening to someone else. Then one night he overdid it. I was so tired I'd fallen asleep and he got into the room."

He wondered why his voice sounded so flat. "I was in the hospital for ten days and I never went home."

"How old were you?"

"Eight."

"They took you into care?"

"I went to a foster family for a while, but that didn't work out."

"Why not?"

"Because there are limits to what folks are prepared to deal with, and I was way beyond those limits. After that I was in and out of foster homes and residential care."

She was silent. "I should never have pushed you to get married. I should have known, guessed, that after everything that had happened to you, you couldn't trust. I should have known it wouldn't work for you."

"I wanted it to work. Marrying you was my one attempt at having a normal life. At being like other people. As if by marrying you I'd merge my background with yours and somehow wipe out who I was and where I came from. I thought you might be the cure."

"If I'd known you felt that way, if I'd understood, I would have realized that we needed more time so that you could learn to trust me."

"That wouldn't have happened."

"Because sometimes not trusting keeps you safe. Is that it? That's what you said about Travis." There was a long silence and then she moved closer. She curled into him, resting her head on his shoulder and curving her arm around him. "I'm sorry." Her voice was choked. "I'm so sorry."

"For what? None of it was your fault."

"Yes, it was. I'm sorry for not looking deeper. For not encouraging you to talk about your past, even a little bit.

I was so sure of us, so confident that we could withstand anything. I told myself that I was protecting your privacy. I was naive and ignorant."

"My past wasn't your problem."

"How can you say that? From the moment we met, it became both of our problems. The present is built on the past and we can never really understand it until we dig down, layer by layer. Instead of ignoring it, I should have talked to you."

"You're beating yourself up over nothing. I wouldn't have talked to you."

"Because you didn't trust me, but maybe if we'd talked properly you would have understood that you *could* trust me. Was that what went wrong with us? Were you keeping yourself safe, Zach? Did you think you needed to protect yourself from me? If we'd talked, would we still be together?" Her voice was clogged with tears and he felt the tension rush through him.

"Don't cry. I hate it when you cry. And none of this was your fault. I blew it."

"That's not true. I was blind. I wasn't a good friend to you."

"We were lovers."

"But we were friends, too. I should have come after you. Even if we couldn't work our marriage out, I should have been there for you. I should have tried harder."

He stroked his hand over her hair, feeling softness and silk. "This wasn't an exam, honey. It wasn't something you could study for and get top grades in. Nothing you did would have changed anything."

"Do you really want to walk in the rain or can we go back to bed?" She lifted her head to his and kissed his mouth gently and he tasted the salt of tears on her lips.

He could feel the warmth of her. Her hair slid over his arm, tickling his skin. "Nothing is going to change, Brit. I'm not going to change. If you're a smart woman, you'll walk out of here and not come back."

"That just shows you don't know as much about women as you think you do, because no smart woman would turn her back on sex this good."

Despite everything, she made him smile.

"If Kathleen had known the things we did in that cottage when she was out at her knitting group—"

"I'm sure she knew. We talked about everything." She gave him a mischievous smile. "Okay, maybe not *everything*, but most things. She warned me about you."

"Of course she did." He wondered why hearing that bothered him so much. "She was a good woman and she was protecting you. She was right to tell you to stay away. You should have listened."

"She didn't tell me to stay away. She would never have done that. But she did tell me that she didn't think someone like you would be able to open up." She paused. "She was worried you wouldn't be capable of intimacy. At the time we were finding ways to get naked on every available occasion so naturally I thought I had sufficient evidence to disprove her theory. I didn't realize she was talking about emotional intimacy."

"So knowing all that, you're still sitting here? How do you explain that, Dr. Forrest?"

"I know a good thing when I see one." She stood up, stripped off her clothes again and climbed onto his lap. Her hair slid forward, forming a dark frame around her wicked golden eyes. "We might be crap at marriage, Flynn, but we're good at this."

"This" was her pushing him back on the bed, guiding him into her and taking him deep in a series of slow, lascivious movements of her hips.

His body was devoured by smooth heat and the breath hissed through his teeth. She gave him a knowing smile as she moved slowly, running her hands over his chest and lower.

"You have an incredible body. Have I told you that?"

Some distant part of him knew he should be delivering another warning, but he'd lost the power of speech. His head spun as all the blood in his body rushed south to enjoy the party. The tight grip of her body created a delicious friction that blew his mind. He was drowning in sensation, and he tried to move, but she laughed and kept him still, the way he had her.

"You're not allowed to move until I say so. If you can torture me, then I can torture you right back."

And she did.

Her hips moved in slow, sinuous movements and the full curve of her breasts filled his vision.

He was so aroused he couldn't form a coherent sentence.

Usually, with sex, he was the one giving the master class but tonight he'd met his match.

And right through the whole intense, erotic experience she watched him, as he had watched her. And because he was watching he saw the moment her expression changed, saw her eyes darken and her tongue moisten her lips. Then she lowered her head to his and kissed him, the movement shifting the angle yet again.

Excitement screamed through him and he tried to hold back, tried to find the control he usually accessed with casual ease but this time she had all the control. He slid his hands down the smooth skin of her back and cupped her bottom, trying to still her writhing hips, but she moved in a relentless rhythm that wound the excitement tighter and tighter until they both shattered.

He felt her tighten around him like a silken fist and he emptied himself into her, his hand locked on the back of her head, his mouth consuming hers as they kissed like demons.

Eventually she eased away from him, a satisfied smile on her face as she delivered a final lingering kiss.

She said nothing.

Asked for nothing.

Zach wanted to warn her again that he was going to hurt her, but clouds of exhaustion rolled in, and when she curled into him like a sleepy kitten, he didn't have the energy to push her away.

Instead he closed his eyes and did what he rarely did.

He slept.

Chapter 15

Brittany opened her eyes as the first fingers of dawn stretched through the screened window and was instantly wide-awake.

Her head and her heart felt heavy with the revelations of the night before. She knew that later she'd go back over what Zach had said and dissect it, word by word, but right now she had a decision to make.

Go or stay?

She knew they'd taken a huge step. She didn't want him to feel suffocated or trapped, or as if he had to run from her. Whole nights were for serious relationships and this wasn't—theirs wasn't—

Shit.

She should definitely go.

She slid out of bed, stumbled over his shoes that had been abandoned halfway across the floor and froze. A quick glance towards the bed told her Zach was still sleeping and she tiptoed across the room with exaggerated care, like a character from a cartoon. Her clothing had been strewn around the place during her striptease and she gathered it up and dressed quickly.

Carrying her running shoes in her hand, she sneaked out of the door and closed it quietly behind her, but not before taking a last look at Zach. He was still sleeping, sprawled on his front with his eyes closed.

Her insides softened and she felt a rush of emotion. He was sleeping. Really sleeping.

And that was good, wasn't it?

That was progress.

As she walked away from the cabin, salty sea air brushed over her face, chasing away sleep. The air smelled fresh after the rain and the ground was damp under her feet.

She was grateful that Seagull's Nest was out of sight of the camp and nowhere near the buzz of the harbor. If she'd had to do the walk of shame along Main Street at this time of the morning, she would never have heard the last of it.

To reach Castaway Cottage from the camp, she had to choose between a long hike through the forest or a blowy walk around the cliffs.

She chose the cliffs.

The sea breeze tangled her hair and shimmered over her skin, blowing away the last cobwebs of sleep.

It was cool, and she zipped her sweater on the second attempt and kicked up the pace.

Her body felt deliciously used, but it wasn't the sex that kept her mind occupied as she walked, it was the other things.

He'd talked to her.

Under the comforting blanket of darkness, he'd finally talked to her. And he'd said more to her in those few hours than he had in the months they'd spent together when she was eighteen.

Remembering those revelations brought a stinging to her eyes and a pressure to her throat.

It had been a tiny glimpse, that was all, but enough to make her realize just how blind and selfish she'd been back then.

With the naivety of youth she'd thought the past was something that could be shrugged off or left behind, like a piece of clothing that no longer fit. She hadn't had the maturity to understand how deeply Zach's past had affected him or to understand how it would impact on his relationships.

She'd thought she'd known him, but she hadn't known the most important thing of all.

At the time she'd been so damn proud of accepting him as he was. Except that she hadn't, had she? She hadn't truly known who he was. She'd allowed him his secrets, hadn't tried to access those dark depths he guarded so carefully.

The ache in her throat grew worse.

How could she have been so selfish and unthinking?

She'd wanted him, and she'd allowed the dizzy excitement of being with him to cloud her brain and obliterate her common sense.

She'd treated him like a goal, something that could be obtained if she worked hard enough, like an A grade in English. And when her marriage had failed, she'd limped away, blaming him, whereas in actual fact, the blame lay firmly in her lap.

Now, finally, she understood why he found it hard to sleep.

He'd had to stay awake to protect himself.

She imagined Zach, little and terrified, moving furniture against the door, afraid to drift into a deep, defenseless sleep. The thought made her nauseous.

When she was growing up, she'd watched her parents argue and ultimately divorce. She'd lived with her grandmother and seen her father on his occasional flying visits to the island. She'd considered herself sophisticated and mature, knowledgeable about the world. It unnerved her to realize how deluded she'd been.

She'd known nothing.

Certainly she knew nothing about how it must have felt to be afraid for your own safety. She'd never been afraid to fall asleep. Never felt the need to stay awake to protect herself.

Zach had told her he'd been removed from his home at the age of eight.

She remembered being eight. On her eighth birthday her grandmother had arranged a picnic on Shell Bay and most of the island had turned up. Everyone had brought food and they'd spent the day playing ball games and scrambling over the rocks.

It had been innocent fun, another happy childhood memory to add to the others, like creating a photo album in her brain. Zach had his own album, his own set of memories, and it made for ugly viewing.

She rubbed at her chest, trying to relieve the ache.

In her job, it took patience and long, painstaking hours to remove the layers and find the secrets of the past buried deep. And the secrets meant little when viewed in isolation, which was why archaeologists constantly clashed with treasure hunters who often removed a find from a site before it could be properly catalogued.

Context.

It was a word she'd used on an almost daily basis over the past few years. Context was essential to building a picture, for establishing a relationship between things. For finding and making connections. Discovering more about a person wasn't so different. You uncovered the past. You made connections and looked for context.

After that short, telling conversation during the night, she felt as if she'd been given a brief glimpse at the album in Zach's head. She'd seen dark shapes and shadows but very little detail.

Feeling tired and low, she clambered to the top of the bluff and sat down on the rocks. It was early, but already there were yachts cutting through the waves and she recognized the familiar lines of the *Alice Rose*, the schooner that had once belonged to Ryan's father and was now run as part of his business at the Ocean Club.

She was admiring the elegant lines of the boat and stewing in her own guilt, when she caught movement out of the corner of her eye and saw Alec running up the path towards her. His T-shirt was damp and glued to his skin, his dark hair ruffled by the wind.

Pirate, she thought and managed a smile. "Good morning, Shipwreck Hunter. You're up early."

"I was going to say the same thing to you." He came to a halt in front of her and she shrugged.

"I'm an early riser. What's your excuse? Running away from your fans? Emily told me a carload of women arrived last week with the express intention of tracking you down."

He took a slug of bottled water, a gleam in his eyes. "Should I move?"

"No. You know the islanders. John told them he'd heard a rumor you'd moved somewhere else. How do the women know where you live?"

"Some damn journalist decided it was romantic that I live on what he described as a 'deserted island' and chose to publicize the fact. I suppose I should be grateful he left off my zip code."

"Deserted?" Brittany lifted her eyebrows. "Makes you sound like Robinson Crusoe. Clearly he's never visited the island in the summer."

"And let's hope none of them do. I need to buy John a drink next time I bump into him. Are you all right?" He lowered his water, his eyes on her face. "You look pale. Wrist bothering you?"

"No. It's—" She felt an overwhelming need to talk to someone but she couldn't do it without revealing Zach's secrets and she wasn't prepared to do that. "It's nothing."

Alec sat down next to her. "Tell me." His voice was kind and her eyes filled.

"Don't give me sympathy."

"I promise not to give you sympathy. Now tell me what's wrong."

"Have you ever totally messed something up because you thought you knew everything and then discovered you knew nothing?"

"Hasn't everyone?"

"Maybe." She shook her head, blinking rapidly, and felt his arm come around her shoulder.

"I'm not sure whether we're talking personal or professional," he said slowly, "but whichever it is, the theory is the same. We make the best judgments we can at the time, Brit. We take the information we have and we use it. That's all anyone can do."

"But what happens when you realize that you were missing the essential facts when you made your judgment? What happens when you realize you didn't know anything at all and everything you thought and believed was totally wrong?"

He stroked her arm with the tips of his fingers. "It happens. New information comes to light all the time, both in history and in science. You know that. The same thing happens in life. You use the new information. You keep moving forward. That's how we make progress."

Progress.

Keep moving forward.

But was there a future for her and Zach? Now that she knew a little about his past, she wanted to know more. She wanted him to share, not because she had a grisly interest in the grim details but because she understood that sharing required trust and more than anything she wanted him to trust her.

She wanted him to know that she was a friend as well as a lover. Someone who would never let him down. Someone who wouldn't walk away no matter what life threw in their path. Even if their relationship was never anything more than a mix of friendship and sex, she wanted him to know it was something he could rely on.

But she was terrified he was going to wake up and decide that telling her had been a mistake.

Terrified he'd withdraw from her.

Aware that Alec was still by her side, she managed a smile. "I don't want to hold you up. You need to nurture that fit body for your adoring fans."

He didn't budge.

Instead, he stared out to sea.

"Can you imagine navigating these waters without GPS and radar? No wonder so many ships hit the rocks. Those poor sailors wouldn't have had a clue what was hidden beneath the surface." He kept his arm around her. "You stayed at Zach's last night."

Tears blinded her and she gave a choked laugh. "Who needs GPS and radar when we have the Puffin Island spy network."

"I'm observant. I ran past your cottage and you weren't there. Which means you walked here from a different direction and that direction happens to come straight from Seagull's Nest."

Brittany wiped her eyes on her sleeve. "I thought you were a historian, not a detective."

"There's an overlap. I'm assuming Zach is the reason you're looking as if your pet has died." He offered her his water and she shook her head.

They'd known each other for years, since Alec had arrived on the island to write his first book on naval warfare. Introduced by Ryan, they'd discovered a surprising number of overlapping interests. Since then Alec's career had soared, thanks to his on-screen charisma and talent for presenting complex information in a way that fascinated the general population.

He'd slotted naturally into their friendship group, although in reality, between her travels and his, they spent very little time together.

"Basically I'm crap at relationships," Brittany muttered and he gave a short laugh.

"Then I'm going to be very short on good advice because I'm crap at relationships, too. There are some things man never seems to get better at, despite studying."

"And woman." She sniffed and leaned her head on his shoulder. "You studied it? Seriously?"

"I read a few books."

Of course he had. Studying was Alec's answer to everything. "But it didn't help? How are things for you?"

"If by 'things' you mean my ex-wife, I can tell you that things have never been better between us."

Knowing how scarred Alec was following an acrimonious divorce, Brittany was surprised. "You've reached an understanding?"

"We have." He spoke in the smooth British accent that had American audiences swooning. "She doesn't contact me, and I don't contact her. It's the happiest we've ever been."

Brittany gave a choked laugh and shook her head in apology. "I'm sorry. I'm not really laughing."

"Laughter is healthy."

"Someone needs to invent a GPS that helps navigate relationships. They'd make a fortune. Do you ever think about your marriage?"

"I try not to."

"Well, for the record, I think your ex-wife is crazy." Brittany gave him an affectionate nudge with her shoulder. "Does she know there are a million women out there who dream about being married to you? You are the original Action Man."

"That was part of the problem. The outdoors was something she liked to admire from the other side of a double-glazed window. If it was something that was going to mess up her hair, she wasn't interested. I can only stay indoors for so long before I want to break out. I'm like a caged tiger. That's why the balance of writing the books along with the TV shows is perfect."

"Do you ever think about what went wrong?" She did. Since coming home, she thought about it constantly. She'd been so upset, it had stopped her from taking a long hard look at her own actions. It had been easier to blame Zach for everything.

"I know what went wrong. Our problem was that we didn't like each other. We had nothing in common outside the bedroom and sex is never enough to sustain a relationship." He glanced towards her and frowned when he saw the tears on her cheeks. "Never seen you cry before. Do you want me to call Emily? Ryan?"

She shook her head, touched by the offer. "I'll be fine, but thanks."

"I hate to be the one to break this to you, but you don't look fine, angel." His kindness was the final straw.

She stood up and pulled herself together. "I will be after a few strong cups of coffee. How about you? Are you going back to England anytime soon?"

"December." He stood up, too. "I have a meeting with my publisher and I'm giving a talk at the Maritime Museum in Greenwich."

"You'll be over there at the same time as Sky. You should give her a call. You could go to her exhibition. Have dinner or something."

Alec gave a faint smile. "I don't think so. I'm doing a twelve-step program to give up my addiction to having dinner with beautiful, high-maintenance women."

"Sky isn't high maintenance. Far from it." It frustrated her how many people took one glance at Sky's blond good looks and made that same judgment.

But what was the point in arguing with him? Sky was in an established relationship with Richard Everson and even if she weren't, Brittany wouldn't have put her optimistic, wildly creative friend with a hardened cynic like Alec Hunter.

She pushed her hair back from her face. "I should go. Thanks for listening."

"Anytime." He paused. "So do I take it you and Zach are involved again?"

"I wouldn't describe it as *involved*, exactly."

"Be careful. I wouldn't want to see you hurt. I don't want you to get in trouble." Unsmiling, he reached out and tucked a strand of hair behind her ear.

She felt the comforting warmth of his touch and thought for the millionth time in her life that without her friends her life would be a barren wasteland.

"I won't be hurt and I'm not in trouble. I'm not one of those women who think the only relationship worth having is one that could potentially end in wedding bells."

He laughed. "If that's true, then you might be my perfect woman."

"Alec, we would kill each other." She gave him a light punch on the arm and carried on walking. "See you around." She threw her parting words over her shoulder and made her way down the narrow path that wound its way down to Shell Bay.

There, nestled on the far side of the beach, was Castaway Cottage.

Despite everything, her heart lifted.

Was there a more perfect place to live on the whole planet?

She didn't think so, and judging from the number of calls she had from real estate agents, she wasn't the only one with that opinion.

She stared at her home for a moment, absorbing the truth.

For the first time in her life she didn't want to leave.

There was no urge to travel, no restless pull or wanderlust.

She wanted to stay.

She wanted to spend Thanksgiving with her friends and have Christmas here, too. Maybe Sky and Richard could be persuaded to join them for a few days.

Mulling over the possibilities, she walked the final distance and took the sandy path that led to the front door.

She let herself in, decided that coffee was her priority and walked through to the kitchen.

And there, fixing the lock on her back door, was Zach. He wore black jeans and a black shirt with the sleeves rolled back and he looked sexier than any man had a right to look.

Her mood lifted and her heart flew.

Shit, she thought. *I am* in *trouble.*

Serious trouble.

He should have stayed away.

When he'd woken and found her gone, he should have thanked his lucky stars she'd made that decision. Instead he'd felt a gut-wrenching disappointment and that unsettled him far more than finding her in his bed would have.

His brain had told him to stay away, and yet somehow he was here, standing in her kitchen, remembering the kindness in her eyes as he'd given her a glimpse into the toxic wasteland of his past.

He was trying to work out how to best make his excuses and leave, when she flashed him a smile.

"Maybe I should just give you a key? Then you could come and go as you please without breaking in."

"I don't need a damn key." His voice didn't sound like

his own. His tongue felt thick and his head was spinning. She'd pulled her hair into a simple ponytail but it was uneven and a little tangled and he knew he was to blame for that. "Everyone can gain access to this place just by giving the door a push. Hilda's right, it's time someone fixed that."

That was his excuse for being here.

It sounded pathetic, even to him, and presumably she thought so, too, because she raised an eyebrow.

"Who is 'everyone'? I'm pretty much on my own out here."

"Which is why you need a decent lock. The world isn't populated by fairy-tale characters." He knew. He'd witnessed firsthand the tarnished side of human nature. It was something he never wanted her to see. Except that she had, and he was the one who'd shown it to her. In a careless moment he'd given her a glimpse into a past he tried never to look at himself.

There was a metallic taste in his mouth and a sick feeling in his stomach.

He wanted to wind the clock back and unsay the words but it was too late for that.

All he could do was wait for her to mention it and then make it clear the subject was closed.

He braced himself, ready to block her attempts to dig deeper.

She didn't mention it.

Instead she walked across the kitchen and pulled open a door. "You don't need to worry about my ability to defend myself. I'm a black belt in karate and I won a couple of medals with this when I was in college." *This* turned out to be a sword, which she kept in a long bag in one of the cupboards. "I'm not as skilled with my left hand but I could still do damage to an intruder."

He'd expected pity. He'd expected sympathetic looks and an awkward conversation where she encouraged him to open up and he struggled to escape like a fish on a hook.

He hadn't expected her to be standing in the kitchen pointing a sword at his chest.

Some of the tension left him. "It's a sabre."

"You fence?"

"No. But I once flew a fencing team to a competition. We were delayed by fog and by the time we managed to take off I knew more than I ever needed to know about that particular sport." His heart rate slowed. "I thought your expertise was Bronze Age weapons."

"It is, but my interest is broader than that. Weapons interest me. The ability to cut was vital for early man. Paleolithic hunters needed to kill and dismember animals, and the distinction between blades for hunting and blades for weaponry was pretty blurred for a long time." She swept the sword through the air in an elegant movement and then returned it to the cupboard.

Zach watched. "Might be simpler just to get a decent lock on the door."

"Don't spoil my fun." She leaned against the cupboard and closed it. "I've been waiting half my life to confront an intruder with a sword. Think I'd give them a shock?"

"Maybe." The thought of her confronting an intruder, with a sword or otherwise, turned him cold. "I hope you won't ever need to find out."

"You don't have to worry about me, Zach. I can take care of myself." Her voice was soft and he knew she wasn't just talking about the physical threat of an intruder.

"The first stage of taking care of yourself is having basic security in place." Choosing to ignore the message she was sending, he returned to the job he'd been doing when she arrived. He'd stopped at the store and bought the best lock Puffin Island had to offer. The best had been pitiful, and he'd felt like making some suggestions to Ted Whittaker, who owned the only hardware store on the island, then decided he didn't need to draw attention to a past that was already part of island gossip.

A past Brittany now had access to.

The cold rush of panic was disturbed by a clatter as she lifted mugs from the cupboard.

"How much do I owe you for the lock?"

"Nothing." He wiped his brow with his palm. "Turns out Ted Whittaker is Grace Green's uncle."

"I know who Ted is, but— Oh!" She filled the kettle and gave a nod of understanding. "You're the hero of the hour and he gave you the lock without charge?"

"I'm guessing Grace has been exaggerating, but so far I'm getting more free stuff than I did when I stole it."

"I love that."

"Yeah, there's an irony there." And there was an irony in the fact that he was the one with the skills of breaking and entering, and yet Brittany had somehow found her way into the locked vault inside him. She'd sneaked in there, around the deadly barbs of protection that had kept him safe for years. He watched as she made fresh coffee and poured it into both mugs. The rich fragrance of roasted beans filled the kitchen. "That's the best thing I've smelled in a long time."

"It's not bad, but I miss Greek coffee. Thick, black and

guaranteed to keep you awake when you're working on a paper in the middle of the night."

Both of them knew he didn't need coffee to keep him awake.

He already spent most nights wide-awake.

Except for last night. Last night, he'd slept.

Not wanting to analyze the reason for that, he removed the screws from the old lock. "Who takes care of this place when you're away?"

"When I don't have a friend in crisis living here, Ryan watches out for it and Susan Miller tends the garden to stop it from getting out of control. Zach, you don't have to—" She winced as the lock fell into his hand. "All right, you've proved your point. I need a new lock. But if you replace it with a shiny, secure version how are you going to get in next time you hear me scream?"

"I'll push twice as hard as I did last time." He ran his finger over the wood of the frame, trying not to think about how he'd felt when he'd heard her scream. "This whole damn door needs replacing."

"Then I'll arrange it. I don't expect you to do it." There was a pause as she added cream and sugar to his coffee. "I didn't expect to see you here today. You didn't have to do this."

Yes, he did. And that was the scariest thing of all. For the first time in his life he had no idea how to stay away.

"Why didn't you wake me?"

"It was early. And I wasn't sure how you'd feel about waking up and finding me there. I know we talked about some stuff you haven't told anyone before. I just want to assure you that I'd never share it. Not with anyone."

He ignored that. "You should have woken me. I would have driven you home."

"It was good to see you sleeping." She sat down at the kitchen table in a graceful movement. "And it's a pretty day. Perfect for a walk. I met Alec on the cliff path."

That bothered him more than it should have. He knew from listening to Ryan's teasing that Alec had a large female fan base. "You two have plenty in common."

"We share some interests, that's true." She sipped her coffee. "He's a good friend. Nothing more."

"It's none of my business."

"No, but I thought I'd clarify before you break that new bolt you're putting in."

"Like I said, your love life is none of my business." He lifted his eyes from the lock and met her steady gaze.

"After last night I would have thought it was fair to say that you at least have a stake in it. I'm not going to push you, Zach. I don't want to make you uncomfortable, but if you ever feel like hooking up again, let me know."

"Hooking up?" He tightened the screws, checked the bolt and decided it should be enough to deter a casual housebreaker as long as they didn't know what they were doing. "Is that what we did?"

"I don't know what we did, Flynn. Do we have to put a name to it? Generally I'm not big on labeling things unless I've pulled them out of the ground." Looking tired, she pushed the mug towards him. "You should drink this before it gets cold."

As it dawned on him that she didn't intend to subject him to an interrogation, he slowly relaxed. Putting down his tools, he sat down opposite her. "Tell me the most exciting thing you've ever found."

"On a dig?" She propped her feet on one of the empty chairs. "It's nothing like the movies. Discovering King Tut's tomb is the exception rather than the rule, but you don't need to uncover a room of sparkly objects to get excited. Standing on a patch of ground, knowing that you're literally going to uncover the past—well, that sets my pulse racing. You find something, maybe just a fragment of pottery, and straightaway you're thinking about the people who used it and how they lived."

He watched the light dance across her eyes. Even sitting still she exuded energy and vitality, as if she believed everything and anything were possible if approached with enough enthusiasm and determination.

"So you're a detective."

"In a way, yes. And I love it. Archaeology is a perfect combination of history, science and mystery. How about you? What do you love about flying?"

"There's not much about flying I don't love."

But that wasn't enough for her, of course. "Is it the technical challenge of understanding the aircraft? The buzz you get from knowing you can fly?"

"Mostly it's the freedom." Zach picked up the mug and drank. It was the best thing he'd ever tasted. Smooth, strong, and with none of the bitter aftertaste that so often marred the flavor of coffee. "When you're in the air there are no walls or doors, just open space." And his need for that open space, for the freedom, was something that came from deep inside him.

"Would you take me up sometime?" She spoke softly. "Not because you're taking me to an appointment, but so that I can sit with you in the cockpit and see what you see?"

He never let anyone sit with him in the cockpit unless he was flying with a copilot, which was rare. And he'd never taken a woman on a pleasure trip, at least not the sort that involved strapping in and cruising at six thousand feet.

But her hand was on his and her eyes, bright and intelligent, were looking at him hopefully and somehow he felt himself nodding.

She smiled, and that smile knocked him off balance and fried his brain.

Sexual attraction he could deal with, it was the other feelings that shook him up like a wind gusting at thirty-five knots. Being with her was like being injected with adrenaline. Pushing women away was one of the few things in life that had come easily to him, but for some reason he'd lost that skill around Brittany.

Instead of pushing her away, he wanted to carry her up to the bedroom, strip her naked and keep her there until she'd told him every single thing she'd done in the years they'd been apart.

It was that last thought that drove him to his feet.

She'd open up. She'd trust.

And then he'd let her down.

"I should go." He gathered up his tools and made for the door, trying not to look at her sexy eyes and her wind-ruffled hair.

"Thanks for fixing the lock. I owe you."

He almost crashed into the table in his haste to leave the room.

It was only as he closed the door behind him that he realized she'd made no move to stop him leaving.

Chapter 16

"It's like trying to cage a lion," Brittany said to Skylar a few days later while they were chatting on the phone.

"You still haven't heard from him?"

"Not a word in three days."

"You could go over there in black underwear."

"No. I don't want to pressure him again. That's what I did last time. This time he has to make the next move."

"What if he doesn't?"

"I die of sexual frustration." Brittany sat in her favorite spot on the rocks above Shell Bay, watching the sea roll in. She'd gone for a run right after waking and was still dressed in sweats and her favorite sports top. "Are you going to visit this weekend?"

"I don't think I can. Richard needs me to be somewhere." Sky was evasive. "What are your plans?"

Brittany stared out to sea. "I thought I'd clear out some

of Grams's things. I haven't been up into the attic since she died. It's full of boxes I've never opened."

"You should wait until one of us is there and we can do it with you," Sky said immediately. "You shouldn't be on your own for that."

"I'll be all right. I've put it off too long already." She glanced back towards the cottage, all familiar lines and welcoming warmth as it nestled on the edge of the bay. "I don't feel ready to leave here."

"So don't leave."

"Staying was never part of my plans."

"Plans change, Brit."

"Do you remember what she used to say to us?"

"Kathleen? Yes. 'Change is part of life, girls.' Then she'd slap down some of her apple-topped ginger cake and I always wondered if the change she was talking about was gaining a hundred pounds in one meal."

Laughter eased the ache in her chest. "She wouldn't be impressed that I haven't even started to sort through her things. I've been a wimp."

"You've been busy. Traveling. Working. Living your life. She would have approved."

"I'm wondering what she would have said about Zach being back. Those first few weeks after he left, I remember her sitting on the edge of my bed trying to feed me chicken soup. She kept saying, 'He's a good man, Brittany, but he doesn't even know it himself.' I had no idea how she could think he was a good man when he'd walked out on me. She said that one day, when time had passed, I'd see it more clearly."

"And do you?"

"I think so, but it's taken me ten years. This is one of those occasions where I'd like to be able to rewind time."

She stood up, tucked the phone between her ear and her shoulder and used her good hand to help scramble down from the rocks. "I'd better go. I want to make a start."

"Are you sure I can't call Em? I don't like to think of you being sad and having no one to hug you."

"I'll be fine. Maybe I'll go up to the shelter to walk Jaws first. He needs the exercise and he likes the company."

"Zach is a bit like you," she told Jaws later as they ambled through the fields that led along the edge of the Warrens' farm. "He doesn't trust easily. I guess deep down he thinks that every human he meets is capable of putting a wire round his neck."

Jaws grunted and stopped to thrust his nose in the grass, apparently unsympathetic to the traumas of humans.

He'd put on a little weight and Sara was delighted with his progress.

"He's going to make a wonderful companion for someone," she told Brittany as she put him back in his kennel along with a bowl of food. "We just need to work out who that someone is. Right now we don't know what will happen to him next."

She and Jaws had something in common, Brittany thought. Neither of them knew what was going to happen next.

For the first time she was grateful for her damaged wrist because she didn't want to admit, even to herself, that Zach was the reason she didn't want to leave.

That would be stupid, wouldn't it?

No matter how much she sympathized with him, it

didn't change the fact that it would be stupid to make plans around a man who had already hurt her once.

Back in the cottage Brittany climbed the ladder to the attic and flicked on the light, a single bare bulb in the center of the room.

Deciding that one of the best cures for sexual frustration was hard physical labor, she hauled box after box into the center of the room. Realizing she couldn't get them downstairs with only one hand, she sat cross-legged in the dusty attic and sorted through her grandmother's life.

It was in the third box, buried under paintings of the seashore and a collage of pressed leaves and flowers that bore her grandmother's signature, that she found the diaries.

There were four of them, each one sturdy and thick, bound in dark red leather and smelling slightly of dust. Opening them, she saw pages and pages of her grandmother's even handwriting.

She found the first diary and started reading. By the end of the first page she realized two things. One, that Kathleen had been a fine writer, and two, that she was holding in her hands a chronicle of her grandmother's life on the island from the day she first arrived.

It was a love story, and one with plenty of bumps along the way.

Brittany's grandfather had been a lobsterman, born and raised on the island at a time when the population was less than three figures and the entire community was focused on fishing. He was one of generations of Mainers who relied on the sea for income.

Her grandmother, raised in Boston, had struggled to adapt to a place where most of the land was national park. She'd found the winters long and brutal, and wrote eloquently about the ways in which the community had helped each other.

Emotion shone through the words, bringing light and color to the descriptions of life on a rural island. There was fear, exhaustion, exhilaration and hope, but underpinning it all was love. It was clear her grandmother would have lived anywhere, learned to adapt to any lifestyle, as long as she was with her husband. It was also clear that none of it had been easy.

Brittany let the diary fall into her lap.

She'd always known her grandmother was a fighter, but she'd never known any of the detail. Her grandmother was the sort who either solved a problem or accepted it. She never complained.

But she hadn't allowed a single hurdle to derail her relationship.

Brittany thought back to those first horrible weeks after Zach had left, when she'd alternated between pounding cliff paths in an attempt to run off her misery and lying in the bed with the covers over her head.

She remembered her grandmother stroking her hair.

Sometimes the timing just isn't right, honey.

Tears scalded her throat and because she was on her own, she let them fall. What the hell was the matter with her? She never cried, and suddenly it was all she seemed to be doing.

She closed the book carefully so that she didn't damage the pages, scrubbed at her face with a dusty hand and then stilled as she heard someone at the door.

Emily.

Sky had obviously called her and Brittany felt a rush

of warmth because if she'd ever needed a hug from a friend, it was now.

Cradling the book under her arm, she scrambled down from the attic, guarding her arm.

Wondering why Emily hadn't just used her key, she opened the door and was confronted by Zach.

"Oh—"

His eyes raked her face and his expression darkened. "What the hell is wrong?"

Crap.

He was the last person she'd expected to see. She hadn't heard from him in three days, and here she was standing in her dusty sweats with windblown hair that hadn't seen a brush or a straightener all day. "Nothing."

"You don't cry about nothing. If something upsets you, you're more likely to shoot it in the butt than cry over it. So I'm asking you again—what's happened?" He used that same firm, patient tone he used when he spoke to nervous children and frightened animals. The tone that told her he wasn't going to give up until she answered him.

He's a good man, Brittany, but he doesn't even know it himself.

"Honestly, I'm fine."

His gaze shifted to the book under her arm. "What's that?"

"It's one of my grandmother's diaries. I found it when I was clearing out her things in the attic."

"You were doing that alone? Why didn't you call Emily or Skylar?"

"Because I was fine doing it on my own."

"Bullshit." Without waiting for her to respond, he nudged her gently back into the cottage and closed the door behind them. "You're not fine. You're feeling sad and lonely and you miss the hell out of your grandmother."

She didn't know whether it was his words or an overload of emotions but her vision blurred, she felt the salty sting of tears build in her eyes and the next thing she knew the diary was being gently tugged from under her arm and she was hauled against Zach's chest and hugged tightly.

Enclosed by the tensile strength of hard male muscle, it was impossible to keep the emotion in. She closed her eyes and let herself sob.

Through the storm of emotion she felt him holding her, felt the gentle stroke of his fingers on her hair and heard the rough tone of his voice as he told her everything was fine, that she should let it out.

And she did. She buried her face against his chest and cried, her tears soaking his shirt. She breathed in the warm male smell of him, felt the secure circle of his arms and wondered how a man who claimed to feel no emotion should be so attuned to the emotions of others.

"Sorry." The word was muffled against his shoulder. She knew she should pull away but she felt safe and warm.

"Why are you sorry? You loved her. You miss her. You don't have to apologize for that." He eased away slightly and dragged the backs of his fingers over her damp cheek. "She was a special woman. Kind and wise."

"Yes, she was." She sniffed. "She always liked you, did you know that?"

He gave a short laugh. "Then maybe she wasn't as wise as I thought." He smoothed her tangled hair back from her damp face with gentle hands. "You need coffee."

"I can't be bothered to make it."

"I'll make it." He urged her into the kitchen and pulled out a chair. Then he fetched a box of tissues from the shelf and placed them next to her. "Sit there and don't move."

She wondered what he was doing at her door.

She was about to ask him when her eyes strayed to the photo of her grandmother, taken on a windy day on the beach.

She'd thought she'd cried herself out, but her eyes filled again and she shook her head, embarrassed. "What the hell is wrong with me? I need a plumber."

"There's nothing wrong with you." Zach reached into the cupboard and pulled out two mugs. "You're grieving, that's all. It's natural."

"It's been three years."

"I don't think there's a time limit on these things and anyway, I bet you kept yourself so busy you barely had time to stop and breathe."

"Maybe." She blew her nose. "I was in Greece. I'd been home just the month before and she was fine. Then I had a call from Agnes Cooper in the middle of the night." Her eyes filled again. "I wasn't even here."

He put the mugs down and sat down next to her. "You were living your life. That's what she wanted." He took her hand between his and she looked down, noticing the contrast between her slim fingers and his rough, calloused palm.

"You don't think I'm going crazy?"

"What I think," he said slowly, rubbing her palm with his thumb, "is that you loved a person enough that losing them left a big hole in your life. That's going to hurt."

"It does. I miss her so damn much." She tugged her hand away from his, grabbed another tissue and blew her nose. "Sorry. Wow. This is attractive. Hysterical woman drenches you. Great way to start your day."

"I've known worse ways to start a day." He stood up and made the coffee. "You shouldn't have cleared the attic on your own."

"That's what Sky said."

"So why did you?"

She sniffed and wiped her eyes on her sleeve. "I guess I was being stubborn and pigheaded."

He smiled and poured the coffee into the mugs with the same smooth economy of movement he showed in everything he did. Then he placed one on the table in front of her. "Drink."

"Do you think I was wrong to read her diaries? I felt like an intruder. I keep thinking that if she'd wanted me to read them, she would have given them to me when she was alive."

"Or maybe she wrote them, put them in the attic and forgot about them. When was the last entry?"

"I don't know. I didn't look." She sipped the coffee gratefully. "I wish I'd asked her more about her past. It wasn't really something we talked about. I never realized how hard she found it when she first came here. It was my grandfather who wanted to make a life here and she loved him so much, she agreed. From what I've read so far, it seemed as if all that mattered to her to begin with was being with him. She thought the rest would figure itself out. And then she fell in love."

"She wasn't in love when she married him?"

"I meant, she fell in love with the island. This place." She warmed her hands on the mug and looked across the kitchen to the sun-filled garden. "They bought this place together."

Zach stared at her for a long moment and then stood up. "Go and fetch a sweater."

"Why? I'm not cold."

"Not here, but you might be where we're going."

"Where are we going?"

"I'm taking you flying."

"Flying?" Her head ached from crying and her heart felt like a lead weight in her chest. She hadn't heard from him in days and she still hadn't asked why he was here. "Why?"

"Because the weather is perfect and that's as good a reason to be up in the air as any I can think of. Because you asked me what I love about flying and the simplest way to explain that is to show you. Better than sitting here digging yourself deeper into misery."

Even though she knew it was dangerous to read anything into it, her spirits lifted. "Give me five minutes to wash off the dust."

Twenty minutes later they were at the airstrip.

"Do I sit up front with you?"

"As long as you promise not to touch anything."

Brittany's tears had dried and she couldn't resist teasing him. "I can't touch anything? Nothing?"

His gaze settled on her mouth. "Not unless you want me to crash."

She sat next to him and took the headset he handed her. "Can I talk to air traffic control? Blue Bird, this is Johnny Boy, come in please."

Zach reached for the controls, a smile tugging at the corner of his mouth. "For the record, this plane is not Johnny Boy. It's female."

"Why?"

"Because that's how I think of her."

"If you're about to say it's because she's temperamental and needs careful handling, think twice. I can do a lot of damage with this cast." She watched as he flicked a switch on the instrument panel. This was his territory. His area of expertise. "So this is an amphibious plane? You can land anywhere?"

"Anywhere from a grass runway in the Vineyard to a frozen lake in Alaska."

She blinked at the array of lights, dials and switches on the instrument panel. "It's pretty. And complicated."

"Not really. Everything has a purpose and it's an easy plane to fly. It helps having the engine instruments on the MFD."

"The MFD?"

"Multifunction display. Shows real-time flight-critical data, including traffic, digital attitude, heading, engine, airframe indication and CrewAlert. You've got three 10.4-inch LCDs, backup instruments, switches and the flight guidance panel." He showed her. "The layout is clean and logical."

It didn't look logical to her. It looked complex and perplexing, but although she didn't understand the mechanics of flight, she understood how it felt to have a passion for something.

"As long as one of us knows what it's all for. Seems like a lot of dials and switches for a small plane."

"Small plane—advanced avionics."

Flying wasn't something she'd ever thought about much. To her, it was a mode of transport and usually not a particularly comfortable one. She was used to being crammed into a small space with her knees bumping the seat in front.

This was different.

She watched as Zach's hands moved over the instruments with quiet confidence. Stealing a glance, she realized how much he'd changed. He had a quiet self-belief that had been absent when she'd first known him.

He must have felt her gaze because he turned his head and raised his eyebrows. "Is this the part where you tell me you really are scared of flying?"

"Spiders, Flynn. It's just spiders." She licked her lips. "Is it going to put you off if I tell you you're hot when you fly a plane?"

For a brief moment his gaze held hers and then he turned his head and focused his attention on the flight deck. "I'm not hot the rest of the time?"

"Maybe it's to do with all the thrust and power that's going on around here."

"If you're having filthy thoughts, you might want to save them until we land. That's unless you want to ditch in the ocean."

There was an increase in engine noise and then they were speeding along the runway and into the air.

As she watched Puffin Island recede beneath them, she realized she was holding her breath.

To the right she saw the *Captain Hook* leaving the harbor on its way to the mainland, the yachts moored in the Ocean Club and the rocky shoreline and inlets that formed the west coast of the island.

Then they turned and flew over the forest. Far beneath her she caught a glimpse of Heron Pond where they'd camped with the children, and then saw Shell Bay and Castaway Cottage. There were people on the beach, tiny figures with no face or form, enjoying the last days of summer. They'd be wearing sweaters, she thought.

Reaching for another layer, commenting on how the weather was turning.

And then the figures vanished and there was only the rippling expanse of the ocean, yachts cutting through the white chop of the water.

They flew over Puffin Rock and then headed north over islands, some inhabited, some not, and she looked down on beaches, lighthouses and mountains. Seated in the cockpit, she had an uninterrupted view of her little corner of the world and that world was breathtaking.

I've never seen it like this.

The thought flew into her head and out again because now they were over Acadia National Park and far below she could see spectacular summer cottages dotted around Bar Harbor. She looked down on Frenchman's Bay, bound by Mount Desert Island and the rocky granite shoreline of the Schoodic Peninsula. Here the shoreline was red granite, the forest dominated by pine, birch and varieties of spruce, cedar and maple.

In the summer the roads were crowded but in the winter the visitor numbers dwindled.

"It's perfect. I understand why you love it." She glanced from Zach's hands to the strong, masculine lines of his face and realized that when she looked at him now, she saw him differently. The past had vanished. There was no sign of the angry boy, the loner who had been suspicious of everyone around him. In his place was a man who had built a life from the rubble of his childhood. "Where are we going?"

"It's a surprise."

For a moment she allowed herself to admire the hard lines of his jaw highlighted by the hint of masculine shadow.

Then she turned her eyes back to the view. To the right she could see a small island, one of many, with a spectacular summer house overlooking a beach and a dock.

When she realized he was intending to land on the water her heart bumped a little faster. "We're landing? I thought this was a flight over the bay."

"It's a flight over the bay, with a scenic stopover." He reached towards the control panel. "Gear up for water landing."

"You're sure about this?" As the ocean grew closer, she felt a flicker of nerves. "You know for sure the plane floats? Because I ate a bagel yesterday and I'm not at my thinnest."

His response was simply to smile and moments later they skimmed the water and came to a halt by the dock.

Brittany breathed again. "Okay, well, that was impressive." She knew nothing about flying but she could see the skill with which he'd handled the plane. "Landing on water must be tricky."

"You want to keep the nose slightly high. If you try to land with zero degrees of pitch as you would when you're cruising, the water could catch the front of your float pontoons and flip the plane." He removed his headset and stood up. "Ready to explore?"

"I don't even know where we are. Or are you about to tell me you've bought an island as well as a plane?"

"It's owned by a guy called Frederick Richardson. He runs a hedge fund. Drags himself out of the madness of Manhattan once a month and comes here for the fishing. I'm his transport." He walked to the back of the plane. "Aren't you going to ask me if we're trespassing?"

"No. You respect other people's property."

He reached for a cooler and a basket. "I didn't always."

Brittany's heart skipped in her chest. Another revelation, but one so small he didn't even seem to realize he'd made it. Warmed by the knowledge that he'd dropped his guard a little, she resisted the temptation to push further.

"Do you have something to drink in there?"

"And something to eat."

"You planned this? I thought it was a spontaneous suggestion." She took the basket from him. "I didn't even ask you why you dropped round this morning. I opened the door, grabbed you and cried all over you. I bet that wasn't quite the greeting you were expecting."

"I seem to remember I was the one who grabbed you." He carried the food down the steps. "And I came round to take you flying. And to apologize for not being in touch for the last three days. I found out Philip was due over at the mainland for some tests. I wanted to be with him."

"Tests?" That news drove all other thoughts from her head. "Is he worse?"

"The pain is worse. They were doing some more investigations. Playing with his medication."

"So you took him over and stayed?"

"I wanted to hear what they said. I can't rely on Philip to give me the whole story. He always pretends everything's fine. A bit like you."

She ignored that. "And?"

Zach lowered the cooler and the basket to the ground. "They're going to try different treatment. Exercise is good, but getting tired isn't. No way is he going to be able to be involved with the camp the way he has been. He has to scale it back."

"That's disappointing news and I'm guessing he's taken it hard. So what happens now?"

"I don't know."

She saw the tension in his jaw and his shoulders and sensed his frustration. "Lucky he has you," she said calmly. "That must help."

"How the hell does it help?" His voice was raw. "I can't fix his joints."

"No, but you can be there for him when he needs it and that's worth a lot. When life gets bumpy, sometimes the only thing that helps is knowing your friends and family are there to support you."

Zach shot her a look. "I'm not his family. We're not related."

And yet you took time off to go with him to the hospital.

She wondered how, after all these years, he could possibly think that he wasn't part of the Law family. She felt an ache in her chest because she knew, despite everything, he was still afraid to let anyone in. And then she thought about Zach's real family, the one who had treated him so badly he'd been afraid to sleep at night. Maybe when you'd grown up with the bad, you didn't ever dare trust the good not to disappear. "Celia and Philip think of you as a son. They're there for you. They've had your back since that first day you arrived here. In fact I think you'd be surprised by how many people have your back." Having planted that thought, she picked up the basket. "I hope you packed plenty of food, because I'm starving."

Without looking back, she walked along the dock and took the path that curved towards a beach.

Did he really not believe his presence made a difference to Celia and Philip?

Why wasn't he offering to help Philip with the camp given that he had the necessary skills?

The questions ran through her head until it was hard to keep them inside.

She forced herself to keep her mouth shut and instead studied the view.

Far in the distance she could see the mainland and Bar Harbor.

"This is incredible." She sat down on a rock and anchored her hair with her hand. "So how did you meet the guy that owns this place? You said his name was Frederick something?"

Zach sat down next to her. "He was a friend of someone I worked for in Alaska. The guy owns a drilling company specializing in Alaskan oil-field construction. Divides his time between Alaska and Houston." He opened the cooler and then the basket. "Help yourself."

She looked down at the pretty green-and-white-spotted napkins and laughed. "No way did you put those there."

"You're right, I didn't."

Brittany reached into the basket and raised her eyebrows. "Heart-shaped chocolates?"

"Didn't put those there, either."

"So who packed the food?"

"It's Ocean Club takeout."

"I didn't think the Ocean Club did takeout."

"I called Ryan and pulled in a favor." He handed her a plate and removed chicken from the cooler.

"Ryan packed heart-shaped chocolates? Doesn't sound like him."

"He was out sailing with Alec and Lizzy so he delegated to Kirsti."

Brittany laughed. "*Now* I understand where the chocolate hearts came from." She nibbled the chicken. "You do know Kirsti is the biggest matchmaker on the island? These chocolates are supposed to be a romantic gesture."

"If I want to have sex with a woman, chocolate doesn't

play a part." His gaze dropped to her mouth and her heart bumped a little harder.

"It could do. Chocolate would soften me up." She scooped her hair back, fighting a losing battle with the breeze. "I know I look a mess. It's your fault. You told me to grab a sweater for a flight around the bay. If I'd known we were having a fancy picnic I would have dressed up and done something with my hair."

"You always look beautiful. Last thing at night, first thing in the morning, angry and happy."

It was like missing a step. Her insides jumped and tumbled. "Well, that's—" Her voice was husky. "Thank you. But I don't look beautiful when I've been crying so hard my face looks like a strawberry."

"Yes, you do." His voice was rough. "But maybe you shouldn't read any more of your grandmother's diaries if they're going to upset you."

"I want to. I want to know everything there was to know about her. I always knew she was determined, but I never knew how much she struggled when she first came here. Now I understand why she encouraged me to work so hard. She wanted me to have options and she believed that studying gave you options. My mother hated it here and couldn't wait to leave."

"You don't talk much about your mother. Are you in touch with her?"

"Occasionally. We email. We talk on the phone. But we're not close. Never have been. I was closer to my grandmother. She raised me." She stared out to sea. "The people who are your real family, the people who you can rely on one hundred percent, are not always your closest relations. But you already know that."

His expression didn't change. "What I know," he said

slowly, "is that the only person you can rely on one hundred percent is yourself."

It felt as if someone was squeezing her heart. "Sure, if you're in trouble, you deal with it yourself, but while you're dealing with it, it's nice to have the support of people who love you. It's like crying. You can cry by yourself but it's a whole lot better if someone hugs you while you do. I couldn't imagine a life without my friends in it."

He gave a half smile. "Why would you need to? You have a thousand friends."

Her breath caught in her throat. "Grams always said that a thousand friends prepared to party with you are worth less than one friend who is willing to stay and help you clear up after everyone else has left."

There was a brief silence. "Then I guess you're fine, because you have friends who would do that."

"So do you."

He gave a soft laugh. "Honey, there are at least a dozen people who would boot me off this island if they had their way."

"Maybe ten years ago that was true, but not now. You need to take another look." She wondered how he couldn't know that so many people cared about him. Trying to lighten the mood, she made a joke. "Mel would love to be in a room with you when the lights go out."

"I need to make a note not to be anywhere near Harbor Stores when the power is out."

Brittany grinned and finished the chicken. "That was delicious. You do know that if it was packed by Kirsti, the rumor mill will be working overtime?"

"I do know. I also know I'm being closely watched."

She helped herself to more chicken. "If you made me cry in public everyone would feel sorry for me and I'd be given free food. Might be worth thinking about." She licked her fingers. "Tell me more about flying in Alaska. I don't understand how you can fly in all that snow and ice."

"Sometimes you can't. If it was light ice, I flew. Severe ice, I didn't. Pilots in Alaska spend a lot of time hanging around checking the weather. Most of the time it was something in between and then you try and get above or below it."

She reached into the basket and took a chunk of the olive bread Kirsti had packed. "How does that help?"

"If you encounter ice, you need to climb. The higher you go the colder it gets, so there's less ice. You can always go back down. NASA has done research on icing and ninety percent of the time climbing or descending three thousand feet will get you out of ice. But it isn't just the ice that's a problem up there, it's the wind, too." He reached down into the sand and picked up a pebble, running his thumb over the smooth surface. "The weather is in charge, just as it is along this coastline."

"So you either freeze or get blown out of the sky?"

He stared across to the mainland, hazy in the distance. "Worst flight I ever had was when I was taking a group to a remote village. It was a bumpy ride right from the start and as I flew over the lakes, I could see the wind shadow."

"What's wind shadow?"

"When you look down on the water you can see the ripples caused by the wind. Look at the shore and you'll see a crescent where the water is calm—that's the direction the wind is blowing. If you have white lines on the water, you don't want to be flying. As landing strips go in Alaska, this was a good one. As I came in to land

I dropped the wing into the wind—" he glanced at her "—it's called cross controlling and it compensates for the crosswind—" He continued to talk and she listened, absorbed by the detail and his obvious love for the outdoors.

"So the wind sock was horizontal?"

"I came in sideways. It was like flying a crab. Landing like that can put a side load on the wheels and blow a tire, but luckily the runway was gravel so there was some give. If it had been a paved runway I would have been in trouble." He drew his arm back and threw the pebble into the water. "I don't know who was more relieved to be alive, me or the passengers."

Finally she asked the question that had been burning inside her. "How did you come to own a plane?"

"It was a gift from the guy who owned the drilling company." He hesitated. "I did him a favor."

"Must have been some favor. What did you do?"

For a moment she thought he wasn't going to answer. Then he reached into the basket and helped himself to some of the bread. "I flew his little girl to the hospital."

"You— Oh. What was wrong with her?"

He turned the bread over in his hands, not eating. "The guy had been away on a business trip for a week. Before he'd left he'd promised her he'd bring her a pair of skates so that they could skate on the lake together. Within an hour of him returning they were out on the ice. Dani fell and banged her head. Knocked herself out and cut herself."

Dani. Not "his child" or "this kid"—*Dani.*

Another connection he'd made that somehow hadn't registered on his radar.

"That's terrible. I bet he blamed himself for giving her those skates."

"He was beating himself up for a long time."

"Still, people don't usually hand out planes when they're grateful. That's a hell of a tip, Flynn, so why don't you tell me the rest of the story? And no editing." She finished the chicken and wiped her fingers. "It was minus-stupid figures, blowing a gale and no one else would fly, right?"

He broke off a chunk of bread and ate it. "Something like that."

Exactly like that, she thought. "So you were a hero?"

"No. I made a judgment. If I hadn't thought I could do it, I wouldn't have offered."

"So you didn't just put the autopilot on and pray?"

"I don't use the autopilot in icy conditions, it can mask cues. I prefer to hand-fly the plane."

And she was willing to bet those hands were as good at controlling the plane as they were at everything else. "But Dani was okay?"

"She was in the hospital for a week, but she made a full recovery."

"And her father gave you a plane." She stretched out her legs and looked at him in awe. "Was there a catch? You had to always be on call or something?"

"No. I carried on flying him and his family while they were there. Then they moved back to Texas and I decided I was ready for a change."

"So you set up a business, flying folk with deep pockets." But what he did wasn't all about the money, she knew that. He'd flown Brittany to her appointments. He'd flown Lizzy to the hospital when no one else would. "Emily thinks you're a hero."

"She's biased. A sick child is a scary thing. They go downhill fast when they're young. It was the same with

Dani. You're grateful to anyone who goes through that with you, even if it's someone at the controls of a plane." He rose to his feet, closing the subject down. "We should be getting back."

"Praise makes you uncomfortable."

"I haven't had much practice at receiving it and I don't see the need for praise when you're just doing something that needs doing." He closed the basket, reached out his hand and pulled Brittany to her feet.

"You're not such a badass, Zachary Flynn. When it comes to the weak and the vulnerable, you're a pushover." On impulse, she rose onto her toes and kissed his cheek, feeling the roughness of his jaw against her lips. "Thanks." She'd intended the kiss as a simple gesture of friendship, nothing more, but between the two of them there was always more. "Simple" had never played a part in their relationship.

His head was bent, his mouth dangerously close to hers. "What are you thanking me for?"

There was a tightening low in her pelvis, a dangerous ache that always seemed to be present when she was near him. "For giving me a hug when I was upset this morning. For bringing me here. I feel better." Unsettled, she started to lower her heels to the ground but he slid his arm around her waist and pulled her hard against him. She rocked off balance, curving her fingers around the hard steel of his biceps to support herself.

His gaze, dark and shielded, was fixed on her mouth. "What do you think your grandmother would say if she knew you were with me now?"

The excitement was agonizing. It rushed through her like a rogue wave, threatening to swamp her. "I think— I know—she'd want me to be happy."

There was a long, pulsing silence and then his gaze lifted from her mouth to her eyes. "And are you happy?"

"Yes." Her heart was pounding and she curved her fingers into the unyielding bulk of muscle to support herself. They stood like that, their breath mingling, eyes locked, and then finally he slid his hand behind her head and drew her face to his.

"I promised myself that I wasn't going to do this again."

"Why?" Her heart was racing. "Why not?"

He didn't answer. He simply lowered his head and took her mouth, kissing her with slow deliberation and erotic skill until she was relieved he was holding her because without the support of his arm she would have slid to the ground in a melted puddle. His kisses were intimate, searching, demanding and every bit as deep as if they were both already naked having sex.

And she wanted that.

She wanted it so badly she couldn't think straight.

"Can we go home?" Drugged and dizzy, she eased her mouth away from his just enough to speak. "Can we—"

"Yes." His voice was thick and he loosened his grip on her, keeping his arm around her until he was sure she was steady on her feet. "Let's go."

Walking on legs the consistency of jelly, Brittany helped him gather up their belongings and carry them back to the plane.

It was the first time she'd taken off from water and she might have been a little anxious had there been room for anything in her head other than sexual awareness.

She heard the powerful sound of the engine and then they were moving across the water, gaining speed.

She watched Zach's hands, hypnotized by the skilled, quiet movements of those fingers.

And then, in the few seconds before takeoff, a lobster boat emerged from the far side of the island.

Brittany wasn't sure whether she screamed out loud or whether the sound was trapped in her head.

Zach yanked off the power and pulled back on the wheel, stopping the plane in a shower of sea spray.

Brittany closed her eyes. "Crap, that was—"

"Yeah, we almost ingested a few hundred crustaceans." He waited a beat. "It would have been our first dinner date. You could have had lobster for supper. Right there in your lap, already diced. Let me know if you want fries or ketchup."

She started to laugh, grateful for his cool and even more grateful for his skill. "Take me home, Zach."

And he did.

Chapter 17

As promised, two weeks later, Zach flew Brittany to the hospital to have the plaster removed and afterwards drove her home.

After weeks of being restricted it was wonderful to feel the air on her skin.

"I have exercises to do, and one more appointment in a few weeks to check everything looks good, but I'm free. Thanks for flying me. I'll cook you dinner as a thank-you."

"We're going out."

"We are?" Surprised, she looked at him questioningly and saw something in his eyes that she hadn't seen before.

"I booked a table at The Galleon."

Her heart did a little dance in her chest. Since the picnic on the beach they'd spent almost all their time together, although little of it had been in public. But although the sex was incredible, she sensed nothing had really changed for him. Even in bed he had an air of cool detachment, as if part of him was separate from all the things they did together. "Is this an actual date?"

The corners of his mouth flickered into a smile. "I thought after ten years, it was about time."

"Right." She tried desperately not to read anything into it but her mind was already throwing out questions. "If you buy me dinner, there will be gossip."

"There's always gossip." Zach took the road that led down to Castaway Cottage. "At least we'll give them something juicy to gossip about."

Brittany smiled. "And at The Galleon we won't have Kirsti telling us our fortunes and slipping a magic potion into our food. Ryan takes Emily to The Galleon when he wants a romantic evening." The moment the words left her mouth she wanted to bite off her tongue. "Not that I'm saying—"

"You don't have to watch your words," he said evenly. "You shouldn't have to look before you take a step, Brittany. I booked the place because we've spent most of the last two weeks naked and feasting off grilled cheese sandwiches at two in the morning. I wanted to show you that your body isn't the only thing that interests me. I wanted to have dinner with you."

She was floored. Speechless. And confused.

She had no idea how to respond in a way that wouldn't send him running, but fortunately she didn't need to because he pulled up outside her cottage.

She wanted to ask what his plans were. Wanted to ask if he'd made any decisions about Philip and Camp Puffin, but she didn't want to push him. She reasoned that if he had something to tell her about that, he'd tell her.

Instead of focusing on that, she focused on the cottage and the bay.

"I love it here. Leaving it seems to get harder every time."

"Then don't leave."

She stared ahead, watching wispy clouds drift lazily across the horizon. Soon the leaves would turn and the temperature would drop. "Now that the plaster is off my wrist, there's nothing to keep me here." And she'd been putting off the decision about what to do next, a tiny part of her thinking, hoping—

Unwilling to accept even to herself what she'd been thinking and hoping, she slid out of the car.

Frustrated with herself, she stretched her hands into the air. "It feels amazing not to have that cast on my wrist—Zach!" she gasped as he scooped her up and threw her over his shoulder in a fireman's lift.

Breathless, laughing, she thumped his back. "What are you doing? Put me down—"

"I'll put you down when I'm ready." Pausing to toe off his shoes, he strode across the sand as if she weighed nothing.

When she realized what he intended to do, she started to squirm. "Don't you *dare* drop me in the sea, Flynn. Put me down. *Put me down!* I'll lose my flip-flops, soak my jeans, it's freezing and—oh!" She felt a tug on her feet as Zach removed her flip-flops and dropped them on the sand and then he was wading into the water and she was laughing and clinging at the same time. "Don't drop me!"

"A moment ago you wanted me to put you down. Make up your mind."

"I'm going to kill you, Zach. I swear I'm going to—

holy crap——" she gasped as he lowered her into the freezing water. "That is *so cold*!"

"All summer you've been telling me how much you missed swimming."

She stood, shivering, as her calves turned slowly numb. "Obviously it was one of those memories I'd built up into something different in my head. Suddenly I'm missing the Mediterranean."

"Wimp." He was looking at her and she was facing out to sea, which was how she saw the wave racing towards them and he didn't.

"Did you call me a wimp?" She held his gaze and timed it perfectly, her push sending him spluttering under the water.

He recovered quickly and grabbed her around the waist and she struggled to keep her balance, laughing so hard she couldn't breathe.

"I'm soaked."

"That's what happens when you swim in the sea."

"But people generally change into something more suitable, like a bathing suit or a wet suit. I can't feel my legs. I'm not sure if that's a good thing or a bad thing. I may have frostbite. You'll have to fly me to the hospital again, Flynn."

"I have other ways of warming you up. Better ways." He grabbed her hand and dragged her out of the water as another large wave rolled in and soaked the only part of her that was still dry.

Her hair was plastered to her forehead, her eyes stinging.

"These are my favorite jeans and now they're stuck to my body and nothing short of a surgeon's scalpel is going to be able to remove them. I swear I'm going to kill you."

"Better do it inside. That way my body won't be washed away." Still holding her hand, he scooped up their shoes and together they walked towards the cottage.

Feeling the cool sand beneath her feet, she felt a pang of nostalgia. "When I was little, my grandmother used to pick me up and wash my feet off outside the door so I didn't bring the sand indoors."

Zach paused. "When your mother left, why didn't she take you with her?"

"She was a single mother and I was settled in school and doing well. I loved the island." She bent and brushed the sand from her feet. "I don't remember my parents' divorce being a great trauma. My father was away all the time when I was young anyway, so the divorce simply made it official. It didn't change my day-to-day routine. And I always knew I was loved. I was lucky." She sent him a look. "Is it hard for you to hear this?"

"That you had a happy childhood? No." He reached out and smoothed a strand of damp, tangled hair from her face. "I'm glad you were happy. You deserve to be happy."

So do you.

She kept the words in her head as she unlocked the door to the cottage. "My jeans weigh a ton."

"I'm happy to help you with that, Dr. Forrest." His hands closed over her shoulders and he lowered his mouth to her neck.

Heat shot through her and she closed her eyes. "How does that help? Or are you trying to melt me out of my pants?"

"Maybe I am." He kicked the door shut behind them, took her hand and led her up to the bathroom.

"This shower is not built for two. It's going to be cozy."

"Cozy works for me." He stripped off her jeans, T-shirt and underwear, followed by his own, and Brittany shivered and ran her hands over the hard planes of his chest.

She felt the familiar knot of scar tissue and pressed her mouth to it.

Tension rippled through him and he lowered his hands to her shoulders. His eyes were flinty dark, like the sky before a storm. "Don't—"

"I wish none of that had happened to you."

A muscle flickered in his cheek and he slid his fingers into her hair, massaging her scalp with his hand. "It's all right." His words were neutral but she felt the distance in him, that distance that she'd never totally managed to breach.

"Trust me, Zach." She rose on her toes and ran her mouth over his jaw. "You don't have to protect yourself anymore. Trust me not to hurt you. Let me in."

There was a glitter in his eyes and an expression on his face that she didn't recognize.

For a moment he stood perfectly still, and then he reached out and switched on the shower. She gasped as needle-sharp hot water cascaded over both of them, warming their skin.

He washed her, his clever fingers leaving no part of her undiscovered, and by the time he finally turned off the water she was trembling.

She tried to speak but tumbled straight into the penetrating heat of his kiss. Sensations blended together, racing over her skin and seeping into her pores. She was no longer cold but hot, feverishly hot, and he licked into her mouth, kissing her with intimate precision. She felt the heat of his palm slide up her rib cage and then he dragged his thumb over the tip of her breast and she went weak and pressed against him. "What time is dinner?"

"When we're ready." He wrapped her in a towel and carried her through to the bedroom, taking ruthless advantage of his superior strength as he flattened her to the bed.

"You're going to make us late."

He gave a slow, wicked smile. "Honey, I'm going to make you come."

"Again? You've pretty much done nothing else for the past few weeks." She laughed and then gasped as he spread her thighs. "Zach, stop—you can't—we already—I don't have time—I—Oh, God—" The laughter turned to a moan as she felt the slow, slippery sweep of his tongue against her most sensitive flesh. He explored her with ruthless skill, holding her captive as she writhed against the explicit torture.

She cried out his name and felt him rise above her, his body hard and heavy as he entered her with a single thrust that took him deep. She slid her hands down the taut muscle of his back, almost sobbing with the relief of being able to finally hold him with both hands. His skin was warm and sleek and she slid her fingers lower, down to his backside, arching her hips to take him deeper still.

He groaned deep in his throat and surged forward, finding a perfect rhythm, filling not just her body but her head and her heart.

In a tiny corner of her mind, appearing like the merest wisp of a cloud on a perfect blue-sky day, was a niggling worry that he'd never lower that barrier enough to lose that control and for once, she wanted him to forget technique and make love with his heart and not just his body. She felt the rasp of stubble against her skin as he kissed her neck, the ripple of muscle and the hard strength of his body and then there was a subtle change in his rhythm and all thought left her as he drove her skillfully to climax.

It felt as if it would never end, her body closing around his, her inner muscles rippling down his shaft. It left them both spent and he rolled onto his back and took her with him, holding her firmly.

Dazed, she lay there, drifting out of a sexually induced slumber, feeling his hand gently stroke the curve of her hip, wanting to tell him she loved him but too scared of driving him away.

As luck would have it The Galleon was crowded, which meant there was no chance their presence would go unnoticed. And anyway, he'd known from the moment Brittany had walked into the kitchen of Castaway Cottage that going unnoticed was an impossibility.

She'd chosen to wear a short blue dress that revealed mile-long legs.

He'd taken one look at her and almost swallowed his tongue.

"I've changed my mind about going out."

She'd smiled and walked past him towards the door. "I'm hungry, Flynn. You need to feed me before we go another round." So now here they were, staring at each other over fine linen, sparkling silverware and the flicker of candles.

They ordered without paying too much attention to the menu or the other people seated in the restaurant.

"A toast to our first proper date?" She raised her glass and smiled, her mouth a glossy curve.

He kept his expression neutral. "I have a distinct memory of buying you a pepperoni pizza from Jack's. I can't believe that moment isn't etched into your memory."

"Actually it is. It was great pizza. We ate it on South Beach. That was the night I decided I was going to have sex with you. It was two days after my eighteenth birthday."

Zach felt hot all over. "I remember that night."

"I dragged you to the cave and tried to get you naked. You showed a frustrating degree of self-control." She leaned forward, silver earrings swinging. "I like the way you look in a jacket and tie. Makes me want to unwrap you."

"So unwrap me." Anything to reduce the sweltering heat. He wanted to fling open a window or demand that the restaurant staff turn up the air-conditioning.

"Not yet. Part of the fun is the anticipation. I bet you were one of those kids who opened all your presents on Christmas Eve." Her merry smile faded and she looked guilty. "I'm sorry. That was so thoughtless of me. I wasn't thinking."

"Why are you sorry?"

"For being tactless." She looked annoyed with herself. "Christmas must have been a horrible time for you."

"It was no different from any other day."

"That's what I mean. It was a thoughtless thing to say." She reached across the table and covered his hand with hers. "Again, I'm sorry."

"You have no reason to be sorry. I've told you, you don't need to watch where you step with me."

"When I hurt a friend, I apologize."

"I can't imagine you hurting anyone."

"Not intentionally, but we're all human. And when I'm

more human than I'd like to be, I apologize." Her light tone was in direct contrast to the firm grip of her fingers.

He glanced down. Her nails were short and gleamed with clear polish, her fingers slim and delicate compared to his.

He didn't know whether it was the warmth of her hand or the compassion in her voice, but something unraveled inside him.

"My first year in foster care, they had a large Christmas tree." The words came from nowhere, without any forward planning on his part. "It was the first time I'd seen one up close. It was covered in huge sparkly decorations and chocolate wrapped in shiny paper."

Her eyes lit up with humor and understanding. "You ate the chocolate. Of course you did. You were a kid. There was chocolate on the tree. It's a no-brainer. And then you were probably sick."

He could stop now.

He could let her leave with that version of the story in her head.

Or he could tell her the truth.

"I'd never tasted chocolate before, but I'd been hungry often enough to have learned that when I saw food it was best to take it. I took it."

"Crap, Zach—" The laughter had gone from her eyes but her hand stayed on his. "You were hungry?"

"Most of the time. Sometimes I managed to steal something from the fridge, but there were plenty of days where there was no food in the house." Days when the vicious gnawing pains in his stomach had been so bad he would have eaten just about anything that could be chewed and swallowed. "There was a grocery store close to our apartment." He wondered if *apartment* was really the right word to describe the cramped, filthy space that had been his home growing up. "I often helped myself to breakfast."

"Did they catch you?"

"No. I made sure they didn't. Or maybe they guessed but decided letting a bony kid eat one meal was their charitable act for the day. I don't know." He shrugged. "On my first day with my foster family, I opened their fridge and it was full of food. I ate everything I could cram into my mouth."

"I hope they refilled the fridge instantly. Did they have kids of their own?"

"Their kids had grown up and left home. I was their first foster kid. Their good deed. The way they were judged by the community. In their own way they kept me as trapped as my mother had. They didn't trust me not to screw up and embarrass them." He sat back as their food was delivered. "They deserved an easier start than me. I didn't fit their notion of a dream child. They were expecting gratitude, but by then I knew that the only person looking out for me was myself. I was all about survival. I ate their food and I slept in clean sheets, but I gave them nothing in return except an almighty headache."

"If they knew your background, then I'm sure they understood." Still she didn't remove her hand and Zach realized he didn't want her to remove it.

"There was no way people like that could have understood."

"Not what you'd been through," she spoke softly, "but they should have understood that after the way you'd been forced to live your life, it wouldn't be easy to gain your trust."

"I think they spent too much time trying to anticipate

what I'd do next to even think about gaining my trust. I stole food from the fridge and I couldn't sleep in a bedroom without moving the furniture in front of the door. I broke two lamps and a chair hauling things across the room. The final straw was when my foster mother crept into the room one night to check on me. It was one of those rare occasions I was asleep. I woke up to find someone leaning over me. That had always been bad news in the past, so I attacked her. Things got a little messy after that. Four months after I arrived with them I was moved to another family, but not before they'd made sure I knew how disappointed they were by my failure to magically transform into the child they'd dreamed of. The social worker told me a while later that they'd adopted a baby. I'm sure that was the right thing for them. They needed a child who hadn't formed any bad habits. A child who wasn't going to rearrange the furniture and store food under the bed just in case there wasn't any next time he looked." While he'd been talking, the food had grown cold and their server had twice approached their table only to retreat when Brittany had given a brief shake of her head. "We should eat."

"I'm more interested in talking to you than eating the food."

"If I'd known that I would have ordered takeout and eaten it on the beach."

"I wouldn't have worn this dress on the beach." She leaned forward slightly, the neckline hinting at the tempting dip between her breasts.

"In that case I'm glad I booked this place."

Zach discovered he didn't care that the food was cold because he couldn't taste it anyway.

When he bought a woman dinner it was usually a precursor to sex. Everything from the exchange of looks to the conversation was leading up to that moment. There was very little that was personal about it.

But tonight felt personal.

Tonight felt different, which was why he'd—

Hell. "I'm sorry I told you all that."

Her gaze lifted to his and he saw kindness and warmth in his eyes. "Why? Because it makes you feel uncomfortable or because you're worried it makes me feel uncomfortable?"

"Both."

"I'm sure it's hard for you to talk about it, but it doesn't make me uncomfortable. Angry, definitely, and a little sick to my stomach if I'm honest, but not uncomfortable. I'm glad you told me. Given your start in life, it's a surprise you turned out so well. You were the human equivalent of Jaws." She finished her food, a delicate tartlet of red pepper and goat's cheese that had been more than happy to wait for her attention. "This is good."

"You think I'm like Jaws?" He appreciated her attempt at humor. "Physically or psychologically?"

"Physically Jaws is by far the most attractive, I'm sure you know that." She put down her fork, and sighed. "You lost trust in humans, and no one would blame you for that. Thank goodness for Philip and Celia. How is Philip, by the way?

"Refusing to believe he needs to give up doing some of the things he loves."

"Has he asked you to take over?"

His stomach was hollow. "Not since the first time."

"When, naturally, you said no."

"Why 'naturally'?"

She kept eye contact. "Because you're afraid of letting him down. They love you, but you won't let yourself trust that love. You're afraid you're going to mess up and that if you do, they'll stop loving you. It's natural not to want to disappoint the people we love, and you love Philip and Celia."

He shifted uncomfortably. "I appreciate what they've done for me."

"You love them." She reached out and picked up her wine. "And they love you. They loved the boy you were back then and they love the man you've become. They didn't give up on you. Not once. And what I'm wondering is, why is one set of evidence more meaningful than another?"

His mouth was dry and he took a sip of water. "I don't know what you mean."

"We make our decisions based on knowledge and experience. When you were young, the evidence told you that you had to look out for yourself because no one else would. You worked out that the way to stop being hurt was not to care. The way not to care was to stop making connections with people, so that's what you did. But that changed a long time ago. You can't live on Puffin Island and not make connections. It isn't possible."

"You're saying I've made connections I don't know about?"

She smiled. "No. I'm saying you've made connections you're not willing to acknowledge. You think you're the same as you were twenty years ago when you came here for the first time, but you're not. None of us are. We're all born with certain character traits but who we are, what we become, is the result of our experiences. If we know there's a chance we'll be eaten by a sabre-toothed tiger, we develop a weapon with which to defend ourselves. Humans change and evolve, not only in a macro sense over centuries but over a single lifetime. And I'm wondering when the last time was you really examined the evidence."

"Evidence?"

"The evidence that there are plenty of people looking out for you. Not just Philip and Celia, but Ryan, Emily. Me. It's the reason I scared you the first time. I cared about you." She paused and then seemed to make a decision. "I loved you."

Plenty of women had been attracted to him because he was the bad boy and he'd been happy to oblige, layering on an extra layer of badness just for them. At least their expectations had been easy to live up to. Walking away had been easy.

With Brittany it had been different.

He hadn't walked away. He'd run.

"You were discovering your wild side."

"I loved you. I admit it was a pretty immature kind of love. And maybe a little bit selfish, but it was love. And because I didn't see any reason to hold those feelings back, I didn't. But that's in the past. Since then you've made plenty of connections, but you're afraid to acknowledge them. You don't want to admit that you feel, because if you feel you can be hurt and you worked out a way to stop yourself being hurt. You switched that side of yourself off a long time ago." She gave an awkward shrug. "Sorry. That was a bit deep for our first real date. Are we having dessert? Because Em told me they do the best blueberry cheesecake."

Zach wouldn't have noticed if they'd fed him ashes.

She'd loved him?

He'd assumed their relationship was physical. That

when he'd walked out he'd done her a favor. He'd assumed that any hurt he'd caused would have been superficial and short-lived.

"You didn't know me."

"I knew enough. Maybe not the details of your past, but I knew *you.* I saw how resilient you were, and how strong. I saw that you were prepared to use that strength to protect people and animals who needed protecting. I saw how you refused to let life crush you, how you took a passion and ran with it. I saw the belief you had in yourself. I loved all that." She gave a half smile and sent him a look that fried his brain. "And I also loved the way you kissed and did all those other things."

He didn't smile.

The one thing that had kept his guilt in check over the years was the belief that their relationship hadn't meant that much to her.

"If you felt that way then why, when you arrived back here, did you pretend you felt nothing?"

She shrugged. "Pride? Every damn person on this island was watching me, waiting for me to fall apart."

"I hurt you." His voice was rough. "How badly did I hurt you? I want the truth."

She was silent for a moment. "Quite badly, but it worked out fine in the end. I went to college, and that's where I met Emily and Skylar. They had problems of their own, and we kept each other going. Supported each other. We used to laugh that we were like a three-legged chair. If one of us left, that would be it. The other two would crash to the ground in a heap."

Pain, guilt, regret mingled up inside him in a toxic cocktail.

"Let's get out of here. We'll eat dessert at home."

She didn't argue, and by mutual agreement they chose to go to Seagull's Nest rather than Castaway Cottage because it was closer.

They made it back to Camp Puffin in record time, their hands and mouths greedy for each other as they stumbled through the door.

He didn't bother removing her dress. Just shoved it up to her waist and drove into her again and again until she cried out his name and sank her fingers into his shoulders. There was a soft thud as one of her shoes fell to the floor and then the other, and then she was wrapping her legs around him urging him on.

If he'd expected the sex to extinguish the unfamiliar emotions, he was disappointed.

Afterwards he lit the wood-burning stove, while Brittany sprawled on the bed watching. "You look like Neolithic man, lighting the fire while woman lies here in wait."

"Is that what happened? Seems to me woman had it easy." He returned to the bed and folded her against him, feeling the warmth of her skin against his.

The glow from the fire sent a golden glow over smooth, bare skin. Her face was bare of makeup, her cheeks and neck slightly flushed from the brutal graze of his stubble.

With a flash of guilt, Zach lifted a hand to his jaw. "I should have shaved."

She flashed him a grin that was pure sex. "No, you shouldn't." She pushed him onto his back and straddled him, lithe as a cat. Her eyes were sleepy and full of intent as she ran her palms over the roughness of his jaw. "I love you just the way you are."

Her words knocked the breath from his lungs.

No one had ever loved him just the way he was. All his life people had wanted him to act differently, speak differently, just *be* different.

Acceptance had been a thing as alien to him as love.

But she, apparently, had accepted *and* loved him.

With a blinding flash Zach realized he'd walked away from the one thing that had always been missing in his life. Not because he hadn't wanted it, but because he hadn't recognized it. Hadn't believed in it. *Hadn't trusted it.*

For Brittany, he hadn't been an outlet for rebellion, a statement, an experiment or any of the other things he'd assumed when he'd analyzed it using his own narrow reference.

She'd truly loved him, and he'd thrown that away. Feelings crashed over him, unfamiliar and disturbingly intense.

He'd had his chance and he'd blown it in spectacular style.

One thing, he thought. There was one thing he knew how to do right.

Rolling her onto her back, he slid down her body and spread her legs.

He clamped her writhing hips between his hands and licked into her, hearing her moan his name as he did so.

This intimacy he knew, and he excelled at the delivery.

She came with an agonized cry and he experienced all of it with his fingers and his mouth and then eased over her and entered her slowly.

Her body tightened around his and he closed his eyes and buried his face in her neck.

Her hair smelled of strawberries and summer rain and

he could feel the warmth of her breath, uneven and fast against his skin.

He felt the gentleness of her fingers brushing against his jaw, heard the soft murmur of her voice as she whispered his name.

And then she whispered something else. Words that until tonight he hadn't thought he'd ever hear. And she whispered them over and over again, like a mantra.

It shook him, unsettled him and he slid his hand under her, trying to find the smooth rhythm that usually came so naturally, but he couldn't focus on anything except her voice and those words. They fell like rain onto parched ground, soaking into those cold hard places that no one, including himself, had ever been able to access. He felt something inside him shift and unravel and he gave a groan and tried to withdraw, but her legs were wrapped around him, her hands behind his neck as she drew his head down to hers.

"I love you." This time she said the words against his mouth, and he kissed her deeply, trying to silence her, hoping that raw lust might burn out all these other feelings that were throwing him off his stroke.

But nothing felt the same.

He felt her arch, offering him more and he tried to give her the experience he knew she deserved, tried to find that smooth technique that never failed him, but every movement felt awkward and uneven.

It didn't feel like technique, it felt like—

Making love.

He stilled above her but she moved against him, her body refusing to release him. He felt her feelings flowing all around him, seeping under his skin and deeper, warming parts of him that had been frozen into ice. The heat was intense and he struggled against it but she was drawing him in, saying his name over and over again, telling him how much she wanted him, how he could trust her, how she would never hurt him. And he opened his mouth to warn her that he was the one who was going to hurt her, that she should protect herself, that she should run, but the only sound that emerged was a fractured groan and still the heat spread, this time reaching those tiny corners of his soul that hadn't seen light or warmth for several decades.

He'd already hurt her once. She should be holding back, protecting herself, but instead she gave and gave, stroking her hand over his cheek and then down over his back.

"I love you." She spoke the words softly against his mouth again. "I still love you, Zach. It's always been you."

The words ripped him open, exposing that raw place he'd protected all of his life.

Emotion came rushing up inside him and he groaned her name, engulfed in sensations he didn't recognize. He tried desperately to focus on her needs, but the mental detachment required was missing and the pleasure came rushing in, crashing over him in hot pulsing waves, drowning them both. He felt her hands tighten on his backside, and he drove into her again, emptying himself inside her. And through it all she kissed him, held him until there wasn't a single part of him that hadn't been touched by her warmth.

And afterwards they stayed locked together, strands of her hair clinging to his damp shoulder, as he held her close.

He knew what she wanted him to say.

He could see it in her eyes and feel it in the heavy, syrupy silence that was an inevitable consequence of what had just happened.

And he wanted to say something.

He wanted to apologize for not having given her the sex she deserved, for having lost his rhythm, his ruthless control, *his mind.*

He wanted to assure her that next time he'd get his head together and be back to his normal self. Wanted to tell her to wait around for an hour and he'd be sure to get his performance back to normal levels.

He opened his mouth to say something and then she reached up and delivered a lingering kiss to his mouth.

"That," she said softly, "was the best sex of my life."

Chapter 18

"There was something about the way he looked at me. For a minute I thought he was going to say *I love you*. How crazy is that?" She was with Emily and Skylar, and they'd opted for a picnic on the beautiful sandy curve of Shell Bay. A little distance away from them Lizzy was playing with Cocoa on the sand. The child threw the ball and the little dog bounded after it, skidded to a halt and then sprinted back with it locked firmly in her teeth while Emily watched them both closely.

"You mean you wanted him to say it." Skylar foraged through the various treats while Brittany sprawled on her stomach on the blanket.

Apart from a family on the far side of the beach, they had Shell Bay to themselves.

"Maybe I did. Yes, okay, I admit it, I did." She gave a groan of frustration and rolled onto her back. "Three little words, that's all. How hard is it to say three little words?"

"It depends on the words. He's not the first person to have a problem with those particular three."

Brittany lifted her hand to her mouth and started to chew the edge of her nail and then let her hand drop as she caught Sky's eye. "Sorry."

"Don't apologize. It's true that I don't see the point in ruining your nails over a man, but nor do I think you're crazy. You two have been pretty cosy. Spending a lot of time together."

Emily unwrapped meat they'd bought from the deli. "I don't want you to be hurt the way you were hurt before."

"That was then and this is now. It's different."

"He's the same guy, Brittany."

"Yes, and I loved that guy! I loved his resilience, his strength, the fact that despite everything—and I didn't even know what everything was then—despite everything, he never lost his humanity or his kindness. And it *is* different now. He's dealing with things differently. He's talking. He's opening up. We're close."

"Naked close." Today Sky was wearing a dress of cerulean blue which she'd teamed with bold silver earrings. With her long golden hair and blue eyes she looked like a summer flower. "Naked close isn't the same as emotional close."

"That's right. Sex is sex, but a relationship is intimacy," Emily said slowly. "It's about knowing someone and allowing them to know you back. That's the really scary part."

"You're talking as if he's a stranger. We were married for God's sake!"

"Were you? Really? You exchanged vows and rings—" Sky caught Brittany's eye and gave a faint smile. "Okay, maybe not a whopping diamond or anything—"

"It was a cheap ring from a gift store. I bought it."

"Whatever. You wouldn't have cared about that if you'd had something real and sustainable. The problem was that you never really shared anything of yourselves."

"That's what I'm telling you. Now we are. And emotional close makes everything different. Better. People evolve. Nothing stays the same."

"Well, then, that's good," Emily said firmly and Sky nodded.

"Really good. Yay."

Brittany looked at her friends and gave a humorless laugh. "You're both crap at hiding your feelings. You don't think it's good. You think this is going to end in tears."

"We care about you, that's all. And we're hoping he'll say those words soon."

"Or we'll kick his butt," Sky said happily, helping herself to more food.

"I have some news, too." Emily handed out drinks. "I went to talk to Doug Mitchell about renting the empty store near the end of Main Street."

Brittany opened the drink. "Is this for you or for someone else?"

"For me. I've been playing with the numbers. I want to open a store that sells a variety of things with a seaside theme. Despite the obvious market, there's nothing like that on the island. The artists who work here take their stuff to the mainland. There's a woman who lives over near Puffin Point who makes beautiful mirrors out of driftwood. And John Harris makes those awesome wooden boats like the one he made for Lizzy. I've already talked to him, and he'd be interested in making more."

"Paintings? Jewelry? I can see that working. I think it's a great idea. I can make you a few pieces to sell." They finished eating and Skylar wiped her fingers on a napkin while Brittany started tidying up.

"It sounds exciting."

She tried to ignore the little pang inside her.

Both her friends knew what they wanted to do. They both had a clear vision of the future, whereas hers was murky and opaque.

For the first time in her life, she had no idea what she wanted to do.

All she knew was that she wanted to stay here, living close to her friends, breathing in the salty air when she woke up every morning. She wanted to walk in the forest, watch the sun go down over the ocean from the terrace of the Ocean Club.

Most of all she wanted to be with Zach.

After a decade of traveling, she was ready to settle down in some form, although she was flexible about how that looked. All she knew was that she was tired of carrying her life in a backpack.

Should she tell him?

Yes. She'd tell him how she felt and ask him to be honest with her.

Hope lifting her mood, she scrambled to her feet and turned her attention back to her friends. "So what are you going to call your gift store?"

"I don't know, but I want something with 'seashore' in the title."

"Something Seashore." Skylar grinned. "Perfect. I'll design you a logo." She sighed as her phone rang. She delved into the bag and the smile faded from her face as she saw the caller ID. "Excuse me. I have to take this."

She scrambled to her feet and walked away from them across the sand, her voice carrying in the wind. "Richard? I wasn't expecting—well, I know that, but I thought you were—"

Feeling as if she was eavesdropping, Brittany caught Emily's eye. "I don't like what being with him does to her."

"Me neither. It reminds me of college."

"When she was trying to escape from the pressure her parents put on her? I was thinking the same thing."

They couldn't hear the rest of the conversation, but when Sky finally walked back to them her smile was forced.

"Sorry. I'm going to have to leave."

"Now?" Emily's tone was gentle as she scrambled to her feet. "We were going to spend a little more time on the beach and then I was going to run you up to the air-field in time for your late-afternoon flight."

"Something unexpected has come up. Richard has booked Zach to fly me."

"Without asking if it suited you?"

"He knows how much I hate planning. And spontaneity isn't practical when it comes to air travel." Without looking at them, Skylar slid her feet into her shoes. "I have to pack. My things are strewn all over the cottage, it's going to take me a while. Stay there. Pete can give me a ride."

"No way." Brittany gathered up their things. "If you're really leaving, then Em can drop you at the airfield on her way home. I'll come, too. I need to pick up some things from the store and I'll walk back across the fields."

Barely responding, Skylar hurried off towards Cast-away Cottage, all long legs and graceful lines.

Brittany watched her go, her own problems temporarily forgotten in her concern for her friend. "He calls and she drops everything. What is that about?"

"I guess she loves him."

"It didn't look like love to me. It looked like coercion. Love is supposed to flow both ways. Have you noticed that Richard never comes with her? He expects her by his side whenever he commands it, but it doesn't work in reverse."

"Yes, I've noticed." Emily reached for her sweater. "I've sometimes wondered if we're the problem. Perhaps he doesn't like us."

"How can he not like us? We're awesome!" Brittany grinned and then shrugged. "Honestly? He doesn't know us. We've only met him twice and on both occasions he was so busy working the room he barely did more than nod."

"We're not important enough to merit a slice of his very valuable time."

"We're important to Skylar. That should mean something, surely? He doesn't like anything or anyone that takes her away from him. It worries me."

"It worries me, too. But what worries me most is that she sometimes seems almost scared of him." Emily stuffed the remains of the picnic into the bag and slid it onto her shoulder. "I've been on the phone with her when he's shown up unexpectedly and she dashes off, even if we were in midsentence."

"You think he's physically violent?"

"No! I hope not." Emily caught her eye and then shook her head. "No, I'm sure he isn't. He cares too much about his public image to ever lose control like that. But she's always a little jumpy when she talks about him, and very careful not to upset him. She's trying very hard to be who he wants her to be and losing who she really is in the process."

Brittany thought about Skylar, so bright, happy and optimistic. "It's like watching someone trying to cage a bird and it doesn't make for comfortable viewing. Think we should say something before she flies back?"

Emily shook her head. "No. She needs to work this one out for herself. She knows we love her and she'll talk to us when she's ready."

"I want to fire an arrow into Richard Everson's butt and I will still want to fire an arrow into his butt if he wins in November. Why is she even with him?"

"I suspect she's still trying to please her parents."

"You'd think that the most important thing to them would be her happiness."

"That's the theory. Not always the practice."

Remembering Emily's own background, Brittany made an apologetic sound and pulled her friend into a hug, the gesture sending bags tumbling onto the sand. "I'm sorry. I'm a tactless idiot."

"You're not. And I'm as worried about Sky as you are. If you're firing arrows into butts, you could add her parents to the list. Now move your feet. You're treading on the blanket." Emily extracted herself and stooped to fold the blanket.

"You can't ever really see inside another person's relationship. Maybe it will all work out," Brittany said doubtfully and Emily gave her a troubled look.

"Maybe. But if it's right, if it's really love, I don't think it should be that complicated, should it?"

"You're asking the wrong person." Brittany took the

blanket from her and picked up her flip-flops. "I'm starting to think that there is nothing in the world more complicated than love."

Emily touched her arm. "You really do love him, don't you?"

Brittany stared out to sea. "I think a small part of me never fell out of love with him. Does that sound crazy?"

"No, it sounds like you. You're loyal to your friends. You stick with people through thick and thin." Emily's hand was warm. Comforting. "Do you think he loves you?"

Brittany thought about the past few weeks, about the gradual shift in their relationship. The laughter, the long talks in the dark while they lay there wrapped together. "I think he does. But it's hard for him to say those words. He's never said them to anyone, Em. And if you struggle to trust people, handing over your heart is the ultimate test of trust."

And she wasn't sure he could do that.

Zach executed a perfect landing on the ocean, and his four passengers, a family from Boston who regularly used his services, stepped from the plane onto the dock of the private island they used regularly over the summer months. The days were growing shorter, the temperature falling and the leaves starting to change. Another storm was forecast, but for now the weather was perfect. Maine was dressed up in her finest for the tourists, the sea sparkling in the sunshine.

He arrived back at Puffin Island in time for his last flight of the day.

This time his only passenger was Skylar.

As he landed, he saw Emily's car swing into the small

parking area. The glimpse of a mahogany ponytail in the passenger seat told him Brittany was there, too.

He made his final preflight check, watching out of the corner of his eye as the three women climbed out of the car and hugged.

Brittany turned her head to glance in his direction, then lifted a hand and waved to him before sliding back into the car.

Skylar walked towards him, dark glasses covering her eyes.

He noticed that her stride lacked its usual bounce and she was quiet as she slid into her seat on the plane.

Reminding himself that there was no obligation on his passengers to make conversation, Zach secured the door, then took a look at Skylar and froze.

She'd removed her glasses and her fingers were pressed to the bridge of her nose.

He'd made enough women cry in his life to know when one of them was near tears.

"Skylar?"

"I'm fine." Her voice was clogged and she turned her head to look out the window.

Zach was prepared to take her at her word. He was paid to fly passengers safely to the mainland. Their emotional well-being wasn't his business and anyway, she had friends. Good friends who were no doubt supporting her through whatever trouble she was in. She didn't need him.

He was about to leave her and walk through to the cockpit when she turned to face him. One single tear escaped from the pool gathering in her eyes and slid down her pale cheek.

"Do you ever find people hard to understand?"

Zach stilled. "All the time."

"He's supposed to care about me, but if he cares, then why does he always want me to be different? 'I don't like you in that dress, I prefer your hair when it's elegant, not loose, try not to laugh so loudly—'" More tears fell and Zach groped in the pocket of the adjoining seat to find some tissues.

He pulled one out of the packet and handed it to her. "Do you want me to call Brittany or Emily?"

"No. I know they're there for me. They're always there for me, but just for once I'd like my man to be there for me and not my girlfriends." She blew her nose. "He keeps hinting at marriage, but he never says he loves me. And we never do the things I want to do, which is weird because when we first met we seemed to have so much in common. I have my exhibition coming up in December. I've asked him to come with me to London. I thought it would be romantic. But he says he can't make it, as if I picked the time on purpose to be awkward. I know the election is November, but just once I'd like to know he was putting me first. He doesn't have to come for long. Just two days would be enough to show me he loves and supports me. Showing it is more important than saying it, don't you think? The words are pretty easy to say."

Zach, who found those words impossible to say, stayed silent. It was obvious to him that she didn't expect a response, so he handed her more tissues and listened as she talked and sobbed.

"I'm being stupid. I'm lucky. He's perfect for me."

Zach handed her another tissue, making a mental note to replenish his stock. "How do you know he's perfect for you?"

"Everyone says so. My parents. My brothers. He ticks every box on their list. According to my father, dating

Richard is the one thing I've done right in my life." She scrunched the tissue into her palm. "My parents introduced us. They were hoping he'd be a stabilizing influence on me. Until I started dating Richard I hadn't done a single thing in my life that pleased them or made them proud."

There had been times during his childhood when Zach had wondered what it would be like to have a normal family, but the more time he spent observing others, the more convinced he was that such a thing didn't exist.

"If you've never made them proud, then your parents are clearly insane."

She gave a watery laugh. "Is that a compliment, Zachary Flynn?"

"It's an observation."

She sniffed. "My dad is a judge. Very serious."

"Then I'd expect him to have a better appreciation for human differences and individuality."

Skylar blew her nose. "Differences are for other people. In our family, conformity is compulsory. Was it Richard himself who called to book this flight for me?"

"His office."

"Right." Another tear escaped. "I really am sorry about this. You have places to be and I'm going to make you late. You've been very kind. Thank you, Zach. I'm very grateful, although just for the record if you hurt my friend, I will kill you."

Ignoring that last part, Zach handed her the rest of the tissues and dropped to his haunches in front of her. He'd never seen anyone more miserable and confused in his life. "What do you really want, Sky?"

She leaned her head back against the seat, her eyes swimming. "I want to be in love. Really in love. And right now I don't think I'm feeling what I'm supposed to feel. I dreamed of something so different. I dreamed of *more*. But what if I'm wrong? What if I'm as idealistic as my parents say I am and this is all there is?'

"If you don't feel the right way, you don't feel the right way."

"I don't know what the right way is. All I know is that I want someone who I know will be there through thick and thin. I want a guy who is my best friend as well as my lover. I want to be with someone who is interested in what I do, and proud of me. I don't want to feel as if I'm just another member of someone's campaign team. I want to laugh and have long conversations that last until morning, but most of all I want someone as reliable as my girlfriends, someone who is going to hold me when life turns to shit and not walk away when things get tough."

He said nothing.

She sniffed, her breathing jagged. "I don't want to build a life on lies and then find it all comes crashing down years later. I want to build a future on firm foundations. I want to slide into old age laughing at the things we've always laughed at." She blew her nose. "You're so lucky having Brittany. No one could have a more loyal, loving friend. If she were a man I'd marry her, and I'm not even that wild about marriage as an institution."

Tension rippled across his shoulders.

He knew Brittany was loyal and loving, and what had he ever given her in return?

Sky cleared her throat. "I can't believe I'm talking to you about this and not Em or Brit."

"Why are you?"

"Because you don't care about me so you're unbiased."

Zach gave a faint smile and rose to his feet. "Maybe

I'm not. I sure as hell wouldn't vote for the guy after what you've just told me."

She gave a choked laugh and then blew her nose again. "Brit always said you were good with anything injured. I guess that's me. You're a good listener. I expect you've had a lot of experience with female tears."

"Causing them," Zach muttered. "Not mopping them up."

"I know. You dumped my friend, remember?"

He remembered.

Sky took another tissue from the packet. "When Em and I first met her, she was broken. And we didn't understand it. After what you'd done to her, we couldn't understand why she didn't just wipe you out of her head. And then we got to know her, and we realized she is the most loyal, loving friend anyone could have and that for her, love isn't something you give and then take back. She never gives up on people, so losing touch with you, having you cut out of her life like that, was torture. It was like trying to live with part of herself missing."

Zach couldn't breathe. "She must have hated me."

"Sure, she hated you, but I can guarantee that if you'd picked up the phone at any point in those ten years and asked for her help, she would have been there for you. She might have yelled at you and slapped you for behaving like a shit, but she would have been there." Sky sniffed. "Brit would never, ever, leave a friend who needed her."

"I wasn't a friend."

"Do you seriously believe that? You dumbass." Sky sighed and rolled her eyes. "I can't sort out my own love life but at least I can try to help with yours. Do me a favor, Zach. If you don't love her, if you want to take the amazing gift of her love and friendship and throw it away, then at least tell her straight. But please, for the love of God, think carefully before you throw away the best thing you've ever had."

Sarah Morgan

down, then at least tell her straight, thoughtless." for the love of God, think carefully before you throw away something you never had.

Chapter 19

The following day Brittany drove up to the village to do some shopping.

She parked at the harbor, wandered along Main Street and picked up a few items in Harbor Stores before making her way back to her car.

She was piling her purchases into the backseat when she heard someone calling her and saw Philip walking towards her.

She noticed his gait was a little stiff and wondered if he was in a lot of pain. "Hi, Philip." She walked to meet him and gave him a hug. "How are you?"

"I'm not going to be running the marathon anytime soon, but I've never really wanted to, so I'm not complaining."

Brittany thought that he looked remarkably upbeat for someone who'd had bad news. "Let me know how I can help. I know how much you love the camp and it must be hard cutting back."

He nodded. "That was my biggest concern of course, but not anymore. I've found someone else to step in and take my place." He was buzzing with excitement and Brittany felt her insides shift. How would Zach feel about that?

"You found someone?"

"Zach came over to the house this morning and spoke to Celia and me. It's the first time we've ever heard him talk like that. He told us that we weren't to worry about the camp, that he was going to step in and take on the bits I couldn't do, but leave me with all the bits I still *could* do. It was a weight off my shoulders. He's always been involved with the scholarship kids of course, and his mentorship has been almost as valuable as the sponsorship he gave us, but seeing him take on more general responsibility is good news."

The world seemed to slow down. "He sponsors the kids?"

"Yes, he's already giving us a huge sum of money, so—" Philip broke off and pulled a face. "Damn it, Brittany, you didn't know, did you?"

"That Zach was personally responsible for some of the scholarship places? No." Her mouth was dry and she told herself that it was typical of him not to reveal something like that. He never revealed anything that made him look good.

Philip raked his fingers through his hair. "You've been spending so much time together, I assumed he'd told you."

"He told me a little about one of the kids—Todd? About how he came here on a scholarship and has now got a place at medical school. Zach told me what a kick it gave him seeing him turn his life around." She kept her voice steady. "Did he pay for that?"

"He contributed funds, along with a few other people he knows. Zach has wealthy contacts and he's good at persuading them to open their wallets for a good cause. I shouldn't have mentioned it. I didn't realize—"

"It's fine, Philip." She ignored the tiny part of her that felt hurt that he hadn't told her. "What else did he say about the camp?"

"He said that we could rely on him. He said that he had our backs and would never let us down. He said that he—" Philip's voice cracked "—that he loved us. Well, would you look at me, making a fool of myself right in the middle of Main Street. No guesses as to what the gossip will be tomorrow."

But Brittany wasn't even aware of the people strolling past them. She didn't hear the shriek of the gulls or the shattering boom of the *Captain Hook*'s horn as it approached the harbor.

There was a dull throbbing in her ears and a chill rushed across her skin.

"He told you he loved you?" Forming the words was difficult. "He actually said those words?"

"Yes. And Celia cried. I told her to stop. Pointed out that if that was the reaction he got, he'd never say those words again."

"No." It was a struggle to smile. A struggle to react in a normal way. "Well, I'm glad he finally said them."

And she was. She really was.

Was it wrong of her to wish he'd said them to her?

She felt as if someone had taken an ax to her heart and chopped it in two.

Questions swarmed into her head. When had he made the decision? Why had he made the decision? What had changed for him?

And why hadn't he shared it with her?

And another part of her brain was already answering, telling her she was a fool, because he'd never shared anything, had he? Not really.

"You of all people will understand." Philip carried on talking, apparently oblivious to her mounting distress. "It isn't about the camp, although of course it's a huge weight off my shoulders, it's about him. He's never given, or accepted, trust. He grew up believing he couldn't be trusted. That he'd let people down. This is a huge step forward."

Aware that a response was needed Brittany nodded. She felt like a wooden doll. "I know. I know it's a huge step forward."

"And it means he's planning on staying on the island. That's the best news Celia and I could have been given."

And the worst news Brittany could have been given.

If Zach was staying on the island it meant that every visit home in the future would be punctuated by this same agonizing, restless pain.

He clearly didn't feel the same way about her as she did about him.

If he did, then he would have told her.

She could no longer pretend to herself that the reason he didn't say those words was because he was afraid.

She couldn't tell herself that he'd never said those words to anyone, because he'd said them to Philip and Celia.

She was right out of excuses and forced to face the truth.

"What about you?" Philip's smile was interested. "Now that your wrist is healed, there's no stopping you. Have you decided what you want to do next?"

"Yes." She made her decision in an instant. "I'm going back to England."

Philip looked surprised. "Really? Because I thought maybe—"

"What?"

"Nothing." He smiled. "I can't thank you enough for your help this summer. Anytime you want a job here, it's yours. I hope you know that."

There was a burning in her throat and a salty sting in her eyes. "I'll do that."

"So it looks as if it's all change."

"Seems that way." And because the burning in her throat was growing more intense, she decided she needed to get away from him. "I need to go, Philip. Good to see you and I'm so happy that everything's working out."

Instead of driving home, she walked the short distance to Harbor House and found Emily in the kitchen, experimenting with a new recipe for waffles while Lizzy covered a large sheet of paper with splotches of paint.

"I can't believe I used to buy these. They're so much—" Emily took one look at Brittany's face and ushered Lizzy into the garden to play with Cocoa. "What's wrong? Is it Zach?"

Brittany flopped onto one of the kitchen chairs. "Who does that? Who makes the same mistake twice? I've only been in love twice in my life and each time it was with the same man."

"So maybe that tells you something," Emily said quietly and Brittany dropped her head into her arms.

"It tells you I'm an idiot. Shoot me. Shoot me now."

"What happened?"

"I've been kidding myself, that's what happened."

Emily, sensitive as ever, didn't ask for the details. "What are you going to do?"

"I have no idea. None." Her emotions were so shaken up she couldn't think straight. "I'm like an addict. I can't stop wanting him even though I know he's not good for me. The only way to keep myself safe is to leave."

"But this is your home."

"And now it's his home, too. And this island isn't big enough for both of us." Brittany blew her nose. "That sounds like a line from a bad movie."

"I can't bear this." Emily sat down on the chair next to her with a thud. "You two have a real connection. I know he cares about you."

"Apparently not. Can I use your laptop? I need to book a flight before I change my mind."

"Where will you go?"

"I don't know. Somewhere I'm not going to find a casserole on my doorstep every day. London. Cambridge."

It didn't really matter, she thought, because wherever she ended up would be somewhere without Zach.

And life without Zach felt like a wilderness.

A few hours later Zach walked into Harbor Stores and loaded a basket with supplies. It was a few minutes before he realized everyone in the shop had stopped talking.

"So you're staying put and helping Philip and Celia with the camp." Hilda patted him on the arm approvingly. "We're all glad to hear that."

He didn't even bother asking how they knew.

He thought, not for the first time in his life, that humans were the strangest creatures in the animal kingdom. "I thought you'd all be locking your doors."

Hilda pursed her lips. "Not much point in doing that, seeing as you're an expert in opening just about anything, Zachary Flynn."

Despite everything, it made him smile. "Anytime you need me to secure that lock on your door, you let me know."

"Philip and Celia must be glad to know you're staying around."

"I hope so."

"And it will take your mind off other things." Hilda gave him a sympathetic look. "We're all sorry it didn't work out this time. We wanted it to. We were all rooting for you."

Zach had no idea what she was talking about and didn't want to know. "I appreciate your concern."

"You shouldn't blame yourself, not this time. Of course last time you *were* to blame. I remember saying to Kathleen at the time, that boy isn't ready for the responsibility. You were too busy watching out for yourself to watch out for the girl you married."

Zach realized they were having a conversation about Brittany. "Hilda—"

"If you hadn't left the island, we probably would have kicked you off. But it's different this time. You're different. It's a shame she can't see that, but I suppose it's hard when you've been hurt once before. I used to see her in here with Kathleen in the weeks after you left, white and skinny. Kathleen worried herself sick over the girl."

"Wait a minute—" Zach felt a pressure on his chest. "What do you mean 'it's different this time'? What are you saying?"

"I already told you—I'm saying I'm sorry it didn't work out." She patted his hand. "We all feel for you."

By the time he reached the checkout, he'd received sympathy from at least eight different people and had ascertained that not only was Brittany leaving, she'd already booked her flight.

Without telling him.

Apparently his relationship with Brittany was over and he was the last person to find out.

Why the hell wouldn't she have told him that?

Mel was the only person who was smiling. "We're all real sorry to hear the news." Not looking in the least bit sorry, she checked out his groceries. "Seeing as the whole island saw the two of you looking all cozy, heads together, at The Galleon the other night, we assumed you were together again but I guess it didn't work out. Some say you should learn from your past mistakes but I suppose this time round *she* dropped *you* so it's not the same thing. If you need someone to talk to, you know where I am."

Zach ignored that. "How does everyone know she's booked her flight?" Had the subject been anything else he would have laughed because here he was, gossiping like a true islander.

"Someone mentioned it." She tucked the fruit into a bag and gave him a sly look. "You'd think she would have told you, given that you've been spending so much time together and all. Looks like running away to me, but what do I know?"

She clearly knew a hell of a lot more than he did.

He paid, drove back to the camp and there, on the deck right outside Seagull's Nest, was a large blue casserole dish.

He stared at it in silence.

If he'd needed confirmation that the rumors were true, he had it now.

Swearing under his breath, he reversed the car and drove up to Harbor House.

Ryan was in the kitchen when Zach walked in.

"Was it you?" Zach's voice was a growl. "Did you leave that damn thing by my door?"

"What are you talking about?"

"The casserole."

Ryan shot him a look of naked incredulity. "Have you been drinking? You think I made you a casserole?"

Zach turned just as Emily walked into the room. "Was it you?"

"Was what me?" She looked stressed and tired.

"It took me half an hour to buy two items in the store because everyone was commiserating with me about Brittany leaving. I thought they'd probably got it wrong." It disturbed him just how much he'd wanted them to be wrong. "Then I arrived home to find a casserole on my doorstep."

"A casserole?" Emily pressed her hand to her chest. "Oh, that's so—Zach, that's lovely."

"What's lovely about it?"

"It shows they care. That they've accepted you. I love this island and the people so much. They're worried about you." Her eyes misted and Zach looked at Ryan with a mixture of exasperation and bemusement.

"Do you have any idea what's going on here?"

"No. But if you want my advice, you should just eat the casserole. If it's too much for one, bring it round here and we'll help. Anything for a friend."

"I'm not talking about the casserole. I'm talking about

Brittany." He jabbed his fingers into his hair, the tension an ache across his shoulders. He turned to Emily. "Are they right? Is she leaving? Why the hell didn't she tell me?"

Her eyes shone. "Zach—"

"I'm putting you in an impossible position, aren't I?" His throat felt raw. "It isn't fair to involve you. She's your friend."

"You're our friend, too," Ryan said bluntly, "although I'm not planning on making you a casserole anytime soon."

Emily stepped forward and put her hand on Zach's arm. "Yes, she's leaving."

Zach drew in a breath. "Why? What happened? Was she offered a job?" He didn't understand why she wouldn't have told him that.

"I thought—she thought—" Emily opened her mouth, looked at Ryan and then shook her head. "You have to talk with her, Zach. You have to ask her about it yourself."

"Go. Do it right now." Ryan gave him a friendly shove. "Come back later and bring that casserole with you. I'll provide the beer."

Brittany pushed the last of her things into the small suitcase and picked up her backpack.

She was used to traveling light, but somehow today everything felt heavy, as if it didn't want to leave Shell Bay and the cottage.

Restless and sad, she walked into the kitchen.

Sun sprinkled light over the countertops and she waited to see an image of her grandmother, standing with her arms dusted in flour. Instead she saw Zach, his dark head bent towards hers as he kissed her.

Closing her eyes, she tried to wipe out the picture in her head.

How would she feel next time she came home?

Would this place always be associated with Zach?

The two things she loved most in the world, the man and the cottage, were inextricably linked.

But she knew it wasn't the prospect of leaving the cottage that was making her sad, it was the prospect of leaving Zach.

Deeply absorbed in her thoughts, she didn't realize the man himself was standing there until she heard him say her name.

"Zach! You almost gave me a heart attack." She dropped the backpack onto the floor. "Why didn't you knock?"

"I did. You didn't answer."

"So you broke in."

"No. Emily gave me her key." He placed it carefully on the kitchen table. "Were you going to leave without telling me?"

"No, of course not! I was going to call you as soon as I finished a few jobs. I have to pack up Grams's diaries. There's a publisher in New York who might be interested, can you believe that?" She wiped her hands on her jeans. "How did you even know I was leaving? I only decided myself a few hours ago."

"I heard it in Harbor Stores."

"But how—?" Annoyance flickered inside her. "No, that isn't possible. I told one person. Philip. He would never gossip."

"Where were you when you told him?"

"We were standing in Main Street, but—" She stared at him and rolled her eyes. "Someone overheard? Who?"

"I have no idea, but everyone knows." He waited a beat. "Everyone except me."

Exasperated, she said, "Right. Well, I'm sorry you had to hear it that way. But yes, I'm leaving."

"Why?"

She didn't look at him. "I spoke to Philip. He told me that you're staying. That you're going to take responsibility for Camp Puffin alongside him. That you're going to be there for him. And I think that's wonderful."

His shoulders were tense. "I don't see what that has to do with you leaving."

Finally she looked at him, unable to hide the hurt. "You didn't share that with me, Zach! That's the problem. All this time we've spent together, the things we've shared and done, but you still didn't trust me with that."

He drew in a breath. "There's a reason for that."

"I know. I know you find it hard. And I didn't expect miracles, but I hoped that with enough love and patience you'd eventually understand that there are people who care about you and have your back and I'm leading the pack. I thought, maybe, that you would have shared some of that stuff with me." Her voice sounded thick and she hoped desperately she'd get through to the end without crying.

"Brit—"

"I'm thrilled for you, Zach. I'm thrilled for Philip and Celia. But I can see now that no matter what I do or say, nothing is going to change for us. And maybe I was hoping for too much. I don't just want great sex, I want trust and intimacy and all those things that scare you."

"You really need to—"

"We're still friends, Zach. We'll always be friends. We can text, video chat and next time I'm home we'll all get together, the six of us and it will be great. But I need a little time—" She shot him a smile that cost her every last shred of emotional energy she had and stooped to pull on her hiking boots, trying to hide the misery she was sure was stamped all over her face. "Call me whenever you like. I want to know what you're doing. If it feels like pressure taking over from Philip, talk to me about it. And I'll let you know next time I'm back on the island and you can fly me. I've developed a taste for private flying." She lifted her backpack onto the chair. It weighed nothing, and it occurred to her that the heaviest thing she was carrying was her heart. It sat in her chest like a lump, pressing hard against her. Crap, she was turning into a sentimental idiot.

"You're not leaving, Brit."

"Yes, I am. My wrist is healing well and I—"

"You're not going to leave. You wouldn't do that."

Confused, she glanced towards him. "Why wouldn't I?"

"Because you'd never leave a friend who needs you."

She felt another wash of misery. "Em will be fine. She has Ryan and Lizzy." She turned away and started packing her grandmother's diaries into the box she'd found. "And Sky has a busy few months with her exhibition coming up."

"I wasn't talking about Emily or Skylar." His voice was husky. "I was talking about me."

She stilled. "We've had fun this summer, but you'll be fine."

"I won't be fine if you leave. You're my best friend, Brittany. I need you here."

"I can't, Zach—"

"I love you."

Her heart pounded at her ribs, as if it was trying to escape. "You—"

"I love you." He walked over to her and cupped her face in his hands. "After everything we've shared the last few weeks, did you really think I didn't?"

"I thought you did, and I was hoping you'd say it but you didn't—" she swallowed "—and instead you said it to Philip and Celia."

"Yes." He nodded, stroking her cheek with his thumb. "And maybe I should have said it to you first, but I knew that it wasn't going to be enough to tell you I loved you. I needed to show you that I meant it. You set a high bar for your friends, Brit. You have their backs, and they have yours. Before I talked to you, I wanted Philip and Celia to know I was there for them. That I'll be there for them in the future, no matter what happens. That was part of my plan to convince you that I've changed. That I can do this."

"But—"

He gave a wry smile. "My plan was to come straight over to you once I'd talked to them, but the Puffin Island gossip-net has apparently upgraded from fast to superfast."

"The islanders told you I was leaving?"

"They commiserated with me." He gave a soft laugh. "I drove home in a daze where I found a casserole waiting for me."

"You're kidding!" She gave a choked laugh and leaned her head against his chest. "This place is—"

"Unbelievable," he finished for her. "And the people are the most meddling, annoying, wonderful people in the world. And living here teaches you that no man is an island, and no island is ever about just one man. It teaches you that life is so much richer when it's lived as part of a community."

She sniffed. "Well, if you've been given a casserole, then I'd say you're officially part of that community."

"If you leave, they will never forgive me." He eased away from her slightly and pulled something out of his pocket. "I should have given you this ten years ago. I hope it's not too late."

She looked down at the beautiful diamond sparkling on his palm and the breath caught in her throat. "Zach—"

"I love you. You've given me all of yourself and you've given me back a part of myself I thought I'd lost forever." He lowered his head and kissed her gently. "Will you marry me again? And this time I'll get it right. Through thick and thin, Brit, no matter what happens I will always have your back."

Tears streamed down her cheeks and she held out her finger. "You'd better put it on, because my hands are shaking. I love you, too, you know I love you. I loved you before I was really old enough to understand what the emotion was, I still loved you when you left me and I love you now."

"I know. Because when you love a person you love them forever. Sky told me that." He smoothed her hair back from her face. "I don't want to stop you taking up the job you found, though. We'll find a way of making it work."

"I haven't found a job. I just needed some space, so I thought I'd go back to Cambridge for a couple of weeks. See some friends. Do some thinking."

"So your only reason for leaving," he said slowly, "was to escape from me?"

"Yes."

"Then how would you feel about staying here and taking that part-time post at the university? I can fly you to the mainland once a week. And the rest of the time you can help out at the camp and help me with the rest of my responsibilities."

"What responsibilities?"

He kissed her and then released her. "Wait there."

Moments later she heard the scrabbling of paws and a grunting sound and Jaws appeared in her kitchen.

Brittany looked at the panting, slobbering dog and started to laugh. "Are you serious?"

"It's not doing his manners any good living in the animal shelter. I thought it was time he settled down and learned to trust people. No more of this glaring suspiciously at every human being that passes. No more snapping and biting. It's time he learned that all you need to get through life is a handful of people who love you." He stooped to give Jaws a reassuring stroke and the dog trotted across the kitchen and settled himself in a warm spot in front of the stove. "For what it's worth, Sara thinks we're a perfect match."

"I've already told you that the physical similarities between the two of you are astonishing, but—"

"Not Jaws and I, you and I." He drew her back into his arms. "I thought we could live here, the three of us. Build a life. How does that sound?"

"It sounds perfect." Choked by emotion, she eased away from him and hunted for her phone. "I need to call Emily and Sky."

"I've got a better idea." He took the phone out of her hand. "We'll go and tell Emily in person. In fact we can share a celebratory meal together."

"What about Jaws?" She glanced at the dog, who had

his head on one side and his teeth in a chewy toy. "We can't leave him. We're responsible parents now."

"We'll take him with us."

"Cocoa will object."

"Cocoa will love him and it will be good for him to make a friend." He lowered his head and kissed her again. "It's important to let good people into your life."

"It's not fair to make Em cook without any warning."

"She doesn't need to cook." Smiling, he slid his arms around her. "We'll drive via Seagull's Nest. I happen to know where I can find a large casserole that needs eating…"

* * * * *

Acknowledgments

Thanks to my wonderful agent, Susan Ginsburg, and the team at Writers House who continue to guide my career.

I'm so lucky to have as my editor the lovely and talented Flo Nicoll, who works tirelessly to ensure every book is the best it can be. Thanks to Dianne Moggy for the endless encouragement and support, and to Susan Swinwood and the rest of the team at HQN for their wonderful work. Special thanks to Lisa Wray for her valuable help with publicity. I appreciate all you do!

My heartfelt thanks to everyone in the Harlequin UK office, including Anna Baggaley, Vicky Tinsley and the whole sales and marketing team. I'm grateful for the dedication they show in ensuring my books reach as many readers as possible.

My love and appreciation goes to my family, who continue to accept my unusual choice of job (and the associated lack of catering) with patience and good humor.

And finally my biggest thanks goes to you, the reader, for choosing this book, thus ensuring that I can continue with a career I love.

We hope you enjoyed reading

THE LADIES' MAN

by *New York Times* bestselling author

SUSAN MALLERY and

SOME KIND OF WONDERFUL

an original Puffin Island story

by *USA TODAY* bestselling author

SARAH MORGAN

THE LADIES' MAN was an original
Harlequin® Special Edition series story!

HARLEQUIN®

SPECIAL EDITION

Life, Love and Family

SPECIAL EXCERPT FROM

H HARLEQUIN®

SPECIAL EDITION

*When tycoon Ben Robinson enlists temp Ella Thomas
to help him uncover Fortune family secrets, will the
closed-off Prince Charming be able to resist the charms
of his beautiful Cinderella?*

Read on for a sneak preview of
FORTUNE'S SECRET HEIR, the first installment in the
2016 Fortunes of Texas twentieth anniversary continuity,
***ALL FORTUNE'S CHILDREN**.*

Ben figured it was only a matter of time before the security guards came to check that he'd exited. But having gotten what he'd come for, he had no reason to stay.

He went out the door and it closed automatically behind him. When he tested it out of curiosity, it was locked.

"Crazy old bat," he muttered under his breath.

But he didn't really believe it.

Kate Fortune was many things. Of that he was certain.

But crazy wasn't one of them.

He looked around, getting his bearings before setting off to his left. It was dark, only a few lights situated here and there to show off some landscape feature. But he soon made his way around the side of the enormous house and to the front, which was not just well lit, but magnificently so. He stopped at the valet and handed over his ticket to a skinny kid in a black shirt and trousers.

He tried to imagine Ella dashing off the way this kid was to retrieve his car, parked somewhere on the vast property. He couldn't quite picture it.

But in his head, he could picture *her* quite clearly.

Not the red hair. That just reminded him of Stephanie. But the faint gap in her toothy smile and the clear light shining from her pretty eyes.

That was all Ella.

A moment later, when the valet returned with his Porsche, Ben got in and drove away.

Don't miss
FORTUNE'S SECRET HEIR
by New York Times *bestselling author Allison Leigh,*
available January 2016 wherever
Harlequin® Special Edition books and ebooks are sold.

www.Harlequin.com

HARLEQUIN®

SPECIAL EDITION

Life, Love and Family

Use this coupon to save

$1.00

on the purchase of any
Harlequin® Special Edition book.

Available wherever books are sold, including
most bookstores, supermarkets, drugstores
and discount stores.

Save $1.00

on the purchase of any Harlequin® Special Edition book.

Coupon valid until March 31, 2016.
Redeemable at participating outlets in the U.S. and Canada only.
Not redeemable at Barnes & Noble stores. Limit one coupon per customer.

Canadian Retailers: Harlequin Enterprises Limited will pay the face value of this coupon plus 10.25¢ if submitted by customer for this product only. Any other use constitutes fraud. Coupon is nonassignable. Void if taxed, prohibited or restricted by law. Consumer must pay any government taxes. Void if copied. Inmar Promotional Services ("IPS") customers submit coupons and proof of sales to Harlequin Enterprises Limited, P.O. Box 3000, Saint John, NB E2L 4L3, Canada. Non-IPS retailer—for reimbursement submit coupons and proof of sales directly to Harlequin Enterprises Limited, Retail Marketing Department, 225 Duncan Mill Rd., Don Mills, ON M3B 3K9, Canada.

U.S. Retailers: Harlequin Enterprises Limited will pay the face value of this coupon plus 8¢ if submitted by customer for this product only. Any other use constitutes fraud. Coupon is nonassignable. Void if taxed, prohibited or restricted by law. Consumer must pay any government taxes. Void if copied. For reimbursement submit coupons and proof of sales directly to Harlequin Enterprises Limited, P.O. Box 880478, El Paso, TX 88588-0478, U.S.A. Cash value 1/100 cents.

® and ™ are trademarks owned and used by the trademark owner and/or its licensee.

© 2016 Harlequin Enterprises Limited

NYTCOUP0116